Chilling, disturbing, and eerily real, *Don't Play With Emily* is the kind of horror story that creeps up on you, grabs you by your unsuspecting shoulders, and shakes you to your core. Not just any ghost story or horror story, *Don't Play With Emily* is frightening because it is based on a true incident-a real five-year-old little girl ghost. As the author o *Angel Watch* and two other collections of spirit intervention in human life, I can attest that dead people do cross through the dimensions and "visit" us.

Phyllis Uzelac employs just the right tone of real and unreal to weave a tale that can happen to any of us. Kidnapped and murdered as a young child, Emily, the ghost, is determined to be reunited with her own bones. To do that, she must make her spirit presence known to her family. Throughout the story, you will find yourself questioning every flickering light bulb, night shadow, and disembodied voice. And you should.

A Tantalizing read that will haunt the reader for years.

Catherine Lanigan

www.catherinelanigan.com

Author of Angel Watch, Divine Nudges, Angel Tales, and coming soon, Angel Guides.

Author of Romancing the Stone; Jewel of the Nile, and Shores of Indian Lake.

Acknowledgements

I am grateful to my family, who've been close to my heart while making this book a reality. My sincere thanks to:

My husband, Ted for all of our journeys so far and those yet to come. I love you, Ted.

My sons, Ted and Dan for giving me the love and encouragement needed to complete my book.

My daughters-in-law, Nikki and Sherry for setting the mold for my female characters.

My grandsons, Teddy and Christian for being my little men and for who I have unconditional love.

My beautiful granddaughter, Brittney for being the little girl on the merry-go-round, demonstrating the reality of a child's innocence and revealing Emily to me.

To my lovely and talented sister, Lizzy, who shared her art with me to bring Emily to life.

And to my dear friend, Catherine, who mentored me for years. She helped evolve from storyteller to writer.

DON'T PLAY WITH

EMILY

BY

Phyllis Uzelac

Prologue

Sarah's eyes darted back and forth between Charles and the merry-go-round. "What do you mean, where's Emily? Get up there and look for her." She pushed her husband in the direction of the ride.

It took Charles a moment to process what Sarah had said. He was trying to focus on the different carousel horses as they passed in front of him, searching for the now familiar purple plume that was perched on the head of the horse that Emily was riding. However, each time the merry-go-round completed a turn, the statuesque steed, on which he had left his only child, was empty.

As nameless fear settled in her, Sarah ordered her husband, "Go around that side of the ride and see if she slipped off her horse. I'll go this way." She spun around and took off running. A deep wrinkle formed on Sarah's brow. There was no sign of Emily anywhere. She was quickly losing the ability to make rational decisions. "Emily Marie, answer me! Where are you?" Sarah shouted. It was getting hard for her to breathe. "Stop the ride. Someone, help us!"

Sarah's rising terror rapidly drew attention from the crowd. She waved her arms in the air and started screeching louder and louder. A vicious knot of unease caught the young mother in the pit of her stomach. Her fear was escalating into uncontrollable panic.

Charles raced around the other side of the merry-go-round, meeting Sarah midway. Her lungs burned and tightened and she clutched her chest, barely able to breathe. They both stopped abruptly, their eyes locked, afraid that if either looked away, they might have to face the truth.

A gut-wrenching scream escaped from deep within Sarah's body. Her voice was filled with equal measures of anguish and disbelief. Her knees buckled, betraying her and she dropped to the ground with a thud, burying her face in both hands. Sarah wailed her daughter's name. It didn't matter that everyone was staring at her. "Has everyone gone crazy?" she cried. She felt as though she was losing her mind.

"You have to do something Charles," Sarah cried while scrambling to her feet. Dark circles shadowed her damp, swollen eyes. She grasped his hands in a desperate attempt to make him understand her passion. There were so many children scampering around them, yet still no trace of Emily.

With renewed desperation, Sarah pushed past Charles and stumbled from one stranger to the next. She grabbed at them and shrieked in their faces. The only words she could get out were, "Emily, Emily, Emily!"

By now, Sarah was exhausted and sweating profusely in the June heat. Her body trembled like a person possessed. Nearly out of her mind, eyes wild from fear, she grabbed hold of an innocent bystander, who was watching her spin out of control. Sarah had no composure as she questioned the woman. "Have you seen Emily? Have you seen my little girl?" Emotion wreaking havoc, Sarah accidentally knocked the woman's glasses off.

The crazed look in Sarah's eyes frightened the stranger, who defensively shoved her away, causing Sarah to fall backward. Charles was witnessing his wife's mental breakdown. It was so unlike his gentle Sarah to create any sort of scene. How can this be happening to us? He rushed to her side.

Letting loose with yet another piercing scream, Sarah begged, "Why doesn't anyone want to help me?" She flailed around in a wild frenzy. Her mind in turmoil, she began to imagine horrifying, nightmare scenarios. Sarah's hair fell down from the twisted vertical roll that earlier laid neatly at the back of her head. A thick lock, moistened by sweat lay limply across her face. Charles didn't know what to do. He felt helpless, as if he were outside looking in at this horrendous situation. He looked at Sarah but didn't dare touch her.

"Do something, Charles! You have to find Emily!" Sarah's mournful, high-pitched cry intensified as she continued to make a spectacle of herself. "There are so many people. How will we ever find her?"

Charles offered no answer. Sarah continued to beg, "Someone, anyone please, listen to me!" She whipped her head around and spoke to Charles with an intensity that burned through him like a hot poker. He had never seen his wife like this before. "Answer me Charles. You have to tell me that this is just a terrible mistake. Go and get Emily. Bring her to me. I'll wait right here."

The sun's intense heat beat on the back of Charles's neck. He stared at his wife sitting in a crumpled heap on the ground. It sickened him when he noticed that the area she was kneeling in was soiled with urine. "I failed you, and I failed Emily," he whispered.

The crowd backed away one by one. Charles felt that there was no way to console his wife, so he turned away from her, moving in a dream, unable to handle his own shock and grief. He could hear Sarah sobbing behind him. Then, he heard her wretch and vomit. He didn't look back. Charles focused on the merry-go-round. "I can't go home without Emily," he mumbled. "This is crazy." He ran alongside the moving ride, grabbed hold of a pole and swung himself up, on to the wooden platform. Charles quickly made his way from one horse to the next, frantically searching in one last effort to find his daughter. "For all that's holy, Emily where are you?" The blaring music coming from the calliope had become maddening.

Totally unaware of the chaos going on behind him, the young man operating the carousel stood up from his chair. His feet had been propped up on the side of the motor box when he noticed a hysterical man sprinting from one wooden horse to another.

"Hey, you there," he called to Charles. "What do you think you're doing? You're gonna fall. Stop running or you'll have to get off."

The caretaker of the merry-go-round grabbed hold of the long wood handle that controlled the motor and pushed it over to the left, bringing the ride slowly to a stop.

Charles ignored the order and continued his frenzied search for Emily. He stepped off of the ride, down into the inner circle where the young man ran the carousel. After running around the entire area, he laid down on his stomach to look under the platform. Charles wanted to believe that there was still a flicker of hope, a logical explanation. It was at that point, he knew. Emily was really gone.

Charles closed his eyes for a moment, feeling a dull ache in his head, not wanting to get up. It would be so much easier to simply disappear into the cool, dark earth. "Why did I leave her alone? What was I thinking? My God, this is all my fault," he mumbled into the dirt.

"What do you think you're doing? You aren't supposed to be in here. You're gonna get me fired. Are you hurt?" The carousel attendant was yelling.

Charles stood up slowly, not bothering to brush the dust off his clothing. Sarah mounted the carousel and wove her way through the horses, looking for him, totally rumpled and disheveled. He saw her reflection in the mirrors, coming toward him like a ghostly disfigurement of his beautiful wife.

"Where's Emily? Did you find her?" Without waiting for his answer, Sarah swiftly turned to the young man, who had no idea what was going on. "Did you find my little girl?" A burning lump seared her throat. "I can't go home without her. I just can't!"

Charles had always been able to fix just about anything. He never failed to have an answer for Sarah. But, he couldn't fix this-not this. The only sound that Sarah would remember from that dreadful day would be the monotonous, deathly tune piping from the calliope.

Charles was first to break the strained moment. "Sarah, Emily is really gone." He squeezed his eyes in an attempt to hold back the tears. Choked-up sobs made it difficult to speak. He could no longer look his wife in the eye; the burden of guilt was too heavy. It was the unfairness of it that threatened to take his breath away. Looking to share some of the blame, he turned and redirected his attention to the totally confused young man, whose only role in all of this was being in charge of the merry-go-round that day. "Our daughter is missing. She was on your ride and now she's gone!"

Chapter One

'Five-year-old Emily Marie Thatcher was pirated from a merry-go-round at the town's annual carnival on June twenty-eighth and as of yet, there is still no trace of her.'

Sarah picked up the morning newspaper and carried it to her room. The article she was looking for was no longer on the front page.

'Sarah Thatcher, the distressed mother of the five-year-old abducted child, pleads with the public and law enforcement to continue to be diligent in their search for her daughter. Missing for over two weeks, she was last seen on the merry-go-round, where her father left her. Statistics show that the most likely time to find a young child is in the first few hours after their disappearance. At this time, there is only a one percent chance that Charles and Sarah Thatcher will ever be reunited with their daughter again.'

Sarah crumpled the paper and threw it on the floor. "Why Lord? Why my Emily?" She sat down hard on the chair by her bedroom window and thought about the day that Emily was born.

It was June 28, 1942. The day had started out warm and sunny. As Sarah's labor progressed, so did the brewing thunderstorm that began over Lake Michigan. The dark, rolling clouds worked their way inland and hung heavily over the hospital.

The storm lingered and by mid-afternoon, the sunless sky appeared menacing. Sarah tried to focus on the electrifying, split-second bolts of lightning that flashed beyond her hospital window.

The nearly unbearable pressure was becoming stronger and Sarah cried out with each pain. The nurse returned to the labor ward, examined Sarah and said, "It won't be long now. The doctor is on his way. I'm going to move you into the delivery room."

Charles paced fretfully in the father's waiting room. Leeza, who had helped raise Sarah and was now their soon-to-be nanny, waited nervously alongside him.

"I hope everything is okay in there. You know, we never thought Miss Sarah could even carry a child, her being so small and fragile. This baby is truly a miracle," Leeza proclaimed. She didn't want to scare Charles with the overwhelming sense of terror that caught her at the nape of the neck, making her tiny hairs stand upright.

Just then, the nurse entered Sarah's room. There was a loud clap of thunder, all the lights went out, and Sarah let out a blood-curdling scream that could be heard all the way down the hall to where Charles and Leeza waited.

"That was Miss Sarah! I'd know her voice anywhere," Leeza cried.

There was one final moment of blinding agony when Sarah thought she would lose her mind. Then, out of the shadowy room came the wondrous sound of a baby's first cry.

Sarah's heart soared. Warm tears of joy streamed down her cheeks. She spoke through the darkness to her precious baby. "Emily, you're finally here."

The storm ended. Slowly, the sun began to peek through the clouds and drifted into the hospital room. It shone directly on Emily like a beam sent from heaven as she lay safe and protected in her mother's loving arms.

Chapter Two

From the moment she came into this world, Emily was positively enchanting with her sky-blue eyes set perfectly above two round cheeks like vaults from heaven. Wisps of blond hair curled around her face and the deep dimple in her right cheek accentuated her smile.

Charles and Sarah doted on their only child. Sarah often reminded Charles how much Emily fulfilled her life. "I don't know what I did before Emily came. Without her, my days would be so insignificant."

By the time she reached the age of three, Emily's budding imagination had become quite apparent. Charles set aside a special time every evening to read to her.

Emily's favorite poem was Winkin, Blinkin, and Nod, a wonderful fantasy about three fishermen who sailed off in a wooden shoe and fished among the stars. When Charles read, Emily was drawn into the expertly woven tale.

"I can see the stars from my bedroom window," Emily exclaimed. "I play with my friends up there." Her eyes shone brightly as she pointed through the dark sky. Unlike most young children, Emily was fascinated with the night. "My swing is shaped like the wooden shoe in my book," she explained.

"How does it stay up there?" Her father asked.

Emily giggled and said, "With ropes, silly Daddy." She stood in front of the opened window and let the soothing breeze feather her hair.

Anyone who met Emily became mesmerized by her crackling personality. However, it was the intensity of her incredibly blue eyes that held them captive.

Another of Emily's favorite stories was from a book that Charles's parents sent to her from Virginia. Every year, a beautiful music box accompanied a new book. This particular year, Emily received a music box with the statue of a magnificent bay. She fingered the reddish-brown high-stepper as her father read to her from the book, *Gi Gi*.

Gi Gi was a story about a wooden merry-go-round horse that got its sturdy body and tireless gallop from his mother, a pine tree in a big forest and his sense of rhythm from his father, who was the wind that swept through the woods where his mother stood. It was all a part of another world, Emily's world.

"I'm going to ride this horse someday, Daddy," Emily said firmly as she studied the figurine. "I'm going to ride him and he'll be mine forever!"

"That's nice," Charles said, ignoring Emily's adrenaline-laced tone.

Being an only child, Emily created imaginary playmates. In the morning, when Sarah asked how she slept, Emily would have extravagant adventures to share.

"I played with my friends last night," she spoke without hesitation.

"Who are your friends?" Sarah asked gently.

"Bo and Cupcake. They come here every night," Emily responded freely. "They wait outside until after I say my prayers with you and Daddy. Then, when you leave, they come in and carry me up to my swing." Emily pointed to her bedroom window. Sometimes Sarah had to rub the hairs down on her arms when Emily told her such things.

Emily learned new games from her nighttime friends and shared them with Leeza during her bath or while she was getting dressed. Leeza laughed out loud and clapped vigorously when Emily danced or showed off what she had learned the night before. However, Leeza held tightly to the amulet that hung from the worn ribbon around her neck when she listened to Emily's stories.

"You're a very special little girl, Miss Emily. I knew there was a reason I was sent to this family. It was to look after you." Leeza shivered in response to the sardonic, sly expression on

Emily's face. Everyone felt that Emily was just an extraordinarily gifted child and excused her behavior; everyone except Leeza.

"I think there's more going on with that child than just an over active imagination," Leeza would say. "She has things in her room that appear out of nowhere."

"Oh Leeza; what are you talking about?" Sarah laughed. She was used to the superstitious ways of her beloved nanny.

"Like the sparkly rocks she keeps in that wooden box of hers," Leeza pressed.

"She probably picked them up when we were at the lake," Sarah answered. But there was a worried look in Sarah's eyes as she watched Leeza leave the room. An unexpected fear surged through Sarah, leaving her breathless. She whispered, "Sometimes she scares me too."

Charles couldn't help but indulge Emily's whims. "She certainly has enormous energy," he said. "You have to admit that there's something incredibly unique about our Emily."

Charles would turn on the radio and watch Emily keep time to the music with her feet. There was one occasion in particular, when Emily was playing ring-around-the-rosy.

"Look at Emily's hand, Charles," whispered Sarah. "See the way she's reaching out. Her little fist is curled. She actually appears to be holding on to someone."

Charles and Sarah watched quietly. All of a sudden, Emily stumbled. Before Charles could reach her, she sprung up with her right arm stretched high above her head, dangling for a moment as if someone was holding on to her. Emily giggled and continued playing. She looked up adoringly to the empty space alongside her.

After that unexplainable incident, Charles felt that it was time for Emily to play with children her own age. He allowed her to visit with Isabel Young, the little girl next door. She was about the same age as Emily.

"Maybe some of Emily's enthusiasm will rub off on Isabel," said Susan Young, Isabel's mother. "She's always whining about a stomachache. I think she's just lazy." Mrs. Young was definitely jealous of Emily and constantly compared the two children. Sarah found Mrs. Young's remarks distasteful. She felt that she was extremely judgmental and unjustly critical about Isabel.

It was only when Charles was home that Emily was allowed to play next door. He would stand on the back porch and watch her run across the yard to the Young's house.

Sarah didn't like not being able to see what her daughter was doing. After an hour or two, she would send Leeza to bring Emily home.

"You can see their house from the kitchen window," Charles would argue. "Give the child some space, Sarah."

"I can't see them when they're in there," Sarah responded in a huff. She hated having to justify her intuitions. "There's something about Susan Young that's very unsettling. I can't put my finger on it, but I don't trust her."

One night Sarah was awakened by loud claps of thunder. She went down to the kitchen and stood by the back door, watching the lightning dash between the clouds. Before the storm ended, a final bolt of lightning flashed and illuminated the sky. It lit up the back yard and Sarah could see the Young's house from where she stood.

In just that split second, when both houses were lit up, Sarah spotted Susan Young standing outside on her back porch. She was staring directly at Sarah. She gasped and quickly stepped away from the window. In an attempt to shrink away from Mrs. Young's line of vision, she turned and found herself face to face with Emily.

"What are you doing down here? Did the storm scare you?" Sarah's voice cracked.

"My friends didn't come tonight. I'm worried," Emily cried. Her small frame trembled.

Sarah took off her robe and wrapped it around Emily's quivering little body. "Oh, you're shaking. The storm got me up too. Your friends didn't come by tonight because of the bad weather. Come on, let's go back to bed."

Sarah led Emily back to her room. The bedroom window was opened, allowing the cold, damp night air to blow in. She quickly went over to close it but a blustery gust of rain and wind hit Sarah, knocking her back and soaking the front of her nightgown.

"Oh, that was cold!" Sarah cried. "Who opened this window?" She turned to find Emily in bed, snuggled down under the covers.

Before Sarah tiptoed out of the room, she heard something flutter hard against the window. She snapped her head around only to catch a glimpse of something brush past the closed pane.

"I'm glad I shut that window when I did. Something is definitely trying to get in out of the storm."

The icy, wet gown clung uncomfortably to Sarah's body. "I'm freezing, I have to get out of these wet clothes." She immediately left the room.

Emily peeked out from under the comforter once she was certain that her mother was gone. Ghostly forms materialized in the dim lit corner where Emily had willed the window to open. She relaxed as a slow, impish smile crept across her face.

Chapter Three

Silver maple trees lined the street where Charles and Sarah lived. The warm scents of summer drifted on soft breezes, in through opened windows. There was the smell of blooming flowers mixed with freshly cut grass as lawnmowers hummed and neighbors could be seen maintaining their beautifully manicured flowerbeds.

The houses sat close together, appearing cloned, except for the occasional Victorian model, like the Thatcher home. It boasted spacious ceilings and two bay windows, both of which had their original stained glass. It was still light outside when Charles got home from work. He enjoyed relaxing on the front porch with a cold drink. It was a peaceful, quiet neighborhood where remarkable occurrences were scarce, yet Sarah didn't allow Emily to play unsupervised without Leeza or herself keeping watch.

"She's too young to go outside alone and unattended." Sarah would argue if Charles interfered. Leeza would eavesdrop on their conversations. She sensed something more than simply motherly concern.

"I don't like that boy, Luke Phillips. He's too big to be hanging around the little girls. It just isn't natural for a boy his age not to be playing with other boys," Leeza voiced her opinion boldly. "I once heard him tell Emily that she looked just like the angel on top of their Christmas tree."

Luke lived across the street from the Thatchers. He was quiet and a few years older than Emily. While the other boys his age were outside playing with toy guns, hitting a baseball or climbing trees, Luke could most often be found hanging around or close to, wherever it was that Emily was playing. He was very polite, almost too polite, with a manipulative, sickeningly sweet way about him.

"He gives me the creeps, plain and simple!" Leeza said. "He's always sneaking around or staring at Emily. There's something, not quite right about that boy."

Luke didn't care what people said. He would watch Emily when she played outside with Isabel. He also noticed how awkward it was for Mrs. Young when the girls were together. Once, Luke peeked into the Young's window when Emily was playing there. He watched Mrs. Young actually pluck leaves from the old hemlock bush next to her house and feed it to Isabel. Emily was too young to realize what was going on, but deep down, Luke knew why Isabel was always sick to her stomach.

Charles and Sarah wanted Emily's fifth birthday to be special. On the morning of June 28th, 1947, they were up early getting ready for Emily's celebration. They planned on taking her to the annual carnival at Wormwood Park, followed by cake and ice cream with a handful of selected neighborhood children and Sunday school classmates. Leeza was to have everything ready when they came home. How could they have known the terrible consequences of their decision?

"Charles, please don't forget the camera and make sure you have plenty of film," Sarah instructed. "I want everything to be perfect. Can you believe our baby is five years old today?" she cried.

Charles paced impatiently across the living room. "Where is she? Come on down here, birthday girl," he called to Emily from the foot of the stairs.

"She's coming, Mr. Thatcher. I just need to tie a bow in her pinafore and she'll be right down. This is the most wigglin' child," Leeza responded.

Leeza was helping Emily get dressed. She loved her as if she were her own. "Where are the new shoes yo mama bought for you, Miss Emily?"

Emily pulled away from Leeza and ran down the hall to the back staircase, meant for the servants. "I'll get them," she called as she broke into a fast dash.

Even though Leeza practically raised Sarah, she had a completely different relationship with Emily. She knew that along with Emily's birth came a danger from the spirit world. The darkness surrounding Emily on the day she was born was more than just a summer storm. To Leeza, it was an omen.

Leeza was the illegitimate daughter of Clairese Boudreaux, a Creole and self-proclaimed, faith-healing Voodoo queen from deep in the bayous of Louisiana. Clairese was a rare, mystical spiritualist. She didn't know who her father was. She was raised in a world of superstitions, curses and spells.

Leeza fell in love with Benjamin Jackson, a Christian from New Orleans. They met at a church revival one sweltering night while she stood outside, listening to boisterous preaching and Southern gospel music. Benjamin convinced Leeza that her way of life was just a bunch of hocus-pocus. Clairese was heartbroken, but didn't stand in her daughter's way.

Before Leeza traveled North with Benjamin, Clairese placed a green opal in her hand. "Certain stones and gems hold great powers," she said. In her other hand, she closed Leeza's fingers around a smooth bead. Leeza uncurled her fingers and recognized the evil eye. The corners of her lips turned upward.

"Promise me that you'll wear this amulet at all times. It will ward off spiritual attackers." A moment of silence passed between them.

Benjamin assured Leeza that they never had a child of their own, because Leeza was being punished for the black magic her mother practiced. Leeza continued to wear the talisman around her neck as she promised, but she never saw her mother again.

Leeza witnessed more than she would ever admit to. She knew for sure that something was in Emily's future that even she wouldn't be able to protect her from.

Sarah was comfortable with Leeza, as she had been her own nanny. Charles grew to depend on her as much as Sarah did and when Emily was born, Leeza took over her care. She was treated like a member of the family. At the end of the day, Leeza waited on the front porch for Benjamin to pick her up in his dark blue truck. She viewed her job as a personal destiny. By taking care of Sarah and now Emily, it helped to fill the void that a childless woman often feels.

Emily came bounding down the stairs. She was excited about her birthday. "Is it time to go? It's my birthday. I'm five years old today."

"Come here and let Daddy give you a birthday kiss," Charles said with opened arms. After squirming out of her father's hold, Emily skipped over to Sarah. She gave her mother a tender hug and took a step backward. Sarah looked down at Emily's feet. "What's on your new shoes?"

Emily looked down at the scuff marks on the toes of her new, white, patent leather shoes. "I was in the back yard," she said.

"What were you doing back there?" Sarah asked.

"I was burying my shiny stars," Emily answered. "Leeza kept taking them out of my box and looking at them. She thinks I didn't know so, I hid them."

Charles smiled. "Where did you hide your rocks...I mean, your shiny stars?"

Emily looked around as if she had a very important secret. She whispered, "I dug a hole under the back steps and I buried them. Now, they're dead!"

Sarah gasped. "That's terrible. You'll have to speak to Leeza about bothering Emily's private possessions, Charles. If Emily tells her not to touch them, then Leeza needs to leave her things alone."

"Okay, I'll tell Leeza to leave your things alone." He pulled out a handkerchief and moistened it with spit before cleaning the smudges off Emily's shoes. The deep dimple creasing Emily's right cheek was Charles's reward.

Her pastel lavender dress complimented Emily's fair skin and brought out the luminescence of her clear blue eyes. There was a haunting enchantment in Emily's eyes. They seemed to speak to whoever they gazed upon, from deep within. The white eyelet pinafore perfectly complimented the dress with lavender ribbons woven through her white lace stockings.

Sarah tied a bow under Emily's chin. "Charles, would you please pull the car up front?" She held her daughter's hands and whispered, "Emily, I want you to know how special you are and how very proud I am of you. Happy birthday darling; you'll always be my beautiful little girl."

Emily giggled and pulled away. She snatched her favorite doll off the window seat and tucked it securely under her arm. They heard the horn outside. "My dolly wants to go to the park too, Mommy." She ran for the front door. "Hurry, let's go. Bye Leeza," Emily called over her shoulder. A tear slid down Leeza's lined, black, angular face.

"You have yourself a good time, baby." Leeza followed them to the front door. Out of nowhere, a burst of cold air hit her in the face sending a bristling chill down her arms. She reached for the amulet that always hung around her neck. It was gone.

Fear encompassed Leeza leaving an uncomfortable flutter in her stomach. She fought the sudden urge to reach out for Emily and pull her back inside. But deep down, she knew that there was no way to stop what destiny had planned. There was no way to prevent what was meant to be. Something else clung to the corners of her mind, twisting in her gut, something bad. Leeza turned and scurried upstairs to Emily's room to search for the box where Emily kept her precious star rocks. She couldn't find them. The box was gone.

Leeza's blood ran cold. She opened the bedroom window and watched as Emily skipped down the sidewalk, alongside her mother. Although it was warm outside, there was an unusual breeze, an ill wind as cold as death. Leeza covered her face with her hands, and shed mourner's tears. Sarah and Emily walked away from the house, hand in hand together, for the last time.

Chapter Four

Sarah helped Emily into the back seat of the car. Emily
stood in the middle with her tiny face peering between her mom
and dad. Charles rolled down the window and rested his left arm
on the car door.

Lurking, waiting, hiding behind a thin, worn curtain, Susan
Young watched as Emily rode away with her parents. Her face
was hot and flushed. She stomped outside and began hacking
away at the hemlock bush, making certain to collect specific leaves
and stems to create the perfect bouquet for a perfect little girl.

"Is it too windy back there for you, Emily?" Sarah turned
and asked. Emily slid over to her father's side of the car. She tilted
her chin upward, letting the wind from the opened window blow
directly into her face.

"Nooo...Mommmyyy," Emily dragged out the words that
were being distorted by the wind.

"Charles, roll up the window," Sarah ordered.

"Sorry, baby. Mommy doesn't want you crying tonight
with a bellyache. You're swallowing too much air," Charles
explained.

Emily thought about it and immediately began gulping air.
"It doesn't taste like anything." She relayed her findings and
opened her mouth wide. Her blond curls flew around her head.

Charles laughed, but compliantly rolled up the window.
"Hey, Em, I hear there's a carnival at Wormwood Park today." He
glanced over at Sarah. She was still scowling at him. Charles
gave her a crooked little smirk, causing Sarah to shake her head
and smile.

"I want to ride the merry-go-round. Can I Daddy? It's my
birthday," Emily squealed.

"Of course you can," Charles said. They found a parking
place in the picnic area right behind the magnificent, newly-erected
merry-go-round.

"Don't go running off," Sarah instructed her daughter. "Make sure you hold her hand, Charles." Emily tugged on her father's hand, pulling him toward the looming carousel.

"Daddy," Emily said as they approached the beguiling ride. "Look," She stared in awe and pointed to one of the incredible wooden statues on the carousel.

Charles was examining the new structure. "Do you mean the one trimmed in purple and gold?" The horses were painted in vibrant colors. Each one appeared to have its own separate personality. There were chestnuts, roans, and dapple-grays posed in a mad gallop, while others looked to be holding their heads high in an arrogant fashion.

The horse in question stood on the outside row of the ride, bedecked with a feathered plume atop its head. Emily's heart beat rapidly at the sight of the steed. "He's my favorite, Mommy. I want to ride that one."

Charles tipped his head to one side and waited for Sarah's response. "Lift me up, Daddy. Hurry, someone else will get it," Emily was jumping up and down.

"Well, go ahead," Sarah smiled.

"Alright honey; let's go."

Emily was ecstatic. In the center of the ride was an exquisite calliope playing, "The Band Played On."

Sarah watched Charles proudly escort Emily to the horse of her choice. He carefully placed her on the elegantly posed statue. Her eyes were wide with wonder and she gripped tightly to the pole that held the horse. The deep dimple in Emily's right cheek could be seen clearly from where Sarah stood.

Sarah noted with pride how Emily distinctly stood out among the other children. Her daughter was ethereally beautiful with her light blond curls hanging down her back, bouncing loosely whenever she turned her head.

"What a great way to celebrate your birthday. Are you happy?" Charles asked. He held his hands protectively around Emily's little waist.

"Yes, Daddy!" she exclaimed. Fidgeting, she searched her father's face before speaking. "I want to ride alone. I'll hold on tight. Please, get off. Go stand by Mommy." She pushed his hands away from her small frame.

Charles was thrown off guard by his daughter's request and didn't respond immediately.

"Come on, Daddy. I'm a big girl now. I'm five years old today," Emily persisted.

Charles paused for a moment. He thought she looked so small on that big, wood horse. For a split second, before dismounting the ride, he had a stabbing feeling of regret.

Just then, Emily said, "It's okay, Leeza."

"Who are you talking to?" Charles turned back and asked.

"Leeza told me to hold on tight," Emily said. "I told her it was okay."

The smile on Emily's face assured Charles that it was simply another rite

of passage. He knew that Emily loved Leeza and was probably pretending that she was there with her.

"Daddy," Emily called out. "I want my dolly to ride with me." She reached out with fingers stretched wide.

Looking at the doll he had clutched in his hand, Charles was glad for the opportunity to hurry back to Emily's side. She snatched the doll and tucked it safely under her arm, all the while looking straight ahead. It bothered Charles the way she could distance herself from him.

"Hang on tight, Em," he repeated.

"I will. Watch me, Mommy!" Emily yelled with a song in her voice. She hung tightly to the pole. When the music started, her tiny knuckles turned white. The tips of her fingers just touched as she gripped the sturdy post.

The young man operating the ride took hold of a tall stick and moved it over to the right. He began pushing the circular contraption by hand, running alongside the horses until it began to pick up speed. The motor sputtered loudly before kicking in and as if by magic, the ride began to glide by itself.

Charles and Sarah locked arms. They looked on with great anticipation as Emily waved and giggled each time the merry-go-round made a complete circle.

"I know that Emily is getting to be a big girl, but how could you let her go on that ride alone?" Sarah complained. "I'm afraid. What if she slips off?"

"Relax. Let her enjoy herself," Charles snapped in a lame attempt to justify his actions. "It's her birthday." While harsh, his words didn't sound very confident. The deep furrow in his brow confirmed Charles's second thoughts about letting Emily ride alone. He cupped his hands around his mouth and yelled, "Hold on tight, Em!" Turning to Sarah, he said, "See. It's okay. She's good."

Sarah was too busy searching the horses for her daughter to pay any attention to Charles. The merry-go-round was circling for the sixth time. The music was blaring so loudly that it drowned out the sudden gasp that escaped from Charles's lips. "Where's Emily?"

Chapter Five

Charles and Sarah were extremely agitated and distraught. They were disruptive and yelling accusations that were both upsetting and threatening to the carousel attendant. He was simply there to operate the merry-go-round.

"She couldn't have simply disappeared," Sarah coughed out a mock laugh. "What's your name? You look like a nice young man. Why don't you help us find our daughter and we'll go home and never bother you again." Sarah's eyes opened wide with terror. He stepped back from her.

Charles spoke in a low tone and moved in closer to him, so close to the young man's face, he could smell his breath. "If you had anything to do with this, you will rue the day you were born!"

"Hey, wait a minute. I just work here, mister." He took a couple more steps back. "I don't know what you're talking about. I have no idea where your little girl is. Hundreds of kids ride this merry-go-round. I don't keep tabs on them. That's their parent's job."

"You don't understand. I'm not leaving here without Emily," Sarah said in a louder, more threatening tone of voice.

The reality of their loss was taking hold. Every time Charles looked at Sarah's face, he knew there had to be something more he should be doing. But he didn't know what. "I don't want to leave either. We can't just go home without our daughter. It's absurd to even think about it." Charles turned and stepped back on to the merry-go-round. He shouted Emily's name. Not knowing where else to go, Charles returned to the horse where he last saw his precious little girl.

"She chose this horse herself. I left her right here." Charles was becoming repetitive. His voice was loud and demanding. The carousel attendant didn't know what to do.

"Emily couldn't have just vanished into thin air. What the hell is going on?" Charles yelled at no one in particular. This was all it took to make the young man take off in a fast sprint.

Sarah walked up to Charles and wrapped her arms around him. Charles made no attempt to return her embrace. He couldn't; he felt numb. *If she could see how scared I am on the inside, she'd be horrified!*

When the police arrived, Charles was still clenching the carousel horse that had infatuated Emily. The officers started clearing the area of spectators and escorted children away from the merry-go-round. The young man, who was responsible for operating the ride returned with the owner of the carousel. They were instructed by the police to step back and stay away from the distraught couple. Charles and Sarah were in shock. By this time, they were unable to think constructively. A young officer stepped forward.

"Everyone back away. I'll make a complete report and give you the information you need to know." He turned back to Charles and Sarah. His well-trained eye and gut instinct told him that this young couple was desperate and in trouble. He knew that they needed to be handled very carefully.

"Hello," he began calmly as he stepped onto the merry-go-round. "My name is Officer Sullivan. I'm here to help you."

Charles still clung tightly to the horse where he regretfully left Emily. "I'm so glad you're here. Now, maybe you can find our daughter and we can just go home," Charles sighed deeply with a false sense of relief.

"I want you to tell me what happened here today," the officer directed his question to Charles. "Take your time. So far, I only know what the young man operating the ride told me. He's pretty upset. He claims that you can't find your daughter and somehow you blame him."

Charles was mentally drained. He was shaking and having a hard time focusing on the police officer. "I'll try to answer your questions, sir," he said, inhaling slowly. "Someone took our daughter. Her name is Emily." Just saying the words out loud was enough to break the composure he was fighting to get under control. *I have to think of Emily.*

Officer Sullivan waited patiently for Charles to get a hold of himself. He placed a firm but empathetic hand on Charles's shoulder. "Calm down and try to tell me exactly what happened."

Charles sighed deeply before going on. "I put Emily on the merry-go-round. She wanted to ride this horse, right here." The seat of the carousel horse felt cold and hard under his hand. "Emily insisted on riding alone. I don't know what possessed her to ask, but it's her birthday today. I wasn't sure but I gave in. I left her here on this horse and stepped off the ride to watch her with Sarah. This is her mother." Sarah simply nodded.

Heat rose in Charles's cheeks. He was unable to suppress his heavy burden of guilt. A sense of doom gripped him in the very depths of his soul. He glanced at Sarah, who was hanging on his every word.

For a split second, Charles thought he heard Emily's voice calling for him. He immediately whipped his head around, but all he saw was his own humiliating reflection in the carousel mirrors. Emily was gone.

"The merry-go-round started and Emily looked like she was having a great time. She was holding on tight enough. Then, about the sixth time around, she wasn't on the horse. She was gone." Charles shook his head in disbelief. "It happened so fast."

The officer was taking notes as Charles spoke. "Is it common practice for you to let Emily make decisions, whether or not it's in her best interest?"

Charles felt bad enough and in his own defense, he retaliated. "It's her birthday. I didn't want to tell her no." Nothing sounded right. "Is it a crime to indulge in a child's whim once in a while?"

"Of course not. I'm only looking for the facts, sir." Officer Sullivan wanted to get the details of what happened while they were fresh in Charles's mind. "There'll be plenty of time for indulging after we find your daughter." He smiled at the ravaged couple.

"Is that it?" Sarah cried. "We have to go home without her? Emily vanished right before our eyes. Something horrible has happened to our little girl!"

Officer Sullivan had to defuse the immediate situation. "One more thing. Before you placed her on the merry-go-round, at any time was Emily out of your sight? Did you see her talking to anyone?"

"No," Sarah stated adamantly. She looked at Charles for support. He nodded in agreement.

"We'll keep in touch with you. Please, go home and stay close to the phone in case Emily or whoever she's with tries to contact you. I have to get to work now. The sooner we get started, the sooner we can bring Emily home." He turned and walked away from the Thatchers with a heavy heart.

Extra police were brought in. A search was completed of the ride and the entire carnival. There were roadblocks set up at all the entrances of the fair where cars were stopped and checked before being allowed to leave.

The owner of the carousel ordered the merry-go-round to be disassembled and put into storage. All of the riders were escorted off of the majestic carousel. It was officially closed to the public, but it gave Charles and Sarah no relief. They still had to go home without Emily.

Next to the now abandoned merry-go-round, in the shadow of a big, old, oak tree, a lone figure lurked, silently watching the hunt for Emily. Subtly blending into the environment with a large baggy hood over his head, the skulking spectator remained quiet and unnoticed as he slithered away into the crowd.

Charles and Sarah took one last look at the breathtakingly beautiful carousel before turning to leave. *If I tell them that I thought I heard Emily calling me, they will simply think I've gone mad. Maybe I have.* Charles took Sarah by the arm and allowed one of the police officers to escort them out of the fair grounds. He turned to Sarah and asked wearily, "How are we going to tell Leeza?"

Sarah's face clouded over and she looked away. "She already knows."

Chapter Six

June, 28, 2005

"Wake up, sleepy head." Angela Michaels sat on her daughter's bed, gently stroking Brittney's hair. "Happy birthday."

Brittney Michaels was waking up to her fifth birthday. She stretched her little arms above her head.

"This is a very special birthday for you. I can't believe you're five years old already," Angela marveled.

Brittney mumbled with a sheepish grin as she burrowed under the comforter, "Where's my present?"

Angela tickled her and rolled her around the bed, making Brittney giggle and scream. "You little piggy. I know a secret. Your daddy has a big surprise for you."

Brittney perked up at the thought of a surprise. "What is it?" she pleaded.

"Well, didn't you tell me that Papa said something about Willows Park and this weekend?" Angel tilted her head to one side and tapped on her chin thoughtfully. Brittney was wide-awake now.

"The carnival?" she exclaimed. "Oh Mommy, is Daddy taking me to the carnival for my birthday?"

"I don't know, Britt," Angela taunted. "It's a surprise, remember?"

Brittney jumped out of bed and ran for the bathroom. She continued chattering from behind the partially closed door.

It wasn't unusual for Angela to catch her daughter interacting with what she thought to be imaginary friends. She didn't think it was odd for a five-year-old to fabricate make believe playmates, especially with her being an only child.

"What do you want to wear today?" Angela asked. "How about your pretty lavender top with the flowers across the front, and your new jeans?"

"Okay, Mom." Brittney liked dressing up, but sometimes she would over-dress. Angela allowed her to make the final decision, but helped her select an appropriate outfit for the day. She started running the tub water for her daughter, smoothed the bed linens and laid Brittney's clothes on top of the bed.

While straightening up, Angela found a strange looking bead strung on a tattered, faded-pink ribbon. It was lying on Brittney's dresser. Angela picked it up and turned it over. She went into the bathroom. Brittney was already in the tub. "Hey, where did you get this?" Angela asked. She held up the strange necklace.

"When I was playing outside in my sandbox an old black lady gave it to me," Brittney answered. "It was in a little box with a bunch of sparkly rocks. She was so nice."

"She came into the yard?" Angela thought for a moment. "It was probably one of the housekeepers taking a walk. Next time you see her, you call me. You know better than to talk to strangers." Angela was concerned about Brittney's experience.

"Okay, but it's mine now," Brittney said.

"I'll put it back on the dresser. Where are the other rocks? I'd like to see them," Angela asked.

Brittney stood up in the tub and announced that she was finished. "I'll show you later. I'm freezing. I want to get dressed."

Angela reached for a towel and wrapped it snuggly around her daughter's head, and quickly patted her dry. "Come on, I have your clothes laid out. You can get dressed while I pick up in here."

Brittney did as she was told and was still dressing when Angela came out of the bathroom. "You're getting so big, Britt. Where's Mommy's baby girl?"

"Oh Mom, I know I'm big. Look how tall I am." Brittney stood against the wall and Angela impulsively picked up a pencil and drew a line above her daughter's head. Brittney turned and stared at the mark on the wall.

"Mom. You drew on the wall." She looked right at her mother and waited for an explanation.

"I know. That's how tall you are now. Don't wipe it off and next year, we'll measure you again to see how much you've grown." Angela gave Brittney a reassuring hug.

Angela thought about the day that Brittney was born. Her thoughts turned to darkness, thunderstorms and fear. "That's weird," she said aloud. "It was a beautiful day when you were born, Brittney. There wasn't a cloud in the sky. I wonder what made me think of thunderstorms and lightning." Angela wanted to shake the gloomy feeling that was trying to overwhelm her spirit.

"Go get a pony-wrap and a brush." She spun Brittney around and gave her a playful love-tap to her bottom. "After you're finished getting dressed, we'll go downstairs and see what Daddy has planned for your birthday."

While sitting on the bed, Angela remembered the rocks that Brittney told her about. She opened the dresser drawer and found the small wooden box, well-worn.

Angela opened it and found five stones. One was incredibly stunning, resembling a green opal. Angela put the box back where she found it and closed the drawer.

Brittney returned and stood in front of Angela. She was dressed and holding a brush in one hand and a scrunchy in the other. Angela brushed her daughter's long brown hair and twisted the scrunchy around it, creating a perfect ponytail. "There. How's that?"

"Did you like my rocks?" Brittney asked.

"Yes, they were very pretty," Angela said, wondering how Brittney knew she had looked at them. She took the box out of the drawer. "Where's that odd looking stone?" Angela asked and was surprised when she looked up and saw that Brittney was wearing the weird bead on an old ribbon around her neck. *I don't remember seeing that when I brushed her hair.*

"Do you really want to wear that today? It isn't very pretty," Angela said in an attempt to discourage her from wearing the strange necklace.

Brittney didn't seem to mind either way, so Angela quickly slid the ribbon over her daughter's head. "There, let's put it away with the rest of the rocks for now. I think we should go downstairs and see what Daddy's up to."

Brittney bounced down the steps and stopped short. Balloons and streamers filled the living room. "Wow! Is this all for me?" It was the perfect distraction.

"It sure is, baby," Ted Michaels came up behind his daughter and knelt beside her on the floor, before planting a kiss on her soft little cheek. "Happy birthday, princess. I have a surprise for you," he whispered in her ear. Ted instantly pulled out a lovely gold chain with a quaint gold cross. He fastened the necklace around Brittney's neck and held her at arm's length, so he could admire it.

Brittney touched the necklace and quietly searched her father's face.

"Well, do you like it?" he asked

"Yes Daddy, but Mom said you had another surprise for me," Her voice trembled as she choked back the rising tears.

"Hmm. Let me see." Ted acted like he was searching his pockets. Then, he noted the look of desperation on Brittney's face. He couldn't continue to tease her. "How would you like to spend the afternoon at the park?"

Brittney was so relieved, she clapped her hands vigorously.

"Nana and Papa won't be coming over until later on this evening and I thought we would do something special for your birthday," Ted announced.

"Oh yes, Daddy! Let's go to the park. Is Mom coming too?" Brittney's voice elevated with enthusiasm.

"What about it, Ang? Are you coming with us?" He threw the unexpected invitation at his wife.

"I have to bake a cake this morning. I'll leave it up to you, Britt. Do you want a store-bought cake or a Mama-made birthday cake this year?"

"I want you to make my favorite chocolate cake." The decision was made.

"It looks like you and your daddy have a date then." Angela smiled at Ted.

The phone rang. Ted answered it and called out, "Brittney, it's for you. Your Nana would like to talk to you."

Brittney ran for the phone. She began telling her Nana all about the carnival at Willows Park.

Angela followed Ted upstairs to discuss the events of the day. "I'd like to go but, you need some time alone with Brittney too. She's with me all day. You only see her for a couple of hours before she goes to bed. It'll be good for both of you," Angela said. "By the way, Brittney told me that an older black lady talked to her in the back yard when she was playing in the sand box."

"Where were you?" Ted questioned.

"I had to have been outside. She's never out alone. I must have been in the garden," she replied defensively. "Anyway, that isn't my concern. The woman gave Brittney a box of what looked to be some nice colored stones."

"Sounds like real criminal activity to me," Ted answered with a note of sarcasm.

Angela ignored his mockery. "One stone actually looked like it might be worth something. It was some sort of green opal. But, the one that bothered me was one of those evil eye beads. It was strung on an old ribbon." Angela lowered her voice.

"You can get those in any gum ball machine, Ang. She was probably lonely and trying to be nice. If you see her again, talk to the old woman. If she makes you uncomfortable, tell her not to come around. Then, if she does, we'll call the police." Ted tried to simplify the situation.

Angela wasn't buying it. "We'll see. Oh remember, your parents are coming over tonight for cake and ice cream. I wish my mom and dad could have made it."

"Did they say what time they're coming? I need to know when to have Britt back home," Ted replied. "We'll most likely be gone the better part of the afternoon and I'd like to go back for the fireworks tonight."

Ted Michaels enjoyed fireworks more than anyone Angela knew. She gave her husband an annoyed glance. "If your parents leave early enough, we might be able to go back to the park and see your fireworks," she said.

"Daddy, what are you guys doing?" Brittney stood fixed in the doorway. "You're supposed to be getting ready to go to the park."

Angela looked at her daughter. "Are you finished talking to Nana and Papa already?"

"Yes Mom. Come on Daddy, let's go," Brittney implored. Brittney put on a satisfied grin when Ted got right up. She turned to get a head start out of the room. "Last one downstairs is a rotten egg!" she yelled.

Angela reached out and gave Brittney an unexpected crack on her butt. "I still owe you four more, birthday girl. You get a swat for every year."

"That's right, but you can't forget about the pinch to grow an inch," Ted growled and chased his daughter out of the room.

Angela lingered with her thoughts. She inhaled the warm summer air that gracefully swept in through the screens. There was something special about the smells of summer that always carried wonderful, childhood memories.

"That's what I want for you, Brittney; memories that you can recall as simply as opening a window on a warm, sunny day," Angela said aloud. She turned to leave the room and was stopped short by a sudden, uncomfortable chill. It didn't appear to be coming from the opened window. In fact, it felt like tiny, cold fingers running down both of her arms.

As she left the room, Angela could almost swear that she heard the soft giggle of a child's voice. "What the hell was that?"

she whispered. Her heart beat rapidly, and then she laughed at herself, deciding that it was nothing. Angela headed downstairs to say good-bye to Ted and Brittney.

"Bye Mom. See you later," Brittney shouted from the back seat of the car.

Angela saw her little fingers waving from the car window and she volleyed back, "Have fun, you two! Hold Daddy's hand." Angela took a deep breath and released a sigh. "Happy birthday."

Turning around, she picked up the newspaper and read the headlines as she carried it into the house. The front page had a picture of a priest. She read aloud, "Father Luke Phillips received a recommendation for the prestigious position of Bishop. 'This is something I've worked for, all my life,' he stated."

Angela tossed the paper on the hall-tree and closed the front door. She glanced up toward her bedroom and mumbled, "It was probably just Brittney." The phone rang and startled her.

Brittney could hardly wait to get to Willows Park. She kept watching for signs of the carnival. Ted was happy about the quality time he was about to spend with his daughter. He glanced at her in the rear view mirror. "What's that around your neck? Where's the necklace I gave you?"

"I have them both on. The nice black lady told me it would keep me safe," Brittney explained.

Before Ted could respond, Brittney spotted the bright colors of the local festival. "Daddy, we're here, we're here! Look at all the rides. Can I have some cotton candy?" She definitely had a one-track mind and began chattering. "I want to ride the real live ponies. I'm big enough. I'm five years old today."

Chapter Seven

Ted found a parking place and pulled in. For some odd reason, he became overwhelmed with dread. *Maybe we shouldn't have come here today.* He got out of the car and opened the back door for Brittney. She was like a pot ready to boil over.

"Before we start, we have to get a couple of things straight. First, there's no running off. You have to stay right by me. Second, let me see that thing around your neck." Ted examined the odd looking stone and the faded ribbon. When he was sure it was just an old bobble that the woman probably gave to all the kids she met, he said, "It really is a beautiful day. Come on, let's get started."

"Okay Daddy," Brittney squeezed her father's hand when she got out of the car. They both smiled. "Look, they have real horses." Ted could feel her trembling. "Let's go over there and pick one out." He held her hand securely in his.

As they approached the ride, there were two young men in charge of the little ponies. They immediately sized Brittney up.

Knowing they were looking at her, Brittney spoke up boldly, "I'm five years old today. I'm big enough to ride a pony this year, all by myself. My daddy said so." She let out a huff and placed her hands firmly on her hips.

Ted chuckled to himself. *She sure looks like her mother when she does that.*

"Is that right?" One of the young men said. "My name is Jeff. Have you picked out a horse?"

Brittney looked at her father with great expectations and a twinkle in her eye. "Go ahead, sweetie. Show the man which one you want. I'll stand right here and watch you," he assured her. "Hey, do you guys walk around with them?" Ted asked the carnival worker.

"We certainly do, sir. These are real live animals, not like the ones on that merry-go-round over there." He shielded his eyes from the sun with one hand and pointed to the carousel.

Ted looked in the direction he was pointing. From where he stood, the sun reflected off the mirrors of a picturesque old merry-go-round. It sparkled like an iridescent gown covered in sequins. "Are you talking about that old carousel?"

"Yes, sir," Jeff replied. "You really ought to let her ride it before you leave. It's one of a kind. I used to operate that very merry-go-round a while back."

"We'll have to do that, thanks." Ted glanced at it again. The merry-go-round was on the other side of the park. It would be a while before they reached it. Ted returned his attention to Brittney and the live pony. He watched as the carnival worker lifted her up and set her on the little horse that was white from its mid-section to his hind legs. Brittney giggled into her hand.

"What's so funny," Jeff asked.

Brittney turned slightly and pointed to the pony's backside. "He looks like he's wearing pants. I'm going to call him, Mr. Pants."

Jeff chuckled. "That sounds like a good name for him."

Ted laughed along with them. "Hang on tight Brittney. That's a real live horse," Ted said nervously. Turning toward Jeff he said, "It's her birthday today. Can I take a picture of her on the horse?"

"Fine with me," Jeff said.

Brittney put on her biggest smile. Ted snapped a picture. He felt so proud at that moment.

After being led around the small corral a few times, Jeff helped Brittney down off the pony. Ted thanked him and they headed back through the midway, hand in hand.

"Are you having a good time, honey?" Ted asked.

Brittney answered without looking up. "Yes Daddy." She was taking in all the food stands, games and rides. The smells were stimulating; the games were just plain fun; but, the rides were alluring.

Ted stopped at one of the vendors to get Brittney a large, freshly made cotton candy, spun on a paper cone. She stood next to him watching the big carousel.

When she turned her head, a little girl, whose long blond curls hung over her shoulders was standing right up next to her. They were literally face to face. The child was staring at Brittney. She didn't speak. For no reason, she reached out and touched the bead, hanging from the ribbon around Brittney's neck. Brittney smiled. The little girl tugged gently on the bead before turning and stomping off in the direction of the merry-go-round.

"That was pretty brazen of her," Ted said. Despite the warmth of the day, he felt an icy chill slither down his back. He shook it off and handed Brittney the cotton candy. She pulled off a wad of the sweet, blue spun sugar with her teeth, while holding tightly to the evil eye bead with the other.

"I hope that sugar doesn't make you sick," Ted said. Brittney lowered her eyes, her face full of gooey remnants of the cotton candy. Ted reached out and picked a piece of the crystallized delight from her hair. "Let's go over to the merry-go-round. I heard it was supposed to be the best ride in the park."

Brittney smiled and took hold of his hand. He pulled her a little closer as she skipped alongside him. The melodious tune coming from the merry-go-round was loud and inviting.

Chapter Eight

Ted and Brittney stood in front of the beautiful carousel, enjoying the splendor of the merry-go-round. The painted, wooden horses sat on a revolving, circular platform. They were painted in vibrant colors that attracted attention from the crowd like a magnet. Intricately carved benches were scattered between the rows of horses. The vintage carousel circled in front of them as the bewitching, painted horses slid gracefully up and down on their sturdy poles in perfect time with the music, which flowed from the calliope. Brittney was completely enamored by the sight of it.

Brittney stared at the majestic steeds in awe. A withered old tree blocked the sun, allowing her to look directly into the individual faces of each carousel horse. The very sight of them circling around and around made her queasy and for a moment, she wanted to turn away. But instead, Brittney took a dangerous step toward the moving ride.

"What the hell are you doing?" Ted instantly jerked her back to his side.

Brittney gasped. "Isn't it awesome?"

"Yeah, it would have been real awesome if you had been dragged under that thing,. You need to start paying attention." The merry-go-round slowed down and Ted was able to get a better look at it.

"It looks old. I wonder where it came from. I don't think I've ever seen a merry-go-round quite like this one. The workmanship is incredible," Ted said. He studied the intricate detail of the horses. "Whoever designed it certainly took pride in their work. Look at that one." Ted pointed to one of the carousel horses that held his head high above the rest. "He must be the lead," Ted chuckled. He felt a sudden urgency to move on to another horse and steered his daughter away from the wooden character that presented as both immortal and enticing.

After the ride came to a complete stop, Ted picked Brittney up and stepped on to the platform. He touched one of the carousel horses and received a shock, causing him to jerk his hand away.

"What's the matter, Daddy? Did he bite you?" Brittney giggled.

Ted set her down and responded with a nervous laugh. "I just got a shock when I touched it." He rubbed the palm of his still stinging hand. *I could swear that for a split second, that horse felt warm and alive.*

Unaware that anyone was listening, Ted startled when a stranger spoke up in a low tone just over his shoulder. "It belongs to my uncle. He bought out an old estate a little north of here and found this carousel in pieces, stored in one of the pole barns on the property. He replaced some of the mirrors, lights and rickrack. I can't really date it, but it's pretty old."

"Nice job," Ted remarked.

"When my uncle had the mechanics updated, he found that the center structure is all one piece. Makes one curious, doesn't it?" The stranger almost whispered his words before backing away.

Ted whipped around to look at him but, he was gone. "What a freak. I wonder what he meant by that."

Redirecting his attention, Brittney said, "Daddy hurry, I want to ride that horse over there."

"Do you mean the one next to the gold and purple horse?" Ted scooped her up and she straddled his hip as he worked his way through the different carved animals.

Brittney squirmed to be put down and scurried over to the horse she had her heart set on riding. "This one Daddy; I want this one."

Ted placed her on the saddle of the carousel horse. He thought about how less than an hour ago, she was riding a real live pony and wondered how this could even compare to such an experience. However, she seemed to be just as happy with the imitation.

"Hang on to the pole. I'll stand right next to you."

The man, who spoke to Ted only moments earlier, reappeared. He had a little girl with him that he sat on the horse next to Brittney, before quickly shuffling away.

She was an exceptionally pretty child with long, blond curls that hung down her back and bounced freely whenever she turned her head from side to side. A deep dimple creased her right cheek when she smiled.

Brittney looked directly at Ted. "Daddy," she whispered. "Can you get off and let me ride by myself?"

"Heck no. What do you mean, Britt? What if you fall off?" Ted didn't understand why she would ask such a thing.

Brittney glanced at the little girl sitting on the horse next to her. "Please, Daddy. I'm five years old now. I can hold on tight," Brittney spoke in a hushed tone so that only her father could hear.

Ted noticed that Brittney was looking at the little girl sitting all alone on the horse next to her. "How old do you suppose she is?" He leaned in to maintain the privacy of their conversation.

"I think she's my age. If she can hold on, so can I! I'm bigger than her." Brittney spoke adamantly and sat up straight on her horse.

"Ah Britt, I don't know. You can't tell your mother that you went on this ride alone. Do you promise?"

Excited beyond words, Brittney answered, "Pinky promise. Now, go stand over there." She pointed to a spot just off the ride. "I'll wave at you when I go past and you can take our picture." The two girls smiled as if they knew each other.

"Forget about waving, you just hold on tight! I'll be right there where you can see me. I'll be able to jump on the ride if you need me." Ted hesitated before turning to leave. Before stepping off the solid wood platform, he heard the girls giggle. It took every bit of his will power to get off of the carousel.

The merry-go-round began to move, slowly at first, and then it picked up speed. Ted watched as the horses slid gracefully up and down the poles. "Hang on tight, Brittney," he shouted. Each time the ride circled, she let go of one hand and waved at him.

Ted held the camera up to his face and yelled, "Say cheese." Taking pictures of the girls was a good distraction and occupied his time as he waited for the ride to end. Both children smiled for the camera. Ted felt he was capturing a very important moment in Brittney's life with every photograph.

The ride circled four or five times before beginning to slow. Brittney was enjoying her freedom. The carousel music blared around her and for that short period of time, she was experiencing another dimension of her life. She could see her father mouthing words to her every time they passed, but she couldn't hear him and didn't particularly care. She simply waved and smiled.

At one point, before the ride was over, the little blond haired girl reached out to Brittney and wiggled her fingers as if to tickle her under the chin. In response, Brittney tucked her face down so that her chin touched the right side of her chest and she laughed out loud at her new friend's gesture. Ted was able to capture the moment with his final picture.

The carousel appeared to be moving in slow motion as Ted leaped on to the sturdy platform and headed straight for his daughter. "Don't try to get off by yourself," he called out. "It's too high."

I wonder where that kid's father went.

When he finally reached them, Ted addressed the little girl sitting up on the horse next to Brittney. "Don't try to get down by yourself. You'll get hurt. Wait for your dad. Do you want me to help you get down?"

The strange little girl offered no response, but simply gave Ted an icy glare that caused the hairs on his neck to stand at attention. A feeling of anger and distaste reared up in him like a tidal wave at the thought of this child's disrespect.

The pretty little girl smiled at Brittney and shook her head back and forth, indicating that she did not want or need any help. The children had definitely struck a bond.

Ted collected his daughter and turned to leave when Brittney grabbed hold of the evil eye bead and pulled the ribbon over her head. She handed it to her new friend.

"Why did you do that?" Ted asked.

Brittney smiled at the little girl and said, "She asked me for it."

Ted was glad that Brittney was still wearing the necklace he had bought for her. However he thought it was very rude for a complete stranger to ask Brittney for her necklace. He quickly reached out and took the ugly old ribbon out of the child's hand. "I'm sorry, but that belongs to my daughter."

Before Brittney had a chance to protest, Ted shoved the necklace down deep into his jean pocket, walked to the edge of the merry-go-round, and stepped off. When he set Brittney down, she called back to her newfound friend, "Good bye Emily, sorry." Emily waved ever so slightly as if it were an extreme effort to raise her arm. She looked straight ahead and stayed on the merry-go-round as the ride started up again.

"How did you know her name?" Ted asked. He couldn't shake the uneasy feeling that Emily gave him.

"She told me her name and I told her mine. Emily is my new best friend."

Ted glanced back over his shoulder at Emily. She was still sitting alone on the purple and gold horse. He clenched his jaw and debated on staying until she was safe with her parents. *I can't worry about every kid with bad parents. They know where they left her.*

Emily didn't look the least bit worried or afraid. Ted took Brittney firmly by the hand and walked away with no intention of ever seeing Emily again.

Chapter Nine

"How would you like to ride the train before we go home?" Ted attempted to redirect his daughter's attention.

Brittney smiled and nodded. Her gaze slid back toward the merry-go-round to see if Emily was still there. Ted tried to ignore her indifference. He held her hand firmly and led her toward the carnival's train depot. The car they stepped into was one of the replicas of the Santa Fe rail cars. It circled the entire park.

"I hope you had a good time." Ted felt that somewhere along the line, he had lost Brittney's attention.

The corner of his mouth pinched and his lips flattened when she didn't answer him. "After this ride, we're going home. I hope you remember to tell Mom that we did more than just ride the merry-go-round and meet that little girl."

Brittney was perplexed by his tone of voice and attitude. "Maybe Mom is finished with my chocolate cake." She inched toward him.

"I'm sure she is," Ted answered, his expression softened. "Nana and Papa will be coming over soon. I wonder what they got you for your birthday." *The present alone should be enough to get her mind off that kid.*

"I want to say goodbye to Emily before we go home," Brittney looked at her father as if she were the parent and he was the child.

"I'm sure she left with her parents by now," Ted said flatly.

"Emily is my best friend," Brittney responded boldly.

Ted tried to ignore her. "By the way, unless you ask Mom or me, don't give anything away. You don't even know that kid and you gave her your necklace. What was that all about?"

"She asked me for it. Emily said that it didn't belong to me. She said it belongs to Leeza," Brittney answered casually.

"Who's Leeza?" Ted demanded. "Never mind. On second thought, just do what you're told. I don't want this to ever happen again. End of discussion!"

Brittney tried to explain, "But Dad..."

Ted was glad that the afternoon was coming to an end. The sound of Emily's name was becoming as irritating as a hovering mosquito. The train pulled into the carnival version of a real train station. Ted attempted to show Brittney around and explain what a train depot was. Usually, she focused on her father's every word, but today her mind was elsewhere. Ted gave up and headed for the parking lot. They had to pass the merry-go-round on the way.

As if suspended in time, Emily remained perched on the carousel horse where they last saw her. Brittney was excited to see Emily and pulled away from her father, walking away from him and toward the carousel.

"Brittney," Ted yelled. He rushed up behind her, grabbed hold of her arm, and spun her around to face him. "Don't you ever walk away from me again. We're going home. Obviously, you don't know how to listen."

Emily didn't show any emotion as she watched Ted and Brittney struggle. She glared wickedly at Ted and he returned the gesture as the merry-go-round continued to blare the repetitious melody that only seemed to get louder and louder. Ted's heartbeat pounded in his head.

"Bye Emily," Brittney called out.

Ted shook his head and glanced at Emily before turning away. She wore a sinister smile and nodded at Brittney. The bond was sealed. The children had connected.

"I can't believe you did that," Ted mumbled. "That little girl has no one watching her. She's on the same horse that we left her on. What sort of parents leaves a child unattended for that length of time? Not a good one, that's for sure."

"It's okay, Daddy. Emily stays on the merry-go-round all the time," Brittney said.

"Her dad did say something about his uncle owning the ride," Ted answered. "That's how he knew so much about the carousel. I suppose the merry-go-round is as good a babysitter as any," he said in a most uncharacteristically sarcastic way.

"We're both five years old. We don't need babysitters anymore," Brittney announced smugly.

Ted made one of his monster faces. "Is that so? We'll see about that." Brittney started screaming and laughing. It was a relief to see her acting more like the Brittney he knew. Ted gave his daughter a hug, but he could feel her wrenching around in the direction of the merry-go-round. It stirred ill feelings. Emily was only a little girl. He couldn't figure out what it was about her that made him so uncomfortable.

When they reached the car, Brittney looked back towards the carousel, waved and blew a kiss. Instead of arguing, Ted said, "Let's go home and see if Mom is finished decorating your birthday cake."

"It's so much fun here. Can we come back?" Brittney asked. "Emily said they're going to be here for another week."

"I don't know; we'll see." Ted's response was short. "Get in the car." He was in no mood to encourage a discussion about Emily. *She is just a child. Why am I getting so upset?*

"Maybe Nana and Papa will be there when we get home," Brittney shouted with renewed excitement.

Ted secured his daughter's seatbelt and planted a kiss on her forehead. As he ducked out of the car, Brittney said, "She's very lonely, Daddy."

"What? Who are you talking about?" He held his hand on the opened car door taking short, quick breaths in an attempt to maintain his composure.

"Emily is very sad. She's been on the merry-go-round for a long time. I promised that I would play with her again. She said that she has a secret. I think her secret makes her sad. Brittney avoided her father's eyes and let out a low sigh.

"Yeah, well I have a secret too. Don't you want to know what you got for your birthday this year? Aren't you excited about that anymore?" Ted was allowing a one sided discussion to turn into a nasty conversation with a five-year-old. It was starting to infuriate him.

Ted had to calm down before saying something he might regret. "It was nice for you to meet Emily and have someone to ride the merry-go-round with. But don't get your hopes up on ever seeing her again."

Brittney held out her hand. "Can I have my necklace back?"

Ted reached into his pocket. He felt horrible when he realized that the strange stone that had caused so much of a disturbance was gone. "Crap, I must have lost it. I don't know how it got out of my jeans."

Brittney settled back in her seat. She had nothing further to say. Ted closed the car door and slid into the driver's seat.

"I'm sorry about losing your necklace. Did you hear me? You know, I didn't do it on purpose." He felt like a heel.

"It's okay Daddy." She met his gaze in the rear view mirror and didn't look like she understood at all.

Ted needed to change the subject. "Can you guess what your special present is?"

"Is it a castle tent for my bedroom?" Brittney's familiar innocence made Ted relax.

"I don't think so. Mom showed it to me when we were shopping for your birthday present and it was so big that I told her it would never fit in your room." He wore a sly grin when Ted returned her gaze in the mirror.

Brittney waited for her father to tell her he was joking. She had been asking for the play castle for weeks now. "Nana said it was just my size. Nana said it would fit perfect in my room." She seemed to be back to her old self. The person he knew her to be before they went to the carnival. "I'm going to call Emily when I get home and she can come over and play with me."

Ted stiffened. *What the heck does Emily have to do with anything? Why does the very sound of her name make me cringe? I can't believe I'm jealous of a five year old girl.*

"Look, Daddy. Nana and Papa are here. I see their car," Brittney cried when they turned down their street. Ted released a long sigh of relief.

"Maybe Emily will come to my birthday party and eat cake and ice cream with me. It's her birthday too. I told her she could come over." Brittney's excitement over her birthday now included a stranger.

Ted refused to respond to her new obsession. Angela was on the front porch when they pulled into the driveway. Elizabeth and Leonard were right behind her singing, *Happy Birthday* all in unison.

"It looks like you have a welcoming committee, Britt," Ted announced.

"Yeah, just for me. I can't wait to tell Mommy all about Emily, my new best friend."

Ted pursed his lips hard. He had to shake the thoughts that were being forced into his mind. A soft childlike voice followed the breeze that floated into the car window. It was only meant for Ted to hear. "You can't stop it. A mysterious mingling of souls has taken place."

Chapter Ten

"Here comes the birthday girl," Elizabeth sang out as Ted helped Brittney out of the car. She was thrilled about being the center of attention.

"Hi, Mom," Ted greeted Elizabeth with a kiss on the cheek.

"You always smell like fresh cookie dough, Nana," Brittney giggled when Elizabeth hugged her. She nuzzled her face into the collar of her grandmother's blouse.

"We'll have to make up a big batch when you come over. They're Papa's favorites, you know," Elizabeth chuckled.

Brittney looked at her grandfather. His familiar smile always gave her a safe, comfortable feeling. "Happy Birthday, Britt," he boomed. She ran over to Leonard and jumped up into his opened arms.

"Be careful, honey. Don't knock Papa down," Angela laughed.

"Sorry Papa," Brittney giggled.

"That's okay," he smiled. "We heard you've been having quite an exciting afternoon."

Brittney skipped over to Angela. "Me and Daddy rode the train all around the park. He had to squeeze in the seat cause he was too big." Brittney glanced at Ted and snickered into her little cupped hand.

"Did you have a good time, honey?" Angela asked, while smoothing back the hair covering her daughter's forehead.

"Yes Mom. Daddy let me ride all the rides. We ate cotton candy, hot dogs, ice cream and everything." Without pausing to take a breath, Brittney continued, "I rode a real horse all by myself." Her arms were flying above her head as she described her afternoon at the park. "I got to ride the merry-go-round with my new friend, Emily." Brittney lowered her eyes and peeked up at her father.

Angela gave Ted a questioning look. He was listening to his daughter carry on about her afternoon at the carnival. It surprised him that she actually seemed to have enjoyed everything they did together. However, when Brittney brought up Emily's name, he clenched his jaw tightly.

"She had a great time," he boasted. "It's her birthday. She rode that pony all by herself like a real cowgirl," Ted said, intentionally leaving Emily out of the story. "I got her home in one piece and with no belly ache. For that, I deserve an award." He bowed gracefully.

Brittney spun around in a little dance as she continued telling everyone about her day. Angela noted the disturbed look on Ted's face every time Brittney mentioned Emily.

Gently interrupting her, Angela took Brittney by the hand and whispered in her ear. "Let's go in and see your birthday cake. I even wrote your name on it." The aroma of sweet, baked chocolate hung heavy in the air when Angela opened the front door.

Elizabeth followed them inside. Leonard took a seat on the porch. "Sit down a few minutes with me, Son. It's beautiful out here today." He pulled an old pipe out of his shirt pocket, lit it and took a few quick puffs.

"That child sure is growing up fast," Leonard began, attempting to make small talk.

"Yeah, she sure is. She has a mind of her own too. It'll be nice in the fall when she starts school and can make some real friends. She's definitely ready for that." Ted couldn't stop thinking about Brittney's obsession with Emily.

"There was this little girl about Britt's age at the park. They met on the merry-go-round. She really took a liking to her." Ted began to vent. "After that, it was all I could do to keep Brittney focused on anything else. She even gave that strange kid her necklace."

"Not her birthday present?" Leonard asked.

"No. It was some piece of junk that one of the neighbor's housekeepers gave her. You know those things they get out of a bubble gum machine?"

"Well, at least she was smart enough to share that and not the beautiful necklace you bought for her birthday. You have to give her some credit," Leonard added.

"She didn't even know the kid, Dad. Brittney was trying to impress her and that bothered me. It didn't matter how much fun we were having. She completely turned her attention to that total stranger and ignored me."

"Children don't have the conscience to know better," Leonard reassured his son. "Their words can cut ya like a sharp knife," he said, obviously speaking from years of experience.

Leonard threw his head back and laughed. "Pay back is hard. You've only just begun. If you think what happened today is tough, I can't wait to see how you handle her when she gets to be a teenager." He gave Ted a playful slap on the back. "It only gets worse before it gets better. Wait until she gets her first real crush on some mop haired boy with tattoos all over his arms and a ring in his nose." The older man shook with laughter.

"You're thinking about Marie's first boyfriend, aren't you, Dad?" Ted smiled.

"Your sister gave me every one of my gray hairs," he said as he stroked the top of his head.

"I thought you said I did that."

"Nope, you're the one who made them fall out." Both men laughed out loud.

"How did you do it with four kids?" Ted was thinking how hard it was raising just one.

"Each one gets a little easier. It's that first one that's the hardest. You don't know how to be a parent until you've had two or three of those little rascals," Leonard laughed. "Plus, I had your mother to take care of the small stuff. You'll learn how to do that." He took a long drag off his pipe.

"We better get into the house before that child explodes." Leonard moaned when he got up. "I never saw anyone so excited about a birthday."

"Okay, Dad. Did you set up the castle in her bedroom? I don't want to tell her about it. I want her to find it herself," Ted warned his father.

"I sure did. It fit perfectly in the corner, opposite the bed. We just moved things around a little. It brought back memories of that old box you spent hours playing in.

I think our washer came in it." Leonard loved to reminisce.

Ted smiled. "I remember. I was sick when Mom threw it out," Ted admitted.

"I know you were. Throwing that box away was really hard, but we were afraid you were turning into a little nut case. You would spend so much time playing in that thing with your imaginary friends." Leonard still tensed up when he recalled Ted's 'playmates'. "We were young and things like that scared us," he said. "Like you, we worried about the small stuff." Leonard tapped his pipe on the side of the porch.

The two men enjoyed a good laugh as Ted put an arm around his father's shoulder and walked into the house. "It's always good to have you around, Dad."

"Daddy...Papa, come look at the big cake Mom made for me. It has a merry-go-round on top. It's just like the one at the carnival. I have to call Emily. She'll be so excited. Can I Mom? Can Emily come over for my party? She said it's her birthday too."

Brittney ran up the stairs to her bedroom. Angela threw Ted a puzzled look. "Who's Emily?"

Ted heaved a long, disgusted sigh. "Some kid she met on the merry-go-round. I think she belonged to one of the carnival people."

When Angela didn't respond negatively, Ted balked. "This kid is traveling with a carnival. No one was watching her. I won't have Brittney hanging around kids like that." The more Ted talked about Emily, the more agitated he became.

"Oh, her parents were probably a lot closer than you thought," Angela challenged.

"Don't go against me on this, Ang. I don't want you encouraging her. Her first friend isn't going to be some carni-kid." Ted gave Angela one of his 'end of discussion' looks.

"It's not likely that she'll ever see her again," Angela said. "Leave it alone and Brittney will forget all about her."

Angela didn't want to get into an argument with Ted in front of his parents. The conversation was becoming uncomfortable and she knew that Ted wasn't about to back down. There was something about the way he was reacting that wasn't right. Something scared him.

Chapter Eleven

It was obvious from the squeals of delight echoing from upstairs that Brittney had found the gift she sought.

Leonard smiled. "Sounds like she found her castle."

Elizabeth was already heading up the stairs with Ted and Angela close behind.

"Mommy, Daddy, it's here. My very own castle. You were fooling me, Dad. It's big enough for me and Emily." Brittney was darting in and out of the little playhouse. "I called her. She's coming over for birthday cake. It's Emily's birthday too. We're going to play in my castle."

Seeing how excited she was over Emily caused Ted to shrink back. He didn't even like hearing that child's name. "How did you call her?" Ted blurted out.

"I called Emily on my phone, Daddy. See, Nana and Papa gave me my own princess phone," Brittney said as she pointed to the pretty pink telephone sitting on the corner of her dresser.

Leonard nudged Ted gently in the ribs. "It's one of those pretend phones. It looks real, but it's only a toy," he whispered.

Ted felt a little better knowing that the phone Brittney claimed to call Emily on was simply a novelty.

"Remember the small stuff," Leonard peered over his glasses.

"I guess so." Ted shrugged.

"Leave her alone. She met someone her own size and is a little infatuated. When did you get so old?" Leonard tried to humor his son.

All of a sudden, the doorbell rang. Brittney's eyes lit up and she ran out of the room yelling, "I'll get it. It's probably Emily."

Angela quickened her step to keep up with her daughter. "You wait just one minute. Don't you dare open that door before I get there! You know the rules."

Brittney knew very well that she was never to answer the door or the telephone. Ted was close behind his wife. "See, it's already starting," he mumbled as they approached the front door. "That carnival brat has her thinking that she can do whatever she wants."

"Oh shut up." Angela couldn't believe she said it, but the situation was becoming overwhelming.

Leonard went over to the dresser and picked up the toy phone. He brought the receiver up to his ear for just a few seconds when he heard the sinister laugh of a young child. "Darned kids anyway," he said as he placed the receiver firmly back on its cradle. "Now he has me acting like a fool." He could hear voices at the front door as he went down the stairs.

"I'm glad you could come, Emily," Brittney exclaimed.

Standing in the opened doorway was the little girl Brittney had met on the carousel. Around her neck was the evil eye bead on the faded pink ribbon.

"I'm glad you found the necklace I gave you. I guess that makes it yours now," Brittney said. She turned to her father and shrugged. "Finders' keepers."

"Let's go to the kitchen, so I can show you my birthday cake." Brittney reached out and took hold of Emily's hand.

Ted turned and looked at his father. He clenched his jaw before speaking. "How did she know where we live?"

Brittney was still chattering as she pulled Emily toward the kitchen. "We can go upstairs later and play in my castle."

Ted and Angela stepped outside to see who dropped the child off. There was no one in sight.

"What's going on, Ted? Why does that little girl have Brittney's necklace?" A deep crease appeared between Angela's eyebrows. She waited for him to explain.

"Your guess is as good as mine," he snapped. "I knew there was a reason I disliked that kid."

They followed the girls into the kitchen. Angela couldn't help but notice how cute they were together. Brittney was so excited. She was holding on to Emily's hand and whispering in her ear. Emily stood quietly, while taking in her new surroundings.

Ted wasn't happy at all about Emily being there and started right in with the questions. "Emily, how did you get here? Who dropped you off?"

Angela stood by Emily and placed her arm protectively around the tiny body. "You don't need to scare her, Ted. Leave the girls alone. We don't even know how she's supposed to get home," Angela said quietly.

"Wherever that is," Ted responded sarcastically. He pulled his wife aside. "This is Brittney's birthday. No one invited her," he blustered.

"Now, that's not completely true. Britt said that she asked Emily to come to her party for cake and ice cream." Angela fidgeted as she tried to make sense of the situation.

"How did she do that? On that phone she has up in her room?" Ted's voice went up a notch.

"Just stop it. I'll talk to her later. Please, get the ice cream and turn out the lights, so we can sing *Happy Birthday* and cut the cake. The sooner we get this over with, the sooner we can take Emily back where she came from." Angela turned her attention to Brittney. She glanced back over her shoulder at Ted. "I'm concerned too. I just don't want to ruin Brittney's birthday."

The two girls were sitting next to each other at the kitchen table. Brittney had pushed their chairs together.

Ted couldn't sit back and not say anything. "Emily, where did you find that necklace? I put it in my pocket and there's no way it could have fallen out."

Emily's stare was cold as ice. Her impudence made Ted all the more furious.

"I don't appreciate your attitude either. You're a guest in my house and I expect you to answer me when I ask you a question," Ted said.

Angela lit the candles. Elizabeth turned out the lights as Ted and Emily stared through the dark at each other. Neither spoke; their eyes remained locked.

"Let Angie handle it," Leonard took a seat next to Ted. "Just enjoy the cake and sit back. You'll see, there'll be a logical explanation for everything," he whispered in an attempt to diffuse his son's badgering. However, it was hard for Leonard to completely disguise the worry in his own voice.

The room was dark. The candle's glow cast an ellipse of light on Emily's face. She had the evil eye bead clutched tightly in her hand and continued to glare steadily at Ted. He was just about to protest, but Emily spoke up first.

"Leeza was supposed to give this stone to me," her voice buzzed quietly. It sounded out of place, like laughter at a funeral, giving everyone a creepy sense of unease.

"What? Who's Leeza and why was she hanging around our house?" Ted retaliated. He wondered if Leeza was the black woman who was roaming around their neighborhood when Brittney was outside playing.

"Leeza made a mistake. She gave the stone to Brittney. It's mine now." The sound coming from Emily held no resemblance to the voice of a five-year-old child.

Angela broke the awkward moment by starting to sing. Everyone joined in and sang Happy Birthday -- everyone except Emily.

Brittney closed her eyes and made her wish out loud. "I wish that Emily could stay with me forever."

No one responded. Brittney opened her eyes and smiled at her new, best friend.

Ted got up from the table and went outside. He was flushed, frustrated and in need of fresh air. He leaned on the front porch railing and looked up and down the street. *Who in the world would drop a little girl off at the home of total strangers?* "This is so wrong," he murmured. "How did she find us?"

Ted took a couple of deep breaths, went back into the house and stood behind his father's chair. "Good cake, Son. You should have a piece," Leonard said as he shoveled another fork full of the sweet pastry into his mouth. "Liz, I could use a scoop of that chocolate ice cream," Leonard called to his wife.

Brittney laughed at her grandfather. "Isn't my Papa funny?" she asked Emily.

Emily didn't answer. She sat quietly in the chair beside her new friend, observing the merriment without actually participating in the festivities.

Ted watched Emily, thinking how profoundly odd the little girl was. Her mouth opened and closed when she spoke, which was rarely, but the words came out just above a whisper. A blanket of silence muffled her carefully selected words. However, it was the cheap necklace that irritated him the worst. Emily wore it so boldly.

Ted bit the inside of his cheek nervously. "What explanation could there be for this kid, Dad?" he whispered to his father. "What are we supposed to do with her?" Ted squeezed the back of the chair. "I'll tell you one thing, someone is gonna answer for this."

Brittney laughed out loud and spoke saucily around her new friend. She was demonstrating a different side to her personality that Ted and Angela weren't accustomed to. Brittney had a good appetite for sweets. Emily on the other hand didn't eat anything.

Ted was keeping a mental notebook of everything Emily did and said. Nothing made sense and he was definitely not used to being out of control with any situation, especially in his own home.

Angela watched the girls play. Brittney danced to her new CD while Emily watched. It was interesting to see how surprised

Emily was at all of Brittney's toys and gadgets. Nothing appeared familiar to her, not the toys, music or even the computer. It was as if Emily had appeared from somewhere out of the past.

Brittney took Emily by the hand and headed for the stairs. Ted wanted the girls to stay where he could keep an eye on them, while Angela was only concerned that Emily hadn't eaten anything.

"Brittney, I know you're anxious to show off your new castle, but Emily didn't eat her cake and ice cream," Angela said with some concern. She walked up behind her daughter and stood in front of the stairs as she spoke.

"It's okay, Mom; Emily doesn't like cake and ice cream, right Emily?" Brittney announced. "Can we go up and play in my castle?" She marched in place anxiously, while waiting for Angela to give them permission.

"I suppose," Angela answered, unable to think of a reason to say no. Ted was coming out of the kitchen with his parents as the two girls ran upstairs. Leonard stood with Ted by the front door. "I don't like to drive in the dark anymore if I don't have to. Do I sound like an old man?" He tilted his head to the side. "I want to go home, pick up my feet and watch some television before we go to bed."

"I don't blame you, Dad," Ted answered quickly. "I'd leave too. You came to see your granddaughter on her birthday and she doesn't have the courtesy to stay and visit. She is being totally rude!"

Elizabeth came up behind the two men. She smiled and kissed Ted gently on the cheek. "There's something strange about that little girl," she said. "Keep an eye on

Brittney. It's just not right when a little one doesn't have anyone looking after her. I can't believe someone would even consider leaving a small child like Emily with total strangers. Be careful, Ted." She patted his shoulder in a motherly fashion. "I'm not trying to tell you what to do, but I get an eerie feeling around that child."

"I know, Mom. I don't like it either. I'll call you later. I love you." Ted gave his mother a hug.

"I love you too, Son. Bye Angie. The cake was delicious, as usual. You should bake for a living. You'd be rolling in dough." Everyone smiled.

Ted and Angela stood outside on the porch and waved at his parents as they drove away. It was getting late. The sky appeared dull pewter. The evening air had cooled off and a mist hung over the water in the birdbath that took on the appearance of a person's breath on a cold day. Still no one came for Emily.

"Brittney didn't even bother to say good bye to my parents. She's usually begging to go home with them," he complained as they walked back in the house. "Why did you let her run off with Emily when she still had company?" Ted was taking his frustrations out on Angela.

"Oh come on, Ted. She's excited over her castle and actually has someone to show it off to," Angela said in a feeble attempt at a poor excuse. "What were you and your mom talking about?"

"Nothing, she thinks there's something wrong with Emily too," Ted said.

The girls were still playing up in Brittney's room, when Ted and Angela entered the house. Ted headed for the stairs.

"Where are you going? Leave them alone," Angela said gently taking hold of his arm. "Give them some time to play. Then, we'll go to the park and drop her off by the merry-go-round. I'll try to find out who she belongs to. You wanted to go back there for the fireworks, didn't you?" Angela steered her husband in the direction of the kitchen.

"I suppose," he sulked. "I'm serious, someone is going to get an ear full when I find out who's responsible for dumping her off like that," Ted fumed. "This won't happen again. You have to agree with me. This whole thing is totally inappropriate. What if we had plans to go somewhere? We'd have been screwed."

Angela was sick of his whining. "Ted, no one said you were wrong. I agree with you a hundred percent. But, there is a way to approach this without acting like them!" Angela tried to keep their conversation from turning into a ping pong match of words. "It's getting late and no one has even checked up on Emily. I'm scared too, but I won't make a big deal about it in front of Brittney. It's still her birthday. Let's not spoil it."

Chapter Twelve

When they finished in the kitchen, Angela went upstairs to get the girls ready to go back to the park. As she approached Brittney's bedroom, she noticed the quiet. *There are two five year olds playing in there. There should be some noise.*

The bedroom light was off, which was definitely not normal for Brittney. Angela stood as still as her trembling legs would allow and literally had to strain to hear anything. She quietly tiptoed closer. It was Emily's voice that finally emerged from inside the castle.

"I couldn't find my mommy. I heard her calling me. The bad person held me under a big coat. The room behind the mirrors was very small. It was hot in there. I kept thinking that my daddy would be so mad. There are doors that shouldn't be doors and walls that aren't safe for little girls."

Angela covered her mouth to stifle her gasp as she crept closer.

"Didn't your daddy help you? My daddy would help me." Brittney reacted innocently to Emily's story.

"I called him but, he didn't come," Emily said sorrowfully. "I heard my daddy calling me. The bad person held my mouth so tight. I was crying, but no one could hear me." Emily sounded so pitiful. "The bad person held my mouth and nose until I went to sleep."

"Did you get hungry? Did they let you have cotton candy?" Brittney's five-year-old mind was trying to put Emily in a happier place.

"There was a salad on the table. I ate some, but I think it was spoiled. I felt sick in my tummy after I ate it." Emily was explaining a horrible experience. However, it sounded like she was simply telling a story.

Angela began to wonder if Emily was actually living in an abusive situation or was she just a little storyteller. The whole thing was very upsetting.

Life-like shadows of Brittney's toys, danced on the bedroom walls from a glow being cast by her night-light. *I don't like it that they shut off the lights in here. It had to be Emily's idea. Britt would never play in the dark.*

Angela didn't want to be caught eavesdropping. She stomped her feet as if just entering the room and quickly pushed aside the soft cloth that covered the entrance into the play castle.

The girls were sitting side by side on the floor, talking. Emily was just a child, yet there was something strong and frightening about her. The glow from the nightlight shined through the opening of the playhouse, illuminating Emily's flaxen blond hair. It was an eerie addition to the strange little girl's face. Emily held tightly to the evil eye bead when Angela spoke.

"What are you girls talking about? Are you all right, Emily?" Angela demanded. "Why are you two sitting in the dark?"

"Emily was telling me a story," Brittney answered, not taking her eyes off her new friend. "Emily said she can only talk to me. She isn't supposed to talk to strangers and you're a stranger, Mom."

The snotty look on Brittney's face and the rude tone in her voice threw Angela into mother-bear mode. It was completely out of character for her daughter.

Angela reached into the toy castle, taking Brittney firmly by the arm. "It's time to go. We're going back to the park. Daddy wants to see the fireworks and we have to get Emily home. She's been here all afternoon. Her parents have to be worried about her by now and if not, well, that's the way it goes."

"They aren't," Brittney jumped in.

"They aren't what?" Angela paused to listen to her daughter.

"They aren't worried. Emily doesn't have a mommy and daddy anymore. She lives on the merry-go-round."

"I don't care where she lives. There has to be someone taking care of her and we're going to find out who that is. Let's go," Angela snapped as she spun Brittney around and pushed her in the direction of the door.

"Can Emily spend the night?" Brittney asked.

Angela glared at her daughter. "No. Now move it, young lady."

Brittney grasped Emily's hand. "We're going to the park now. Maybe you can come back tomorrow."

"We'll see about that," Ted said from the doorway. "The car is running. Let's go. I want to get a good seat for the fireworks."

Brittney was ashamed of her mom's behavior. She rolled her eyes and dragged her feet. "Emily doesn't like the fireworks. They're too loud and they scare her."

"Sorry, Emily, we don't get to see them very often. I've planned this all day," Ted responded sharply.

As Angela reached for the light switch, she glanced at the place on the wall where she marked Brittney's height. There was another pencil mark just below it. "Oh Britt...why did you do that?" Angela sighed. She turned out the light and went downstairs.

Chapter Thirteen

Ted already had Brittney and Emily in the car before Angela shut and locked the front door. After sliding into the passenger seat, she turned to look at the girls. "Is everyone ready? Emily, put your seat belt on. I'm sorry, but I don't have another booster seat for you to sit on."

Emily gave Brittney a puzzled look. Reaching over, Brittney helped her friend buckle up.

Ted backed the car out of the driveway and headed for Willows Park. He glanced in the rear view mirror and saw Brittney chattering away. He didn't see Emily in the mirror. Ted turned and looked back to make sure she was still there.

"You must be a lot shorter than Brittney," he said. "I can't see you in the mirror. I thought you fell out," Ted chuckled, making light of the incident.

Emily smiled at Brittney, exposing the deep dimple in her right cheek.

"Does anyone mind if I stop at the store real quick? I want to drop off the film I used today for Brittney's birthday. I'll do the one-hour developing and we can look at her pictures tonight when we get home," Ted suggested.

"Go ahead," Angela said. "I'm in no hurry. It's been a long day. A nice hot bath with candles and scented water would be wonderful."

Angela laid her head back on the headrest when Ted pulled into the parking lot.

"I'll only be a few minutes. Maybe, I'll pick up some bath salts for you." He smiled.

"That would be great," Angela said and closed her eyes.

"When we get to the park, can Emily watch the fireworks with us?" Brittney asked.

Ted stiffened and shot Angela a look that could have stopped a clock. "Please handle it," he said before shutting the car door.

"Brittney, we need to get Emily back to her parents. She's been gone all afternoon. No one has even bothered to call or check on her. They don't even know us. The answer is no. You'll stay with Daddy and Emily will go with me when we get to the park."

"Geeze! Not fair," Brittney whined and slumped down in her seat. She glanced sideways at Emily.

Emily began humming an unusual, yet familiar tune. Angela listened intently. What an odd child. If I didn't know better, I'd swear there's more than one voice humming back there. "That's a pretty song you're singing, Emily," she began. "What is it?"

The little girl stopped singing, but didn't answer Angela. Angela continued to try to make small talk with her. "Is it really your birthday today, too?" she asked.

Brittney was quick to answer. "Her birthday is almost the same as mine. We are both June twenty-eight."

"What do you mean, almost? Today is June twenty-eighth. You're smaller than Brittney. Are you four years old today, Emily? Do you know what year you were born?" Angela asked.

The girls leaned in toward each other and began whispering. Again, Brittney took it upon herself to answer for Emily. "Her birthday is June twenty-eight, like mine, and nineteen forty two."

Angela laughed. "I don't think so, Britt. That's impossible. Your Papa was born in nineteen forty-seven. Is she older than Papa?"

The girls began whispering again. They didn't have anything more to say about the year that Emily was born. Angela accepted it as a mistake. "What's your last name, Emily?" Angela continued, but this time, she added, "Brittney, let Emily speak for herself. It's very rude of her not to talk to me when she just spent the better part of the afternoon in my house."

Angela's abrupt tone was meant to display her annoyance with both girls. "It's disrespectful of you, Emily; not to mention the way you've been acting, Brittney. You know better."

To Angela's surprise, a breathy voice drifted from the back seat. It sounded very delicate, like it came from somewhere far away. The hairs on Angela's arms stood up.

"My name is Emily Marie Thatcher. I went to the park for my fifth birthday with my mom and dad. Just like Brittney, but I never got to see them again. A bad person took me away. I couldn't tell them what happened to me because, I died."

A wave of nausea consumed Angela. *What if part of what she is telling me is the truth? I can't be certain. She's only a child. But, she's obviously a very disturbed child.*

"Emily, do you realize what you're saying?" Angela asked as calmly as she could.

"Yes, Brittney's mommy. I want everyone to know what really happened to me that day. I want my mommy and daddy to know that I didn't leave them on purpose. I miss them," the child replied sincerely. "I've been trying to find them for a long time." Emily's voice vibrated ever so lightly, like the strings of a harp.

If she's lying, she's awfully good at it, Angela thought as icy chills caressed her spine. "Emily, when we get to the park, I want to meet your parents or whoever it is that is taking care of you right now," Angela instructed. "Brittney, you are to go with Dad. I'll meet up with you later. Do you understand?"

"But, Mom...can't Emily sit with us?" Brittney pleaded.

"No, she can't. Plus, didn't you tell us that Emily doesn't like the fireworks? You'll do as you're told. I don't want to hear another word out of you."

More than upset, Angela was terrified. *Where the heck is Ted? How long does it take to drop off a couple rolls of film?*

Angela turned around in her seat and stared at Emily. She was rolling the bead that Brittney gave her around in her fingers. She didn't look frightened at all. In fact, she appeared to be wearing a slight smirk. The police could be looking for her right now.

Angela was deep in thought when Ted pulled the car door open and bounced into his seat. "It's almost time for the fireworks."

"You startled me. I didn't see you coming," Angela said as she repositioned herself.

"They never do," he laughed. Ted was in such a jovial mood. Angela hated to ruin it. She thought about not telling him what Emily had just said.

Before starting the car, Ted tossed a little bag over to Angela. "These are some of the best smelling salts on the shelf. Sorry I took so long, but I didn't realize how many different salts, pellets and candles they have out there," he spoke like a true connoisseur. "I hope you like these."

"I'm sure they'll be wonderful, honey." Angela was having second thoughts about keeping Emily's story from Ted. "Emily was telling me some horrible things about being kidnapped and not knowing where her parents were. I don't know what to make of her," she blurted out.

Ted's mood darkened. He spoke just above a whisper. "I think we'll drop this kid off at the merry-go-round with whoever claims her and be done with it. She can cause us a lot of trouble. These carnie-kids are taught early how to spin these yarns. It's a tough life but, I don't want any part of it."

"We don't even know who dropped her off at our house. They could have followed Brittney home from the carnival this afternoon," Angela said, her disapproval catching a worried glance from Ted.

"This might be a set up. They most likely want money. I've read about these scams. They probably use her in all the small towns they go to." Ted was just grabbing at straws.

"Poor kid," Angela said under her breath. "I'm not so sure though. I can't turn her over to just anyone. What if she's telling the truth? Even if it's partially true, we can't put her back in harm's way. What kind of people would that make us?"

Ted started the car and turned to Angela. "Think about it, Angie. If you were a kidnapper, would you take the kid and drop her off at some stranger's house so she could turn you in to the cops?" he huffed. "Take her back to the merry-go-round and leave her there."

"I'll take her over there, but I'm not going to just dump her off. I have to find out who's responsible for Emily."

Before long, the lights from the carnival could be seen glistening throughout the park.

"We're here." Ted pointed to the fairgrounds. "It sure looks different at night, doesn't it Britt?" He pulled in and was able to find a good parking space, close to the midway.

Ted opened the back door and helped Emily out of the car, then gently pushed her toward Angela. "You go with Brittney's mommy, Emily. Come on Britt; let's find a good spot to sit." He grasped her hand firmly. "We'll save a place for you, Angie; hurry up."

"Fine, you come with me, Emily," Angela said as she reached for her little hand. "It's like holding on to nothing," Angela remarked when she walked away with Emily.

Emily turned her head and watched Brittney walk away with Ted. She called out, her voice echoing, "Brittney, come ride the merry-go-round with me. We never have to get off."

"Can I Daddy?" Brittney squealed.

Ted jerked his daughter in the direction of the fireworks. "You're coming with me. Take that kid back where she came from," Ted hollered over his shoulder.

Angela gave Emily a perplexed look. "You're quite the mystery, aren't you?"

"Bye Emily," Brittney called out.

"I'll see you soon," Emily breathed the words in an unearthly voice that carried clearly on the breeze.

"Not if I have anything to do with it," Ted mumbled. "Turn around and keep your eyes open for a good place to sit." He was practically dragging Brittney by this time. She had to run alongside her father to keep up with him.

"Let's try to find your parents. Is there someplace they told you to meet them? I guess they assumed we'd bring you back here. Am I right?" Angela demanded.

Before she could take another step, Emily slipped free of her hold. "Wait, Emily; where are you going?" Angela tried running after her. She shot a look back at Ted and Brittney, but they were already out of sight. She couldn't have gotten far. *The little snip ...where could she have gone?*

Angela walked briskly over to the merry-go-round. The closer she got, the more her attention was drawn to the captivating carousel. Suddenly, she spotted her. Emily was sitting on one of the horses.

"How did she get on that ride? There's no way she could have made it to the merry-go-round and found someone to put her on there that quickly. What's going on?" Angela expressed her thoughts out loud.

It was hard to miss those long, blond curls bouncing around her little face. The music coming from the old fashioned calliope was playing loudly. It was the tune that Emily was humming in the car and Emily appeared quite comfortable in her surroundings.

"You little stinker. I guess you know this place pretty well. Ted was right. Whoever you belong to can take over now." Angela was relieved to see Emily safe and at ease on the merry-go-round.

She didn't appear to be in any sort of danger. *That child is no more afraid of this place than I am.*

Angela spun around on her heel and walked away from the elaborate carousel and away from Emily. "I can't believe she was able to make up such a horrible story. I'm glad to be rid of that problem," Angela said out loud. "She lies too well for one so young, not to mention her absentee parents. What a gimmick."

Feeling confident that it was the last time she would ever have to deal with Emily, Angela left to join Ted and Brittney.

Chapter Fourteen

The fireworks display began shortly after nine P.M. and lasted an hour.

"Those were some of the best fireworks I've seen yet," Ted laughed boisterously. "Aren't you glad we came?"

"We had good seats," Brittney laughed along with her dad.

"I have to agree with you this time, Ted. They definitely were some of the best I've ever seen." Angela kept the conversation light and away from Emily.

"How was that for a terrific ending to your fifth birthday?" Ted asked his daughter.

"You weren't this excited the day she was born," Angela laughed.

"Oh, now that's not true," Ted responded with a grin. "I just love the fireworks; especially the grand finale."

"We know," Angela and Brittney spoke simultaneously.

Ted took hold of Brittney's hand and they headed for the parking lot. Angela continued to divert Ted's attention away from the merry-go-round. Brittney, on the other hand, began searching for Emily. She twisted her neck back toward the brightly-lit carousel.

"What are you looking for?" Ted asked, noting her distraction.

Angela knew what was coming and tried to intercept, but it was too late.

"I hope Emily wasn't too scared. She doesn't like the fireworks," Brittney expressed with true concern.

"I didn't ask you if Emily liked them; I asked if you did," Ted said bluntly.

"That's enough, Ted." Angela stepped between them and pulled Brittney gently to her. "You aren't going to solve anything by being a bully."

"I liked the blue ones," Brittney looked sheepishly at her father. Her remark was neither sassy nor challenging. It seemed to work for the time being. Brittney continued discussing the different shapes and colors.

"I'm glad that you both had a good time. It amazes me that you can actually recall a certain display. I don't want to be a party pooper but, I'm ready to go home," Angela whined. "You have to be exhausted, Britt."

"I'm okay, Mom." Her reply was followed by a long yawn.

"What's that tune you're humming?" Ted asked in a softer tone, trying to make up for his earlier dramatic display.

"Emily taught it to me. She sings it all the time. She said that her mom used to have a music box that played it." Brittney continued humming the catchy tune as they approached the car. Ted just shrugged and let it go.

"Did you find Emily's folks?" Ted asked Angela.

"No, as a matter of fact, I didn't. However, that little whippersnapper took off on me. When I found her, she was riding the merry-go-round and appeared to be okay."

Angela shook her head. "I don't know what to think about that child."

"Did you talk to anyone about her?" Ted probed.

"No, I'm starting to think that you were right," Angela lowered her voice. "Maybe, we should talk about this later."

"Who put her on the horse?" Ted probed further.

Angela leaned in closer. "Someone had to lift her up and put her on the ride. I realize that. She's too little to get on by herself, but that isn't what freaked me out," she said, trying to keep Brittney from hearing what she had to say.

"Why, what happened?" Ted stopped and turned to face her.

Angela hesitated a moment. "When I saw her, I immediately ran up to the merry-go-round to see if she needed help. Whether she meant it or not, Emily not only infuriated me; she really scared me."

"If you were afraid she'd fall off, forget it. That kid rides the merry-go-round all the time," Ted said. He saw firsthand how they put her on the ride and left her there.

"No, it wasn't that at all," Angela said meekly.

"What do you mean?" Ted frowned.

Angela's breathing got shallow. "I don't want to talk about it in front of Brittney."

"Put her in the car. I want to know what you think you saw," Ted insisted.

Angela secured Brittney in the back seat of the car and shut the door. She dropped her face and lifted her eyes slowly to meet Ted's.

"It all happened so fast. Emily appeared to transform, right before my eyes," Angela began.

"How?"

"Emily's skin turned pale, almost transparent. Her face became elongated with this gaping, howling shaped mouth." She trembled. "It was awful."

"It was dark, Angie. Maybe you didn't really see Emily like that," Ted said softly with trepidation.

"No Ted, I know what I saw. Emily's features converted from the fragile little girl we saw earlier, to a creature with dark sunken eyes and a large, bulbous chin," she said. "It happened quickly and didn't last but a few seconds. The weird thing was, I couldn't tear my eyes away," Angela said, finding it difficult to admit.

"Before I left, there was this awful smell," she added.

"What kind of smell?"

"Like something rotting. It was the smell of death," Angela had tears coming from the corners of her eyes. She was relieved to be able to unload her horrible experience. "I don't ever want to see that little girl again."

Without another word, Angela turned, opened the car door, and slid into the passenger seat, leaving Ted standing outside, horrified.

Chapter Fifteen

Brittney dozed off in the back seat. Angela checked on her before continuing her conversation with Ted.

"I just can't believe that a five year old could make up a story like that. She really had me going. There's something terribly wrong with Emily." Angela kept her voice just above a whisper. "Maybe we should talk to Father Luke about it."

Ted spoke adamantly. "I don't want her anywhere near Brittney. If she shows up again, tell whoever it is that's trying to pawn her off on us that we aren't babysitting! And...don't tell anyone about her. We don't even know how she got to our house. Leave it alone, Ang."

"The problem is, we don't know who dropped Emily off. What if she does show up again? What can we do?" Angela shook her head.

"I'll tell you what we can do; we can call the police. There are laws protecting people against things like this. We don't know what these people want." Ted was raising his voice.

"Shh." Angela glanced back at Brittney. She was still asleep. "I don't want Brittney to hear you."

"What worries me the most is how they found us and why did they pick Brittney?" Ted's voice was low. Angela could tell that he was scared too.

"Think about it Ang, they set up the carnival, spot a kid about Emily's age and match them up. They follow the family home and the problems begin." Ted tried to explain things from his point of view. "By the way, when did that strange black woman come by our house? Emily seemed to know her. She recognized the cheap bobble that woman gave Brittney. Maybe that's how they tagged her."

"It was the day before yesterday. As a matter of fact, it surprised me that she was able to talk to Brittney without me seeing her. I never leave her outside alone." Angela was really starting to worry.

"The only thing to do is call the police," Ted said.

"No Daddy. Don't call the policeman on Emily. She's my friend. Don't put Emily in jail," Brittney cried.

"Oh honey, we won't do anything to Emily. Don't worry, Daddy was only talking. He's just wondering why Emily's mom and dad left her with us without even knowing who we are. We would never leave you with strangers." Angela tried to reassure her daughter. "I've always told you, if you don't recognize someone and they want you to go somewhere with them, run and scream for help."

"Why did you talk to that black lady when she came in our yard?" Ted asked.

"I didn't," Brittney cried. "She talked to me."

"What's done is done," Angela cut in. "I'll just have to be more alert and careful from now on.

"Emily is my friend." Brittney continued to whine. Angela winced at Brittney's words. *Emily has too much influence on her.*

"We love you very much and we don't want you to believe everything Emily tells you," Ted piped in from the driver's seat.

Brittney simply sighed. It was obvious that she wasn't going to reject her new-found friend. Emily had definitely reached her.

Angela leaned her head back and opened the window to allow the cool night breeze to brush gently across her face. There was a hint of honeysuckle in the air. Her eyelids were getting heavy, and she let herself relax and closed her eyes.

All of a sudden, standing in the middle of the road, Angela saw Emily. She screamed, "Stop the car! Ted...!"

Instantly, Ted hit the brake and swerved the car to the side of the road. "What the hell?"

"My God; did you hit her?" Angela opened the car door, jumped out, and ran back to the spot where she thought she had seen Emily.

"Stay in the car," Ted yelled at Brittney. He opened his door and ran back to where Angela was frantically searching for Emily. "What are you doing, Angie? What do you mean? Hit who?"

Brittney sat quietly in the car. She didn't know what was going on and turned her head to find Emily sitting next to her. "What are you doing here?"

"I want you to come and play with me. You have to come with me, so that I can find my mommy and daddy." Emily didn't look the same. Her eyes were dark and her hair was tangled. The look on Emily's face scared Brittney.

"No, I won't. My daddy told me to stay in the car. You, go home," Brittney said, adamantly. Her voice trembled.

Brittney's response infuriated Emily and she looked at the gearshift. Slowly, Emily willed the car to slip into drive and it began to roll forward. Brittney screamed, which grabbed her parent's attention.

"Brittney!" Angela cried out and took off running after the moving car. It was picking up speed when the wheels suddenly turned sharply, sending the car into the ditch.

Angela scrambled down into the trench and jerked the car door open. She quickly undid Brittney's seat belt and dragged her out of the car.

"Are you okay?" she cried hysterically.

Ted came running up behind them. "What the hell happened?"

Angela continued to cling to her daughter. "You must not have put the car in park. It rolled away. We're lucky she wasn't killed."

"My God...I've never done that before. Are you okay, sweetie? Daddy would never do anything to hurt you. I love you."

Everyone was badly shaken, but no one was hurt. They called for a tow truck and Ted called his father to come and pick them up. After settling in Leonard's car, Brittney looked out the back window and saw Emily standing in the middle of the road. She shrunk down and buried her face in her mother's arm.

Angela thought about seeing Emily in the road and horror paralyzed her mind. *I think I've actually looked in the face of death.* She tightened her hold on Brittney as she thought about the hideous, distorted features that hid behind Emily's facade. Emily's voice hissed through her brain. 'The bad person had his hand over my mouth. I was crying.' Angela moaned silently, yet loud enough for Ted to hear her.

"What's wrong? Are you okay?" he asked.

"I'm sorry. I must have dozed off. I need to get home and go to bed." She lifted her eyes and saw that they were in their own car. It had just been a bad dream.

Angela mumbled, "A very real and disturbing dream."

Chapter Sixteen

The front of the house was dark when they pulled into the driveway. "I forgot to leave the light on," Angela said. "I hate going up to a dark house."

Ted led the way to the front door. "There's a package on the porch."

"I wonder what it is," Angela said and reached for the box.

"Let me take that. Open the door," Ted said. He took hold of the carton and followed her into the house. Angela turned on the lights and Ted went into the dining room, setting the package on the table.

"Who's it for?" Brittney pushed her way past her parents and stood directly in front of the mysterious box. "Is it another birthday present for me?"

"We don't know, Britt," Angela said gently. "The wrapping paper looks a little faded. I don't see a card, do you?"

"It's my birthday. It has to be for me." Brittney reached for the uniquely wrapped parcel.

Ted impulsively grabbed her wrist; his suspicious nature was always on alert. "It could be anything. Maybe there's a note inside."

"Who do you think left it?" Angela questioned.

"I don't know." Ted began picking at the fragile paper. It fell away from the box like chipped paint. Inside was a sealed carton, with a faded picture of the contents.

"Wow, look at that. From the look of the packaging, I'd say it came directly from the factory," Ted said as he opened the box carefully, almost reverently. When he removed the lid, they found an elaborate replica of a merry-go-round.

"How weird. It looks just like the one at the park," Angela let out a nervous laugh. "What do you think?" she asked, stepping closer to the table.

"I don't know," Ted said as he continued to examine the box.

Jumping into the conversation with a shrill to her voice, Brittney announced, "I'll bet it's from Emily. It's Emily's merry-go-round. She sent it to me for my birthday."

Ted and Angela stared at each other in disbelief. "What the hell?" It was all Ted could say.

"Watch your mouth, Ted. She's going to repeat that and you're going to yell at her," Angela spoke to Ted, but never took her eyes off the package. "Let's just talk about this. Take it out of the box and we'll look at it," she suggested, trying to sound rational.

Ted lifted the miniature merry-go-round out of the carton and set it carefully on the table. Angela's eyes widened with surprise.

"It's gorgeous," she said. "Look, there's a key. I think it's a music box. Could my parents have sent it?" She picked up the ornately decorated brass key and found the keyhole. "It fits," Angela said and turned it five times. They each took a step back and waited with anticipation.

Angela's mouth dropped open as the now familiar melody filled the room. "Oh Ted. It's the same tune Emily was humming in the car. How can that be?"

"I wonder where it came from," Ted said. "Brittney, it's late. Get ready for bed."

"But Daddy," she cried. "Can't I play with the merry-go-round for a little while?"

"I told you to get ready for bed," Ted barked, his tone startling her.

"Oh Daddy, it's my birthday," Brittney withdrew. A tear welled up and hung daringly on the edge of her eyelid.

"I don't care what day this is. It doesn't mean that you can start disobeying me," Ted snapped. He couldn't take his eyes off the enchanting carousel.

Angela took Brittney by the shoulders and turned her toward the stairs. "It's been such a long day, honey. Do what your dad told you. Go upstairs and get ready for bed. I'll be there in a minute to tuck you in." Angela kissed her face. "Happy birthday, honey; I'll be right up."

"Okay, Mommy." She walked away slowly, dragging her feet.

"Ted, you don't have to take it out on Brittney. She doesn't know what's going on any more than we do," Angela scolded. Angela paced around the table with her arms folded protectively across her chest.

"I'm really upset. Who in the world would send a gift like this?" Ted, of course, contemplated foul play.

"If it is a gift." Angela's remark came spontaneously.

"What do you mean?" Ted asked.

"Well, what if it's some sort of intimidation?" She answered, choosing her words carefully. "I mean, what if this is only the first of many ploys to try to scare us? You know, like in one of those mystery thrillers where the crazy killer tries to drive the family insane before kidnapping their child." Angela's imagination escalated toward the end of her thought.

"You watch too many movies." Ted was level with Angela's eyes when he spoke.

"I'm serious. You hear about this sort of thing all the time and there are a lot of copycats out there," Angela insisted.

Ted toyed with the delicate little horses that followed each other on the carousel. "What should we do with it?" he asked. "You don't think your mom and dad sent it, do you?"

"No, but I'll call them and ask. They didn't say anything about it. I'm not going to tell them anything else though. They don't need to worry," Angela said as Ted boxed up the questionable gift. "I'm going upstairs to tuck Brittney in. I want to tell her good night and try to salvage the last part of her birthday."

Angela felt drained as she headed for Brittney's room. When she neared the top of the stairs, those feared voices rose from behind her daughter's closed door. She clutched the stair rail and held her breath, straining to hear the children. "Dear God, please don't let it be what I think." Everything inside her froze.

Chapter Seventeen

Angela knew that Brittney hated to have her bedroom door closed. She grimaced when she took a step and the board beneath her foot creaked loudly. She stopped and held her breath. She wanted to hear what was being said.

"Thank you so much for the present, Emily. The merry-go-round is beautiful. It looks just like your big one at the park. I'm sorry if I was mean to you." Angela's heart sank as she listened to Brittney.

Pursing her lips tightly, Angela turned the doorknob ever so slowly and gently pushed on the door with her shoulder. She peered in to find Brittney sitting on the side of the bed, talking on her play phone.

A smile edged across her lips and she sighed with relief. "What are you doing?" she asked nonchalantly. "I thought you were supposed to be getting ready for bed." Angela crossed the room and sat down next to her daughter.

"Sorry Mom," Brittney said, with the phone on her ear. "I have to go, Emily. I'll talk to you later."

A prominent line creased Angela's forehead. Brittney pulled the phone away from her ear and reached past her mother to hang it up. A voice projected clearly from the hand piece of the toy telephone. "Bye Brittney. I'll see you soon."

Angela snatched the phone out of Brittney's hand and brought it up to her ear. "Is someone there?" she asked, feeling somewhat foolish.

Brittney watched Angela examine the toy phone. Without looking at her daughter, Angela turned the telephone over and over before demanding, "How does this thing work? Did Papa put batteries in it?" She was totally immersed in the workings of the occulted toy.

Brittney answered Angela as honestly as she knew how. "It works like yours, Mommy. I pick it up and talk to Emily."

"And does Emily talk to you?" Angela dared to ask. There was more sarcasm in her voice than reason. "Are you pretending to talk to Emily on this phone or do you really think she is answering you? Brittney, I need you to tell me the truth. You know this is a toy, don't you?"

Brittney didn't answer right away, which frustrated Angela even more. "Answer me, Brittney. Your father and I have had just about enough."

When Brittney refused to answer her mother, Angela stormed out of the room, taking the toy phone with her. She called back to Brittney from the hallway, "Get your

pajamas on like your father told you. I'll take care of this."

Brittney plopped down hard on her bed and came as close to a tantrum as Angela had ever witnessed. She behaved incredibly out of character, flailing her arms and kicking her feet on the bed. "That's my phone! It's mine!" she screamed.

The venomous tone in her precious little girl's voice brought tears to Angela's eyes. She ignored Brittney's protests and pulled the door shut hard. Exhausted and upset, Angela leaned back on the closed door. "Damn it, it's her birthday, and now I'm acting like Ted."

Angela turned the phone over, trying to find a place for batteries. There was none. It was simply a plastic toy.

At that moment Angela became aware of a presence. Although she couldn't see Emily, she felt her sweet, light air, breathing by her ear.

"All you have to do is believe." The voice no longer came from the toy phone. It blew gracefully into her ear as if Emily were standing right next to her.

Emily's voice became intoxicating. Angela could actually feel tiny fingers running up and down her back. She knew that she had to snap out of it. "Okay, this can't be happening. There's no such thing as ghosts."

The telephone receiver hung carelessly from her hand. Just as she was about to replace the plastic replica in its cradle, a child's giggling voice spilled from the toy.

Hearing Emily's ridiculing tone coming from Brittney's toy phone caused bile to rise up to her throat. "Oh my God...what are we going to do?" She took a couple of slow deep breaths to prevent herself from throwing up.

Angela didn't want to tell Ted. She felt it was better to keep the incident to herself, so she opened the hall closet door and shoved Brittney's toy phone as far back as she could on the top shelf. *Out of sight; out of my life.*

The door was still closed when Angela passed Brittney's room on her way back downstairs. She paused for a moment and gently pushed it open. From where she stood, she could see Brittney's face sticking out from under the comforter. Her eyes were closed. All was quiet. *That's the first time she ever rebelled so strongly. I can't encourage that sort of behavior. It just isn't acceptable.* Leaving the bedroom door ajar, Angela went down the stairs to where Ted was waiting in the kitchen.

"What was all the noise about?" Ted asked. "It sounded like you two were playing awfully hard for it being bedtime." Ted was unaware that Brittney had just thrown a full-blown tantrum and Angela wasn't in the mood to discuss it.

"What about those pictures you took of Brittney? We forgot to pick them up," Angela complained.

"I don't feel like going back out," Ted said. "I'll pick them up in the morning when I cash my check, if that's okay with you," Ted suggested.

"That's fine," Angela answered. "I'm beat." She took one last look at the decorations and wondered if she had handled the situation with Brittney correctly.

"This was one hell of a way to end her birthday," Angela balked.

Ted spun around instantly in retaliation. "It wasn't us that ruined anything. Blame Emily if Britt's birthday turned to crap." His mouth twisted with each word.

Telling him about the phone now would just wind him up tighter. "What did you do with the merry-go-round?" She asked.

"It's in the garage. I put it on a shelf over my workbench." Ted noticed that Angela looked a little pale. "Are you alright?"

"I guess I'm just tired. Let's go to bed." Angela looked at her watch. "Tomorrow, I'll call our parents and see if any of them sent the merry-go-round. I want to ask your dad how that toy phone works anyway."

"Why? What's up with that now?" Ted asked. The tone in his voice sounded like he was on his last thread.

"There were no directions in the box. Maybe he took them out when he set up the phone. Simmer down," Angela said as she walked toward the stairs. She hoped he hadn't seen the color rise in her cheeks. She wasn't good at lying.

When Ted didn't push the issue further, Angela was relieved and went upstairs. "I'm going to peek back in on Brittney one more time and kiss her goodnight."

"I'll be right up. I want to double check the doors before I go to bed." He winked at her from the foyer as she leaned over the railing to hear him.

Angela paused in front of Brittney's room. Through the darkness, she could see her curled up on her side. Her breathing was slow and easy. "Well, at least someone is able to sleep soundly."

She tiptoed up to the side of the bed and knelt down beside her daughter. "I love you so much," Angela said. Brittney's eyes remained closed.

Angela passed the hall closet on her way to her bedroom. There has to be a reasonable explanation for everything that happened today. Maybe I should just take a hammer to that phone and be done with it, she thought sighing.

Angela went into the bathroom to brush her teeth and Ted was already in bed when she came out. "Don't bother with that nightie tonight. Just drop your clothes on the floor and climb in here," he snickered playfully as she approached the bed. "I shut the window so you wouldn't complain about being cold. Close the door."

"Not tonight, Ted. I want to be able to hear Brittney if she wakes up." Angela refused to close the bedroom door. "I feel horrible that she went to sleep before I could tell her goodnight."

"Oh Angie, she'll come in here if she wants you," Ted moaned as he held the covers back.

"You know, I was thinking, maybe we've been a little selfish with Britt. She really likes having someone her own age around. Maybe we should think about signing her up to some sort of class where she can play with kids her own age instead of being with us all the time." Angela's thoughts were jumbled as she lay down.

"She'll be starting school in a couple of months. Isn't that soon enough?" Ted said.

Angela closed her eyes. Out of sheer exhaustion, they both fell asleep in each other's arms.

The room was dark and her eyes were closed, yet in Angela's subconscious mind, deep emotional scars were beginning to form from the images of Emily's face, the feeling of her cold breath on her neck, and the eerie, haunting sound of her voice.

Chapter Eighteen

The room slowly brightened as the sun's rays peeked through the slats of the mini-blinds. Angela opened her eyes, feeling warm and cozy all snuggled beneath the down-filled quilt. Squinting through the gaze of morning's first light, she spotted the clock on the nightstand.

"Eight thirty?" Angela moaned. "I slept through part of the morning." She sat up at the side of the bed and stretched her arms over her head. The pillow next to hers was crumpled and empty. Angela tipped her head back and took in a deep breath. The smell of coffee drifted up from the kitchen. "Ah...a man after my own heart. I can almost taste it."

Angela didn't want to think about how Emily had ruined Brittney's birthday. The fifth one was supposed to be a crossroad. She was no longer a toddler. Now, she'll remember it as the day she met Emily. "Ugh!" Angela muttered at the thought of that strange little girl.

"This is a new day. I have a five year old daughter and she'll be going to school in the fall." She smiled and sighed.

Slipping on her robe and pulling the belt snugly around her waist, Angela passed Brittney's room and peeked in. "Are you awake, sweetie?" She whispered while tiptoeing up to the bed. A soft glow, casting shadows from the hall light, shown on the empty bed. Angela left the room and headed downstairs for the kitchen. The sound of laughter drifted up to her.

"Morning, you two. Am I invited to this party?" Angela walked over to Ted and kissed his cheek. "How does it feel to be five years old?" She smiled at Brittney.

"Fine," she answered as she curled her legs and sat on her feet. She didn't appear to be as playful as usual.

"When are you going to the office?" Angela asked Ted.

Ted worked for a large appraisal company in town. He had an office at home that enabled him to do much of his work right there.

"Actually, I took the entire weekend off to be with our little princess," he replied, throwing two more eggs on the skillet. "I hope you two are hungry. I do have to stop at the office, and then I'm going to the drug store to pick up Brittney's pictures. Do you want to ride with me, Britt?"

"Sure," she replied through a mouthful of food.

Ted piled the toast, bacon and scrambled eggs on a big dinner platter and set it on the table. "Dig in girls. Get it while it's hot."

Angela walked over to the counter and poured herself a cup of steaming hot coffee. "I don't know how you two can crawl out of bed and start eating." She crinkled up her nose.

"It's easy Mom. We do it all the time; don't we, Daddy?" Brittney looked at her father. He winked at her and nodded. His mouth was already full.

Angela shook her head. "You're teaching this little lady some very bad habits."

Brittney raised her shoulders up and glanced sideways at her dad. They both started laughing.

Thinking back to how bad yesterday turned out, Angela sighed with relief. Things seemed to be back to normal.

After everyone was finished eating, Brittney headed for the stairs. "I'm going to play in my castle for a little while."

Ted lingered over his cup of coffee. "Do you want me to help clean up the kitchen? I have to shower yet. I'll take Britt with me."

Angela noticed the dark circles under Ted's eyes. He must not have slept well. Emily really upset him yesterday.

"I'll take care of this. Go ahead and get ready. You look like you could use a good hot shower. Let Brittney play in her castle for a while, then she can get dressed."

By the time Angela was finished cleaning the kitchen, Ted and Brittney were ready to go.

"Do you want to go with us?" Ted asked as Angela came out of the kitchen.

"Wow, I can't believe you're already dressed, Brittney. I thought you were going to play in your castle first," Angela remarked.

"I changed my mind. I'll play in it later when Emily comes back," she said.

It was just about that time that Angela noted that Brittney was wearing the evil eye bead on the tattered ribbon.

"Where did you get that necklace?" Angela demanded. She walked up to Brittney and confronted her with a stance that let her know she needed to come up with an answer.

"It was on my dresser next to my telephone," she answered innocently.

Angela looked at Ted, unable to suppress her fear and anxiety.

Brittney saw the change in her mother's face. "Are you okay, Mommy?" she asked. Angela ran through the living room, past Ted and up the stairs to Brittney's room. She switched on the light and found the telephone back on the dresser. Angela pressed her fist to her mouth, stunned by what she saw.

When she turned to leave the room, Brittney was there, standing in the doorway.

"Where did you find this phone?" she asked.

"I thought you put it there, Mommy. I thought you weren't mad at me anymore." Brittney's mouth turned down in a pout as if she were about to cry.

"I'm not mad at you Britt; I just want to know where that phone came from, because I took it out of here last night and I didn't put it back. I want to know who did and I want to know right now," Angela's lips were quivering and her body shook with rage.

Ted came up behind Brittney. "Are you ready to go?"

"Yes, Daddy," Brittney kept her eyes on Angela waiting to see if it was still all right for her to go with her dad.

"Go downstairs and wait for Daddy by the front door. We'll be right there," Angela instructed in an anxious and insistent tone.

Brittney did as she was told and Angela turned to Ted. "Did you see what she was wearing? How did Brittney get that that necklace back? Sometime between the time she went to bed and this morning, she was able to get her hands on that damned piece of crap necklace," Angela picked up the toy phone and slammed it down on the dresser. She hadn't told Ted about the phone incident.

"Maybe Emily came by early this morning, when I was making breakfast. Brittney was told not to open the door to anyone. She might not admit to letting her in," Ted said. "I don't know if one of her newly acquired habits is lying to us or not."

"Ted, be careful. Don't let Brittney out of your sight," Angela instructed. "Not even for a minute."

"Don't worry; if Emily comes around again, we're calling the police. There is no way she's going to come in and out of our house without us knowing about it. We're just going to have to watch Brittney more closely now." Ted turned to go downstairs. "Maybe she'll mention it on her own. I won't bring Emily up while we're out."

Angela put her hand on his shoulder. "If Emily is having Britt lie and hide things from us, she can also make her steal. Brittney is very vulnerable right now. I hate to use the term peer pressure, but she really likes Emily," Angela remarked with deep concern.

"Okay, but that carnival kid is street smart," Ted answered. "Look how she was able to manipulate her way here and into our home."

When they got downstairs, Brittney was waiting by the front door. She was relieved to see that her parents were both smiling.

"I'll see you two later. Don't forget to pick up the pictures. I think I'll soak in a hot tub while you're out," Angela said nonchalantly. "I'll be ready to do something by the time you get home." She turned and headed for the stairs. "Take your time."

When the door closed, Angela went back to Brittney's bedroom. She took the play phone off the dresser and put it back on the top shelf in the hall closet. Then she went into the bathroom to run the water for a steamy hot bath.

"A little peace and quiet, with a few drops of sweet smelling bath oil should make me feel like a new woman."

Angela went back downstairs while the water was running. She double-checked the front door to be sure it was locked. Returning upstairs, she stopped at the hall closet to get a clean towel and wash cloth.

Glancing up to where she had just moments ago placed the toy phone, Angela found the spot empty. Immediately, she felt weak and light-headed, as if all the blood had drained from her head at once, leaving her defenseless. She closed her eyes for a moment and leaned on a stack of towels to prevent herself from sliding down to the floor.

The jingling sound of a ringing telephone snapped Angela back to attention. It was coming from Brittney's bedroom. "What the hell is going on?"

The house was silent except for the persistent ringing of the toy phone. Angela walked cautiously toward the room. Her breathing came shallow and rapid with her heart beating so fast that she could feel it pulsating in her neck.

She crept up to the dresser and stood before the audacious toy. Knowing full well, whose voice would be at the other end, Angela's hand shook as she picked up the receiver and brought it reluctantly to her ear.

The voice on the other end of the line belonged to a child. She was humming the now familiar tune from the merry-go-round.

"Emily, is that you?" Angela asked calmly. She held the phone tightly, fighting the urge to scream.

A ridiculing cackle screeched from the phone. Angela didn't want to make matters worse by responding out of fear and anger. She didn't want whatever it was on the other end of the line to completely sense her terror.

"What do you want? Why won't you leave us alone?" Angela spoke with as much control as she could. There was no further communication from the miserable toy.

In a moment of anger, Angela snatched it and headed for the garage.

"I'll take care of this. No disrespectful little imp is going to terrorize my family," she mumbled as she stomped toward the garage with heavy feet.

Brittney's phone was tucked tightly under her arm as Angela rummaged through Ted's workbench until she found a thick roll of silver duct tape. She wound it tightly around the play phone over and over.

"There. That should take care of your sassy little tune," Angela said as she climbed on the step stool and placed the bound plastic phone on the shelf next to the boxed up merry-go-round.

After carefully stepping off the stool, Angela spoke to the inanimate object as if it could understand her.

"I plan on soaking in that warm tub." Dusting her hands off on her robe, Angela turned to leave the garage.

The muffled, ruthless chiming started again. However, Angela refused to respond and marched into the house, not daring to look back.

Chapter Nineteen

Once back in the house, Angela thought to herself, the war may not be over, but I just won this battle. For the time being, Angela felt she had immobilized Emily's means of communication with Brittney.

"I'll have to tell Ted about the phone when he comes home," Angela said aloud. Then, closing her eyes, she yelled the words, "There is no such thing as ghosts!"

She waited for some sort of retaliation, but nothing happened. That wasn't the way it worked. Emily's attacks came without warning and left one in a state of terror.

Goose bumps trickled up Angela's arms when she stepped into the hot silky water. Letting out a sigh, she closed her eyes, lowered herself slowly into the comfort of the hot bath and moaned, "Oh, this was so worth the wait."

Allowing the therapy of the warm soak to enfold her, Angela drifted off into a semi-deep sleep. She was startled awake by the sound of Ted's voice.

"Angie, where are you? Come down here. I have something to show you," his voice sounded urgent.

"Crap, I didn't figure on falling asleep for so long. This water is freezing," she cried through chattering teeth.

The heat from the hot bath that once soothed her was now gone. Angela swiftly stood up, shivering as the bone-chilling water dripped from her body.

Snatching a thick bath towel, Angela rubbed herself vigorously and wrapped her hair up tightly. She slipped into her terry-cloth robe and slid her feet into a pair of warm comfy slippers, then padded off to see what Ted was yelling about.

"I can't believe I fell asleep in the tub for over an hour." Angela was shaking as she spoke to Ted, who was sitting in the kitchen, totally immersed in the photographs he had spread across the table.

"Come here, Angie. You have to see this," he said anxiously, without as much as looking up.

"Where's Brittney?" Angela asked.

Ted glanced at her, the usual twinkle gone from his eyes. "I dropped her off at my mom and dad's house. I thought it would be better if we looked at these pictures alone."

"Did you warn them about watching her?" Angela immediately questioned.

Ted didn't bother answering her. He was totally engrossed in the photographs he had taken at the carnival.

"Look at these. I want you to really pay attention."

"Okay, let me see." She began going through the pictures one at a time. Ted drummed his fingers on the table impatiently, with restless excitement.

"I don't see what the problem is, Ted. They turned out great. I hope you made doubles so I can send some to my parents. Your mom and dad will want copies too."

Ted was getting frustrated with Angela and snatched the pictures out of her hands.

"What are you doing?" Angela retaliated.

"I want you to see something," Ted clamored. "See this one of Brittney on the merry-go-round?" He pounded his finger on one of the snapshots. Before Angela could actually look at it, Ted quickly flipped to the next one.

"Look at this one and this one." He tapped on each one firmly with his index finger. "Look at this; see how Britt has her chin tucked to the side? Her eyes are closed and she's giggling."

Angela was trying to make sense of what he was saying. "I'm not good at guessing games. I wasn't there, remember? You have to tell me what it is you want me to see."

Ted was unable to settle down. "Listen to me, Ang. Brittney wasn't alone on that ride. Emily was sitting on the horse right next to her. Now do you understand? She isn't in any of the pictures I took. She isn't there! Where is she?" Ted raked his fingers wildly through his hair.

"I'm talking about this horse, the empty one right next to Brittney. It wasn't empty yesterday. Emily was riding alongside her the whole time." It wasn't funny, but Ted kept spitting out little bursts of hysterical laughter.

"Why were Brittney and Emily on the merry-go-round alone? Where were you?" Angela questioned.

"She begged me, Ang. It was her birthday and I was right there taking pictures of the two of them," he began. "Emily was left alone on the horse next to Brittney by this guy who sat her there and took off. Brittney saw her and felt she was big enough to ride alone, too. I didn't see any harm in it, but the hell with that. Aren't you getting it yet? Don't you see what I'm trying to tell you?"

Angela continued to thumb through the pictures while Ted talked. She concentrated on what he was saying before looking up. "Emily isn't in any of these pictures. Why is that?" Angela nearly screamed.

"Bingo!" Ted exclaimed with satisfaction. "That's what I've been trying to tell you," he yelled. "Several of the pictures should be of Emily and Brittney. But only Brittney showed up in every one of them. The damned kid didn't photograph." Ted nervously rocked back and forth from one foot to the other.

Angela didn't know what to say. Then, all of a sudden with a mocking smirk, she started to laugh. "You're kidding me, right? That is totally ridiculous. It just isn't possible."

Ted pushed his chair next to hers and sat down. "You haven't heard a word I said. This may seem like an insignificant matter to you right now, but considering what's been going on around here, it is very significant! Look at this picture and this one and this one." He shoved them at her. Though his frantic actions were upsetting Angela, the absence of Emily in the photographs coincided with the paranormal implications they were experiencing since they met the strange little girl.

"I want you to look at this one in particular. See how Brittney is acting? Emily was reaching from her horse and tickling her under the chin. I saw her do it, Ang! I took the picture! I'm not making this up! You can tell by the way Britt's neck is twisted and she's giggling." Ted was pleading his case. He pounded hard on the picture with his closed fist.

"There...that's the horse Emily was sitting on. Brittney is right here on the horse I put her on. So, where is she? Where's Emily?" Ted pushed the pictures at Angela for the final analysis.

It took Angela a few seconds to ingest everything Ted had just thrown at her. Nothing like this had ever happened to them before, and it was a discovery that seemed to make sense of what was going on in their house.

"What the hell?" she responded.

"Precisely!" he volleyed.

"Do you think Emily is a ghost?" Angela tacked on the evidence in her mind. "It seems to makes sense. Emily showed up out of nowhere with no means of transportation. Her appearance alone should have told us something. Those lifeless, blank eyes and that translucent skin...oh my God, what have we done?" Angela mumbled with her eyes cast down.

"Who is she, Ang? What is she? We don't even know Emily and we allowed her to come into our house and play with Brittney." Ted slumped back in his chair. A deathly hush came over the room.

"I'm glad that Brittney is at Mom and Dad's right now. I don't want Emily anywhere near her." Ted's voice relayed his fear.

"I totally agree," Angela's thoughts were racing in an attempt to compile everything that had transpired over the past couple of days. "It explains why we couldn't figure out who dropped her off. I'm scared, Ted. If she was able to appear on our front porch without anyone bringing her here, how are we going to keep her away from Brittney? She could be with her right now!"

Horror engulfed the couple as they realized what Emily actually was.

Ted looked at Angela and said, "What scares me worse than the fact that Emily might actually be some sort of freak of nature that wasn't able to stay dead, is why did she pick Brittney, out of all the other kids on the merry-go-round? Our daughter didn't find Emily...Emily found her."

Chapter Twenty

Leonard and Elizabeth Michaels lived in the country where the sky was untouched by city lights. Their house sat isolated on a ridge, in the middle of a green meadow, surrounded by fields of wild flowers.

The two-story white farmhouse could be seen clearly from the unpaved gravel road. A cluster of soft white pine trees sat away from the house, allowing the sun to flood every window with light. Leonard's favorite spot was the welcoming front porch, complete with swing. He could usually be found there, relaxing with his pipe.

Elizabeth wiped her hands on her apron and pushed open the screen door leading to the wrap-around porch. Brittney was swinging on the white, wooden swing.

"I thought you'd like to come in and help me make some cookies this afternoon," she said, casually. She sat down next to Brittney. "What are you thinking about? You've been so quiet since your daddy dropped you off."

"Nothing Nana," Brittney pouted.

"I don't go for all that sulking," Elizabeth said. "You should know that by now. If there's something on your mind, spit it out and we'll go around with it until we find a solution."

"I don't know Nana, I'm bored." Brittney picked at the chipping paint on the corner of the swing.

"Don't go making a big mess with that chipped paint. If you're bored, I've got plenty of things for you to do inside besides sitting out here feeling sorry for yourself," Elizabeth scolded. "If you don't want to talk to me about your problem, maybe you'd like to tell Papa."

"No Nana. I just want to play with Emily and Daddy doesn't like her," Brittney whined.

"And why do you think that is, honey?" Elizabeth coaxed.

"I don't know." Brittney continued to sulk. "Mommy says that no one watches Emily. She can't help it, and Daddy won't let her come over anymore."

"I don't think your daddy would say that without a very good reason. He loves you so much. Why do you suppose they're so worried about Emily?" Elizabeth tried to encourage the conversation.

"Emily has a secret. You can't tell anybody when someone tells you a secret. Don't you know that?" Brittney poked her chin out so far that Elizabeth grabbed hold of it with two fingers and shook her little face back and forth.

"I do know that little girls aren't supposed to keep secrets from their mommy and daddy and I don't think that Emily is a very good girl if she tells stories that aren't true." Elizabeth folded her arms unyieldingly across her chest.

Brittney jumped off the swing. "You don't know her, Nana," she said defiantly. She took a stand in front of her grandmother and mirrored her stance with arms folded snugly across her small chest. "Emily is my friend. She wants me to play on the merry-go-round with her," Brittney stomped her foot. Her menacing facial features scared Elizabeth. For a moment, the child standing in front of her didn't even resemble her granddaughter.

"Don't you use that tone with me, young lady," Elizabeth erupted. Fear overwhelmed her thoughts as the words spilled from Brittney's mouth. "You're big enough for Papa to take you out to the woodshed. Now get in the house and go up to your room. You sit and think about that smart mouth of yours." Elizabeth was so rattled, she took Brittney by both shoulders and directed her through the front door.

"I'm calling your father. I won't have that sort of behavior in our home. I never let my children act like that and I'll be darned if I'm going to let you get away with it." Elizabeth was furious at Brittney.

Brittney knew she was in trouble. It was too late to take back the words that seemed to spill from her mouth faster than she could control them. Hanging her head, she drug her feet across the kitchen floor and headed for the stairs leading to the bedroom.

"Go on. Get yourself up to that room. I'm ashamed of you Brittney," Elizabeth was hurt and disappointed. She went to the back door and hollered, "Leonard, come in here!" Turning abruptly, the screen door slammed shut behind her.

Elizabeth took a few slow deep breaths in an attempt to calm herself as she stood trembling in front of the wall phone in the kitchen.

Leonard came up to the front porch and tapped his pipe on the side of the swing. A couple of paint chips fell to the floor and he pushed them through the slats of wood with the toe of his shoe. He glanced at the door. Elizabeth didn't see what he did and Leonard sighed with relief before going inside. His wife was standing at the kitchen sink vigorously scrubbing a chicken.

"You're going to scrub the skin right off that bird," he joked. "What are you fussing about? Where's Brittney?" Leonard took a seat at the table.

Elizabeth dropped the plucked chicken into a big kettle of boiling water and dried her hands on her apron, before sitting down.

"Brittney got sassy with me," she began. Her voice was quivering. "I can't let her get away with that sort of thing or it'll only get worse the older she gets. Teddy and Angie don't like us reprimanding her, but they didn't see how arrogant she got with me."

Leonard noted the deep-set worry lines around her mouth. "Tried to stand up for herself, did she?" Leonard asked. He lowered his head and peered over the top of his glasses.

"Now, don't you go taking sides with that sort of behavior," Elizabeth shook her finger hard in Leonard's face. "Those sharp little tongues can become habit forming. It's one thing to stand up for herself, but Brittney was downright rebellious and disrespectful. I've never seen her act like that." Elizabeth's face was flushed. A crimson color rose from her neck and settled across her cheeks.

"You aren't going to let this thing rest, are you?" Leonard asked.

Elizabeth shook her head adamantly. "I can't back down. I told her to go to her room and wait for you to come up and talk to her. She has Teddy all shook up over that little girl she met on the merry-go-round. Something just isn't right. Maybe you can find out what's going on. I think those children have some sort of secret between them," Elizabeth whispered.

"A secret, huh? Okay, I'll go up and see if I can crack this case." Leonard mimicked the voice from an old detective show.

"Go ahead and make fun all you want," Elizabeth retaliated. "You'll see what I'm talking about. There's something wrong with that little girl from the carnival. Brittney hasn't been the same since they met." Elizabeth pushed her chair away from the table. "I'll call Teddy and tell him and Angie to come over."

"There are always two sides to every spat. I'll talk to Brittney and see if I can make heads or tails of this before they get here," Leonard said in Brittney's defense.

He took a deep breath and started up toward Brittney's room. With each step, the air around him became more and more stagnant making breathing a chore. Elizabeth is right about one thing. Something isn't right. I hope Brittney is okay.

The banister creaked when Leonard leaned on it for support as he climbed the wooden steps to Brittney's room. He thought about what he was going to say to his granddaughter. *She's only five years old. The poor kid is probably scared to death.*

The door was opened when he reached Brittney's room. She was sitting on the bed facing the window. "What's that you have there, Britt?" Leonard asked casually.

She didn't answer. He noticed that she was cradling the doll Elizabeth had made for her a couple of years ago.

"You still have that old rag doll Nana made for you? She pieced her together from our old quilt. Every one of those stitches was sewn with love. Did you know that?"

Leonard stepped closer to the bed. "If I remember right, I think you named her Abby."

Brittney sat quietly with her back toward the door. Her head was bowed.

Leonard recognized the sullen behavior that Elizabeth was so worried about. The closer he got, the more uncomfortable he became.

"What's going on with you, Brittney? How come you aren't playing outside? I thought you were going to help me work on the front gate," he said. Brittney just stared at her doll.

Leonard pulled up a chair and sat down near the foot of the bed. What he saw upset him. He folded his hands on his lap and searched for the right words to relay his feelings of frustration.

"What did you do to your doll?" he asked. There was a bright red mark scribbled across Abby's face. "You never destroyed any of your toys before. Nana worked hard on that. She sewed every stitch herself.. It's really going to hurt her feelings when she sees what you've done."

Leonard pushed his chair back and stood up. He waited for Brittney to give him some sort of excuse. Anything would be better than the thick silence that hung between them.

The scared little girl inside Brittney wanted to scream out in her own defense, but she remained quiet.

Leonard took the doll from her hands and picked up the red marker lying next to her feet. "What's the matter with you? Turn around and talk to me," he said impatiently.

Leonard was about to leave the room. When he reached the doorway, he paused.

"Nana yelled at me," Brittney blurted out.

He was relieved to hear her finally respond. "So you ruined your doll because Nana yelled at you?"

"No one likes Emily and she's my friend. Do you like her, Papa?" Brittney searched his face, making Leonard feel uncomfortably challenged.

"I don't know her. I can't make a fair decision."

Brittney mulled over his answer. "Nana doesn't know Emily either and she said she doesn't like her."

"I thought you loved your Nana," Leonard fished for a little loyalty or sentiment.

"I do love Nana," Brittney said. Her eyes were filled with tears.

Leonard held up the doll. "It was mean of you to color on Abby's face. That was a permanent marker and will never come off."

"I DIDN'T DO IT!" Brittney exploded. She began to cry and covered her face with both hands.

Leonard didn't know what to say. He didn't want to believe that she would lie; however, he saw the scribble on the doll's face and found the red marker by her feet.

"Do you know what a lie is?" he asked.

"Yes, Papa," Brittney sobbed. She glanced at the doll she loved so much. It was hanging by a leg from her grandfather's big hand.

"No one else is here. I found the red marker on the floor by your feet. If you didn't do it, then who did?"

Brittney looked up to meet his eyes. Tears were streaming down her cheeks. "Emily did it! Emily drew on Abby's face. I told her not to. She said that she's mad because no one will listen to her."

Not willing to play games with Brittney, and not having a reply, Leonard put the chair back by the desk. As he left the room, Leonard called back over his shoulder, "It was bad enough that you lied to me, but it's worse for you to blame someone else for something that you did."

Leonard was sure that it was Brittney who drew on the doll's face. However, deep down, he also believed in his granddaughter and knew that eventually, she would do the right thing. It wasn't right for her to ruin the doll's face and Elizabeth was going to be furious, but more important to him was for Brittney to preserve her integrity and own up to what she did.

Brittney continued to maintain her innocence. "I DIDN'T DO IT!" she cried.

"I don't like a liar, Britt. This is the first time you've lied to me and I'm really disappointed in you," he looked at the doll's face again; unable to believe that she wouldn't admit to what was so obvious.

"I'm going to put Abby away until I can figure out how to tell Nana. I can't imagine what she's gonna say," he left the room with the doll.

Brittney screamed after him. "PAPA! I SAID I DIDN'T DO IT!" Her cries cut through him like a sharp knife.

Chapter Twenty-One

Leonard let out a long sigh. He headed for his room, thinking to himself that maybe everyone was right about Emily. This definitely was a side of Brittney he had never seen.

Leonard went to his dresser and shoved the doll face down under a stack of shirts that he rarely wore. When he turned to leave, what he saw caused him to stumble backward onto the bed.

Walking out of the room, ahead of him, was a little girl with long blond curls. The sight of her took his breath away. It was Emily. He recognized her from Brittney's birthday party. *How could she be here?*

Leonard sat still a moment in an attempt to compose himself. When he felt strong enough to stand, he rose and faced his own reflection in the dresser mirror. What he saw was horrifying. His face had turned a chalky white.

Brittney wasn't lying after all. It was Emily that drew on her doll's face. He didn't dare speak the words out loud. Something was different about the little girl who looked back at him with an icy glare that chilled him to the bone. "My God...Brittney!"

He had to get to his granddaughter. Fearing for her safety, Leonard pressed the back of his knees against the bed for support before attempting to take a step forward.

The bewitching face of a black woman peered back at him from the dresser mirror. Leonard brought his hand up to his chest. "What the hell is going on around here?"

The woman had a peaceful, gentle appearance and nodded in the direction of the door, "Go to her. Your granddaughter needs you. You must hurry."

Hearing her words gave him the strength to step into the hall where he met Elizabeth coming up the stairs. She rushed to his side.

"What's the matter? Are you sick?" Elizabeth cried when she saw him. "Should I call an ambulance?" She had never seen Leonard look this way before. "What happened? Where's Brittney?"

"Never mind. Are Ted and Angie here yet?" Leonard asked. He tensed up as he headed for Brittney's room. The image of the dark skinned, older woman stayed with him. It was impossible to escape her words and the eerie sound of her voice.

"Leonard, what's wrong? Talk to me," Elizabeth cried.

Leonard didn't feel any better and shook his head back and forth. "I have to get to Brittney."

"What are you talking about? I thought you were with her," Elizabeth twisted the front of her apron nervously.

"Wait a minute. Let me grab that doll," he pushed her away and went back to his dresser, careful not to look into the mirror. Leonard opened the drawer and reached under his shirts, but the doll was gone.

Elizabeth followed him into their room. Leonard didn't look well at all. His watery eyes were fixed on the opened drawer and rumpled shirts.

"I just put Brittney's doll in here and now it's gone," he said weakly. Without saying another word, Leonard slowly raised his eyes and looked directly into the mirror. But this time, all he saw was his own reflection.

Leonard fought for control of his legs and headed for Brittney's room. He found her standing in front of the opened window, holding the doll in her arms.

It was a long drop to the ground below and he didn't want to startle her. Leonard held his breath and quickly moved up behind her. He reached out and snatched Brittney to him, terrified of what would happen if she fell. His heart was beating rapidly as he dragged her away from the window and spun her around to face him. Before speaking, he sat down on the bed to catch his breath.

"You have been told since day one, never to open that window. It's too high and if you fall out, you'll break your neck or die. What in the world were you thinking?" Leonard's words were harsh and abrupt. Brittney had never been treated so roughly or spoken to like that, especially from her grandfather.

She stood stiff with fear as Leonard held tightly to both of her arms. The look of terror in her watery eyes brought Leonard back to his senses. His features softened and he released his grasp. It made him sick when he noted the red marks where his thumbs had pressed into her soft flesh.

Leonard rubbed the marks on Brittney's arms. "I'm sorry. You scared me to death when I saw you leaning out of that window. I don't feel very well right now."

"Look Papa," Brittney said sweetly. Her tears had left streaks on her round little cheeks. "Emily fixed Abby's face." She held the doll up for her grandfather to see. Brittney waited anxiously for his approval. "Now everyone can be happy with her."

Leonard glanced around the room. "Where did you get that doll? Tell me who opened the window." He tried to remain calm. The paranormal activities going on around him were overwhelming; however, Leonard wasn't going to let anything happen to Brittney, not while there was still a breath of life left in him.

He saw something move, out of the corner of his eye. "We have to get out of here, Brittney. I want you to take my hand and help me down the stairs. Don't ask any questions, just listen."

Elizabeth had already gone down to the kitchen to see if Ted and Angela were there yet. Leonard had a firm hold of Brittney's hand. "I believe you about your doll. I apologize for doubting you about Emily. I should have known that you would never lie to me. I hope you can forgive me," He kept Brittney's full attention as they headed downstairs.

Elizabeth was looking up at them from the kitchen. "My God, Leonard...what the hell is going on?"

"I found Brittney looking out of that window in her room. It was open. Can you can believe that?" he said.

"I don't know how she could have gotten it open. I painted it shut years ago," Elizabeth said defensively.

Leonard turned to go back upstairs. "Stay down here with Nana. I feel like some homemade cookies. You can help her make them." He gave Elizabeth a stern look. She didn't know what to do. Leonard looked horrible.

Brittney obediently skipped off toward the hook where Nana kept an apron for her to wear when they baked.

How easily they forgive and forget at that age. Leonard gave his granddaughter one last look before turning to go back up the stairs to Brittney's bedroom. "I have to check that window."

When he entered Brittney's room, Leonard found that the window was closed. "I'll be damn. I had a feeling it would be closed," he mumbled aloud and stepped over to examine it. Leonard studied the area closely. It remained sealed shut from several coats of paint.

He looked out at the grassy area under the window. Positioned directly below, was the little girl Emily. She stood straight with her arms hung down by her sides and rose steadily up to meet Leonard, face to face.

Emily wore a twisted, sinister sneer that turned his already weakened stomach. The horrible sight of the wretched child caused him to quickly step back away from the window.

Leonard whispered aloud, "What, in God's name are you?"

He didn't look out the window again, but hurried down to the kitchen where Elizabeth had opened all the windows. A cool breeze whirled around the room, providing a refreshing atmosphere and Leonard filled his lungs with it.

He noted Elizabeth's worrisome expression, but he was happy to see Brittney digging out bowls and getting the mixer out of the box. The tension between Leonard and his wife remained heavy. He couldn't tell her what he had just seen from the bedroom window. Not in front of Brittney, and not until Ted and Angela were there.

Elizabeth continued scrubbing the kitchen table. It was something she did when she was nervous or upset and that was all right with Leonard.

"Don't let Brittney out of your sight...not for one second. I'll explain everything to you later when the kids get here. I don't think I'm capable of going through everything twice," he said.

Elizabeth didn't question him. She got out the cookie recipe she used when Brittney was visiting and began reading it aloud to her.

"At least go sit down," she said. "You look like you just saw a ghost." Leonard went out the front door to wait on the porch for Ted and Angela. "I'll be on the swing. I'd like a cup of coffee."

Before he sat down, Leonard looked around to the side yard. No one was there. *I don't want another confrontation with that awful little girl. Not now and not alone.*

Once on the swing, Leonard pulled out his pipe. The breeze felt good against his wet brow. He had a few minutes to try to organize his thoughts before Ted and Angela arrived. "What in the world am I going to say to them?" he moaned. His thoughts were all over the place, looking for answers, reasons, something solid to cling to, something real.

Leonard remained outside. He couldn't bring himself to go back indoors. There was an uncomfortable stillness in the house. Emily had invaded their home and disrupted their lives. She tormented Leonard and made him sick, both physically and mentally. *How can I explain any of this? Brittney's doll, that wretched little girl in my room, the bedroom window, the evil.*

Chapter Twenty-Two

Leonard was deep in thought when Ted and Angela pulled up on the gravel driveway. Ted hung his head out of the window and yelled to his dad, "Hey...what's wrong? Mom sounded upset on the phone."

He and Angela hurried out of the car. "What's going on?" Ted asked.

"Where's Brittney?" Angela asked as she quickly climbed the wooden steps.

"Calm down. Brittney is in the kitchen with Nana. Go on in, Angie," Leonard answered. "I think they're making cookies."

Angela didn't wait for chitchat. She opened the screen door and went right inside.

"What happened, Dad?" Ted questioned.

Leonard didn't know where to start. . "Sit down," he patted the seat next to him on the swing. Ted couldn't help but notice how bad his father looked.

"I used to be the strong, young father that you are now. I hate feeling old and weak," Leonard began.

"Gosh, Dad. What happened after I dropped Brittney off?" Ted wasn't used to seeing his dad like this. It was obvious that something bad had happened.

Leonard looked down at his feet. "You know, these old feet have taken me places I'll never see again," he stomped his foot lightly. "I walked through dense jungles in Viet Nam and murky swamps where I didn't know when or where the enemy would attack, but I never felt the terror that I experienced today."

"My God, did something happen to Brittney?" Ted jumped to his feet.

Leonard looked at his son with a complete loss of reason or understanding. There was no other way to approach this inevitable revelation than to jump right in. "I think you were right to be concerned over that little girl that Brittney met at the carnival."

Ted frowned. "What are you talking about?" He crossed his arms in front of his chest. "Do you mean Emily? What does she have to do with this?"

Leonard took a deep breath and let it out slowly. "Your mother and Brittney had a few words out here on the porch. It wasn't anything your Mom couldn't handle."

"Is Brittney starting to get smart with you and Mom? I'll definitely punish her, but I'm surprised that Mom didn't nip it in the bud herself!" he said with a slight chuckle.

Leonard shook his head back and forth. "I wish it were that simple."

"If Brittney is acting up, I need to know about it. This all started when she met Emily. Is that all?" Ted was hoping that his father had blown everything out of proportion.

"I wish it were," Leonard said. His entire demeanor had changed, not to mention the pale tone of his normally ruddy skin.

"I've never seen you so upset Pop," Ted said sincerely. "What happened to all that 'small stuff' crap you handed me? Quit beating around the bush and tell me what happened."

"I don't know how to tell you," Leonard confessed. "We have a really big problem," he shifted in his seat. "Brittney's friend isn't...well, she just might be..."

"Emily was here?" Ted shot back. He was furious. "Did you see who dropped her off? Is she here now?" Ted headed for the front door. "I'm calling the police. They have to be stalking Brittney to know how to find her."

It was difficult for Leonard to come right out and tell Ted what had happened. There's only one way to do this. He'll either believe me, or he won't. "Son, do you believe in ghosts?"

Ted looked closely at his dad. "Do you mean like...dead people?" He was glad it was his father who brought the subject up first.

Leonard struck a match on the side of the swing and held it in his pipe. He took four or five short, little puffs before going on. The air was permeated with the familiar aroma of his tobacco.

"I don't know how else to explain it to you," he said.

"Explain what?" Ted asked cautiously.

"I'm usually a pretty rational man, wouldn't you agree?" Leonard bit down on his pipe.

Ted sat back down on the swing with a renewed interest. He didn't take his eyes off his dad. "What happened here today?"

"I already told you that it started out when Brittney and your mom had some words. The little one never stood up to her like that before and she really got her apron in a bunch. She sent Britt to her room. You know the routine," Leonard added.

"I sat on my bed many times 'thinking about what I did'." Ted smiled.

"Your mom called me in to talk to Brittney. She was madder than a wet hen!" Leonard was relieved to be sharing his experience.

"What did Brittney have to say?" Ted asked, feeling that he was pulling every word out of his dad.

"When I got to the room, she was sitting on the bed, facing the window. She was clutching that old rag doll, your mom made her."

"She loves that doll," Ted added.

Leonard continued. "I looked closer and saw that there was a dark red mark scribbled across the doll's face. I was really surprised. It showed a side of Brittney that I didn't know."

A deep crease formed across Ted's forehead. "That isn't like her. She never did anything like that before. What did she have to say for herself?"

"She denied doing it," Leonard lowered his eyes.

"Wow...that's worse," Ted was at a loss for words. "If she said she didn't do it, who'd she blame?"

Ted knew what his father was going to say. He simply wanted to hear it.

"She told me that her friend, Emily did it," he spoke just above a whisper. "The fact is I think she was telling me the truth."

"Why? Was Emily here? Did you see her?" Ted asked impatiently.

Leonard's hand was shaking when he reached for his pipe. "I feel like I'm talking to someone who doesn't understand the English language. You don't catch on very fast."

"Thanks a lot, but I don't know what you're trying to tell me. First you ask me if I believe in ghosts and then you sit here looking like you've just seen one. Get to the point," Ted demanded.

Leonard leaned forward and through a shallow breath, he said, "I took the doll away from Brittney and went to my room. I was gonna hide it from your mom until everything cooled down."

"Good idea," Ted said. "What happened, did Mom catch you?"

"No, it wasn't that simple," he responded warily.

"Come on, Dad. Spit it out!" Ted urged.

Leonard's eyes looked almost glazed over. He became lost in thought as he recalled the incident. "I turned to leave the room and she was there."

"Who, Brittney?" Ted probed.

"No, Emily. That little girl with the long blond curls was upstairs in my room. I thought I was going to have a heart attack. She didn't look like a normal child. She glided with no effort at all, like there was some sort of breeze carrying her along." Leonard paused for a moment. "I must sound insane."

"I never saw you like this. Did you talk to her and ask her what she was doing there? Did she tell you how she got there?" Ted asked.

Ted was furious about Emily; however, the sick look on his dad's face was something he would never forget. He looked like someone who was almost frightened to death.

"I'm so sorry, Dad. I'm here now. Just tell me exactly what happened. I'll deal with that carnie-kid," Ted said sharply.

"That's just it, nothing actually happened," Leonard replied. "I followed her down the hall and then, she was gone. I went to Brittney's room and she was holding the doll in her arms. I had just tucked it under some shirts in my dresser drawer. It was like some sort of magic trick."

"What do you mean? How did Brittney get the doll without you seeing her take it?" Ted asked.

"It wasn't Brittney. You aren't listening to me." Leonard was getting restless. "I'm telling you, Emily took the doll. Somehow, she was able to remove it from the drawer without me seeing her. She cleaned the marker off the doll's face and gave it back to Brittney. Then, she disappeared. I saw her...I saw Emily. She was here one minute and gone the next." The two men looked at each other, each searching for the right words.

"What about Brittney? Did she say anything to you about Emily?" Ted asked.

"That's another thing," Leonard continued. "When I got to Brittney's room, I found her standing in front of the window looking out. The problem was the window was open." His eyes were wide as saucers. "That window has been painted shut for years. I can't even open it. If you go up there right now, you'll find it's still painted shut."

"Are you kidding me?" Ted asked. A chill ran up his spine so fast, it caused him to shake. "Did you see where Emily went?"

"I saw her again outside Brittney's window. She was levitating on the other side of the closed pane with an evil grin on that angelic little face." Leonard heard his own words, but couldn't believe what he was saying. "She isn't real, Teddy. As sure as I'm sitting here in front of you, I'm positive that Emily is a ghost."

Chapter Twenty-Three

Ted Michaels sat quietly next to his father on the porch swing, following his dad's horrendous recollection of his encounter with Emily. They sat together in silence, as they glided peacefully back and forth, listening to the rhythmic creaking of the interlocking chains of the swing.

"You realize that what you told me is impossible?" Ted said.

"I would have agreed with you one hundred percent, yesterday," Leonard replied.

"Do you really believe that Emily is a ghost?" Ted asked.

Leonard sat forward, holding the swing still with his legs. "I saw her appear out of nowhere and simply vanish before my eyes. I witnessed that terrifying little girl hovering just outside of Brittney's bedroom window. Now, unless you have a logical explanation for me, other than the possibility that I've gone stark raving mad, then yes, I believe that she is definitely not of this world!"

"Did you tell Mom about Emily? Did she see her, too?" Ted asked.

"No, I didn't want to talk about it in front of Brittney. She doesn't realize what's actually going on with her new friend. She simply found someone her size to play with." Analyzing the horror of what occurred seemed less threatening when Leonard was able to discuss it with Ted.

"Brittney is intimidated by Emily. She must have seen her scribble on that doll's face," Leonard continued. "Brittney really didn't want to tell on Emily at first. It wasn't until I actually accused her of doing it and she realized how badly I felt that she stood up to me and told on that little...whatever Emily is."

Ted thought about it. "Brittney loves you and Mom. I'm glad that she was strong enough to stand up for herself and tell the truth. I thought something was weird when Mom called me and told me there was a problem with Britt."

"There isn't anything wrong with Brittney. The problem is Emily. I don't know exactly how dangerous she is or what to make of her. The bad thing is that Brittney feels good about Emily again because she fixed her doll's face. All is forgiven and we are back to square one," Leonard said.

"Great, now Emily is the hero," Ted concluded.

"Emily is not what she appears to be. I think she's something we have to protect Brittney against," Leonard stated firmly.

"How are we gonna do that if what you said is true?" Ted asked. "By the way, are you all right?"

"It isn't going to be easy to get that wicked little grin out of my mind. When I found Brittney leaning out of her bedroom window with that doll, it literally made me sick," Leonard admitted. "I don't know what I would have done if she would have fallen out." Leonard put his hands over his face.

"If Emily can open a window that has been painted shut for years, what else is she capable of? She could have pushed Brittney out and we'd have never known. My God, what are we going to do?" Ted became panic-stricken.

Leonard thought about the black woman, who stared back at him from his bedroom mirror, but didn't mention her. For now, he didn't feel that she was a threat. It might have just been part of his shock over seeing Emily.

The events of the day had taken a toll on Leonard. His eyes darkened and his face was pale and weary. "I took the doll and put it in my dresser drawer, like I told you. When I saw Brittney holding it, I actually felt my chest tighten."

"I'm so sorry that you had to go through that, Dad," Ted said. "You didn't actually witness Emily give the doll back to Brittney, did you?"

"Oh, trust me...she gave it to her," Leonard plunged deep into his story. His eyes widened as he spoke. "I watched her walk away and I can't explain how she did it, but I guarantee you... Emily took that doll out of my dresser drawer, somehow cleaned the face and gave it back to Brittney, all in the matter of a few minutes." Leonard was sticking to his story.

"Was Emily in the bedroom with Brittney when you got there?" Ted asked.

"No, Brittney was alone, but she had the doll," he answered.

"So, from what you experienced, you truly believe that Emily is a ghost?" Ted stated.

"In a nutshell!" Leonard answered.

"That's quite a story. Do you know where Emily is now?" Ted asked.

"The last time I saw her she was floating around outside of Brittney's window. I told your mom to keep Brittney downstairs with her until you and Angie got here. That little girl comes and goes as she darn well pleases. I don't want her around here. I don't know what we're going to do."

Leonard shook his head. "Brittney doesn't realize what's going on. Under ordinary circumstances, there wouldn't be a problem with two five-year-old children playing together. But we aren't looking at a normal situation here."

"Brittney started showing an unusual infatuation with Emily immediately after she met her. I didn't like it, but I thought it would end as soon as we left the carnival," Ted said.

"We should have known something was wrong right away, when she showed up at your house all alone," Leonard speculated. "Then there was that necklace. What was the deal with that?"

"I don't know. Brittney told us that a black lady gave it to her when she was outside," Ted said.

Leonard knew it was time to tell Ted about the woman he saw in his dresser mirror. "You might find this difficult to believe."

"I don't see how it could be any harder than what you've told me so far." Ted tensed up.

"When I was in my room, about to have a heart attack over Emily, I looked into the mirror over my dresser. For a moment I saw a woman." Leonard hugged his trembling body with his arms.

"What woman?" Ted asked.

"A black woman. She looked back at me from my mirror and..."

"Spirits," Ted interrupted. "That wasn't a woman you saw. It was some sort of spirit. If Emily is a ghost, then it makes sense that there are other spirits hanging around for whatever reason."

"My God, we sound like a couple of nutcases," Leonard groaned. "There's no other explanation. Emily is a ghost."

Ted turned to his father. "Now might be a good time to ask you what you think about the pictures I took of Brittney and Emily on the merry-go-round."

"I don't really feel like looking at pictures right now, if it's all the same to you," he responded with a deep sigh.

"Come on, let's go inside. I have to show you something. I think you'll change your mind if you give me a minute to explain." Ted held the screened door open for his dad. Together, they went back into the house to share what had just transpired with the women.

Chapter Twenty-Four

Elizabeth, Angela, and Brittney were all in the kitchen making sugar cookies. Angela looked at her father-in-law when he walked in. "Everything all right?" she asked. "Mom was telling me that you had some problems here today."

It was out of character for Leonard to be rude. "I'm fine. Why don't you take Brittney into the den and let her watch television or set up one of those games she plays. Ted wants to show us something and we have a few things we need to discuss that Brittney doesn't need to hear."

Elizabeth gave Angela a sideways glance and slid a pan of cookies into the oven. "I'll clean off the table if we're going to look at pictures," she said.

"Let's get on with it if we're going to do this," Leonard answered. He still wasn't feeling a hundred per cent.

Elizabeth turned to Leonard, "I don't know what happened to you upstairs, but if you don't feel good, maybe you should go lay down."

Ted rushed up behind his dad. "Is the table dry, Mom?"

"Yes, I just finished, now let's see those pictures." Elizabeth dried her hands on a dishtowel and took a seat at the kitchen table.

Angela left Brittney in the den watching a cartoon station. "So, what happened here today that was bad enough for you to call us?" she asked.

"Go ahead and tell them what you told me outside, Dad," Ted coaxed his father gently.

Glancing toward his grand-daughter; making sure that she wasn't able to hear what he said, Leonard repeated everything that had happened upstairs when he went to talk to Brittney. The women both listened intently without interruption until he was finished. Elizabeth rubbed the hairs on her arms that were standing at attention. "Okay, Ted. I'm not feeling too good about any of this," Angela said.

"Now, with that said, I want you to look at these pictures that I took of Brittney at the carnival on her birthday. This is the day she met Emily on the merry-go-round," Ted said as he took a seat next to his wife.

Ted began going through the snapshots taken at the carnival. Angela sat anxiously watching for their reactions.

After Ted separated the photographs, he started to narrate. "Please, don't say anything until I'm finished explaining. I think you'll appreciate this, Dad. I listened to everything you told me on the porch. I had a reason for wanting to know exactly what happened here today."

"You have the floor," Leonard said.

Ted began, "When Brittney and I got to the merry-go-round, I put her on one of the horses." He pointed to a picture of Brittney sitting on the merry-go-round.

"Emily was sitting on the horse right next to her. As a matter of fact, it was this horse right here." He touched the photograph of the empty carousel horse. His index finger was shaking.

Leonard pulled out his pipe. He didn't light it, but held the tip in his mouth.

"Now, listen carefully," Ted instructed. "I thought that the girls looked cute together in the beginning. Emily and Brittney hit it off right away. Brittney was so excited about having another little girl to ride the merry-go-round with. I took a few pictures of them. I even took one of Emily reaching out to tickle Brittney under her chin. See this one where Brittney is curling her neck down and giggling?"

As Ted continued to explain, he laid the pictures out side by side, in order of his story. Then, he waited for their response.

"I know exactly what Emily looks like," Leonard said.

"Wait a minute Pa," Elizabeth interrupted. "Let me see those pictures again." She began going through the photographs one by one.

Elizabeth stopped and looked at Ted and Angela. "You said that you took a picture of Emily with Brittney. Where's Emily?"

With his interest now evolving, Leonard said, "What are you talking about?"

"Look at these pictures again. What's missing?" Elizabeth asked.

"Emily isn't in any of them, but you claim she was there when you took them?" he questioned.

"Exactly," Ted answered.

"I met Emily at your house the night of Brittney's birthday party. The little girl I saw here today is the same one I saw at your house," Leonard stated.

"I believe you Dad, honest," Ted said and took the pictures from his mother.

"It's downright spooky, if you ask me," Angela added. "I'm afraid for Brittney."

"After what happened here today, I'm afraid for her too. I'm afraid for all of us," Leonard admitted.

Elizabeth sat forward and frowned. "What are we gonna do? What could she want?"

"I personally don't like the thought of that hobgoblin coming into our homes," Leonard complained. He was feeling more confident, now that he had some support from his family and it was obvious that he wasn't losing his mind.

"How did she know where to find Brittney?" Elizabeth asked.

Angela sat down at the table where she could still keep an eye on Brittney. "I read an article once about the spirit of a dead child. It said that the unwelcome spirit can't haunt your home unless they're actually invited."

Ted froze. "I never thought about that. Out of all the children on the carousel, why did she choose Brittney?"

Angela thought about it for a moment. "They do have the same birthday. Remember, Brittney asked Emily to come over. She invited her into our home. Now, how are we going to get rid of her?"

"I feel defenseless against Emily," Ted admitted.

Leonard felt pressured. He remembered how arrogant Emily had been upstairs and how bold it was of her to come into his home and exercise her powers. He spoke up emphatically. "You call Brittney in here right now and tell her, no matter what, don't play with Emily!"

Chapter Twenty-Five

"Brittney needs to be warned about Emily," Elizabeth stressed.

"I know, but we can't tell her not to play with Emily without giving her a good reason. She's a smart little girl and already feels that everyone hates her first real friend," Leonard reiterated.

"We can't worry about upsetting her. My only responsibility is to protect her. If Brittney gets mad, so be it," Ted said adamantly.

Angela hadn't had much to say, up until now. "I agree with both of you. No matter how Emily came into our lives, we're all involved with her now and we have to keep her away from Brittney."

"Do we know what we're actually dealing with? The paranormal implications being made here fall so far out of the realm of anything we've ever had to deal with. Shouldn't we consider calling a professional in to help? Maybe we could ask Father Luke from St. Patrick's parish for his advice," Elizabeth suggested.

Ted spun around and the sharpness of his words stung Elizabeth, causing her cheeks to flush. "What do you suggest we tell him, Mother?"

"That's quite enough." Angela stood up, eye level with her husband. "We aren't going to settle anything with that sort of attitude. We have to work together; there are no options here. The only one who matters right now is Brittney."

Ted clenched and unclenched his jaws as he started to speak, "Just let me handle it. You know I hate this sort of crap. I don't believe in ghosts and I can't stand not being in control. Father Luke isn't going to listen to us if we run in there and tell him we are being haunted by a little girl with long blond curls. He'll never look at us the same."

"Oh crap," Angela said. Brittney was standing in the doorway listening to the steamy conversation.

"What's wrong?" Brittney asked, causing the loud group to stop talking. "Are you mad?"

Leonard glanced at his son. "Answer the child."

A loud crash interrupted them. "That sounded like it came from Brittney's room." Leonard stood quickly knocking over his chair.

Ted scooped Brittney up and sat her firmly on Elizabeth's lap. "Keep her here with you, Mom. Right here! Don't let her follow us," he ordered. "Dad and Angie, come with me."

Angela gently touched Leonard's shoulder. "Are you sure you can handle this?"

"I'm fine. This is my house. I may not understand what's going on here, but I'll be damn if I'm going to knuckle under to a ghost," he replied.

"All right, but if you feel overwhelmed, remember, you don't have to do this. I would feel much better if you stayed here with Mom and Brittney," Angela reassured him.

Leonard puffed up his chest. "Let's go!"

When they entered Brittney's room it was immediately apparent where the noise came from. Ted went in first and saw the shattered window. "It looks like this was done from the inside. There are only a few pieces of glass on the floor. If Emily did this, she is becoming more and more dangerous."

Ted peered out of the shattered window to the ground below. Angela and Leonard stood behind him looking down.

"Isn't that Brittney's doll down there?" Angela asked. "What the heck is going on around here? Why would anyone throw a doll through a window?"

Leonard took a deep breath. "Mom and Brittney are alone downstairs."

While Ted and Angela continued examining the broken window, Leonard moved into the hallway. He caught a glimpse of the back of a light blue dress and the leg of a child going into his bedroom and followed her, his anxiety as sharp as one of Elizabeth's knitting needles. When he saw Emily standing by his bed, Leonard forced himself to stand firm as the destructive imp snarled fiendishly at him.

"What do you want, Emily? You aren't welcome here. I'm aware that if a spirit is not invited in, they can't stay. You were never invited here, so why you are in my house and what do you want with my granddaughter?" He spoke as calmly as he could and leaned against the doorframe for support.

Angela stopped and placed her hand on Ted's arm. "Listen. Who's your dad talking to?"

"I don't know. Where is he?" Ted followed Angela into the hall. Leonard was just about to stumble backward as Ted ran up behind him. "What's wrong, Dad?"

Leonard didn't have to answer. Emily simply glared at them through cold lifeless eyes. Silence is a natural environment for the dead.

"I think we need to get out of here," Ted said.

"No, we're going to settle this once and for all!" Angela positioned her hands firmly on her hips, refusing to budge.

"My dad doesn't look good. I have to get him downstairs," Ted insisted. "You come too!" He placed his hand under the older man's' elbow and turned him in the direction of the stairs.

"Come on, Dad. Let's go. I know you want to help, but you have to admit that this is just too much for you." Ted led his father away from Emily.

"We can't leave, Angie." Leonard looked at Angela over his shoulder. His face was twisted and as white as the belly of a whale. "We don't know what that is in there, but we do know what she's capable of. Evil can take many shapes and forms. Emily is not here on a social visit. She's here because she died."

"Angie, come on." Ted was more frantic in his request. "We need to get Dad downstairs, right now. I can't believe you're being so stubborn." He headed for the stairs with his father.

Angela couldn't break eye contact with Emily. She held her ground with the wicked child and continued talking to her.

"I stood up for you, Emily. Why would you want to hurt my family? What do you want from us?" Angela confronted her with the aggression of a mother bear. A thrill and challenge accompanied the horror Emily emitted as she retaliated against Angela.

Emily began to levitate, in an attempt to intimidate her opponent further. She rose slowly, her arms close to her sides and her eyes in constant contact with Angela's.

It was difficult for Angela to mask her terror. "You have to leave. It was evil of you to scribble on Brittney's doll and break her window. Get out of here and go back to wherever it is you came from!"

Ted and Leonard were halfway down the steps. "Can you make it from here, Dad? I have to go back and get Angie."

"Of course, go...go!" Leonard held on to the railing and continued slowly.

Ted turned and bolted back up the stairs, taking them two at a time. He stopped abruptly when he reached Angela. She was still focused on Emily. He grasped her arm. "Please," he begged. "Come with me."

Emily glared at the two of them with malice. Her eyes narrowed and she pursed her lips as she held up the doll that had become a pawn in her game.

Angela didn't let Emily's antics rock her. She had just seen the doll outside of the broken window. When Angela didn't move, Emily began to float toward her. Neither would budge.

Ted gasped and clutched Angela tighter when he witnessed Emily suspended in mid-air, floating toward them. Angela wouldn't back down and the terrifying presence passed right through her, causing the color to drain from her face. Her body temperature dropped drastically and Angela fell heavily to the floor.

Ted knelt beside her and felt a puff of frigid air leave her body. "My God, what do you think you're doing?" Ted protested in fear. "We have to get out of here. Are you crazy?"

He helped her to her feet, but Angela pulled away from his hold. "I can't let her get control," Angela insisted as she struggled to follow the little banshee.

"Get control?" Ted cried hysterically. "She has control. You're only functioning on pure adrenaline and sheer stupidity!" Ted argued with Angela as she scooted after Emily. "What do you think you're doing?" His voice had reached a level of panic.

Ignoring Ted, Angela stormed into Brittney's room. She bent down in front of the broken window and began picking up the shattered glass. Emily sat on the bed, cross-legged, holding the rag doll on her lap.

Ted stood in the doorway, bewildered by his wife's actions. He didn't understand what she was trying to prove, but he couldn't leave her. "I hate this spooky shit!" Neither Angela nor Emily looked his way.

Angela remained on her hands and knees cleaning the mess Emily had created. Emily watched her, showing no emotion.

"I asked you where you got that doll. We aren't impressed with your cheap little magic tricks," Angela spoke boldly, though her insides felt like jelly. Her teeth chattered from the paranormal cold which made her even more furious

Ted was becoming more and more agitated. "What are you waiting for? Fire and brimstone, pits of tar, Beelzebub himself? Can't you see that something bad is going to happen?"

Ted's ranting distracted Angela and she put her hand on the window ledge to push herself to a standing position. When she pressed down, she cried out in pain as a large chunk of glass cut deep into the palm of her hand.

Ted rushed to her side as the blood ran down her arm and splattered to the floor. "Now look what you did," he yelled while rummaging around in the dresser. He found a loose sock and wrapped it tightly around her bloody appendage.

Angela searched frantically around the room for Emily. "Where did she go?" she demanded, completely outraged.

"To hell with that kid. Look at your hand. We have to get that glass out and there's no way I can do it. Now we have to go to the emergency room," Ted said in a total rage, as he forcefully took hold of Angela's arm and pulled her away from the window and out of room.

Angela leaned against Ted. He pulled her close as they headed for the stairs. She cradled her hand and Ted stroked her hair in a slow, soothing rhythm. The sun streamed through the broken window behind them, forming a column of light. Emily stood in the center of the light, staring after them. She appeared transformed into a radiant vision of someone who once was truly beautiful. Angela looked back and saw the full, childish curve of her lip. She was like something gifted back from darkness for a brief, miraculous moment.

Chapter Twenty-Six

"Ouch! Let go," Angela cried. She jerked her hand away from Ted.

"I'm sorry, but you're acting like a stubborn child. You're coming with me," Ted paused a moment and focused on his wife. "Stop acting like a fool and look at me. You're badly hurt and you don't even care. Emily has robbed you of all reason. You're in no position to argue."

When they reached the head of the stairs, Emily appeared before them and blocked their descent. Angela boldly walked toward her, holding her now throbbing hand.

"You're dead, Emily. There's nothing here for you and I am going to protect Brittney. You aren't a good little girl. Good girls don't hurt mommies." She held her hand directly in front of Emily's face.

Emily's expression wasn't altered by Angela's dramatic attempt to sway her. Without a trace of remorse, the ghostly child turned her head from side to side studying the blood as it dripped from Angela's hand. She continued to block Ted and Angela.

Angela recalled the morbid sensation of ice cold death that Emily caused when she passed through her body. She didn't want to ever feel that again.

"WHAT DO YOU WANT!" Angela's exaggerated scream echoed through the house.

Emily reared her head, her mouth stretched wide and the volume pounded their ears like a sledgehammer. The sound that rolled out of Emily's distorted mouth thundered turbulently.

"I...WANT...BRITTNEY!" Her words were drawn out slowly and enunciated with staunch determination.

Elizabeth clung to her granddaughter as Brittany buried her face in Elizabeth's chest. Leonard watched, horrified, while Angela stoically held her position at the head of the stairs. Ted yelled at Emily to stop it as he held his hands over his ears.

The force of Emily's words echoed throughout the house. The noise brought a thunderous, pulsating banging, like a heavy, beating heart. Angela held tightly to the banister and screamed back at the dreadful spirit, standing firm against her opposition. "You can't have my child! You'll never take Brittney!" Her voice was venomous.

Ted realized that if he didn't make a move soon, Angela would tumble down the wooden stairs. He lifted his hands in an attempt to grab Emily. The small spirit of a child spun around abruptly and faced him.

"Oh shit!" Ted exclaimed. His hands remained above his head.

Her face twisted with the stubborn willfulness of a spoiled child. "I WILL TAKE BRITTNEY. I NEED HER!"

The house shook on its foundation. "I NEED BRITTNEY TO COMPLETE MY LIFE FORCE. MOMMY...DADDY!" Emily wailed like a lost child.

Angela was completely thrown off guard. The sound of Emily's sobbing for her parents might have touched her heart except for the vision that stood in front of her. Angela began inching her way down the stairs. She bumped into Leonard at the bottom. Ted was moving quickly behind her.

"For all that's holy...stop this infernal racket! Hurry, let's get out of here!" Leonard yelled to Angela.

"Grab Brittney," Angela instructed Ted. "Come on, Elizabeth. We have to go...NOW!"

A gale-force wind began whipping through the house, as Emily's mouth remained gaped wide. The pantry door was torn off its hinges and flung across the kitchen with tremendous velocity, destroying everything in its path.

The wind swirled around the kitchen, preventing the Michaels family from leaving. They stood in the center of the room, huddled tightly together.

Angela called out, "Emily, I'm so sorry. I feel your pain and turmoil. But why are you releasing all your anger on us?"

The dishes clattered in the cupboard. "You can't have my daughter! Go away Emily. I'll fight you with all the love I have in me for Brittney! Someone committed the unholy act of taking you from your parents. I won't let you do that to my little girl."

Ted worked his way back through the living room and up the front staircase in an attempt to sneak up on Emily. From behind, she appeared small and fragile. He hesitated as he brought his arms up over his head.

Emily spun around and stood face to face with him. An unseen force made it impossible for him to bring his arms down. He was close enough to Emily to get a good look at her. She looked like a mannequin, staring through dark, lifeless eyes. For a brief moment, Ted wondered if she really saw him.

Emily closed her mouth. Immediately, the wind stopped and she began to fade slowly as if from exhaustion.

Elizabeth stood next to Angela with Brittney wrapped securely in her arms. Everything was still. No one dared move. They were utterly stunned.

Leonard looked around at the mess Emily made. "What just happened?"

Ted came down the steps feeling lucky that things turned out the way they did. "She could have thrown me across the room like that cabinet door!" he said. "My God Angie, your hand!"

They noted that the sock around Angela's hand was drenched in blood. "We have to get Angie to the emergency room. She has a chunk of glass in her hand."

"I'm not leaving Brittney," Angela protested.

Elizabeth suggested with a shaky voice, "Then, let's all go together. There's safety in numbers."

"Good idea," Leonard sighed. "We all need to stay together until we decide what to do about that awful child."

"I want my doll," Brittney cried.

Elizabeth surprised everyone when she started up the stairs. "I made that doll with my own two hands. I sewed every single stitch. No impudent little brat is going to walk into my house, go through it like a cyclone, and take it."

Ted attempted to go after his mother, but Leonard took hold of his arm. "Let her go. She's just what that little monster deserves," his weak voice still had a hint of humor.

Ted shook his head and let out a quick burst of air. He followed his mom up the stairs taking them two at a time. "I don't think it's safe for you to go up there right now."

"Safe for who?" Leonard called after his son.

Ted met his mother coming out of Brittney's room. He touched her shoulder. "Please, let's go. We need to get Angie to the hospital right now!"

Elizabeth held up the rag doll. "It was on Brittney's bed, just where I left it."

Ted put his arm around Elizabeth's shoulder and accompanied her down to the kitchen where everyone was waiting.

Brittney ran to meet them when she saw Elizabeth carrying her doll.

"Well, I'll be damn," Leonard said.

Everyone was allowed out the front door. Leonard was the last to leave. As he pulled the door shut, Leonard glanced in and looked around one last time. Lines seamed the corners of his deep set eyes. The pretty little girl with the long blond curls stood staring at a pot of tea roses that Elizabeth kept on the table. She leaned over to smell the tiny flowers. As she did, a lone tear fell from one of Emily's hollowed out, darkened sockets and dropped onto a beautiful rose petal. The miniature flower instantly shriveled and died. Emily turned her head toward Leonard and glared at him through the now putrid, yellow eye-sockets. Her bitterness carried a warning.

Leonard lowered his eyes so as not to be caught in her gaze. He turned to Ted, "I have never felt such terror. That is no human child in there. We have been visited by the devil himself. Whatever it is has displayed an independent will with a deep-seeded malice." Before the door clicked shut, he heard the soft voice of a child. The words blew in his face like a warm breath and caressed his ears, "Death is supposed to be brothers with peace. I have no peace."

Chapter Twenty-Seven

The emergency room was crowded when they arrived. Ted and Angela went to the desk to sign in. The girl sitting behind the counter fired off questions methodically showing no apparent concern over Angela's hand or the blood soaked sock.

"How long do you think it will be before she can see a doctor?" Ted asked.

"Take a seat over there." The girl motioned without looking up. "Someone will come and get you when it's your turn."

"In the meantime, do you think you can trouble yourself to get off that chair and bring us a towel or something to wrap around my wife's hand?" Ted let the clipboard with the routine paperwork drop loudly on the countertop.

The overweight young woman pushed her chair back and glanced unimpressed at Angela's blood-soaked, makeshift bandage. She stood slowly, sighed and looked around for someone to delegate the chore to. It was obvious that she was completely annoyed with them. "Hold on, I'll find something."

"Come on Ted, let's sit down. My hand is really starting to hurt," Angela moaned.

"You're dripping blood all over the floor!" Ted complained.

"They'll just have to clean it up!" Angela raised her eyebrows along with her voice. They walked over to the designated waiting area.

Leonard and Elizabeth were anxiously waiting with Brittney. "What did they say? Does Angie need stitches?" Elizabeth asked.

Angela took a seat and Ted paced in front of her. "They told us to sit down and wait."

"I don't know what this world is coming to," Leonard said. "People just don't care anymore. There's no more compassion. All they want is money! When I was a boy, the doctor came to our house."

The pain intensified as Angela tried to lessen the discomfort by changing positions. "I'm going to go rinse my hand in the sink. I have to get rid of this sock." Angela stood and walked toward the restroom.

"Do you want me to go with you, honey?" Elizabeth offered. Brittney jumped up and ran after her mother.

"I'll go with you Mommy!" she cried out.

"Thanks anyway, Mom. Brittney will come with me. See if you can find something else to wrap around my hand. If that girl ever shows up with a towel, bring it to me."

Angela had to pass the desk on the way to the bathroom. She noticed that the heavyset receptionist was back in her chair with her face glued to the computer screen.

Angela cleared her throat, "Excuse me."

The girl was deeply involved with whatever she was doing on the computer and didn't look up.

"I said, excuse me! Did you ever find something to wrap around my hand?" Angela raised her voice. Everyone seated in the waiting room looked at her.

"If you haven't noticed or simply don't give a damn, I'm still bleeding." Angela was in a lot of discomfort and aggravated by the rude young woman's lack of empathy.

Before the unit clerk had a chance to respond, Angela unloaded on her. "We have had a horrendous day. While you were sitting here on your big butt doing whatever it is you do on that computer, I was chasing ghosts and having glass driven into my hand by a force that was able to open a window that has been painted shut for nearly ten years! Now, what do you think about that?"

The look on the secretary's face was priceless. She sank back in her chair and reached for the large drink that was sitting on her desk. She didn't appear to consider the logistics of what

Angela had just thrown at her. All the young woman could mouth in response was, "Ghost? What ghost?" She handed Angela a towel that she had retrieved from the triage area.

Angela wrapped her throbbing, blood soaked hand in the rough, starched piece of terry cloth. "Please, find someone to assist me. I'm in a lot of pain and I'm not leaving here until you come back with help."

When she didn't move fast enough, Angela's voice reached a crescendo, "Now! I'll be in the bathroom trying to wash off some of this blood."

The young woman left her chair and walked off through the swinging, double doors leading to the triage area.

Angela rinsed her hand under the tepid water in the sink and cringed at the pain it caused. She gently wrapped the towel around her throbbing hand, careful not to apply too much pressure to the sharp piece of glass that protruded from her palm.

On her way back to the waiting area, she passed the desk. A handsome, young male nurse with a pleasant smile was standing there waiting for her.

"Is there something I can help you with?" he asked calmly.

Angela smiled. "Where did that lazy one go that was sitting out here?"

The young man laughed. "You gave her quite a start. She said that you were talking about being attacked by ghosts. It really scared her."

It was Angela's turn to smile. "Well, it got her out of that chair, didn't it?"

Angela noticed his nametag. "Are you my nurse, Jon?"

"Yes, I am. It looks like you had some sort of accident. Let me get you back to one of the cubicles. Give me one minute; I'll be right back." He was very cordial and sincere.

Brittney smiled sweetly at the nurse. "Thank you for helping my Mommy."

"You're welcome, young lady." Jon disappeared through the swinging doors.

"Come on Brittney, let's go tell Daddy what we did. He'll be proud of us."

Brittney laughed. Before they finished telling everyone what happened, the receptionist called Angela's name.

"Now that's service," Ted said sarcastically. "Brittney, I want you to wait here with Nana and Papa. I'm going back there with Mommy."

Elizabeth put her arm around her granddaughter and began telling her a story.

Ted and Angela walked over to the nurse who was waiting by the door to take them back to the examination area.

The look on Angela's face was grim and her color was pale. "I'm starting to feel nauseated and dizzy," she leaned on Ted.

Jon pushed a wheelchair up behind her. "Sit down. Take a couple of deep breaths and keep your eyes opened," he instructed. Ted followed nervously.

Angela took a deep breath and turned her head just as they passed through the swinging doors. Before they closed, she caught a glimpse of a black woman with a brightly colored scarf on her head. She was standing next to the desk looking after them with a comforting smile. The woman nodded at Angela just as the doors closed.

Chapter Twenty-Eight

Once in the treatment area, Ted and Angela found it to be a bustling world of gurneys, doctors and nurses. Jon pushed Angela's wheelchair into one of the cubicles and pulled the curtain closed around them.

"Do you think you can stand up?" he asked.

"Yes, I'm fine." Angela attempted to stand and sat right back down. "I'm sorry, I feel dizzy and I feel like I'm going to throw up."

Jon reached in his pocket and pulled out a pair of latex gloves. Once donned, he instructed Ted, "Help me get her to the examination cart."

Ted quietly did as he was told.

"Lay down, please. I'll put your head up a little if you'd like," Jon said and handed her a basin to throw up in, if need be.

"Thank you. I'm sorry, I don't know what happened," Angela said weakly.

"Don't worry about it. Pain and blood loss have that sort of reaction on people," he smiled.

Jon sat down next to the cart and pulled up a small computer. "I'm going to quickly run through some routine questions before we get started. I'll need to find out if you have any allergies or previous injuries, name, rank and so forth," he said. Angela liked Jon. His bedside manner was comforting.

It didn't take Jon long to get through the admission formalities. Ted stood next to Angela and held her uninjured hand. Jon put on a blue plastic gown and changed his gloves.

"Now, let's have a look at that cut." The young nurse explained everything to Angela as he went along. He gently unwrapped the bloody towel and threw it into a red container. Jon changed his gloves again before continuing.

"It looks as if you have a good size piece of glass imbedded in there. I have to clean your hand before the doctor comes in," he said. "This will be uncomfortable."

"What about you?" Jon glanced at Ted. "I don't need two patients right now. Do you want to sit down?"

Ted looked at his sweaty palms. "It sure looks nasty, doesn't it? I'll be fine, but thanks anyway."

Jon brought in the sterile instruments and set up a work tray for the doctor before he started to clean Angela's hand.

Ted felt his face getting warm and his stomach was queasy as he tried not to focus on what Jon was doing. It was hard not looking at the pool of blood in the center of his wife's hand.

"Maybe I should go and check on Brittney. I'll be right outside the room if you need me, Ang," he whispered into her ear and gave her a quick peck on the cheek before stepping out from behind the privacy curtain.

Before calling the doctor in, Jon spoke seriously to Angela. "Were you telling Cindy the truth about seeing ghosts?" he asked.

Angela smiled. "Why do you ask?"

Jon laced his fingers and took a step in closer, so as not to be overheard. "I've never told a patient this before," he began. "I don't know if I should say anything to you."

"Let me guess," Angela jested. "You see dead people," she laughed out loud and waited for him to join her.

Jon waited for her to stop laughing. "As a matter of fact, I do. Maybe I shouldn't talk about it."

"No, please. I'm sorry I laughed; I thought you were joking." Angela tried to sound sincere. "I didn't mean for it to sound like I was ridiculing you."

Jon wasn't exactly sure why he was telling this stranger something so personal, but he went on. "Actually, I have a gift," he said.

Angela leaned on her right side and asked curiously, "What gift is that?"

"I'm not crazy or anything," he smiled. "I just see things that other people don't have the privilege to see."

Jon glanced over to the corner of the cubicle. "I see the spirits of people that have died and for some reason, they haven't passed over yet."

"Doesn't it scare you?" Angela asked.

"Not anymore," Jon answered. "It did when I was a little boy."

"What did the girl at the desk tell you?" Angela asked with the corners of her mouth turned up in a slight smirk.

Jon frowned. "I just thought that I could talk to you about it. I can't tell very many people. I could get fired. Someone might freak out."

"It's okay. This is all new to us," Angela smiled. "The reason I got hurt today is because of a little girl that we fear is a ghost." Angela blurted out the words. "I'm taking a chance by telling you this. However, I wasn't the only one in the house to witness her. You'd have to lock up my whole family!"

Jon smiled and continued to glance towards the corner. "Does your little ghost happen to have long blond curls?"

Goose bumps rippled up Angela's spine and the hairs on her arms stood at attention. With her uninjured hand, Angela grabbed the front of Jon's shirt, pulling him close enough to smell the fresh stick of gum he was chewing. "How could you possibly know that?" Angela looked him straight in the eye.

"If you let go of my shirt, I'll try to explain." Jon spoke calmly. "She's been coming in and out of this cubicle ever since I brought you in here."

"Why haven't I seen her?" Angela asked, anxiously looking all around.

Jon shook his head. "Spirits are able to reveal themselves to whomever and whenever they wish." Below his brow, his eyes narrowed.

Angela's hand was hurting more since Jon cleaned the wound. She brought it to her chest and moaned unintentionally. The medication he gave her wasn't working very well and it was becoming harder and harder to concentrate on what he was saying.

Jon's response was casual and confident. "I have the gift of discerning spirits."

Angela was riveted but confused. "I'm sorry, but I don't know what that means."

Jon looked at his watch. "I really have to get the doctor in here. If you and your husband would like to talk more about this, I'll be happy to discuss it further with you when I'm off work."

Jon walked over to the curtain, paused and turned back to Angela. "If that little spirit is capable of doing this to you," he said as he tipped his head toward her hand. "You might want to seriously consider seeking help."

Angela asked desperately, "What sort of help do you suggest?"

Jon took a moment before answering. "You need to find out what that spirit wants. It's obvious that she isn't going to leave you alone and is able to find you, no matter where you go. Think about it." Jon slipped out of the room.

Angela looked around with a frown. "You've been here all this time, Emily. You might be able to conceal yourself from me, but it looks like we've found someone that you can't hide from."

The doctor startled Angela when he pushed back the curtain and marched in. He introduced himself in a curt, professional manner.

Angela was jolted from her thoughts and more aware of the searing pain in her hand. "Where's Jon? Is he going to be in here?"

The doctor snapped on a pair of gloves and began assessing her wound. Jon had a gentler touch than the doctor did. Angela grimaced.

"I'm going to have to give you a few shots in your hand before I can remove the hunk of glass," he stated. "It will numb the area."

"I'm scared," Angela admitted nervously. She was starting to tremble.

The doctor called for Jon. "I need some Lidocaine and you can give her a Valium and some Zofran before we get started. I think she'll do better after that." He removed his soiled gloves.

The doctor went to the sink and scrubbed his hands. He put on fresh gloves as Jon administered the medication to help make the procedure more tolerable, then sat down on a stool next to the cart. He rapped his knuckles on the arm board that Jon had attached alongside Angela, then looked at her as if she automatically knew what he wanted.

Jon moved in closer and gently positioned her arm. "Lay back. The medication should kick in any time now. Just keep your palm up and let the doctor fix your hand. The doctor can avoid sending you to surgery if he's able to remove the glass here." Jon's voice was soothing. He medicated her through an IV and kept talking softly, informing Angela of everything that was happening.

She laid back and began counting the small holes in the ceiling tile when the doctor said, "Small pinch." The pain was excruciating as he inserted the needle into her hand and pushed the viscous fluid into her inflamed tissue.

Angela gritted her teeth. She wasn't sure exactly what she saw, because of the tears that blurred her vision, but there appeared to be an older black woman with a bandana on her head wearing colorful attire in the corner of the room. She smiled at Angela and moved through the examination room.

Jon saw the woman of color follow Emily into the hallway. Angela had fallen asleep. The Valium did its job. The black woman in the colorful attire would simply be remembered as a vision she had dreamed.

Chapter Twenty-Nine

When Angela woke up, she was still laying on the cart, alone in the emergency room. Her hand was bandaged neatly in a large, clean dressing.

"Where is everyone?" she called. When she tried to sit up, her head felt fuzzy from the after effects of the medication.

Jon came in and turned up the lights. "I see you're finally awake. I gave you something to help you relax. Dr. Pilla was able to get all the glass out without it splintering. Your hand is going to hurt quite a bit once the numbing medication wears off. The doctor wrote you a prescription for pain pills. I'd advise you to take them before the pain gets too excruciating."

"How does it look? Did I get a lot of stitches?" Angela turned to her side and raised up on her elbow, not feeling quite steady yet.

"That was a big piece of glass in your hand. The doctor had to go pretty deep to get it all out. You have ten stitches in all," Jon said. "You'll have to keep the dressing on and avoid getting it wet for a few days. The stitches will need to come out in ten days. You probably won't remember everything I said, so I'll give your husband some follow-up instructions."

Ted stepped into the room just as Jon had finished explaining everything to Angela.

"I was just telling your wife what to expect. She should try to keep her hand elevated." Jon said.

"How do you feel, honey?" Ted asked.

"She still has some medication on board. But it will be wearing off soon. There's a prescription for pain pills in the envelope with her discharge papers. Make sure you get it filled before you go home," Jon instructed.

Ted nodded at the nurse. Angela cradled her injured hand securely across her chest and Ted helped her to a sitting position.

"What happened to you? I thought you were coming back," Angela asked.

"I'm sorry, but I couldn't watch the doctor stick that needle in your hand and I know I wouldn't have been able to stomach him digging that hunk of glass out," Ted pleaded for forgiveness. "I waited with Brittney."

Just then, Elizabeth, Leonard and Brittney burst into the cubicle. Brittney ran to her mother as Angela protected her bandaged hand from Brittney's lunge and wrapped her good arm around her daughter.

"Be careful Britt," Ted warned. "Your mom just had ten stitches put in her hand."

"Wow, can I see?" Brittney climbed up on the cart.

Ted swooped her up in his arms and away from Angela. "Not now, maybe later," he said. Ted handed the car keys to his mom. "Can you take her to the car? We'll be right out."

"Certainly," Leonard said. "Come on Britt, we have to see how many red cars are in the parking lot. I bet I count more than you do."

Brittney giggled and took hold of Leonard's hand. They walked out together and Elizabeth followed.

Angela was still feeling some effects from the medication and didn't feel like discussing Emily or the black woman with Ted. "I want to go home. I need a strong cup of coffee and something sweet."

Ted smiled. "I'll stop at the store next to the pharmacy and get you some chocolate."

Jon brought a wheel chair in for Angela since she wasn't very steady on her feet when she attempted to stand. "How do you feel?" Jon asked.

"I don't think I do well on drugs. I've never taken anything more than a Tylenol," Angela answered. "I don't like this feeling at all."

"It'll wear off and you'll feel better," Ted said.

Jon held the wheelchair and Angela sat down. "If you have any questions or problems, don't hesitate to call or come back. There's always someone here."

Angela thanked Jon and passed him a note when she shook his hand. Ted went ahead to get the car and pulled up to the door.

Jon wheeled Angela to the emergency room exit and Ted helped her carefully into the car. "Thanks for all your help," he said and shook Jon's hand.

Angela smiled. "I wouldn't have gotten through it without you. Thank you so much."

"It's what I do," Jon answered modestly.

After they drove away, Jon opened the note. Please call us. Our number is 219-888-5061. We need help! He tucked the note in his jacket pocket and shook his head.

Angela was glad for the sling holding her arm. It gave her a break from having to elevate her hand.

"You're going to need some help for a few days, Angie," Elizabeth said.

"I'll take care of Mommy," Brittney said, holding her nose so high that Leonard laughed and flicked it with his fingers.

"You're lucky it isn't raining," he told his granddaughter. "The way you're holding that snoot, you'd drown."

Everyone laughed and Brittney just flipped her head in the other direction.

"Thanks Mom, I'll be all right. I just need to go home and relax. It's been a long day," Angela said.

Ted drove slowly out of the hospital parking lot. "I think we'll all go to our house. You and Mom don't really want to go back to your house tonight, do you Dad?"

"Your mother is pretty set on going home. She doesn't think there's anything at our house that Emily really wants," Leonard said, referring to Brittney.

"Nana was brave. She saved Abby for me," Brittney said.

"We seem to forget about little ears when we're talking," Elizabeth said. "That's an awfully big bandage. Does your hand hurt much?"

"It's still sort of numb right now. The doctor gave me a lot of medication. He warned me that it'll hurt a lot later on, but Ted is going to stop and get my prescription filled. I still can't believe it happened," Angela whined.

"I think you'll be able to rest better if we go home and you lay down," Elizabeth said. "We'll call later on tonight and see how you're doing. We can always come over if you need us. I'd rather we have our own car."

"I'll check in with you too. I'm only a phone call away if you need me. How are you feeling Dad?" Ted asked.

"I'm fine now. I hope I never have to go through anything like that again." Leonard met Ted's eyes in the rear view mirror.

Ted took his parent's home and walked them to the front door. "Do you want me to come in?" he asked.

Leonard opened the door and stepped in first. "I'll be damn. Everything is back where it was. It looks like nothing ever happened."

Ted walked around the outside of the house and looked up at the bedroom window. It was intact and there wasn't any glass anywhere. "Unbelievable!"

"Be careful. Take care of Angie and watch Brittney closely. Call me if you need help. I don't think we'll have a problem here. Emily will go wherever Brittney is. I'll call you later," Elizabeth looked at Ted. "I'm very strong in my faith. You need to start praying."

"Okay, I love you Mom. Call me right away if Dad doesn't feel good. Don't listen to him," Ted instructed.

"Don't worry about us. That little girl of yours is who we all have to worry about!" Elizabeth scowled.

After closing his parent's door, Ted thought about the fact that Emily wasn't a real little girl. It was difficult for him to truly grasp the idea. *Unlike the lurid creature that made my knees liquefy in my father's house, she seemed so small and powerless when we met her on the merry-go-round.* He glanced around, hoping she wouldn't show up in another terrifying form. "I'm still not exactly certain what you are, Emily, but I realize that you are something more than human and somehow, I have to put a stop to all this."

Ted got in the car. Angela was dozing peacefully. He closed the door quietly so he wouldn't wake her. He turned around and looked at Brittney, who was lying, curled up on the back seat. Placing his hands over his eyes, Ted cried silently for only a moment. God help me protect them.

Chapter Thirty

Angela was still asleep when Ted stopped at the pharmacy. "Brittney, I want you to stay in the car with your mom. I won't be long," he whispered.

"Don't forget the chocolate," Brittney reminded him.

He smiled and closed the car door gently. Brittney sat in the back seat quietly listening to her mother's deep rhythmic breathing. She watched a squirrel scamper across the sidewalk. When she turned her head, she found Emily sitting next to the window opposite her.

"Where did you come from?" Brittney whispered, making one of her mean faces.

"I've come to play with you," Emily said. "They're going to take the merry-go-round apart in a few days. Come and play with me." Emily stared at her, unblinking.

"No. My mommy said that you're a bad girl. I'm not supposed to play with you anymore. You hurt my mommy's hand. I'm mad at you!" Brittney argued with Emily.

The children's voices woke Angela. "What's the matter, honey?" Her voice was groggy. She was still fighting the effects of the Valium. Brittney climbed over to the front seat.

"Be careful. Watch Mommy's hand," Angela said holding her arm protectively.

"I'll be careful. Can I sit by you?" Brittney said, curling up next to Angela. "I want to sleep with you tonight."

"We'll see, Britt. I don't want you bumping my hand. It's starting to throb," Angela said. "Did Daddy go into the drug store?"

Brittney smiled. "He's getting us some chocolate and your medicine."

"I hope he hurries. I want to go home." Angela leaned her head back and tried to rest. "The numbing medication must be wearing off. It feels like my heart is beating in my hand."

"How did your heart get in your hand, Mommy?" Brittney asked.

Angela didn't feel like explaining and simply didn't respond to Brittney's question. "Just let Mommy rest right now."

Brittney looked in the back seat. Emily was gone. She leaned on her mother's shoulder and snuggled up securely next to her. Angela simply thought that she was being protective of her when in fact it was just the opposite. Brittney was beginning to fear Emily.

Chapter Thirty-One

By the time they reached home, Angela's pain had risen from a four to an eight on a scale of one to ten.

"My hand really hurts. I need to take one of those pain pills, but, I'm so nauseated."

Ted got out of the car and opened the door for Angela. "I think it's a combination of all the medication you've had. You aren't used to taking anything." He helped her out of the car and put his arm around her waist. They walked down the sidewalk together with Brittney close at their heels.

"Can we have our chocolate?" Brittney asked.

Ted unlocked the door. "Why don't you wait for Mom? She doesn't feel good." Brittney slowed her pace and hung her head. "Okay."

Angela wasn't sure when she would feel like eating. "You don't have to wait for me, Britt. Go ahead and eat yours. Save mine for when I feel better."

Ted carried the bag of goodies into the kitchen and set it on the table. "You can take a piece now, and then you can share some with your mom when she gets up from her nap," Ted suggested.

Brittney picked through the selection of chocolates and popped one into her mouth. "I'm going upstairs to play in my castle," she said. Without waiting for her parents to respond, she skipped off toward the stairs.

Angela wasn't paying attention to her daughter. "Ted, give me one of those pills, please. Then, if you don't mind, will you go out and get something for dinner? I don't think I'll be up to cooking." After expressing her concerns about dinner, she took a pain pill and headed for her room.

"Just go lay down. Don't worry about Brittney and me. We'll whip something up," Ted said. He didn't want to leave them alone. Then, trying to sound sincere, he continued, "Can you make it up the stairs by yourself?"

"I didn't break my leg." Angela's sarcastic response was spoken from discomfort. "I'm going to turn off the phone in our room. If anyone calls for me, please don't wake me up."

Angela reached the top of the stairs and could hear Brittney playing in her room. The door was open and she peeked her head in before heading for bed. "Everything good in here?" she asked wearily.

"Yes Mom. I'm playing with Abby. She likes my castle," Brittney answered.

"I'm going to lie down and take a nap. Daddy is downstairs if you need anything. Stay in the house. I don't want you to go outside." Angela waited for Brittney to confirm her orders. "Did you hear me?"

Angela repeated herself in hopes that Brittney would respond. Again, she didn't answer. It wasn't like Brittney not to acknowledge her, but a lot of things had changed since Emily showed up. Unable to let it go, Angela went into her daughter's room and sat down on the bed. Brittney ignored her and continued playing with her doll.

"Brittney, did you hear what I said?" Angela's voice was shaky.

Brittney continued playing in front of the dresser. She stood up and faced the wall where the pencil marks displayed the girl's height.

Though her thoughts were a bit cloudy from the pill, Angela glanced at the pencil marks. *She only stands as tall as the lowest mark. That's the one Brittney made when Emily was here.*

Angela sucked in her breath slowly, not wanting to reveal her suspicions. A mother knows her own child. This little girl is not my daughter.

Emily stood directly in front of Angela. Her small arms hung limply by her sides and the doll swung negligently from her left hand. Angela began to look frantically around the room. It was Emily's eyes that gave her away. They were not the eyes of an innocent child. They were as blue as the sea and set deep in the dark recesses of her eye sockets. But there was no light behind them. This was definitely not her daughter. Her thoughts were spinning.

What has she done with Brittney? I have to get to the hall and call for help. I'll never be able to handle her with this bandaged hand. I need Ted.

Angela scanned the room and froze when she saw the princess phone sitting on the dresser. "Where did you find that telephone?" she asked. Angela stood nonchalantly and walked slowly toward the door. Before she reached the only escape from the bedroom, the door slammed shut. Angela spun around to face Emily.

"Where's Brittney?" she cried and held her injured hand protectively against her chest. At that moment, the toy telephone began to ring.

Emily looked at the menacing novelty, but made no attempt to answer it. She let a smile drag the corners of her mouth up into a sneer. It was terrifying.

The lights on the toy phone blinked on and off as it rang out, demanding attention. Emily watched as Angela slowly picked up the receiver and brought it to her ear. She held it a moment and listened.

"Mommy...Mommy where are you?" Brittney's cries echoed from the play telephone.

Angela remained motionless for a moment. "This can't be happening." She spun to face Emily. "What do you want? I can't take this anymore, don't you understand?" she screamed.

Impulsively, she grabbed hold of Emily with her left hand and pinned her under her arm. The struggle began. Ted came up the stairs and tried to open the bedroom door. He could hear the commotion, but couldn't get the door open.

"Unlock the door, Angie. What's going on in there?" he yelled, shaking and twisting the doorknob vigorously.

Angela pushed Emily down on the floor and straddled her. She tried pleading with the little girl. "Please, I know you aren't Brittney. What have you done with her?

I want my daughter."

Emily didn't put up a fight. She lay still looking up at Angela. The sides of her mouth remained curled up in an obnoxious grin.

"You aggravating little brat!" Angela cried out. She pinned Emily's fragile little arms down with her knees.

Emily's facial features appeared to morph between those of Brittney's and her own. It blurred Angela's vision, causing her to feel dizzy and sick. She leaned forward toward the child. Their faces were close and Emily's words brushed past Angela's cheek with a taunting eeriness.

"I don't want to ride the horses anymore. I want to be your little girl. Brittney can ride the merry-go-round now," Her words caused bile to rise up into Angela's mouth.

"My God, this isn't happening. Get out of here. I don't want you here," Angela cried. The way she was holding Emily's body on the ground would have hurt an actual living child.

Ted had no luck jimmying the lock. He backed up toward the middle of the hall and with a running start, put all of his weight behind his left shoulder and hurled himself through Brittney's bedroom door and into her room.

The door gave way easily to the impact and Ted went tumbling into the room.

"Angie," he yelled. "What the hell are you doing? Get off of her," he demanded.

With tremendous force, he grabbed Angela by her good arm and yanked her to her feet. She was hysterical. Emily remained on the floor continuing to impersonate Brittney. Ted instantly pulled the child up and examined her. "Are you hurt?"

Angela rocked her pulsating limb with her good hand and tried to calm down so she could explain. Tears streamed down her face and out of her nose.

"If this is how you're going to act when you take one of those damned pain pills, you can just suffer. Go to bed and sleep it off," Ted yelled. He pulled the little imposter close to his side.

"Look at her, Ted! It isn't Brittney. It's Emily!" Angela screamed between sobs.

"What are you talking about? You're stoned." He held the deceiver closer. "I'm telling you, it's that pain pill you took. You don't do well on drugs, Angie."

Angela was beside herself. The pain pill was beginning to take the edge off her discomfort. "My God, Ted. Ask her where Brittney is. And that telephone -- it has something to do with all of this too. Brittney tried to call us for help on that stupid, toy phone. You have to listen to me."

Ted shook his head. "Please, don't do this Ang," he pleaded. He began studying the little girl. "You are Brittney, aren't you?"

Angie paced back and forth in front of them. "I'm not stoned, I'm just hysterical. I want my daughter. That little impudent charlatan knows where she is. Ask her. She told me that Brittney is on the merry-go-round." Angela wasn't about to back down.

Ted turned the child around and studied her face. "Brittney?"

Angela moved over to the wall next to the dresser. "Look here," she pointed to the two pencil marks. "On Brittney's birthday, I stood her up against this wall and marked her height with a pencil. See, right here." It was difficult to control the sobbing as she desperately fought to prove her point.

"I was upset after the girls played in here, because Brittney marked Emily's height on the wall, under hers." Angela moved her finger down to the second pencil mark and cried, "This isn't

Brittney. I know my own child. It's Emily and she's done something with our daughter."

Angela snatched Emily out of Ted's arms and pushed her up against the wall.

Angela was getting sick to her stomach. "What have you done with Brittney?" she screamed.

Emily stood in front of the bewildered couple with no sign of emotion.

Angela shook her head, unsure if it was the effects of the medicine or all the crying as Emily began to fade away. Ted was quicker to react and tried grabbing the ghostly image.

Relief flooded Angela as she realized that Ted was finally on her side. Sincerity rang out in her voice as she pleaded, "Please give her back. Don't do this Emily. Please, I beg of you!"

It was too late. Emily slowly disappeared.

Chapter Thirty-Two

Ted and Angela searched the bedroom frantically for Brittney. "Where did she go? Damn it Angela." It frustrated him that he wasn't able to hold on to her. Ted got down on his hands and knees to look under the bed.

"I don't know. Why didn't you believe me? Don't you think I know my own daughter?" They were fighting with each other at a time when they needed to stick together and find Brittney.

"I thought it was the drugs! If it was Brittney, you'd of hurt her," Ted argued. "What was I supposed to do?"

"We have to do something. We have to get Brittney back right now!" Angela insisted.

Ted bent down and helped her up. "Angie, get hold of yourself. I'll find her if I have to tear this entire house apart." He had no choice but to make false promises. "Life is all about being in a certain place, at a certain time. Our problem is, we aren't dealing with life. Emily is dead. How do we fight a ghost?" Ted tried to rationalize the situation.

Angela stopped abruptly, her face was beet red. Ted saw her swollen eyes and the tortured look of a desperate mother.

"Let's call Jon." She swiped at her dripping nose with the back of her hand.

"Jon?" Ted asked.

"Yes, the nurse from the emergency room. He told me that he saw Emily. She couldn't hide from him. He has some gift where he can see ghosts," Angela felt revived.

Ted was against it at first. When Angela's realized that he didn't know about Jon, she began to plead with him and took hold of his sleeve. "Come on, you have to take me back to the hospital right now. We're wasting precious time."

Ted guided Angela to the door and down the hall to their bedroom. He gave Angela a mirthless smile. "You aren't going

anywhere, but to bed. Lie down and try to get some sleep. I'll get
Jon here somehow, I promise." Ted shook his head. "I hope he
doesn't turn this around and treat us like a couple of criminals.
Remember, we have to explain why our daughter is missing."
Silence surrounded the couple like a closed tomb.

Ted spoke under his breath, "I should have never taken
Brittney to that blasted carnival. This whole thing is my fault."

Angela was too exhausted to argue. She sat down on the
bed. Ted was right about one thing; she was in no condition to go
anywhere. The room felt like it was moving around her.

Brittney's picture was in a decorative frame on the bedside
table. For a moment, her beautiful, straight brown hair appeared
blond and curly. Angela grabbed the photo. "No you don't, Miss
Emily Thatcher. You are not taking the place of my baby." Angela
slammed the picture face down on the nightstand. Ted spun around
at the sound of breaking glass.

"Angie!" he yelled. "Are you crazy? You didn't have
enough stitches today? What in the world are you doing?"

She slowly turned the photo over and was relieved to see
Brittney's sweet smile looking back at her. "I just want my baby,"
Angela cried. "Find her, Ted."

He helped her lie down on the bed and covered her up.
Angela's eyes were heavy from medication and exhaustion.

"I'll be back," Ted whispered through his own tears. "I
want Brittney home too." His tongue was thick from the lump that
had formed in the back of his throat.

Ted's head jerked in the direction of the window. A sudden
movement caught his attention. He thought for just a moment that
he had seen the figure of a black woman watching them. *Who is
she?*

He took a breath, "I better hurry. It'll be dark soon and I
don't want to leave you here alone for too long. I can call my
parents. I hate to put them through any more than they've already
been through. But, if you want them here, they'll come."

Ted tiptoed down the stairs and quietly pulled the front door shut. He sat a moment after starting the car. "Now what? Jon might be a complete crackpot or he might take me for one. He did claim to see Emily though. I have no other choice."

"How do I make this guy believe me?" Ted had to pull himself out of the trancelike state common to people who have just suffered a psychological trauma.

The sky was gray and overcast. Ted's lack of confidence and the prospect of a confrontation with a man he only met briefly made him anxious. How was he going to approach Jon, a perfect stranger and convince him of something he didn't even believe himself?

Chapter Thirty-Three

"A nurse working in the ER, who claims to see dead people. What a resume," Ted thought out loud as he headed for the hospital.

"It's twilight, the time just before dark. The witching hour," he feigned a halfhearted laugh and for a split second, took his eyes off the road.

"Oh my God!" he yelled and hit the brakes. "Where the hell did he come from?" Ted's heart pounded as a dark-clothed figure pedaled slowly on a bicycle in front of his car.

Ted laid on the horn for what seemed long enough to let the rider know that he was pissed off without having to actually roll down the window and cuss him out. He wiped the sweat that had beaded up on his forehead and gripped the steering wheel with both hands. "Thank God I didn't hit him. I didn't see that idiot until he was almost under my car!"

The man continued pedaling his bike, oblivious to anything or anyone around him. He led the line of cars behind him at a funeral's pace.

The biker's lack of interest in anyone around him irritated Ted, causing his adrenaline to soar. Unable to control himself, he rolled down the window.

"Get out of the road, asshole," he barked at the sluggish moving figure.

The rider glanced at Ted and slowly faded into the gray evening. He vanished just as mysteriously as he appeared.

"What the hell was that all about?" Ted was rattled by the entire ordeal and continued driving at a snail's pace, worried that the guy might dart out in front of him again. Ted swallowed hard. He felt his pulse thump in his neck. *That guy looked like the man who put Emily on the merry-go-round.* "How could that be?" he said aloud. "Where'd he go?"

Ted turned into the hospital parking lot and lingered a moment before getting out of the car. "What do I even say to this guy?" He drug himself out of the car and slammed the door a little harder than he meant to. "Crap!"

Ted was grateful to find a different receptionist behind the desk when entered the emergency room. "Hi, how can I help you, sir?" she smiled at Ted. Boy, what a difference just a smile makes.

He took a deep breath and began. "I'm looking for the nurse that took care of my wife's hand today. His name was Jon," Ted's voice emitted an unmistakable note of tension.

The girl's entire demeanor immediately changed. She shook her head no and said, "He isn't here right now. Jon worked the day shift."

Ted bit the inside of his mouth. Of course he did, how stupid of me.

"It's really important that I get hold of him. Is there any way I can contact Jon?" Ted asked sincerely.

"I'm sorry, but we aren't allowed to give out any information about the staff. Did you want to speak to a supervisor?" The smile on her face went from friendly to professional. She scooted to the edge of her chair.

"Jon told us that he would be able to help us with something. He gave my wife permission to contact him. It has nothing to do with the hospital or anything." Ted was beginning to sound like he was drumming up excuses. He could hear himself pleading as his voice unintentionally escalated. *Oh my God, I'm sending up one red flag after another.*

The young woman began looking around as if seeking help. *Great, I'm blowing this.*

"I'm sorry if I sound out of line," Ted tried starting over, but it was obviously too late. "Would you consider calling Jon and asking him if he'll speak to me?."

The receptionist was uncomfortable with Ted's persistence. "I could lose my job for doing something like that. We aren't allowed to call the staff at home and I can't give out any information. Those are the rules."

Ted thought about it for a minute and then attempted another line of reasoning. He took his wallet out of his back pocket and pulled out a fifty-dollar bill. The girl was immediately on her feet. Ted had obviously insulted her.

"I better get someone from the back that can help you," she said. "I think the doctor that worked days today is still here. I'll be right back." She quickly escaped behind the double doors before Ted could say another word.

"That's nice, she's probably getting security," Ted mumbled.

Just when things couldn't look any worse, Ted spotted Jon. He had just entered the building. Ted was ecstatic and called out, "Jon! Jon!" He waved his arms in the air in a feeble attempt to gain the young man's attention.

The receptionist came back through the swinging doors, followed by two security guards. Ted was heading toward Jon a little too quickly, wearing a look of desperation.

Jon glanced up just as the two officers took hold of Ted, one on each arm. "Is this the man?" The larger of the officers asked the receptionist, who by this time, was badly shaken.

"What's going on?" Jon asked.

"This man was asking questions about you and your whereabouts. Jennifer was worried about your well-being and felt that we might be needed. It appears that she was right." They kept a tight hold on Ted's arms, just above each elbow.

"I don't know. Is there something I can help you with before these two gentlemen escort you out of here?" Jon wore a pleasant but concerned expression.

"I'm Ted Michaels. You took care of my wife's hand today, here in the ER. She received ten stitches after a large piece of glass, embedded in her palm, was removed. Do you remember her? Her name is Angela Michaels," Ted was speaking much faster than he could think.

Jon remained calm and nodded at the officers. "It's okay. I'm off right now. I came in for a meeting, but I'll speak to this man. Thanks for your concern." Jon didn't feel at all threatened by Ted's presence.

Ted was relieved when the two officers walked away. "I need to talk to you. It's an emergency!"

Jon was touched by the urgency in Ted's voice. He glanced at his watch. "I actually didn't want to go to this meeting anyway."

"I'm really sorry about this. I hope you won't get into any trouble," Ted said trying to sound like he cared about Jon missing his meeting.

"Don't worry about it," Jon said and led Ted to a small canteen at the end of the hall. He stepped over to one of the vending machines. "Would you like a cup of coffee?"

"Thanks, I could use a cup right now," Ted answered.

Jon brought two cups of hot coffee back to the table and motioned for Ted to sit down.

Ted was relieved that Jon was willing to talk to him, even though he wasn't sure how he would start or what all he would say that wasn't going to sound like they were some sort of crackpots. Ted's face and body language expressed a colossal burden that he was more than anxious to share.

The tension between the two men was heavy enough to be weighed. The air felt thick and stagnant. Ted didn't feel he had sufficient time to plan what he needed to discuss with Jon. He had to tell him the truth about Emily, however he didn't want to actually refer to her as a ghost, as they suspected. But that's what she was, wasn't she?

Jon waited a few moments before saying anything. He observed Ted for that time, trying to figure out where he was coming from and what it was he wanted from him. He cleared his throat and three small lines formed on his brow when he wrinkled his forehead. "Well, you wanted to talk to me, here I am. For some reason, the timing was perfect for us to meet. So, let's talk."

Chapter Thirty-Four

"Is this okay for you?" Jon began. "We can talk in here without being bothered. Most of the time, people are just in and out of here for a quick snack."

"I want to thank you for talking to me," Ted sighed and held out his hand in a friendly gesture.

Jon grasped Ted's hand and shook it firmly. "How's your wife doing? She really had a nasty cut." His expression was comforting. "She spoke briefly about an encounter with the ghost of a little girl."

Ted started right in. "This is the first time anything like this has ever happened to us. I was against talking to you, but Angela insisted. She said that you saw Emily."

Jon bit his bottom lip. "Yes, I did tell your wife that I saw a little girl with blond curls come in and out of her room. You knew her? You called her Emily." He tipped his head and spoke with a questioning tone.

"Something happened after we left here. We need help and we don't know who else to turn to," Ted lowered his eyes as the reality of what was happening began to wash over him. His thoughts rushed to Brittney.

"We thought about calling Father Luke from St. Patrick's, however I don't think he will understand or believe us," Ted explained. "We have no one to turn to."

Jon paused a moment and recalled overhearing his brother, Dan talking about how Father Luke used their rare abilities against him in the church. "I personally don't think very much of Father Luke Phillips. My brother and I have a very unusual gift."

Ted raised his eyebrows. "What would that be?"

Jon's dark eyes appeared to bore right through Ted as he shifted in his seat. A twitch of a smile formed at the corners of his mouth. "I don't know if it's a gift or a curse," he chuckled. "It's hard for most people to comprehend. But in your case, I think I can just come right out and tell you about it."

Ted leaned back and crossed his ankles. "Go on, I'd like to hear what you have to say. I don't want to bring some phony home with me. We have enough problems right now."

"I understand," Jon said matter-of-factly. He leaned forward and rested his elbows on the table. "I do want you to know that I don't reveal this to many people."

Ted waited patiently for Jon to explain. He folded his arms across his chest, not saying another word.

"I was always fortunate enough to have my older brother to share this with. He also has the ability to see them." Jon spoke as if he were telling a campfire story.

"I feel like I'm tempting fate, but what exactly are we talking about? What do you see?" Ted asked.

Jon scanned the room quickly before going on. "I'm able to discern the spirits of dead people. That's what Emily is, isn't she? We're talking about a ghost, are we not?"

Ted inhaled deeply. "And I was worried about you believing me."

"Actually," Jon said. "They're the spirits of those who either don't realize they're dead or they're searching for something. I'm not sure. Maybe they're simply lost." He appeared to enjoy talking about the supernatural.

"Is that what you were doing when you were looking around the room and out into the hall a minute ago while I was talking?" Ted asked.

Jon's expression didn't change. "Yes. By the expression on your face, it doesn't appear that you believe me a hundred percent. I thought you and your wife needed help. You came to me, remember? "

Ted was feeling all the unbearable weight of his decision. He realized that Jon was right. There was no way he could go home and tell Angela that he spoke to Jon and didn't accept his help.

"By the way, can you explain the man that has been loitering around you since we sat down?" Jon mustered a half smile. "Or the elderly black woman?"

Ted glared anxiously at Jon. "I don't know. Is he wearing a hooded coat? I have to go home and explain all this to Angela. How did you know about him?" Ted looked around. "Is he here now?"

Jon's eyes were fixed on the area directly over Ted's left shoulder. "There's a figure in a dark hooded coat that has followed you since you walked up to me."

"I saw him on the way here. He just appeared in front of my car, on a bike of all things," Ted said. "It scared the hell out of me. I didn't see him and when I did, I thought I was going to hit the idiot. It was very upsetting. And now you tell me, it's just another ghost? Well, you do seem to be right on target."

Jon sat forward and spoke calmly. "I understand your skepticism, but I need to know if you want my help or not. By the way, the black woman doesn't mean you harm."

Ted spun around and repositioned his chair with a rough gesture that demonstrated his nervous reaction to the spirits.

"I realize that this is a slippery topic for either of us to be discussing. All I can do is offer my assistance." Jon couldn't help it; his eyes kept following the suspicious character that concealed his face with the brown baggy hood.

"You actually see them, don't you?" Ted's eyes narrowed and met Jon's.

Jon nodded his head ever so slowly. "All the time."

"Is there any way you can come home with me and talk to Angela? She's frantic. Something happened to our daughter, Brittney," Ted buried his face in his hands and held it there, unable to bring himself to talk about what happened.

"What do you mean? What happened to your daughter?" The little girl, who had so graciously thanked him for helping her mommy, now captured Jon's attention.

"One minute she was in her room playing and the next, she was gone. Emily was there in her place for a while, but she just faded away. Now, they've both gone. There's no explanation for any of it," Ted trembled as he searched Jon's face.

"Your daughter is missing?"

Ted nodded his head and stared into his coffee mug. "We don't know what happened. I was serious when I said she was in her room one minute and then gone the next. She was here with us at the hospital. You met her. That damned Emily seems to have something to do with everything that's happening to us. Can you help us?"

When Jon didn't answer right away, Ted panicked. There was no way he could go home and tell Angela that he wasn't able to get Jon to listen.

"Please, I'm begging you; at least follow me home and talk to Angie. We're desperate!" Ted pleaded.

Jon drummed his fingers on the table. "I suppose I could try. I'm not sure how much help I'll be, but there's no way you and your wife are going to be able to deal with this yourselves. I'll tell you the truth and see what happens," he continued staring over Ted's shoulder.

Ted turned completely around. "I hate this spooky shit! I never asked for any of it."

"I don't know what it is we're dealing with, but I'm concerned with the fact that Emily was able to replace your daughter," Jon said. "I think we'll find that things aren't as bad as you think. Emily might have shown herself to you and your wife and taken the form of Brittney. If so, then Brittney should be home when we get there. Emily is playing with you. It isn't very funny and I hope that's what this is all about. She's very cunning but there's a reason for her mischief. I hope we can figure it out."

Ted felt a little more confident when Jon used the word 'we.' "Then you'll help us?" Ted pushed his chair under the table showing that the conversation was over either way.

Jon breathed deeply. "I can't promise you anything. If we're unable to find your daughter, we'll have to notify the police. You can't argue with me about that."

Ted's voice was full of dread. "How? What can we possibly tell the police?"

"You have to consider my position. I don't really know you or your wife, but I do know one thing for sure. There are definitely spirits trying to contact you. I'm just trying to be up front with you from the start. Don't worry about the police yet. Not until we've exhausted all other angles." Jon didn't want to be too encouraging.

"I'm parked in the back. You can follow me," Ted motioned to Jon. He didn't want him to change his mind. Ted glanced around the emergency room. "Are there many of them?"

Jon nodded. "Hundreds; it looks like a bus terminal. I used to think they were waiting for the good old gospel train," he snickered without a smile. "But they never leave. They just keep roaming."

Ted and Jon left the hospital together. Jon noted the hooded spirit riding a bike out of the parking lot but kept the ghosts whereabouts to himself. He followed close behind Ted who kept him in his rearview mirror.

Chapter Thirty-Five

On the way home, Ted saw no sign of the hooded stranger riding the bike although he kept looking for him. Things were different for Jon. He kept a close watch over the dark clothed character as he rode the old bicycle right alongside Ted's car. "I wish I could see his face. He wears that hood like a monk," Jon muttered.

Jon noted three different crosses with flowers planted alongside the road, to mark the spot where someone had lost their life. "But not their souls," Jon remarked aloud as he observed three teenagers walking aimlessly around the grassy area just past the white crosses. "More lost, wandering spirits. I'll never get used to their eyes. Those empty sockets still send a chill down my spine," he said as he drove past.

Jon was thinking that he didn't want to lose sight of Ted, when all of a sudden, Ted stopped his car and jumped out. Jon rolled down his window as Ted approached his window.

"We're going to turn here and take another route. Something's going on up ahead and it's causing a traffic jam. Just follow me and stay close," Ted said.

"Can you tell what happened?" Jon asked.

Ted looked down the road, pointing as he spoke. "I can't tell, but it looks like an accident. This road is so busy. I can see flashing lights up ahead."

Jon rolled up his window. When they made a left turn, he glanced down the road. In the middle of the street was a small boy. He was wandering between the cars. His eyes hollow, yet searching in that way that was all too familiar to Jon. He shook his head. "Poor kid."

It was another twenty minutes before they pulled into the driveway. Ted noticed that the upstairs lights were on. "Angie must be up. Come on, she'll be glad to see you," he continued talking as they hurried to the front door.

"I hope she's feeling better," Jon remarked.

"Yeah, so do I," Ted said.

Ted anxiously opened the door as if he had brought home the goose that laid the golden egg. "Angie," he called. "I'm home and Jon's with me. Are you dressed?"

In all his excitement, Ted left Jon standing in the foyer while he took the stairs two at a time, barely touching their surface.

The door to Brittney's room was open. Ted's heart was beating rapidly as he approached it. He placed his hand over his chest to try to steady himself.

"Hi Daddy," Brittney said when she spotted him standing in the doorway.

Ted looked at Angela for an explanation. She appeared relieved, but emotionally drained. There were dark circles under her eyes. He released a long sigh of relief.

"What's going on in here?" he questioned with a serious tone. His eyes were riveted on Angela.

Brittney was busying herself with dressing and undressing her doll. "I was on the merry-go-round with Emily. I tried to tell her that I wasn't supposed to go to the park without you or Mommy, but she wouldn't listen. The nice black lady brought me home."

Ted was amazed at the simplicity of Brittney's story and her incredible acceptance of everything. "Just like that? Can tell me how you got there. How did you get home, Brittney?" He was not giving her a chance to respond.

"Stop it Ted," Angela stepped up next to Brittney.

Ted was enraged. He was so full of emotions over everything that had transpired. "I hope you had fun at the carnival, because it's the last time you're going there!"

Brittney tucked herself under Angela's arm. Ted continued ranting. "We were scared to death. When we couldn't find you, I didn't know what to do. I've never been so frightened in all my life," Ted broke down. He sat on the bed and buried his face in his hands.

Brittney didn't understand. She held tightly to her doll and pointed to the closet. "Emily wanted to play in the closet. We went in there and played with the other little girls. Then we all stood together in a circle and Emily took us to the merry-go-round," she cried.

Angela spoke calmly to Ted. "I'm not letting her out of my sight. I have a lot to tell you, but I'm not going to talk in front of Brittney; do you understand?"

Ted looked up at Angela. She continued, "I called your mom and dad and asked them to come over. We're going to have to take shifts, so Brittney will never be left alone until we find a solution to this mess."

Jon tapped on the doorframe. "Hey, forget about me? Where'd you find her?" he asked as he stepped into the room.

Ted stood up and immediately asked Angela, "Are you sure it's her this time?"

"I was able to spot that little fraud the first time," Angela said proudly.

"I know my daughter," she was confident that the little girl in front of her was Brittney.

Ted felt a mixture of relief and confusion over everything that was happening.

"I'm so glad you're here Jon," Angela said. "We can't thank you enough for coming."

She turned back to Ted. "We'll talk about this once your parents get here. We'll all sit downstairs. She appears calm now, but Brittney was definitely rattled when I woke up and found her sitting next to me on the bed. You can't imagine how I felt. It was like waking up from a horrible nightmare."

"Well, the fact still remains that it wasn't a bad dream. It really happened and it isn't over yet," Ted said.

The doorbell rang. "It's Nana and Papa," Brittney exclaimed as she ran past Ted and Jon. Angela was right on her heels.

"Brittney!" she screamed, all the way down the stairs. Angela was terrified of losing sight of her for even a moment. The nightmare had only just begun.

Ted glanced at Jon. "I'm sorry. I'm not sure what transpired here. Please, stay and hear us out. I'll make a couple of sandwiches and put on a fresh pot of coffee if you'd like. I'm hungry."

"I'll take you up on that sandwich, but I think I'll pass on the coffee. I never finished the last cup I started. I think I like the smell better than the taste. Water will be just fine."

Jon lingered in the hall after Ted went downstairs. He stepped back into Brittney's room and looked around. Spirits were tricky. They could make things appear distorted or leave false trails.

When Jon was a little boy, he remembered a particular child spirit that would lead him astray with echoes and lights. It was very unsettling to his mother, because she didn't understand the spirit world and just thought Jon was a naughty little boy.

In the corner of Brittney's room, huddled closely together were four little girls that each looked to be about five years old. They all were of the spirit world with those same lifeless eyes, looking lost and forlorn.

Jon silently observed the children. He noted that whenever they moved, a soft yellow light traveled with them. Intrigued by the light, he watched it move with the children. When he tried to look away, he caught a glimpse of someone else in the light. For a split second, Jon saw the figure of a black woman.

He stopped and focused on the image. Her attention was on the children. He was able to make out some of her attire, such as the scarf she wore on her head and the long colorful skirt that moved gracefully around her legs as she moved in the light.

There was something in her hand. He was not able to make out exactly what it was, but it appeared to be connected to some sort of tattered ribbon. Whatever it was, she kept it secured in her closed fist.

Jon decided to go downstairs as the tantalizing aroma of freshly brewed coffee drifted up from the kitchen. When he turned to leave Brittney's room, he all but collided with the hooded figure that usually hung close to Ted. Jon stayed and witnessed the children being herded toward the closet where they disappeared.

"The closet is their gateway. Another part to the puzzle," Jon mumbled. He left Brittney's room and followed the voices to where the Michaels family waited.

Chapter Thirty-Six

Ted was standing in the foyer with Leonard when Jon reached the bottom stair.

"This is Jon. He was Angela's nurse in the emergency room. I don't know if you remember meeting him," Ted said.

"Of course," Leonard shook Jon's hand and they walked into the kitchen.

"That coffee smells good," Jon said, changing his mind about having a cup.

Angela poured him a cup and placed the pot in the center of the table so everyone could help themselves. "I have flavored creamers too, if you prefer them," she sat down after putting everything on the table.

"Ang, you still look uncomfortable," Ted said with a note of sympathy towards his wife.

Jon nodded in agreement. "It'll be a few days before all the inflammation subsides. I'm glad to see you're using the sling."

"It helps some," she acknowledged. "Does everyone have what they need, because I'd like to get started."

Brittney sat at the counter coloring in one of her new activity books, where Angela could keep an eye on her.

Brittney had a short attention span unless she was watching one of her videos. "Ted, would you please go upstairs and bring Brittney's portable DVD player down here so we won't be interrupted? I don't want her to overhear our conversation," Angela added.

Ted had just finished his sandwich. "Sure, that's a good idea. I'll be right back."

Jon got up and followed Ted as he left the kitchen. "I'll help you."

"That's okay, it isn't very big," Ted said.

"I need to talk to you anyway," Jon exchanged looks with Ted.

Ted shrugged. "Come on then."

As the two men headed upstairs, Jon stopped in front of Brittney's room. "Ted, wait a minute. I saw something in your daughter's room that you should know about," Jon could hear the muffled cries of children coming from the closet.

Ted didn't appear to hear anything. "What's up?"

"You don't hear anything?" Jon asked.

"No, should I?" Ted cocked his head and listened closer.

"I don't know," Jon answered. "Earlier, when I was in here alone, I saw four little girls. It was unbelievable, because they all seemed to be dressed differently. It was like they were from another time or place. I can't quite put my finger on it. Nevertheless, I can still hear their cries, but I don't see them right now." He was excited and yet frustrated by it all.

"I think they went into your daughter's closet," Jon pointed to the partially closed door. "They seemed to be dressed in outfits from as early as the nineteen forties. One little girl had a type of school uniform on," Jon said as he scanned the room. "I have to admit, I've never experienced anything quite like this, but Brittney's closet appears to be some sort of portal."

"I'll get Brittney's DVD player and we can talk about this downstairs," Ted suggested.

"I'm not sure exactly what's going on around here, but you have more than one ghost," Jon said. "Emily has something that she's trying to convey in a big way and she isn't alone."

"But what does she want with Brittney?" Ted asked.

Jon spoke seriously. "There are only two things Brittney has that Emily could possibly want."

Ted hesitated to ask. "What's that?"

"Her body or her soul," Jon replied.

An icy breeze sliced through Jon as he stood with his eyes closed in the opening of the doorway. "They're all here," he stated calmly. "Emily might have been the first. She's definitely the strongest, but she isn't alone."

Ted stared with a quiet reverence. "You're creeping me out, man. I always hated spooky books or movies. Now, I'm being forced to live it," he rubbed his arms vigorously. "You will help us, won't you?"

"I'm committed now. Those little girls all met with some sort of tragic ending at about the same time in their lives. I think they're all a part of Emily's plan. At least they're sticking together. We have to do something to help them," Jon said sincerely.

"What can we do?" Ted asked.

"I'm not sure. It might be something as difficult as finding their bodies, you know, their remains. It might be the only way we can help your daughter," he mulled over the thought. "For some reason, they're trying to recruit Brittney. Maybe they need her life force, for energy."

"What can we do?" Ted asked in all earnest.

"I don't know. I'm not certain of anything at this point. I can feel their pain and I hear their pitiful cries for help. We can't stop now. They won't let us."

Ted took Brittney's portable DVD player and left her bedroom. He pulled the door closed behind them, stood for a moment and inhaled deeply, in an attempt to digest what Jon had just revealed.

"This isn't going to be easy, is it?" Ted asked.

Jon could only shake his head as they went back downstairs to share their thoughts and findings. Jon braced himself for the night ahead. "You have no idea what we're dealing with. No idea at all."

Chapter Thirty-Seven

Ted and Jon entered the large country style kitchen where the rest of the family awaited them. "Thanks for being so patient, Jon."

"No problem," he said and slowly scanned the kitchen, as he normally did for unwelcomed visitors.

"Thank you," Angela said. She set up the portable DVD player so Brittney could watch her movies and still be within view.

Angela set a few of Brittney's favorite movies next to the convenient portable DVD player. Brittney immediately began sifting through the selections trying to decide which one she wanted to watch.

"You have to be quiet so we can talk. Do you hear me?" Angela addressed her daughter.

"Yes Mom," Brittney said. On the surface, everything appeared to be back to normal.

Angela made a big bowl of popcorn for Brittney and took a seat next to Ted at the table.

Jon glanced through the kitchen doorway to the staircase. The stranger in the dark hooded cloak lingered on the bottom step. He didn't want to mention him to anyone just yet. Jon felt he had to observe the hooded stranger for a while first.

"Ted," Jon spoke softly through a mouth full of partially chewed food.

"What is it?" Ted asked.

Jon took a long refreshing drink of cold water before speaking. "I don't think that I'm going to be able to do this alone."

"Do what? What do you mean by alone? You have all of us," Ted questioned anxiously.

Jon glanced back toward the stairs.

"I thought you were used to this sort of thing. We can't tell anyone else about this. It was hard enough dragging you into it," Ted complained.

Elizabeth shook her head. "We aren't used to airing dirty laundry in this family. Actually, we've never had any so called skeletons in our closet."

"What are you talking about? We didn't do anything and Brittney is definitely the victim here," Angela retorted. She pulled her injured hand snuggly to her chest. "We're all victims for that matter."

Jon ignored the defensive stance the Michaels family was taking. It was a normal response. "I keep seeing things in this house that lead me to believe that something horrible happened to Emily and all those other little girls."

Leonard leaned forward. "What would make you say a thing like that?" he asked curiously.

Elizabeth looked over at Brittney. "Ghost or no ghost, I'll wring Emily's neck like a chicken."

Jon shrugged. "You have no idea what you're dealing with. This isn't something that any of us are capable of handling in a normal, everyday fashion."

"What sort of animal would hurt a child? And furthermore, what sort of child would create all this havoc?" Elizabeth spoke up.

"This is very serious. If it were a mortal man that we were dealing with, I'd be able to defend Brittney. But it's not and we need help," Ted said. "Jon, you have to understand why we're all so devastated and how totally defenseless Emily has made us feel."

Jon shifted in his chair. "First of all, I was invited here to see if there was something supernatural going on," he looked at Angela to support his statement.

"You were quite comfortable talking about Emily in the hospital and told me to call you if we needed help."

"I know my limits and what I'm capable of doing," Jon said.

"You are going to help us, aren't you?" Ted asked, concerned. ". I don't want a lot of strangers involved in our private business."

Jon took a deep breath and exhaled slowly. "You have several ghosts in this house. Emily is one of many. I've witnessed these lost souls for so many years. It didn't seem like a big deal when you first asked me for help."

"What makes it different now," Angela asked. Her eyes were penetrating. Jon avoided her desperate stare.

"It isn't that I don't want to help you," he spoke earnestly. "I don't know if I'm capable of handling this alone. Whoever it is that's been following your husband has something to do with Emily."

Elizabeth looked at Ted. "What's he talking about? How many ghosts did you see in here?"

Jon took another deep breath. "I have to contact someone that I know is capable and more knowledgeable to help you out of this complicated, paranormal travesty."

Agitated and bitter, Ted asked, "And just who might that be?"

"I want to call my brother, Dan. He's twice as gifted as I am both spiritually and telepathically. His gifts, if you will, are stronger than mine. He's dealt with this sort of thing before. I haven't," Jon humbly admitted.

"Why did you lead Ted and Angie to believe that you would be able to help them?" Elizabeth confronted Jon.

Jon went on to explain. "I didn't say that I could help them. I only claimed to be able to see the spirits of people who have died and for some reason haven't been able to cross over. Emily can make herself seen whenever she wants. She can also make herself invisible and still be present. Emily isn't able to hide from me. That's what I'm good for. I can tell you where she is and if there are others around."

"So, there are more?" Elizabeth was skeptical.

"Yes," Jon answered. "I counted at least four or possibly five other little girls that were somehow able to follow Emily.

They don't appear as brave. They huddle pitifully together," Jon said.

Jon laced his fingers and laid his hands firmly on the table. "The hooded character is the one I'm concerned about. In some unexplainable way, it appears that Emily is collecting the souls of other children in order to build a strong spiritual force. She's becoming increasingly stronger. I assume she's doing this to eventually overpower the hooded figure. That's why I have to call my brother, Dan. I don't know the extent of what I'm dealing with. To tell you the truth, it scares the hell out of me."

Ted looked over to his father. "What do you think, Dad? You haven't really said anything yet."

The older man paused a moment before he spoke. "There is something terrifying and forceful about Emily. It's stronger than our feeble, human bodies. She's evil. I would love to be able to claim the role of protector, but she showed me my limits," Leonard wasn't ashamed to say it. He turned to Jon. "Call your brother. The only one I'm concerned with is Brittney. I don't give a rat's ass what other people think."

Brittney walked over to Angela and sat on her knee. "Mommy, can I go play in my room?"

The voices from everyone seated around the table rang out in unison, "No!" It brought tears to Brittney's eyes and she buried her face in Angela's chest.

"Oh honey, they aren't yelling at you. We all simply agree that we don't want you out of our sight for now," Angela looked sternly at everyone. "Now we're scaring her. Call your brother. We need help!" She cradled Brittney on her lap.

Angela moved Brittney in front of the DVD player in an attempt to lead her away from the conversation. "Pick out another one of your favorite videos. I'll get you a glass of chocolate milk and some cookies."

When Ted felt it was safe to start the conversation again, he continued. "We have a ghost that is terrifying our family. I feel a horrible burden for taking Brittney to that blasted carnival and starting this whole mess."

"That's not necessarily true." Jon added. "You have to remember that there are similar things here that match Emily up with Brittney."

"Such as...?" Leonard asked.

Angela interjected a thought before Jon could speak. "Emily told me that she was born on June twenty-eighth, the same date as Brittney. However, she said she was born in the year nineteen forty-two. I thought she made a mistake, but now..." Her voice trailed off as she realized the implications. n."

Jon nodded his head. "That's what I mean. Think about it. One way or another, Emily would have selected Brittney with or without your help, Ted."

"Thanks, but it doesn't make me feel any better. The point is, if you're willing to call your brother, just do it. But if you don't mind, I'd like to know a little about him first. Is he a professional, does he charge an arm and a leg, what can we expect?" Ted never was one to mince words.

"My brother's name is Dan Markos and he doesn't run a little voodoo shop in downtown Chicago, if that's what you're getting at," Jon puffed up at Ted's remark.

"Dan is an honorable person. He's an ex-priest. Right after he graduated from high school, he went to the seminary and worked in the church for twelve years. He's always been twice as gifted as me with the supernatural, but he never flaunts it."

"Was a priest? What happened? Did he leave the church or did they ask him to go?" Ted questioned.

"Ted please," Angela protested.

"I'm serious. I have to ask. It's better than sitting here wondering. I want to know who he is before I go spilling my guts to this guy. We have a huge problem and I can't let someone come into my home and expose my family to some fly by night freak! There I said it." Ted looked directly at Jon.

Jon was offended, but realized the position Ted was taking. "I understand that you already feel bad about taking your daughter to the carnival and now you're just being cautious and tripping on guilt. However, my brother Dan is a good and exceptional person. I won't allow anyone to cast aspersions on him because of his gifts."

Ted had no reply but Leonard spoke up. "We do need to know if he does this sort of thing for a living. Is he working now that he left the church?"

"Dan is very generous and empathetic. He didn't agree with all of the rules of the church, but he still loves his religion and practices it faithfully. Dan felt that he could work better outside of the church, away from the judgment and prejudice. He couldn't hide his gift, so he continues to help those who need his talents. My brother gives lectures, does freelance writing and counseling. He loves working with troubled kids and with exceptional situations, such as yours," Jon defended his brother.

After a pause to access the reactions from his listeners, Jon continued, "He uses his education and training for counseling people who need extensive therapy, Dan is very serious about the people he helps. He also has strong paranormal senses, a lot stronger than mine. " Jon said proudly.

The look in Jon's eyes let Leonard know that Dan was someone to be trusted. "He sounds like a good man to me. Go ahead and call your brother. Maybe he can come over right now while we're all together," Leonard prompted.

Jon studied the faces of the troubled family sitting around him. "I had to be sure that everyone would accept Dan before I asked him to come all the way out here."

"Where does he live?" Ted asked.

Jon smiled. "My brother stayed in Italy after his studies in Rome. He fell in love with the country.

Angela searched Ted's face. The silence was unnerving.

When no one spoke up, Jon said, "It's up to you. I'll call my brother right now, but you all have to agree. Otherwise, the best I can do for you is wish you the very best of luck and remember you in my prayers."

"I'm sorry for our hesitation," Angela said. "We're under a lot of stress and having to call someone all the way from Italy has just added another twist to the tension on our last nerve."

Jon nodded and pushed his chair away from the table.

"It just sounds so far away. Of course we need all the help we can get right now. But what if your brother says no? We need help right now!" Angela began to cry.

Jon chose his next words carefully. "If I call my brother, he'll be here within the next day or two. He won't ask questions until he gets here and certainly won't judge anyone. Just give me the word and I'll have him here within the next twenty four hours" Jon glanced at the stairs.

Elizabeth just shrugged. Leonard addressed Ted. "It's your call. This is your house and your family. If it were up to me, I'd have him call this Dan Markos right now."

Ted inhaled slowly and stood alongside Jon. He looked at Angela. "Go ahead and call him. Tell him we would very much appreciate his help." He never took his eyes off Angela as he spoke.

"It's settled then." Jon held out his hand to Ted. "I'll call Dan when I get home. As soon as he gets in, we'll be back. I'll give you my phone number and if you need me before we get back, please feel free to call. I don't know how much help I'll be, but I'll do whatever I can."

Ted walked Jon to the front door. "How much money is this going to cost us?" he spoke under his breath

"What do you mean?" A deep crease formed on Jon's forehead.

"Well, it isn't cheap to fly all the way here from Italy. Then there are his expenses and services," Ted looked very concerned.

"I just need to have some sort of idea on what you think this might cost."

"Don't worry about it. Dan uses any excuse he can find to come home to visit. As far as his services, he won't charge you anything. I guarantee you, once he finds out what the problem is he'll be more than happy to confront these demons with you. He can stay with me." Jon flashed Ted a big toothy grin.

Ted was still shaken. "I can't believe that your brother would want to do this for nothing."

"He isn't doing it for nothing. Dan works for the satisfaction and knowledge that he is either freeing another lost spirit or condemning another demon to hell."

Ted and Jon shook hands at the door. Jon noted how Ted trembled when he took hold of his hand. Angela, Elizabeth and Leonard came up behind the two men. Jon turned to say goodbye. "I'll see you soon. In the meantime, it might be wise for all of you to stay close together. By the way, do you know any prayers?" Jon asked

Ted nodded. "Of course we do, why?"

Jon held the door with one hand. "I suggest you start saying them."

Chapter Thirty-Eight

Dan Markos was overjoyed to hear Jon's voice. "Hey, little brother! To what do I owe this pleasure?"

"Hi Danny. How's everything in Italy?"

Looking for the real reason for the call, Dan asked, "How's everything at home? Are Mom and Dad okay?"

"Yes, everything's good here. I'm still working in the ER and Mom is over compensating for you leaving home and me moving out of the house by treating Dad as if he were four years old," Jon chuckled at his own analogy. Dan joined him with a loud hardy laugh.

Dan sighed with relief. "I get a little nervous when you call."

"Why is that?" Jon asked.

"Mom and Dad aren't getting any younger and I get so involved with my work that sometimes I tend to neglect them." There was definitely a note of remorse in Dan's voice. "That, plus the fact that you're generally pretty cheap. So, what's up Jonny?"

Jon jumped on the opportunity to ask his brother to come home. "Maybe you ought to come home more often. You only have one mom and dad. I know, because Mom tells me that all the time."

They both laughed. "Okay, seriously, what's up?" I know you didn't call me to chit chat about our parents."

Jon inhaled deeply. "I need your help."

"Anything. Are you in some sort of trouble?" Dan probed. "You can always stay with me here in Italy if you need to get out of the country for a while."

"Thanks but no, it's nothing like that. I don't need to get away. I need for you to come home," Jon stated emphatically.

"Sounds urgent," Dan fished for some facts. He was almost certain it had something to do with the paranormal, but he didn't want to be the one to bring it up.

"I guess I should start from the beginning," Jon began and in a very short time he had told the entire story about his first encounter with Angela, why she was in the emergency room, and seeing Emily at the hospital. "There's a lot more. There isn't just one spirit and they aren't simply lost like most of the ones I see."

Dan noted a slight tremble in Jon's voice. He knew that he had no other choice but to go. "It sounds serious."

"It is Dan and I don't know what to do for these people. I can't just walk away from them. There's a little girl involved. I don't know what Emily's spirit wants with the Michaels child. It scares me to think that she might be looking for a body to house her soul. Where would that put Brittney's soul? See what I mean?"

There was a long, strained moment of silence. Dan's delayed response caused Jon to panic. "I told the Michaels that you were the only one that could help them. I told them you'd come. I even promised them you'd be here within the next twenty four hours," Jon blurted it all out.

"Oh, you did?" Dan wore a smirk that his brother couldn't see.

Jon wasn't able to tell if Dan was mad about the commitment or not. He waited as long as he could before pleading. "I didn't know what else to do. Plus, you haven't seen Mom in six months and she's just about to put those old yellow rubber duckies and bubble bath in the tub the next time I go over there," Jon laughed nervously, hoping that his last remark would smooth the way for him.

Dan had to laugh at his brother's lame attempt to justify his actions. "Rubber duckies?"

"Yeah, you know how Mom would put them in the bath tub every time we took a bath until we finally started taking showers and locking her out?" They both relaxed and had a good laugh over it.

After a moment of silence, Jon said, "It really is bad, Danny. I know that Brittney Michaels is in grave danger. I can see the different spirits, but I don't know what to do. You have to help that family."

More silence.

"So, what do you say? Is there any way you can make it here tomorrow?" Jon reasoned.

"Of course, you know I'll do my best to get a flight by tomorrow. By the way, you're absolutely certain that these people didn't stage any of this? I know you said that you actually saw the little girl at the hospital. I suppose I'm being somewhat skeptical as a defense mechanism right now. I'll come, one way or the other," Dan said softly.

"This is the real thing. There's no doubt in my mind. Once you get here, you'll understand. I just hope there's something we can do to help these people," Jon breathed heavily into the phone.

"I'll call for my ticket as soon as we hang up, then I'll call you later to let you know when to pick me up at the airport. We can stop and see Mom and Dad before we go to the Michael's house. That way, I can change clothes and get something to eat," Dan was already making plans which pleased Jon. "And maybe, I can give you a better idea of what we're actually up against."

"I don't know how to thank you," Jon said. "I mean it. I really hated getting involved, but there didn't seem to be a way out."

"Don't worry, no paybacks necessary," Dan suddenly felt like he wasn't alone. He kept it to himself, because he wasn't certain what was happening. "Let me go, so I can make arrangements. I'll call you later."

"Thanks again," Jon sighed with relief.

"It'll be fine. Just remember what I told you when we were kids," Dan said.

"I know. I'll stay strong. Just hurry home. I'll feel a whole hell of a lot better once you're here." Jon hung up the phone, but continued to stare at it. "I really mean it this time. Hurry home, Dan."

Chapter Thirty-Nine

The air in Dan's small apartment suddenly felt thick and ponderous, making it difficult for him to breathe. He felt like he was being watched by something unearthly. He was thinking about the conversation with his brother when an overwhelming sensation of dread hung over him like a dark, heavy shroud.

"I know you're here. I feel your suffocating presence," Dan said calmly as utter gloom attempted to consume his body. The silence felt like secrets being whispered through an eerie, black fog.

Dan was familiar with these feelings, having experienced them when he decided that it was impossible to totally comply with the laws of the church. He truly wanted to be a priest. He had worked hard, but someone, another priest, had complained. His own parish priest was up for Bishop and he was being judged by his peers for the paranormal gift that he never sought after or asked for. Wanting to be a priest just wasn't enough.

"The Catholic Church states that a priest can't marry or have children. How can this be when the Bible tells us to be fruitful and the family is one of God's biggest pleasures?" Dan said aloud as he had done many times before.

"Tormenting me with false accusations and doubts won't work. I've found peace with myself," Dan spoke aloud. "The Catholic Church says that a man can't have it both ways. He can't love a woman and crave her in every way possible and still declare himself a man of God. Love and lust are separate emotions, never to be intertwined." The words were being forced into Dan's thoughts.

"I beg to differ! These are the feelings of a normal, healthy man. They wanted more than just my every waking hour. They wanted my very soul and in turn, made me doubt my God and myself. Yes, I know you well and I have defeated you before," he professed boldly.

Dan knew that he had to get control quickly before the evil one weakened him with feelings of doubt that would only serve to consume his emotional state of mind and render him submissive to the demons. He wouldn't only be unable to help himself, but all the people who were counting on him.

"You know me," he spoke in a sinister tone to the uninvited spirit. "You know me as well as I know you. You also know that I have been empowered by one you can never defeat," Dan felt strong against the foul visitor.

"Yes, we know each other well. We have a personal relationship, having fought many battles, you and I," he continued with confidence. "No matter what form you take, you are still the same loathsome, filthy gatherer of innocent souls," he stormed fearlessly.

Dan always had a way with words, embellishing them, and loving the strength found in being able to structure ideas and thoughts. He found an inner strength in lecturing with the energy built from words and he was using that very energy now to speak to the unknown entity that was attacking his mortal spirit.

"Wicked one," Dan called out. "There's nothing you can do to keep me from making this journey."

Dan stood next to his desk and thumbed through his Rolodex, looking for the number for the airline he frequently used, when very methodically, the neatly organized cards began to fan out and shuffle. He was familiar with the immature, but annoying antics of an unfavorable spirit.

"It's human nature to become aggravated by your presence. You weren't invited here and you are not welcome!" he said loudly.

Dan gathered the papers that had been strewn around his desk like a hand of badly dealt cards. He found the one with the phone number he was searching for. When Dan picked up the telephone to call the airline, a searing pain shot through his arm as if he had received an electrical shock. It forced the receiver out of his hand and it dropped to the floor. At that very moment, he saw the dark, hooded cloaked figure hovering above him.

Dan forced himself to stand and face the apparition. He realized that this was not simply a visit to scare him into staying away from the Michaels family. This was a challenge of his faith.

"I sense your evil. You've received no invitation and yet you stay," he stood firm. "You stand the chance to lose everything if I choose to call upon the one to whom I owe my very soul," Dan turned in the direction of the shadowed figure. "You must admit, he's your creator too. He banished you from Heaven. How humiliated you must have been. You are doomed to eternal damnation. I will not succumb to your idol threats."

Dan prayed, with his eyes open. "Our Father, who art in heaven. Be with me now as I stand before this vile form. Grant me the strength and power to fight he who dwells among us."

The retaliation was violent. The room turned so cold that ice formed on the inside of the windows. Dan's teeth started to chatter uncontrollably. The air surrounding him burned his lungs. Moving was torturous as his clothing became a weapon. It brushed fiercely against him, with every movement slicing into his skin like the thin cold blade of a sharpened knife. Dan had no choice but to remain motionless to avoid the stinging, icy fingers all over his body.

Dan called out in anguish. "Merciful Father, I beseech you to surround me with your warring angels. Keep me in your arc of safety, oh Lord!" he cried as he fought with the only weapon he trusted, his prayers. Slowly, the cold began to subside.

"There's no mistaking the forces of evil. You are still no match for our heavenly angels when in battle," Dan thought about Jon. I have to get home as soon as possible.

"You only made my decision to go home even stronger. I stand with you, face to face on holy ground. You're helpless here and you must be on an incredibly important journey to come this far from your place of torment. Nothing will stop me from making this trip."

Like loving arms enfolding him securely, the warmth began to creep back into Dan's body. In all the years of dealing with the supernatural, he had never encountered anything this powerful.

As things began to return to normal, Dan slumped down into his chair. He reached for the telephone and dialed the airline's number, anticipating another painful jolt. Nothing happened and he smiled. "Oh, ye of little faith."

The well-trained voice of an airline employee answered and he scheduled an early morning flight back to the states.

Dan pulled out his travel bags and quickly threw together enough clothes for a few weeks. "If I need anything else, I'll just get it there." He knew that his mother hated change. "I'll bet my room will be exactly the way I left it."

Dan called his neighbor, Felicia. She was an attractive young Italian woman who lived alone in the apartment directly across the hall from his. "Can you come over for a minute? I need to go back to the states for a few weeks. It's a family matter and I'd like for you to bring in the mail and watch the apartment, if you don't mind."

"Of course, I'll be right over." Although fluent in the Italian language, Dan always spoke English to Felicia. He enjoyed listening to her thick Italian accent.

There was no explanation for how his once torn and bloody clothes were now mended. The painful cuts were miraculously healed. Dan was relieved that he didn't have to explain any of it to Felicia.

Not knowing what to expect next from the unearthly spirits, Dan stepped into the hallway and pulled the door to his apartment closed behind him. He timed it well as he met his neighbor in the hall.

"Hi Felicia; I really appreciate you doing this for me." Dan handed her a short list of things to do and the phone number where he could be reached in case of an emergency.

Dan and Felicia had grown to be very dear friends. He moved into the apartment right after he left the rectory. It was a dark time in Dan's life and he had been very impersonal when they first met. Felicia sensed the hurt and sorrow Dan carried and kept their relationship simple. She was taking care of her ill mother and from time to time, they would share intimate conversations outside in the garden. After her mother passed on, Dan made it a point to visit Felicia a couple times a week to support his friend. He told her about his decision to leave the priesthood and found her to be an unbiased listener.

"Do you have time to come in for a glass of wine?" she asked.

Dan glanced back at his apartment. "No; not this time. I have an early flight and I have to get to bed." He didn't want to tell her what happened.

"I would love to see America someday. Maybe I can go with you on one of your trips to the states," she coyly remarked.

Dan smiled and raised his eyebrows. "You have my key. I can't thank you enough. I'll call you when I get back." He turned and faced his apartment wondering what awaited him. Reaching for the doorknob, he noted a shadow pass by under the door.

This is going to be a long night. He pushed the door open. Nothing appeared to be out of place. In fact, his suitcases were back in the closet where he kept them and all of his clothes were unpacked and put away.

Dan blew out a burst of air in disgust. "That's nice." He repacked his bags, got ready for bed and turned out the light. Dan knelt next to his bed before climbing in. "Dear Lord, bless me as I offer up my prayers. Hear me, oh God and forgive me for centering my requests on myself and neglecting the praise and thanksgiving.

But I need you to watch over me and comfort me throughout this night. Give me peace and allow me to rest. Amen."

Chapter Forty

Dan arose just before dawn, swung his legs around to a sitting position and turned off the alarm that never had a chance to go off. He ran his fingers through his thick head of hair. "I'm awake now; I might as well get ready to go."

The apartment building was old and so was the plumbing. It was always cold in the morning. Dan thought about the horrible arctic blast he experienced after Jon's phone call. It caused him to shiver. He would have to let the water run a few minutes before attempting to touch it.

Dan shed his pajamas on the bathroom floor and pushed aside the shower curtain. Huddled closely together in the corner of the bathtub were four little girls with darkened eyes. "Merciful Father," Dan gasped. He quickly reached for a towel to cover his nakedness. Out of the center of the group, a stronger, more defiant spirit stepped forward. Her lifeless eyes told Dan who she was.

"You must be the infamous Emily," he breathed her name. "What have you got there?"

Emily held a doll in her hand. The head was torn off and hanging by a single piece of material.

"Someone is going to be awfully sad over that doll. It doesn't affect me one way or the other, but it might help if you told me what you want," Dan attempted to step closer to the terrifyingly bold little girl. She didn't move, but held Dan in a hypnotic stare, wearing a chilling, malevolent sneer. The other children faded away.

A horrific noise emerged from the delicate little form standing before him. It was deep and guttural as if arising from an echo chamber. It was startling and obviously an attempt to terrify Dan.

"Stay away from Brittney. You can't stop me. I've come too far to have a pathetic, has been like you try to practice his failed religious beliefs on me."

Dan couldn't let Emily's cruel words sway him. She was strong; there was no doubt about it. He tried to reason with Emily, using kindness and training. "Maybe I can help you, if you let me try. I'm definitely stronger than Brittney," he didn't want to show how intimidated he was by the rogue poltergeist. He tried focusing on something else, in case she could read his thoughts.

"Help me, Dan Markos. There's a secret room where we're all hidden. There are doors that shouldn't be doors and walls that aren't safe for little girls," Emily's voice became a whisper. She disappeared into a misty remnant of what was once her image.

Dan reached out and tried to grab her. His hands went right through the illusion.

"For all that's holy, what happened to you?" Dan spoke to the empty space while searching for Emily and the other children. "This is all the more reason for me to go home."

"Forget the shower." Dan ran a comb through his hair, washed his face and threw on the clothes he had laid out the night before. He called for a cab and went downstairs to wait for it.

A dark calico cat brushed past him when he stepped outside. Her back arched and she screeched loudly at Dan before running away, sending goose bumps down his spine.

"There is the light and the darkness," Dan said as he stood alone. "Good shines through the light and evil lurks in the shadows of darkness. Why are you lurking with the evil one, Emily? I have to make sure that the darkness doesn't win. I will fight to bring you through the light."

Chapter Forty-One

The airport terminal was crowded. Everyone was scrambling to get to their destination.

"I hate travel days," Dan mumbled. He waited in line to check his luggage, and worked his way to his assigned gate. The security alarm screeched as he passed through the metal detector. A young officer stepped forward and took him aside.

"If you'll let me reach into my pocket, I think I know what the problem is," Dan said with a warm smile and a calm voice.

Another uniformed guard noted the situation and walked over to them. "What's the matter?" he asked the younger officer.

"This man activated the alarm and I asked him to step aside," the younger officer responded proudly. Dan recognized a power struggle between the two men.

"Excuse me, but I can settle this right away if you'll simply reach into my jacket pocket," Dan said. "I have a large crucifix that I carry because it gives me a sense of security. You see, I used to be a priest."

The older officer held out his hand palm up. Dan took the crucifix out of his pocket and handed it to him. The officer examined the icon curiously as he ran his wand over it. The unrelenting chirping resumed.

"We'll hold on to this while you go back through x-ray," the younger of the officers instructed.

Dan was compliant with his instructions. There was no further noise and he held out his hand to the officer. "May I have that back please?"

The man smiled at Dan. His eyes glowed a putrid shade of yellow. A foul odor emerged from the officer, causing bile to rise in Dan's throat. No one else appeared to be affected by what was going on. The younger of the two men had already walked away.

Dan realized what was happening and continued to hold out his hand. The counterfeit law enforcer submitted the crucifix for Dan's taking. It was twisted and bent out of shape.

"This crucifix was blessed by the bishop. Nothing you can do will deplete its power," Dan could feel his heart pumping in his chest, however he held his ground and stood toe to toe with the large contemptible form.

He watched as the cross returned to its original shape. When he looked up, the officer was gone. Dan caught a glimpse of the hooded stranger scrambling away and fading into the crowd. *What in the world have you got us into, Jon?*

Dan took a deep breath, blew it out slowly, picked up his carry-on bag and continued on to the boarding gate. He was able to board the plane without further incident.

Dan moved clumsily through the aisle with his luggage, waiting for something else to happen. When nothing more occurred, he found his seat, settled in and fastened his seatbelt. Before putting his bag under the seat in front of him, Dan opened it to make sure he had remembered to pack a book to read during the long flight back to the states.

He searched deep into the bottom of his luggage. This is ridiculous. I remember distinctly packing a couple of books. I put them right on top.

All of a sudden his fingers closed around a soft, unfamiliar form. He pulled it out and found himself staring at the rag doll Emily was carrying when he met her in his apartment.

"Where in the world did this come from?" he said. The doll was intact, including the head that at one time was ripped off and hanging by a thread. Dan turned it over and read the inscription on her back. 'To Brittney from Nana.'

Dan tucked the doll back in his bag and noted his books sitting right on top where he originally put them. He quickly closed the carry-on as the captain began his well-rehearsed speech. Dan tugged on his seatbelt one more time and slid his bag under the seat in front of him. He leaned his head back and settled in for the long flight.

The takeoff was smooth. After about half an hour, he was able to doze off. His mind was cluttered with visions of the worrisome group of little girls. It troubled Dan how they huddled tightly together. Their large darkened eyes that held no life frightened him, yet their pathetic, lonely image tugged at Dan's heart.

Dan opened his eyes. His neck was stiff and he was uncomfortable in the cramped airline seat. His legs were long and they felt numb. He turned to see if the well-dressed older gentleman sitting next to him was awake. It startled Dan to find the cloaked figure bent over in the seat.

It was impossible to make out the face under the hood, because the head was bowed and the hood hung loosely in front of his face. When the cloaked figure began to move, Dan quickly unfastened his seat belt and began to look around for another place to sit. He decided to take a walk and ask the flight attendant to find him another seat. It wasn't a full flight. She should be able to help him.

When he turned to rise, Dan was forced back into his seat by the malicious expression Emily wore as she floated toward him.

"Doesn't anyone see her?" he said loudly.

The flight attendant looked up. She didn't appear to notice Emily.

The rustling sound that came from this childlike manifestation, whispered each word vas her lips brushed past Dan's ear. "There are doors that shouldn't be doors and walls that aren't safe for little girls." Her closeness and the sound of her voice sent chills down his back like fast, icy fingertips.

Dan snatched his travel bag and pushed himself up and past the apparition. The flight attendant noticed his pallid color and anxious expression. "Is there something I can help you with?" She asked him in a soothing tone.

"I don't feel well. I noticed there isn't anyone up here in the bulkhead. Would it be all right if I sat here for a while? I think I need a little more room," Dan smiled and the airline attendant was quick to accommodate him.

"Certainly, that will be fine. This isn't a full flight. You can sit just about anywhere you want. If you need anything else, just let me know." She bent down close to him when she spoke and Dan could smell the fragrance of soft musk. "Are you sure you're going to be okay?"

"Thanks, I feel better already. I could use a drink." His mouth felt parched as he spoke.

"What would you like?" The young woman smiled sweetly, yet remained totally professional.

"I'd like something warm if possible." Dan was still trying to shake the horrid chill and took note that whenever the apparition appeared, there was a notable drop in temperature.

"We have coffee, tea or would you like something a little stronger?" she asked with a slight lift to her voice.

"You know a glass of wine sounds good right about now. It might just help me relax," Dan replied.

The flight attendant nodded and went to her cart. She returned with a small bottle and a glass. "That'll be five dollars." She put down his tray and set it up for him.

Dan nervously began to fumble for his wallet. The young woman reached out and touched his hand. "Don't worry about it. This one's on me." Her fingers lingered on his hand a moment before she slid them gently away.

Dan smiled and thought about Felicia. He reached into his bag and pulled out a freshly baked biscotti that she surprised him with before he left his apartment. He took a bite and washed it down with the wine. It was a good combination. Dan sat back and began to feel more relaxed.

The book was a good distraction. It helped pass the time. Dan read until his eyes began to blur. He leaned back in the seat.

His eyelids began to feel heavy. *There isn't anything that can keep me from sleeping now, not even the nightmares dancing in my thoughts. It will all have to wait until I get back to the states.*

Just before sleep captured him, Dan glanced at the person sitting directly across from him. He smiled at the old black woman and she returned the smile with a nod. What a gentle spirit, Dan thought.

The wine served as a mild sedative and helped him rest. Soon he would be home. Soon he would have to face whatever war these spirits were waging. But for now, Dan slept.

Chapter Forty-Two

There is a seven hour time difference between Ciampino Airport in Rome and O'Hare Airport in Chicago. When Dan left Italy, it was four o'clock in the morning, and eleven A.M. for Jon. After a ten hour flight it was close to nine o'clock at night as he approached O'Hare.

As they began their descent into the airport, Dan marveled at the city lights, which were positively enchanting. It reminded him of his mother's miniature Christmas village. Dan's thoughts were of home and family as he pressed his head against the cool windowpane. While reminiscing, he reflected, we're always so anxious to get out into the world and leave the security of our parent's home, but somehow we're drawn back to that comfort zone by memories.

"I wonder if this is what death feels like," he whispered.

"There's a thin line between life and death. Both are alluring." Emily's voice penetrated his ear like the buzzing utterance of an annoying mosquito.

Dan shook his head and sat upright. His lower back ached from hours of sitting. His thoughts were set on seeing his family and he tried to ignore the bothersome, spirit world. There would be plenty of time for them.

"We'll be landing in Chicago in approximately twenty minutes," the pilot announced. The flight attendant walked down the aisle one last time checking seatbelts. She bent down next to Dan. "Are you meeting anyone in Chicago?"

Dan looked up into her soft hazel eyes. "Oh yes, my brother is picking me up. We're going straight to our parent's house. My Mom is cooking dinner."

There was a look of disappointment in her eyes. "I'm sorry to hear that."

"What? That my brother is picking me up or that my mom is planning to feed her oldest son?" Dan flirted back.

"Both, I suppose," she giggled in a teasing, yet provocative manner.

Dan tipped his head to one side and shrugged his shoulders as he raised his eyebrows simultaneously. "This is a tightly booked trip for me."

The young woman forced a smile. "Maybe I'll catch you on your way back."

"Who knows?" Dan said lightheartedly.

He leaned back, checked his seatbelt and prepared himself for the landing. It was the part about flying that Dan disliked most.

Out of the corner of his right eye, Dan caught a glimpse of a ghostly blur on the seat next to him. He tried closing his eyes, but was still able to visualize Emily with that deep dimple that oddly mirrored his own facial characteristic.

"How peculiar," Emily tried breaking into Dan's thoughts. He put on his headphones and turned up the music. However, she was quite the fighter. Emily got so close to him that Dan felt the bitter freeze of death. He sat perfectly still and refused to give in to her intimidation.

When he felt the first bump of the wheels on the runway, Dan turned his head, expecting to see Emily's face. Instead he heard her fading words. "You will learn my secret, Dan Markos."

Dan reached for the crucifix that always comforted him and clutched it tightly, until the plane came to a complete stop.

When the fasten seatbelt sign went off above his head, Dan took a deep breath and sighed. He immediately released his security belt and stood up.

The flight attendants waited for the captain to give them the okay to open the door. Everyone was impatient and Dan was no exception. The plane was getting warm and stuffy. Just as the passengers began to get irritable, the doors were opened. Everyone exited the plane slowly, in single file. The procedure seemed to take a lot longer than it actually did.

Once off the plane, Dan found his way to the baggage claim area and made it through customs unremarkably. He had nothing to declare, so the process went smoothly, unlike earlier that day when he boarded in Italy. Once through customs, Dan spotted Jon through the glass exit doors. He picked up his pace and waved his arms in the air. "Jon," he called out loudly.

Jon's face lit up when he saw his brother. They gave each other a big welcome hug. "I thought you'd never get here," Jon said. "How was your flight?"

"Long," Dan remarked. He looked tired. "I didn't get much sleep last night. I had a couple of unexpected visitors."

Jon's voice dropped to a whisper. "Do I dare ask? I'm assuming that you met Emily."

"I understand why misery enjoys company," Dan smirked. "We'll talk about it on the way home. Where's your car? I'm starving. What's Mom cooking?"

"She's making her huge holiday dinner. We're going to eat good, thank you very much." Both laughed.

"Oh, I better tell you, Mom's been pulling out old photos." They simultaneously let out a long wail.

"Seriously, what are the plans?" Dan asked.

"I'm not really sure. We'll know more after we visit with the Michaels," Jon answered.

Dan really wanted to meet the Michaels family and find out what was going on. "Did these people have any problem with you calling me?"

"Not once I told them that I couldn't do anything. They need help and I don't know what to do for them. I can tell you that they aren't lying. There are definitely ghosts tormenting those people. But that's not the extent of it. I can't do anything about it," Jon confessed. "The little girl, Brittney, is in some sort of danger. I believe that. There are others as well. I just don't know what it all means." Jon took on a solemn note.

"You know, I'm not an exorcist," Dan said. "I'm not even a priest anymore. What did you tell them I could do?"

"Let's just take it one step at a time. If we can discover what they're here for, we just might be able to come up with a plan to help these people. That's why you're here," Jon conveyed.

Jon took Dan's suitcase and they headed for the car. "Is that all you brought?" Jon asked.

"That's it. I travel light. If I need anything else, I'm sure I can find it in my old bedroom. It's exactly the way I left it. Am I right?" he laughed.

"Right down to the Tom Sawyer wall paper." Jon rolled his eyes.

"I have to admit, I love my old mattress. I always got a good night's sleep in that bed," Dan admitted. "It's good to be home."

"I'll be staying there too," Jon confessed. "Mom changed all the linens in my room."

Dan grinned. "How do you know?"

"Dad called and warned me," Jon laughed. "He said that Mom is anxious to have her boys home again."

"What does that mean?" Dan raised one eyebrow and tilted his head to the side.

"I don't know, but I wouldn't be surprised if she asked us to move back home. You know the old line. We could save a lot of money if we'd move back. She would never charge her own sons rent and she'd do all the cooking and laundry," Jon repeated his mother's words.

"I wish things were that simple," Dan said with a faraway look in his eyes. Jon let it go at that.

After they found the car and were on their way home, Dan changed the subject. "How are things at work?" he asked. The truth was his mind had been racing ever since his encounter with Emily and her entourage. He needed a break from it before diving in full force.

"The same. Well, it was the same until Angela Michaels came into the ER," Jon said. There was just no way to skirt around it. "I don't know what's going on. It's not the same. I've seen spirits of dead people all my life. I'm used to it. They walk around the hospital all the time. It's never bothered me before."

"And now?" Dan asked.

"I don't know. Emily is different. She's here for a reason and there's nothing good about her," Jon went on. "She's not here alone."

Dan finished his brother's thought. "The hooded figure?"

Jon nodded. "You know about him too?"

"I met him a couple of times since you called. I've seen the group of little girls and of course, Emily," Dan explained.

"We really have our hands full with this," Jon said. "I'm sorry I dragged you into it, but I didn't know what else to do."

"Don't worry about it. I'd have done the same thing," Dan admitted.

Jon turned on to the highway. "We'll be going through it all when we see the Michaels. Then, we can start from the beginning and they'll tell you everything. For now, let's get home and get something to eat."

"One more thing," Dan said abruptly. He reached for his carry on and pulled out the rag doll.

Jon was surprised to see it. "Where did you get that?"

"Actually, I let my guard down for a short time and Emily took the opportunity to harass me," Dan spoke with a renewed sense of strength.

"What happened?" Jon asked

"Emily showed it to me in my apartment. She was trying to terrorize me with her antics. I guess she thought if she could scare me, I wouldn't come home,"

"There was an ominous hooded phantom around too. He was at my apartment, he showed up at the airport and again in the plane." He took a deep breath.

"I'm sorry, Dan," Jon expressed his empathy. "But how did you get your hands on that doll?"

"I'm not really sure," Dan admitted. "I found her in my carry-on bag. Is she important?"

Jon turned his head and looked at Dan. "It belongs to Brittney. Her grandmother made it for her. I saw it at the Michael's house the day I called you."

"That would explain the marking on her back." Dan turned the doll over and read the inscription. "It says, 'To Brittney from Nana.'"

"You're involved now, whether you like it or not," Jon stated in a flat tone. "For some reason, we're both supposed to be included in Emily's plan."

"I think you're right. There's more to this than simply a poltergeist aggravating a family," Dan recalled Emily's voice on the plane. The thought of her deathly, mocking voice so close to his ear caused an uncomfortable, icy chill to dance up his spine. He fingered the spot on his face where the familiar indention creased his cheek. "Odd isn't it?"

Chapter Forty-Three

"Isn't it you who always says that a watched pot doesn't boil?" Robert Markos spoke to his wife from behind the protection of his newspaper.

Grace and Robert waited impatiently for their sons. Occasionally, she would run to the living room, pull back the lined drapes that covered the large bay window and look first to the driveway and then up and down the street. Robert shook his head.

"Yes, Mr. Wisenheimer. Those boys could be in a ditch some place waiting for you to come and help them." Grace wiped her forehead and upper lip with the dishtowel she kept draped over her shoulder.

Robert put down the paper. "Get away from the window Grace," he ordered. "The boys aren't in a ditch. Jon has his phone. He'll call if there's a problem."

The words sailed right over her head. "Maybe the plane is late. Jon could still be waiting for Danny at the airport. I better turn down the oven so the turkey doesn't dry out."

"Good idea. We can't serve a dried out turkey to our boys. What would they think of us?" Robert laughed at the cleverness of his remark as he slowly rose from the recliner and nonchalantly stepped over to the window. "They should be here any time now."

Grace went after the turkey with her basting brush, lowered the temperature of the oven and looked over the table. It felt good to see four place settings again. "Those were the good days," she sighed. "Where are those boys?"

"Mmm...something smells good," Dan's voice echoed from the front door. Grace's heart almost leaped out of her chest.

"Hi Mom, I'm starving!" Jon held up his nose and followed the smell.

Dan stood with his arms stretched out. Tears were streaming down Grace's cheeks.

"Come here and let me give my best girl a big hug," Dan said.

Grace surrendered to her oldest son's open arms. She dabbed at her eyes with the dishtowel. "I hate it when I cry," she blubbered.

Dan laughed and gave her an affectionate squeeze. "It really is good to see you, Mom."

Robert was just as excited to see Dan as Grace. He approached his son with a grin that stretched from ear to ear. "Hey, boy; thank goodness you showed up. Your mother was about to call the National Guard."

"I was not," Grace said as her cheeks turned a bright shade of pink.

Everyone laughed. Dan shook his dad's hand and gave him a hug.

"I wasn't worried," Robert declared. "You still have that weapon in your pocket?" He beamed.

"That weapon, as you call it, is a big comfort to me. I still depend strongly on my faith. Just because I had issues with some of the church politics doesn't mean I don't rely on God. I didn't quit believing," Dan said.

"That decision is totally up to you," Grace interrupted. "Don't start, Robert!"

"Let's eat," Jon called from the kitchen.

The inviting aroma stirred pangs of hunger and Dan seconded the motion.

The corners of Grace's lips curved up as she listened to the sounds of her adult children talking. This is my day. Nothing can spoil it.

"Someone help me get that turkey on the cutting board," Grace sang out.

Jon took hold of the turkey while Robert sharpened the knife. Then, everyone was silent as Dan said the prayer.

Grace couldn't stop smiling at her family as they helped themselves to second and third servings.

Jon stuck his fork into a piece of white meat. Dan snatched it in midair before his younger brother could get it to his plate.

Everyone laughed. "I could always catch you with your guard down," Dan boasted.

"Don't overeat. You have to leave room for desert. I made lemon meringue pie," Grace said.

The mention of desert didn't seem to slow down any of the gorging that was going on in front of her. Grace continued to enjoy the time she was having with her family all together.

"Your rooms are ready. After dinner, I'll clean the kitchen and you boys can get ready for bed." Her words stopped everyone in midair.

"We have something to do after dinner," Jon glanced at Dan.

"What's so important that it can't wait until tomorrow?" Grace complained.

"I have to see one of Jon's patients who is dealing with some spiritual problems," Dan said.

"Her family needed help and I volunteered Dan," Jon announced, attempting to simplify things. "That's why he's here. He wanted to see you and Dad before we stopped by the Michaels' house. We'll be back. We shouldn't be gone too long."

Grace couldn't hide her disappointment. She went to the kitchen sink and began rinsing the empty dishes.

Dan followed his mother. "Don't feel bad, Mom. I know you've been waiting for me to tell you why I quit being a priest. You never came right out and asked. I appreciate that."

She spun around, wiped her hands on the dishtowel and laid it on the back of one of the chairs to dry. "I didn't want to pry. I knew you'd tell me when you were ready," she said. "Did Father Luke have anything to do with it? I only ask because he has been quiet and stand-offish with us ever since you left your position. If I didn't know better, I would guess that he was acting guilty of something."

Dan's response was well rehearsed. He ignored the part about Father Luke Phillips. "I began craving the family environment that you and Dad made such a big part of my life. At first I thought that I could live without all that," Dan paused.

"It's a big decision," Grace smiled.

"I want to get married some day and have my own kids. Wouldn't you like to have a few grandkids?" Dan turned on the charm.

Grace's eyes lit up. "What are you trying to say, Danny? Is there a girl in your life? Did you meet her in Italy? You wouldn't get married and raise your children in a foreign country, would you? How could I be a part of their life?"

Dan winced when he realized what his mother was fishing for.

"What did you do now, Dan?" Robert heard only part of the conversation. "Is it something we should know about?"

"Oh my gosh!" Dan exclaimed. "I don't even have a steady girl yet. I've just been thinking about it," he turned to Jon. "What time did you tell those people we'd be there?"

"I'll call the Michaels family and tell them we're on our way," Jon said wearing a huge smile.

Dan took advantage of the opportunity to escape the interrogation and followed Jon into the living room.

Jon called the Michaels. "We'll be over within the hour. Is everything okay there? Good, see you then."

Jon hung up the phone and snatched his car keys off the table next to the hall tree. "It takes about fifteen minutes to get to their house. I'll fill you in on some of the details on the way over," he addressed Dan.

"Should I wait up?" Grace asked.

Robert interceded. "Better put on a pot of coffee. I want a piece of that pie, Grace."

"We'll see you two later," Jon announced. "I don't know when we'll be home."

Grace stepped outside and stood on the porch as the boys drove away. When she turned to go back in the house, Grace saw what appeared to be a group of small children huddled together in the darkened corner.

"Who's there? Come out here right now," she said.

Just before the little ones vanished, a sorrowful looking black woman appeared. She seemed to be herding the little girls in an attempt to keep them together. Her eyes met with Grace's for but a split second and then, they were gone.

Grace gasped. Nothing like that had ever happened to her before. She hurried into the house and locked the door. "Shadows. That's all it was. It was nothing but shadows from the neighbor's big, old oak tree."

Chapter Forty-Four

After arriving at the Michaels' home, Dan and Jon sat for a moment in the driveway as Dan bowed his head. Jon quietly allowed his brother to finish his prayer.

Dan lifted his head. "Are you ready?"

"Oh you have no idea," Jon said.

They slid out of the car and began walking up the sidewalk towards the house. Dan stopped, finding it difficult to breathe and placed his hand on Jon's forearm. "The air feels incredibly heavy. This home is gravely oppressed."

Jon nodded and continued to the porch. He rang the doorbell.

Ted and Angela answered the door together. Angela looked back at Brittney. It was obvious; she wasn't comfortable putting any space between herself and her daughter.

Brittney was sitting at Elizabeth's feet.

Ted immediately took hold of Jon's hand and shook it vigorously. "Come in," he said with a gentle tug.

Dan gave Jon a sideways glance and followed him into the house. The air was even thicker inside. Once again, Dan felt the evil oppression.

"Let me introduce you to my brother Dan," Jon said. "He just arrived today from Italy. I hope there's something he can do to help you," Jon tipped his head in Dan's direction.

It was obvious from their appearance that the Michaels family was worn out from the stress of their unwelcome visitor. "We've been sleeping in shifts on the living room floor, so there's always someone looking after Brittney. We don't want to leave her alone," Angela explained in hopes of creating a little empathy for their plight. She didn't need to say a word. Her eyes told the story. They looked like teabags that had been used more than once.

Dan looked at Brittney and thought how innocent she looked compared to that wicked little monster he'd met at home and on the plane.

There was an uncomfortable moment when everyone simply stared at Dan. It was as if they expected him to do something dramatic and everything would be back to normal again.

Dan decided to get things started. "Is there someplace we can sit and talk?"

"I'm so sorry, of course. Let's go to the kitchen," Angela beckoned.

"I just put on a pot of coffee. It'll be done in a few minutes," Elizabeth said.

"I need to talk to each one of you individually. I'll be able to understand it better if I can hear how you each individually comprehend this nightmare you're living in," Dan began.

"I hope you don't think we're making any of it up," Ted stated defensively. He appeared to be hanging on by a solitary nerve.

"On the contrary, I need to know if you are able to handle this ordeal and how it affects you," Dan responded. "You're all under a lot of stress; but we have to know all the facts before tackling what I know is going to be a difficult spiritual battle. Something one of you might forget, another could possibly remember."

Dan put the supernatural aspect of their dilemma into prospective, taking away any doubts they might have had.

"Whenever a family is placed in a compromising situation that detours your lives and threatens the safety and security of the home, your natural defenses kick in and you prepare yourself for battle." This wasn't the first time Dan came face to face with the spirit world.

"You have to understand right from the beginning that I'm on your side and we have to work together. The demon will try to

turn us against each other, because we're stronger as a whole."
Dan spoke slowly and clearly to the distraught family.

"I can't fight you and them. It will only weaken me. That's
what Emily is counting on," Dan explained.

"We'll do whatever it takes," Angela said.

Dan had to figure out everyone's role in this dilemma as he
listened to them speak. He realized immediately that Angela would
be the easiest one to work with. Ted, on the other hand, had a
negative, defeatist's attitude.

Jon had filled Dan in on what had happened to Angela's
hand, but it was important for her to give a separate, personal
account of the terror she experienced. There was no doubt that
what they were saying was true. Dan simply needed to make sure
that there was no one among them, working with the evil one and
in effect, creating the problem. That wouldn't be hard for him to
figure out once he talked to each of them.

Ted sat directly across from Jon and Dan. Angela placed
cups on the table and Elizabeth put out a plate of cookies and set
the coffeepot on a hot plate.

"Help yourself," Elizabeth said and took a seat.

Dan accepted a cup of coffee. "We just finished dinner at
our parent's home. I'm anxious to get started.

Ted took a deep breath. "Brittney, why don't you bring
your paper and crayons in here." There was already a play area set
up for her from when they spoke with Jon.

"Okay Daddy. I left it in the living room," Brittney said and
headed for the kitchen door. Angela jumped up.

"I'll help you," she said. "Wait for me."

"It's okay, Mommy. Emily went upstairs. She doesn't like
Jon and his brother," Brittney answered innocently, giving them
much needed information.

Silence closed snuggly around the table like a well-fit glove
as Brittney skipped out of the kitchen. Angela only had time to

throw the young men an apologetic glance before racing after her daughter.

Ted looked down at his hands. "How did she know that?"

Dan stood and pushed his chair back from the table. "Do you mind if I go upstairs?" he specifically directed his question to Ted.

"You don't even know what's going on. Why not wait to hear what we have to say first?" Ted asked.

"If I'm going to help you, we have to start working together. You're emitting some negative vibes and I'm not exactly sure why. Maybe we need to clear that up first," Dan confronted Ted.

Angela returned with Brittney just in time to witness the challenge. "Don't even start, Ted. I won't have any more of your macho attitude. Either work with these young men or send them away. Everyone isn't going to continue to walk on egg shells around you."

"I agree," Leonard spoke up.

Ted's face turned a distinct shade of pink. "Fine," he said.

Brittney slipped out of the room during the discussion. Angela spun around. "Brittney, where are you?"

"I'm here," she answered and came back into the kitchen.

Dan opened his briefcase and retrieved the rag doll. "Has anyone been missing this?" He waved the doll in the air like a magician pulling a rabbit out of a hat.

Everyone in the room was startled. Everyone, that is except for Brittney.

"Where'd you get that doll?" Ted questioned.

Brittney jumped up and grabbed at the doll. "Hey! That's my Abby. Give her to me."

Dan brought the doll down so it was within Brittney's reach. She snatched it and studied the doll's face before clutching it tightly to her chest.

Dan observed everyone's reaction. Ted wasn't one to hold back his feelings. "Jon, did you take that doll from the house when you left?"

"No!" Jon spouted defensively. "Why would I do that?"

"I don't know, but I had to ask," Ted said. "I have to be able to ask questions without you getting all defensive. This working together has to go both ways."

"Fair enough," Dan said.

"It isn't that we doubt you," Leonard added. "You have to admit that it's very odd that you showed up with that doll. I don't think Ted was out of line to ask about it." Everyone agreed.

Ted held his ground. "I never believed in this sort of thing. Now, it's being shoved down my throat. I'm not only expected to believe in ghosts, I'm being forced to live with them."

Jon turned to Dan. "I don't know what to say."

"I'm not surprised by your response. I realize that we just met and it's difficult to allow a complete stranger into your home. I can tell you what happened in my home in Italy and how I ended up with the doll. Then we need to get started on finding a solution to your problem."

Dan needed to get to know the Michaels family and he didn't have a lot of time to do so. He decided to approach them in a more subtle way. He continued with his experience at the apartment, beginning with the hooded figure, meeting the little girls and Emily, then finally with their attempts to prevent him from making the trip. After explaining how he ended up with the doll, even Jon was amazed by what Dan said.

"The most important thing to remember right now is that we have to trust each other. We need to work very closely in order for us to find a solution to this problem, but it is your problem and you will have to work hard to get rid of Emily." Dan took in the intense expressions of his silent listeners.

"These spirits are very cunning. They're watching us individually and will take advantage of any weaknesses. If distrust is among us, it will become one of their strongest weapons. They will use whatever they can to defeat us," Dan said with incredible control.

"Whatever you decide, I have to tell you that we not only need to work together, but quickly. From what I've already observed, I know that your daughter is in great danger. It's up to you where we go from here." Dan looked from one face to the next, waiting for the connection that would pull them together as a group.

Jon put his hand on his brother's arm. "I'll do whatever you need me to do."

Angela smiled. "We'll cooperate. Just tell us where to start."

"Brittney, take Jon and Dan upstairs and show them your room. You need to tell them where Emily is," Ted said.

"I'm sure if Emily or anyone of them is up there, we'll be able to find them," Jon stated confidently.

Dan put a comforting arm around Ted's shoulder. "It'll be alright. Come on, let's go confront Emily together."

Chapter Forty-Five

Brittney led the way up the staircase to her bedroom. She swung the rag-doll aimlessly by its arm, so unlike her usual motherly fashion.

Angela followed close behind. "Brittney, hold Abby right. You're going to tear her arm off if you drag her around like that."

Dan followed closely behind Angela and Brittney. He paid close attention to how they spoke and acted around each other. It didn't appear that Brittney's feet were touching the steps. . Something was very wrong and Dan could feel a powerful resistance with each step.

Brittney stopped when she reached the top and turned to face everyone. In a morbidly acidic tone, she spewed her words at Dan. "There are doors where there shouldn't be doors and walls that aren't safe for little girls."

Angela's mouth dropped open in disbelief and horror. She held tightly to the banister, tears burning her eyes. It was difficult to form even the simplest words. Ever so slowly, she approached the little girl, who held a strange resemblance to her daughter.

"Brittney?" her voice cracked. "Honey, are you in there?"

Ted and Jon were coming up the stairs behind Dan. Dan didn't take his eyes off the child before him. He held his hand up to his brother in a gesture signaling for them to stop where they were.

"What's up?" Jon asked.

Dan brought his index finger up to his lips. "Shh, don't move too fast. Keep your eyes on the little girl," he whispered.

Brittney's features became kaleidoscopic as she changed from one face to another. Dan now recognized her as the same child he met in his apartment in Italy and again on the airplane.

Angela's entire body was shaking. She backed away from Emily as the little girl continued her sepulchral transformation.

"Angela," Dan spoke calmly. "Don't be afraid. Who is it you see in front of you?"

"I don't know," she managed to answer. "I thought it was Brittney, but now I'm not sure. I was hoping it was just the pain pills."

Jon was standing behind Dan and leaned in. "That's not Brittney Michaels. What do we do?"

Dan locked his eyes on Emily. "What about you, Ted? Who is the child standing at the top of the stairs?"

"What are you talking about? It's Brittney. We followed her from the kitchen," Ted answered anxiously. "What's going on?"

"I want you all to stand perfectly still," Dan instructed. "Jon and I are both able to discern spirits of the dead. You asked us to help; now you have to start trusting us."

Ted was on the verge of hysteria. He called past Jon and Dan to Angela. "What are they talking about, Ang? Isn't Brittney with you?"

Angela was close enough to witness the creepy expressions that slid across the little girl's face as she whizzed through different dimensions.

It terrified Angela beyond belief, but she spoke sincerely to the apparition.

"Where is Brittney? Please answer me. You can't continue to do this to us," she pleaded.

Ted wasn't going to wait for Emily to make the first move this time. He bulldozed his way through the small group on the stairs and took hold of the child, who was using his daughter's body so irreverently.

As soon as he had Emily in his grasp, an unexpected force elevated him in place. Ted kicked his feet wildly before he went sailing down the hall. It was quick and the landing was hard. He collided with the wall and ended up flat on his back in front of the closet door.

The violent surge that vaulted Ted's body down the hall left him stunned. He barely heard the muffled ringing that appeared to be coming from inside the hall closet. Ted remained dazed, unable to move.

Angela recognized the toy phone as its chiming got louder and louder. She began to sob uncontrollably.

Jon and Dan ran over to Ted and helped him to his feet. Angela stepped up cautiously behind them and grabbed hold of the door knob. The closet door opened with no effort on Angela's part.

The telephone that she knew was tucked away, high on a shelf in the garage, bound with duct tape, now sat eye level with her. It continued to ring.

"Don't answer it," Dan instructed firmly.

Ted reached for the phone. Angela turned on her husband violently. "Do what he says." There was an undertone to her voice that Ted was unfamiliar with, which caused him to retreat.

Dan turned back to Emily. "I guess we're playing a game now, aren't we?"

Emily remained emotion free and ignored Dan's remark. She looked back and forth between Ted and the ringing telephone. When she finally spoke, her voice sounded exactly like Brittney.

"Answer the phone, Daddy." Emily was doing her best to manipulate Ted.

Ted glared frantically back and forth between Dan and the toy phone. His eyes stopped when they met with Angela's and he starred at her, waiting for her permission.

Angela screamed, "Don't touch that phone. I'm warning you, Ted. You'll listen to Dan or you have to leave." Angela was reacting like a mother bear protecting her cub.

The temperature in the house dropped to freezing. Dan was aware of Emily's use of the deep freeze to demonstrate her power and control. He continued to speak to the Michaels family though his teeth were clanking so hard, he was afraid he'd crack a tooth. It only made him more determine to succeed.

"Ted and Angela, listen to me. Let's all go into Brittney's room like we planned." Dan's eyes remained on Emily as he redirected the desperate family.

Emily baited Ted. Her voice sounded stronger and more demanding. "Answer the phone, Daddy. If you want to talk to Brittney, you have to answer the phone."

Ted's entire body was vibrating when he broke free from Dan and Jon. He grabbed the plastic phone and clutched it tightly to his chest. His eyes were crazed as he looked frantically from one face to the next.

Jon felt sorry for him. He didn't know what to do.

Dan's arms were heavy from the ice that was holding him bondage. It appeared that Emily's attack was zeroed in on him. He remembered the last time he encountered Emily's wrath. His clothes had actually become weapons that sliced into his skin.

Everyone just watched when Ted brought the phone to his ear. The words that rang out from the toy caused his knees to buckle as he listened to the cries of his only child.

"Daddy, where are you? Help me, Daddy!" Hearing Brittney pleading for him to save her was like driving a stake into his heart.

"It's dark inside the merry-go-round. Daddy, I'm scared." The sobbing trailed off and Ted stared at the phone in shock. The receiver dropped from his hand when the familiar carousel melody began flowing from the toy phone like a wound up music box. It haunted him to the depths of his soul.

Leonard and Elizabeth clung to each other at the foot of the stairs. They could hear the whimsical tune.

"My God, what's happening up there?" Elizabeth called out.

Dan knew that he had to do something fast. Everyone around him was in a stupor. He looked at Jon, who was the only one not emotionally involved. "Get Ted away from that phone. It's not real. It is just a pawn in Emily's sick game. Don't listen to it."

Jon placed a hand under Ted's elbow and helped him to his feet. "Put down that phone and don't touch it again," he ordered gently but firmly.

His spirit broken, Ted looked deep into Jon's eyes and did as he was told.

"We have a lot of work to do and if we don't all cooperate, we aren't going to be able to help Brittney," Jon reiterated.

Dan glanced over to Brittney's bedroom. An old black woman stood partially in the shadows. She held out her hand to Dan and motioned for him to follow her. He wasn't sure what her exact role was, but didn't feel threatened by her presence.

Dan began to move his limbs as the thaw came about slowly. Water puddled the floor around his feet. Angela grabbed a couple of towels from the closet; threw one around his shoulders and the other around his feet.

"Just hand them to me, don't touch me," Dan pleaded. "It's very painful and I still have some superficial wounds from my last encounter with Emily."

"What the hell have you people gotten yourself into?" Jon went to Dan's side, but didn't dare touch him.

They all watched Emily glide down the hall. She no longer held Brittney's likeness. Her long blond curls swung back and forth as she floated into Brittney's bedroom and into the closet.

Though only one small child was seen going into Brittney's room, a thunder of footsteps could be heard running past them.

"Emily's powers are getting stronger," Dan said. "Now it's imperative that we find out what happened to her and help her cross over or we're going to lose Brittney forever."

Chapter Forty-Six

Leonard and Elizabeth weren't able to stay down stairs a moment longer. They made their way up to where everyone was gathered.

"Where's Brittney?" Elizabeth asked.

No one answered. The closet door stood ajar and Emily could be seen in the shadow of the darkened room.

"You wicked little brat," Elizabeth cried out.

Angela grabbed her mother-in-law firmly by the arm. "Don't say another word. She holds Brittney's life in her hands. We can't antagonize her."

Elizabeth stepped back next to Leonard, who was watching everything from the doorway.

"They can't handle Emily like they would a normal child, Liz. She isn't real. They're dealing with the supernatural and we need to mind our own business and just be here for them in case they need us," Leonard explained carefully.

Dan and Jon stood with Ted and Angela directly in front of Emily. Dan spoke first.

"What is it you want, Emily? I think you know that Jon and I are capable of seeing you and the others. You can't hide from us. You're here for a reason. What is it?"

Dan's position was clearly more than simply a mediator. He fingered the crucifix that was nestled in his pocket. When Emily didn't respond, Dan pursued the issue. "What do you want with this family? How are we supposed to help you?" Dan's composure with this unknown entity was remarkable.

Emily simply turned away and moved deeper into the closet. Sweat formed across his forehead as Dan quickly moved toward Emily, waving everyone else to stay back.

"Be careful Dan," Jon said.

Dan didn't take his eyes off Emily when he answered Jon. "Keep everyone back. Emily is making some sort of connection with me right now. I can feel it."

"Find my Mommy and Daddy, Dan Markos," Emily's voice was weak although her flaccid features remained staunch.

There was something mesmerizing and alluring about her. Dan allowed himself to stay focused on Emily, though he was fully aware that he had to remain cautious.

Every moment was precious. Dan spoke softly, "What does Brittney Michaels have to do with you finding your parents?"

"We all share the same birthday. The more innocent souls I obtain, the stronger I become," she answered.

Dan became concerned for Emily's soul. "When did you die? How did you die?" he asked. Dan took a step closer to her. "Where did it happen, Emily? What can I do?"

Emily raised her arms as if it were a burden to do so and reached out for Dan. Her movements made him feel euphoric. For a split second, Emily moved inside of Dan's body. Their souls meshed and a connection was made.

If this was life after death, for that single moment, he was almost willing to give up his ghost right then and there.

He opened his eyes and Emily stood next to Dan. She looked up at him and he noted her appearance. She was truly nothing more than an illusion, similar to a bad reaction to a new medication.

In life, Emily couldn't have been more than forty pounds. Yet in death, she was capable of tossing a man across the room. Emily was in control. There was no doubt about it. She was able to create a force after death to walk amongst the living.

Dan raised his eyes and witnessed the little girls huddled closely together.

"Did you take these children from their parents?" Dan asked Emily. "Are you as much a monster as the person who took you from your Mommy and Daddy?"

Emily was not one to be tampered with. Though her soul remained in the shell of a five-year-old child, she replied with sarcasm. "Father Dan Markos, did you forget the vows you took in front of God? I witnessed you taking them. You were so humble and earnest," she mocked. "If you can't keep a simple promise to your God, how can I trust you?"

Emily's voice was smothered with malice and power. She tested Dan boldly by stirring up the depths of his personal life and failures.

"What I choose to do with my time here on earth is my decision. I'm sorry that you were robbed of your life at such an early age. It wasn't fair, but I don't have to answer to you. You are nothing to me but a distressed, lost spirit."

Everyone silently waited for Emily's response. She moved deeper into the closet and beckoned Dan to follow her.

Emily waved her hand toward the other children. "We all carry the same fate. We all visited the forbidden merry-go-round on our fifth birthday."

Dan watched as Emily levitated and hovered a foot above him. She was getting stronger by the minute. Impressed by her display of strength, Dan was fully aware of the danger she presented.

"A lot of children celebrate their birthdays by going to the carnival. That doesn't make them yours for the taking. You're stalling, Emily. You aren't telling me what happened to you. Now, where is Brittney Michaels?"

Dan was getting impatient. Though he had fought with demons before, Emily was different. Somehow, her secret included him. Their thoughts were becoming one. He could feel her determination to live again.

Suddenly, Emily cried out, "It was the merry-go-round. Find my Mommy and Daddy. There are doors that shouldn't be doors and walls that aren't safe for little girls." Her words were nettlesome.

The bedroom was cold. "Heck, you can hang meat in here," Ted complained. He could see his breath when he blew into his cupped hands. Ted rubbed Angela's arms and back in an attempt to warm her trembling body.

Dan tried to yell above the pounding noise that reverberated with Emily's voice. It echoed like the constant beating of a hammer. "Who are you talking about? Who took you from the merry-go-round? Let me help you, Emily. Maybe we can put this all to rest."

"There isn't much time left. Soon, I will have to walk the earth for eternity. Help me to rest, Dan Markos or I will haunt you till the end of time," Emily cried. Her voice floated on the warm air that was creeping back into the room.

They were gone, the children, Emily, even the unknown hooded fiend.

"Where'd she go?" Leonard asked.

"I don't know," Dan was emotionally drained. "Leave the door to this closet open. It appears to be the portal to wherever it is they come from. Plus, Brittney might need it open to get back."

Angela snapped her head around sharply. "Is that it? Is Brittney going to be one of those pathetic little girls we just saw?"

"I don't know any more than you do," Dan said. "She wasn't with them just now. Emily seems to be using her to get to us. To me. I think Emily is just hiding Brittney right now. If that's the case, I don't believe that she's in any immediate danger," he spoke calmly to Angela.

Jon took a deep breath. "What did she mean by doors that shouldn't be doors?"

"I'm not sure," Dan pondered. "But, I think we need to go to that carnival and check out the merry-go-round."

Ted jumped in. "The only time it will be safe to go is after the park is closed."

"Why is that?" Elizabeth asked.

Jon chimed in quickly. "Good thinking, Ted. If we go out there after the park is closed, we'll be able to examine the merry-go-round closely and see if we can find that door Emily keeps talking about."

"What about that miniature merry-go-round that someone left outside on Brittney's birthday?" Angela asked.

"What merry-go-round?" Dan asked

Ted was following everyone down the stairs as the conversation intensified. "We came home from the carnival and found a box on the front porch. It looked old and worn. Inside was an exact replica of the merry-go-round that Brittney met Emily on at the carnival."

"Was there anything odd or different about it?" Jon asked. "Who sent it to you?"

They all headed for the garage. Angela pushed the step stool over to the shelf where Ted had put the old box and answered, "We still don't know. There wasn't a card."

"Of course, there wouldn't be," Dan said.

Leonard stood in the doorway leading to the house. "Why would you say that?"

"Bring it into the house. It's a start," Dan responded. "Maybe the replica will give us some sort of clue before we head over to the park."

"All I know is that we don't have much time," Dan said. "Emily definitely made that clear."

"I'll get some paper and pencils. We need to write down everything we remember about that day, from the time Brittney got up the morning of her birthday," Angela said. It felt good to be doing something.

"Ted, this is going to weigh heavy on you remembering details about the carnival," Dan told him.

Angela broke down and started crying. "I just want my daughter back," she cradled her bandaged hand. It was obvious that the pain medication was wearing off.

Ted placed an arm around her shoulder. "Why don't you take another pill? It should be about time. The sooner we get started, the sooner we'll have Brittney home."

"I saw that wound, Angela," Jon said. "It isn't a paper cut. You're going to have to keep taking the medication to be able to function. If it makes you groggy, let me know and I'll see about getting you something else."

Elizabeth left the kitchen and sat on the couch. Leonard stood at the foot of the stairs looking up. Something bothered him about the house now.

Jon came up behind him. "Do you see anyone?"

"I don't see anyone," Leonard answered. "I just feel uncomfortable here and I never felt that way before."

Jon didn't expose the hooded fiend. He just steered Leonard away from the stairs.

Elizabeth had already cleared the table in the kitchen. She didn't want to be a part of the investigation at that time. Ted noticed that she looked tired.

"This might be a long night for us. If we're going to sleep in shifts, why don't you go ahead and get some sleep while we stay up and talk?" He spoke quietly to his mother.

"I would feel better if you and Dad were here, but I want you to be rested in case we need you," Ted added.

"I hope these men can help," Elizabeth said.

Leonard walked up to Ted and Elizabeth. "Me too! We just don't know what we're up against. I think Dan is right about Brittney's closet being some sort of portal," Leonard rubbed his face with both hands to stir up some circulation.

"You and Mom sleep first," Ted said. "You had a rough time too, Dad. You really look tired. I'm going to let Angie sleep whenever she wants. There's no telling how those pills will affect her."

"By the way," Leonard said. "Your mom found that rag doll at the bottom of the stairs. She tucked it in her apron pocket."

"That's right and I'm not letting it out of my sight until this is over and done with." There was a flicker of sorrow in Elizabeth's eyes.

Ted smiled. "Get some rest. I'll check on Angie and talk with Dan and Jon for a while."

"Dad and I will sleep downstairs, if it's all the same to you. Dad loves that recliner and I'm comfortable on the couch. I'll feel better out in the open instead of cooped up in the guest room."

Angela took some fresh linens to Brittney's room for Dan and Jon. They decided to spend the night. Dan wanted to be there when Emily made her next appearance.

As she was leaving the bedroom, Angela noticed the box of precious stones that the elderly black woman gave to Brittney. It was sitting out on her dresser.

She walked over to the box and opened it. It was empty.

A black woman wearing a bright colored scarf on her head stood next to the dresser. She smiled sweetly at Angela and unfolded her hand, palm up. Brittney's precious stones encircled the evil eye bead that lay nestled in the center. The dark skinned woman plucked the evil eye from the center of the stones and handed it to Angela. "Hold tightly to this bead. It will protect you against my darling Emily." She was gone as quickly as she appeared.

Angela stood alone, bewildered by the incident. She wondered if the pain pills were causing her to hallucinate or if what she saw really happened; but when she opened her hand and looked down, the evil eye bead was there, strung on the same worn ribbon.

"It's true. There really is such a thing as life after death. Ghosts are real."

Chapter Forty-Seven

Ted joined Dan and Jon in the kitchen. Knowing that a minor detail might actually help them, he was desperate to remember everything that happened at the carnival. "Emily seemed like such an ordinary little girl when we first met her."

"I've always felt that if something bad is going to happen, it's going to be in the middle of the night," Elizabeth said. "I'm going to get the couch ready and see if I can close my eyes for a few hours without seeing that awful child's face."

"Emily's not after you, Mom," Angela responded bluntly recalling the words of warning from the mysterious black woman. It wasn't like her to be unkind, especially to her mother-in-law. The stress was getting to her. Elizabeth quietly excused herself.

"I'm going to stay up and listen to what Dan and Jon have to say. We're all tired, but maybe we can get a few more things covered before turning in," Angela told Ted and gave him a gentle hug. "By the way, how's your back?"

"I'll have to be more careful around Emily. It's still sore," he mumbled.

"I'm sorry, but it doesn't surprise me after that trip you took down the hall. That was awful. You can have one of my pain pills if you want," Angela offered.

"No thanks. I don't want to take anything that might muddle my thoughts right now," Ted shook his head. "You have a reason for taking those pills. I'd have to admit that a five-year-old ghost picked me up and threw me down the hall. Plus, one of us has to keep a clear head."

"Dan feels that Emily's strongest point is in Brittney's closet. I agree with him," Angela said. "Somehow, I should have known that."

"How could you have known?" Ted asked.

"I'm the mother. This is my house," Angela said.

Ted pressed his lips together, hard. "Damn it! I'm sick of this whole mess. I don't know how to handle this paranormal crap."

"Who does?" Angela yawned.

"Come on. Let's go see what our ghost busters are up to." He wrapped his arm around Angela's shoulder.

Jon met them on the stairs. "We need to talk in Brittney's room. I think if anything is going to happen tonight, it'll be in there," Jon led the way, anxious to get the spiritual fight started. They could not have predicted what happened next.

When they reached the doorway of Brittney's bedroom, Jon, Ted and Angela were shocked as they watched the phenomenal event in total amazement..

"Where's Dan?" Angela whispered.

Jon pointed to the opened closet. "In there!" he mouthed the words. Jon placed a finger up to his lips and made a soft shushing sound. The room was silent except for the occasional whizzing of an object past their heads. Brittney's lamp hovered over the dresser and blinked on and off. The low chatter of unintelligible voices appeared to be coming from Brittney's group of dolls and stuffed animals.

Ted made an attempt to enter the room. Jon held up his hand abruptly, shaking his head adamantly back and forth as he motioned Ted to get back.

Jon leaned in closer to Ted's face and in a low tone whispered, "Stop. Don't go in there. Dan is in another realm right now. He's trying to communicate with Emily on her level." It was an order, not a request. Jon had to keep Ted from interrupting one of the most phenomenal events he had ever witnessed. "Emily is in complete control and Dan is at her mercy right now. I can't allow you to do anything that might interrupt their encounter."

Ted reluctantly and very slowly slipped back to where Angela stood, just inside the door.

Brittney's toy phone defied gravity as it casually passed the group of flabbergasted onlookers. Brittney's dolls all simultaneously turned their heads and stared at Jon, Ted and Angela, holding them in place. The corners of their mouths twisted into smirks and their eyes moistened as they kept watch over the three interlopers.

Terror-stricken, Angela began to tremble. She whispered in Jon's ear. "Where's Brittney?"

"I'm not sure. But I'm certain, if anyone can find her, Dan will. What's happening here is a form of telekinesis." Jon's voice, though barely above a whisper, vibrated with excitement. Mesmerized by it all, his eyes were wide with wonder.

"What's telekinesis? Are we in danger?" Ted asked.

Jon pressed his finger to his lips as a reminder to keep it down. "I don't think so. Telekinesis is the movement of objects by a powerful, unexplainable energy. It's a rare occurrence and takes great mental or physical strength. I've read about it, but this is the first time I've actually experienced it."

Ted and Angela held their breath and held tightly to each other as they cautiously crossed over to the bed and sat down where they could see Dan. Jon remained standing.

Emily stood directly in front of Dan. In the far corner of the closet, huddled tightly together, were the other little girls whose souls Emily had selfishly embezzled.

Without breaking eye contact with her, Dan spoke to Jon. "I have to go with Emily for a while. Don't ask why."

"Where are you going?" Jon asked fearfully.

"Just listen to me," Dan ordered. "You have to stay here and make sure that no one moves or touches anything in this room until I'm able to come back. Everything has to remain the same so I can be certain of reentry."

Jon was terrified. "I don't understand."

"Don't question me," Dan ordered. "I can't stop now. Just listen carefully. We were brought together for a reason. I don't have much time. You have to do exactly what I tell you. I'm working solely on faith right now."

"Okay, I understand. Just tell me what you want me to do," Jon's voice cracked.

Dan didn't hesitate. "This journey was inevitable. I don't know if I'll be able to get back. I'm going with Emily to the carnival where she was abducted from the merry-go-round on her birthday, in 1947."

Dan was pale. Standing up to Emily drained him.

"Is this really necessary?" Jon asked desperately in one final attempt to stop him.

Dan was totally focused on Emily. "I promised."

"It was a foolish promise," Jon's response was harsh.

Dan ignored him. "Don't make it any harder on me. I'm going with Emily."

Jon knew there was nothing he could do or say at this point to stop his brother. Tears welled up and spilled down his cheeks. He didn't bother to wipe them away.

"What's he talking about?" Angela pleaded as objects in the room continued to spin and swirl.

Ted deflected a flying Frisbee. "What the hell is going on?"

Jon looked back and forth from his brother to Ted and Angela. A lump in his throat made it difficult to speak. "I should never have come to this house. I wish I never met you people. My God Danny," he cried into his hands.

Leonard and Elizabeth heard what they would later describe as a windstorm. They hustled upstairs to see what was going on. Elizabeth clutched the rag doll to her chest and stepped boldly into the room. Leonard stayed safely just outside the bedroom door and peered in.

When Jon saw Elizabeth he marched right up to her. "Give that to me!" he demanded and snatched the doll from her grasp. Jon turned as fast as he could and bolted to the closet as if in a relay race. Fighting the resistance that was forcing him back, Jon stretched his arm toward Dan. "You'll need something to connect you to this place."

Dan reached for the doll and wrapped his fingers around her body just as he and Emily faded away into the darkness of the now, cold and drafty closet.

Everything in the room was still. Jon stared in shock, into the empty closet in monumental shock. "They're gone."

Chapter Forty-Eight

Dan traveled at an electrifying speed. It left him woozy and lightheaded. He stopped abruptly and found himself sitting on a bench with his head cradled in his hands. "This must be how Alice felt when she tumbled down the rabbit hole." Dan lifted his head and opened his eyes, bewildered by his surroundings. "What in the world? I wonder what Father Luke would say if he could witness this phenomenon."

It was impossible to describe the magnitude of emotions Dan felt when he discovered that he was smack dab in the middle of a carnival. The music coming from the magnificent and enticing carousel that stood directly in front of him rang out loudly. The horses were carved from wood with realistic detail and color. Painted flowers and ivy wound under and around the horse's hooves. It was positively breathtaking.

His attention was drawn to the people meandering lightheartedly around him. It was like watching a play from the 1940s. But it was more than simply their appearance. These people were real and somehow, Emily was able to bring them all back to this day. The day that tore Emily's spirit from her body and left it lost and wandering.

A group of men stood a few feet away. They wore their hair slicked down and parted in the middle like in old photographs. "I'm actually here. This is where it happened. She did it. Emily took me back in time."

There was a flyer lying on the ground by Dan's feet. He stooped and picked it up. It was an advertisement for the carnival.

"Dear God. There's the date," he laughed. June 28, 1947. It was really happening.

Dan carefully folded the carnival flyer and slipped it deep into his pants pocket. "I'll need this for proof when I get back home."

"Please Daddy, may I have a nickel?" A child jumped up and down next to a young man who appeared to be no more than Dan's age and was definitely not quick to surrender the five-cent piece.

"What do you need a nickel for?" he questioned the little girl as if the child were asking for the keys to his car.

"I want to ride the merry-go-round," she pleaded. "Please, Daddy."

The wonder of the experience was immediately replaced by doom and dread as he was brought back to the reason why he was there. Dan realized he was still holding tightly to Brittney's doll. "I better tuck this thing away. Someone might get the wrong idea if they see me walking around, carrying this thing." He spotted a paper bag lying by the carousel. Dan snatched it and quickly crammed the doll in the bag.

A nice looking young couple stood in front of the merry-go-round, only a few feet from Dan. He listened to their conversation.

"I know she's getting to be a big girl Charles, but how could you let her go on that ride alone? I'm afraid she'll slip off her pony." The young woman was wringing her hands and pacing back and forth in front of the merry-go-round.

Dan looked up at the children riding the carousel. He spotted Emily. "Oh dear God!" he whispered. Dan looked back at the two people standing in front of the ride and realized they must be Emily's parents. He leaned in closer to listen.

"Relax Sarah, let the child enjoy herself. It's her birthday." The man never took his eyes off the circling horses. His face and voice were filled with anxiety. Emily's father searched the individual horses nervously each time they passed him. Dan realized that Charles Thatcher was clearly upset over allowing his daughter to ride alone.

"This is why Emily brought me here. She's trying to show me what happened to her that day. I must try to warn them," Dan said.

Dan cautiously placed his hand on Charles's shoulder. "Excuse me, Sir." He didn't want to startle the already anxious man.

There was no response from Charles. Dan deliberately tightened his grip on Emily's dad, but it didn't matter. Charles didn't feel Dan's touch. Dan circled him and stood between Charles and Sarah. Neither one of them saw him.

Dan tried speaking louder and soon, he was yelling into Charles's face. "Is that your little girl on the merry-go-round? Come on! Answer me. There's no time!" Dan looked anxiously back and forth between Emily and her parents. No one showed any sign that he was present.

"God in heaven; I'm only here to observe. I can't do anything to help Emily. I haven't been born yet. I don't exist in this time or place," Dan concluded. He waved his arms wildly in front of the Thatchers. "They can't hear me. They can't see me. This is totally insane." He stood directly in front of Sarah's face. "Why does this woman look so familiar?" He recognized her but couldn't place the young woman. "I know we've met before."

Dan laughed out of sheer hysteria but finally settled down. "There's no way for me to communicate with them. I have to think." He looked back at the merry-go-round and spotted Emily. There was a distinct difference between the beautiful little girl sitting on the merry-go-round and the one he met at home.

"It's 1947. There's no ghostly apparition on that carousel horse because Emily is alive!" Dan shouted and leaped onto the moving ride, fighting to make his way to Emily. His movements were heavy and sluggish.

"Emily," he called. "It's me, Dan Markos. You brought me here, remember? What am I supposed to do?" Dan yelled above the blaring music.

244

As the ride revolved, Dan could briefly see Charles and Sarah each time he passed them. Their body language and facial expressions revealed their overwhelming stress.

Dan made it to Emily's side. She was holding on tightly to the pole that held her painted horse securely to the ride.

As Dan approached her, he could see Emily's soft golden curls bounce and tumble while the wind blew them gently around her angelic little face. Her big blue eyes twinkled with excitement. She was so beautiful, so alive.

A boy, a couple of years older than Emily, sat a few horses behind her. He was watching Emily intently. He called her name a couple of times, but Emily ignored the young man. Emily turned her nose up and continued looking straight ahead, waving and screaming out to her mother and father every time she passed them.

"My God, you can't let this happen. What a waste of a precious life!"

"Mommy! Daddy! Look at me," she squealed. It broke Dan's heart to hear her sweet little voice. He watched as Emily experienced a wonderful rite of passage. She was five years old and riding the merry-go-round all by herself for the very first time. The look on her face was priceless. Her enthusiasm each time she went up and down on the wooden carousel horse was contagious.

Suddenly, something caught Dan's attention. Just past the horses, inside the center of the circle, he noted the mirrors. They were sculptured and framed in lovely patterns with picturesque etchings of angels. However, each time he passed a mirror, the reflection staring back at him wasn't his own.

"It's Emily as I first met her," Dan gasped. "She's watching me. This is it...this is what you brought me back here to see," he screamed out of horror at the ghostly reflection. It was Emily, as he knew her now...dead. Her tortured face twisted in a demonic grimace that dared him to move.

"Something awful is about to happen to you, and you want me to witness it, but why? Why, when you know I can't stop it. What happened to you, Emily? Your parents are here watching you."

He searched frantically for a stick or something to grab that he could use as a weapon. "Is she going to fall off? Maybe I can somehow prevent that." He studied the area surrounding her horse wondering what would happen if Emily actually fell in front of him. He tried touching her arm, but she didn't respond.

"It isn't fair," he cried. "Why am I here? What do you want from me?"

Dan tried holding on to Emily one more time. "I can't feel you because I don't exist yet. I can't help you." he screamed at the mirrored image of Emily's distorted face. "I have to stay focused and calm down.

Dan remembered the carnival flyer in his pocket. "That's odd," he continued talking out loud. "My hand goes right through you Emily, but I was able to pick up that piece of paper. Did you do that?"

Chapter Forty-Nine

Looking around, Dan saw a beautifully carved, wooden bench after every second row of carousel horses. He saw someone rise up from the bench in front of Emily's horse. A man dressed like a Franciscan monk in a long brown robe, stood with his hands hidden under baggy sleeves. His face was obscured by a draped hood.

He turned slowly and deliberately began to move toward Emily. Dan felt as though he were in slow motion as he tried to put himself between Emily and the man.

Dan was weakening. He knew that he was wasting the energy he needed to get back home, but he felt that he had to do something.

"Please, don't do this, Father! Why did you allow this heinous act to take place?" Dan cried. "Emily, hang on to the pole. Help her, someone. There has to be something I can do."

The cloaked figure was just breaths away from Emily. "Emily!" Dan screamed so hard his throat hurt. There was no more sound after that. I'm so sorry. I can't help you. Tears formed as he helplessly watched the brown hooded figure standing next to her. Emily was totally oblivious to him.

It happened very fast. Dan found himself being pulled back, away from the merry-go-round. Through a fine mist, arms stretched out, reaching for the innocent little girl, he could vaguely see what was happening. The large cape that hung loosely around the hooded figure opened and for a split second, before it covered her tiny body, Emily's eyes locked with Dan's; then she was gone, leaving the carousel horse empty. The kidnapper stepped off the merry-go-round into the inner circle of the ride and disappeared into one of the mirrored panels. Just like that, it was over. Emily was gone.

A teenage boy sat back on a wood chair with his feet propped up on the control box. He was reading a comic book and didn't appear to witness the distressing abduction.

Every mirror on the carousel projected the image of Emily's tormented ghost. Her face was twisted and distorted, her screams deafening. Dan covered his ears. He felt her anguish. No one else was able to hear Emily's blood curdling screams. No one but Dan knew what happened to Emily.

He could vaguely see the chaos evolving after the merry-go-round circled for the sixth time. He was drifting away, ever so peacefully. His free-flowing tears warmed his chilled face. Dan watched as Charles and Sarah discovered the empty horse and started their painful search for Emily.

Dan was angry and frustrated over his thwarted desire to help her. He stared warily at Charles and Sarah before redirecting his frustration at Emily.

"Why did you bring me here? What was the purpose of me witnessing this horrible crime if there was nothing I could do to help you?" His emotions ebbed. He was fading faster and faster from the scene. All Dan felt was a profound sorrow. Every part of him grieved for Emily. His turmoil and confusion about the overwhelming mystery caused Dan pain and despair.

Through despair and defeat, Dan surrendered to the safety of slumber. He drifted further and further away from the carnival, no longer able to hear the music from the merry-go-round. Emily and her demise swirled around in his mind with one last thought lingering from the words Emily had spoken back home.

"Now someone knows what happened to me. Find us Dan Markos. Find our remains and help us to rest in peace." Emily's words were tucked away in Dan's dreams. His eyes remained closed as he drifted off into oblivion.

"How can I find you?" Dan mumbled through his state of partial consciousness.

"My journey has been long and arduous. Find me and you'll find Brittney. Give me peace and you'll save her," Emily's voice faded.

Dan was about to succumb to his state of rest when Emily's lifeless voice skimmed his ear. "Remember that there are doors where there shouldn't be doors and walls that aren't safe for little girls."

Dan slept.

Chapter Fifty

Brittney Michael's bedroom was on the east side of the house, facing the morning sun. Jon opened his eyes to the bright rays and spontaneously looked at the closet, where he last saw his brother.

It was still early. No one else was wake yet. They had stayed up late talking about what happened to Dan and questioned where he and Emily might be.

Jon sat up on the side of the bed and looked around. Everything was just as they had left it. The stuffed animals lay motionless where they dropped from their positions on the ceiling the night before.

There was a morning chill to the air. Jon stepped over to the window to close it, then stopped when he remembered that Dan had told him not to move anything.

Did I dream everything? No, Dan's still gone. How am I going to explain it to Mom and Dad if he doesn't come back? As Jon turned away from the window, he noticed that the door to the closet that had been partially open, moved slightly. He froze in place and waited. All of a sudden, Emily emerged from the wardrobe, held up her arm and pointed to the inside of the closet.

Jon expected the room to begin its kaleidoscopic activity again, but everything remained motionless.

"Where's my brother?" He questioned with false bravery and then braced himself for Emily's retaliation. Jon towered over the little wisp of what was once a five-year-old girl, but he knew what she was capable of.

Emily didn't move. She just continued pointing at the closet.

Jon kept close watch on the ghostly child and inched his way toward the closet. He looked away long enough to peer in and found Dan lying motionless on the floor. His eyes were closed.

Huddled tightly around him were the five little ghost girls that Emily had been controlling.

"I need help in here!" Jon yelled loudly. He rushed to Dan's side, grabbed him by the shoulders, and began shaking his brother, repeating his name hysterically.

"Danny! Danny wake up!" he cried. "Help me! Dan's back."

Ted and Angela followed Jon's cries into the bedroom.

"Where are you?" Ted called out, anxiously searching the room. He found Jon kneeling beside Dan in the closet. Jon had his arms wrapped around his brother, but Dan didn't appear to be moving.

Angela pushed her way into the narrow closet. She placed her cheek next to Dan's nose and said, "I don't feel anything." When she put her fingers on the side of his neck, it triggered Jon and jolted him into motion.

"I can't believe this. I'm not thinking straight." He positioned himself over Dan.

"His pulse is strong," Angela reassured Jon.

Jon quickly bent over Dan's face, tilted his head back and pinched off his nose. He took in a deep breath but Dan opened his eyes just as Jon was about to cover his mouth with his. He shoved Jon's hand away from his nose.

"Ouch! What are you doing?" He tried pushing himself up on his right elbow, but fell back down. He was surprised by his own weakness.

"You weren't breathing," Jon exclaimed! "I was going to give you mouth to mouth."

"You weren't?" Dan shook his head and screwed up his face in disgust.

Jon was relieved to see Dan coming around. "You scared the crap out of me. I thought that little imp killed you."

"I can be a witness to that," Angela said in Jon's defense.

Leonard and Elizabeth entered the room. "What's going on in here?" Leonard asked anxiously. "How did you get back in the closet?"

"How long have you been in there?" Elizabeth added.

Angela moved out of the way and let Jon help his brother recover from the traumatic re-entry. Dan stood up as soon as he felt strong enough, swaying unsteadily.

Once confident that he could bear his own weight, Dan took a deep breath of relief.

"How do you feel?" Jon held tightly to his wobbly brother.

The air coming in from the opened window smelled sweet and clean. Dan gave Jon a playful nudge, but allowed his brother to walk him out of the closet. "You won't believe what happened. Emily took me back to the carnival where this all started. I was with her when she was alive in 1947. She showed me everything that happened to her on the merry-go-round. I even saw her parents." He recalled how familiar Emily's mother was when he stood face to face with her.

Dan was excited about his time travel and anxious to share his experience with everyone. "This has been the most extraordinary thing I've ever been privileged to encounter."

Dan appeared to have a new relationship with Emily. Ted and Angela listened respectfully before interrupting.

"What about Brittney?" Angela asked.

Dan stopped abruptly. "I'm sorry. I didn't see your daughter. But, you have to remember that Emily took me back to the year 1947. Brittney wouldn't have been born yet. What I saw was Emily as a vibrant, living child. She was on the merry-go-round. Her parents were there. They couldn't have been standing more than five feet from the ride."

Angela looked at Ted with an anguished scowl.

"I'm no less concerned about Brittney than I was, but it's difficult not to be emotional over what I've just experienced.

Emily's parents were arguing about letting her ride the merry-go-round alone," he continued.

"Her mother didn't seem to be very happy about leaving her on the ride without an adult. I guess, true to character, Emily was able to convince her father that it was okay. He didn't seem very comfortable with his decision, but still gave in to Emily's wishes."

Elizabeth went down to the kitchen and put on a pot of coffee, hoping to help Dan clear his head. Her voice drifted up from downstairs, "Coffee's ready."

"A hot cup of coffee sounds terrific right now," Dan said.

When everyone left the room, Jon looked back to see if Emily or the other children were behind them. The room was empty. "Where could they all be?" He found Emily's inconsistency to be confusing.

Elizabeth had everything ready. "Sit down Angie and rest your hand. I'll take care of everyone. It makes me feel useful."

"Thank you, I appreciate it," Angela said with the intention of making up for her abrupt attitude last night. Her mind felt numb. All she cared about was Brittney.

Everyone's attention was riveted to Dan. The steaming coffee sat in front of him and he continued to discuss his journey.

"The travel experience itself was awful. It was fast and intense. I had absolutely no control over any of my movements." Dan's eyes widened as he spoke.

"Everything I tell you may seem impossible. It's like a dream to me right now, but it really happened. I was there and I saw Emily Thatcher." Dan's exuberance was next to contagious.

"How can you be sure that you weren't just here in limbo somewhere under Emily's spell? How do you know it was actually the year 1947?" Jon asked.

"I'll get to that in a minute," Dan answered.

Elizabeth tipped her head. "I'm curious about something. How did you know her last name was Thatcher?"

"I guess I heard it from one of you," Dan said.

"Isn't Thatcher Mom's maiden name?" Jon asked.

"Yes, what difference does that make? Thatcher is a fairly common name," Dan answered.

"You have to agree, it's a little strange," Leonard added.

"On the contrary, it's actually quite a coincidence, in fact," Ted added.

"Do you want to hear what happened to me or not?" Dan was tired and irritable.

"Of course we do," Angela said. "Let him talk. This has to somehow lead us to Brittney, doesn't it?"

Dan went on about how horrible he felt when he was swept out of Brittney's closet. He didn't like the way the Michaels family looked when they questioned him about the Thatcher name. It also bothered him that it didn't even dawn on him that his mother's maiden name was Thatcher. What could the correlation be, if any? He would discuss it later on with Jon, privately.

For now, all Dan wanted to do was to share his time travel and regain some of his strength. His throat was dry and parched, but it didn't stop him from talking about Emily.

Chapter Fifty-One

Like Ted and Angela, Elizabeth and Leonard were worried about Brittney. Finding out what Emily wanted was the main objective.

"Please go on Dan," Leonard said. "If we're going to find out where Brittney is and how we're going to get rid of Emily, we have to find out what role we play in her plan. Don't you agree?" he addressed everyone.

Angela sat down and cradled her throbbing hand. Ted stood alongside her.

At this point, Dan was anxious to share his ordeal. "Imagine, at a terrifying and aggressive rate, the lone spirit of a young child, who has been dead for almost sixty years; walking the earth in search for not one, but three things: one, her parents, two, her mortal remains, and three, most horrifying, a host body. The average mortal person doesn't stand a chance against such a supernatural force."

Dan was grateful for the hot cup of coffee. He took a long slow drink and continued. "The movement back in time was swift and sickening. Once we stopped, I got nauseated and my head felt like it was going to explode. I still don't feel well. I'm just glad to be back. When I finally opened my eyes, I was sitting on a wooden bench in front of the infamous merry-go-round. It was simply captivating."

"Why did Emily want to take you back to the year 1947? Couldn't she just tell you what she wanted you to know?" Ted asked. "She's quite the manipulator. How can you be sure that you actually went back in time?"

Dan dug into his pocket. When his fingertips felt the paper, he smiled with relief. Careful not to rip it, Dan pulled the crumpled sheet out of his jeans and laid it on the kitchen table, gently smoothing it out.

"What's that?" Angela looked at the now yellowed flyer.

"It's an advertisement for the carnival. I found it lying on the ground by the carousel," Dan smiled. "For some reason, I was able to pick it up. I took it for proof of where I'd been. Look at the date?" he exclaimed. "It was really weird though."

"How's that?" Leonard asked.

"I couldn't touch anything else. No one responded to me or saw me. Emily must have been responsible for that too," Dan said.

Everyone took turns looking at the flyer.

"It's clearly a public notice announcing the annual carnival," Leonard said.

"June twenty eighth, nineteen forty-seven," Elizabeth read aloud. "That's what it says."

Ted sat down next to Angela. "I guess it doesn't matter what her point was. What did you see?"

Dan had to select his words carefully. He was very upset over what happened to Emily and didn't want to show too much sympathy for her.

"At first, I was fascinated by the people and the surroundings. It was as if I'd stepped onto the set of an old movie. I was captivated. The clothes, the prices, even their hair. I was taking it all in," Dan said. "Some kid was actually bartering with his father over a nickel. It was absolutely amazing."

Everyone listened intently. Ted and Angela kept waiting for Dan to tell them something that would help them find Brittney.

Dan finally addressed Ted and Angela. "I was there on a very important mission. I was looking for Emily. I'm not sure, but I feel that there's a reason that she wanted me to witness her abduction."

"Her abduction?" Angela gasped. "You actually saw that happen?"

"Yes and there was nothing I could do to stop it," Dan added.

"Go on. I want to know exactly what happened," Angela said with a somber expression.

"It made me sick," Dan began. "First, I spotted her parents. I already told you that they were arguing over Emily's dad letting her ride the carousel alone."

Ted lowered his eyes guiltily and bit the inside of his cheek.

"That's understandable. I would never let Brittney go on any ride alone. She's too young," Angela said.

Ted changed the subject quickly. "Go on Dan. Let him finish his story, Angie."

Dan continued. "I glanced up at the merry-go-round, because I was looking for Emily."

It was obviously becoming difficult for Dan to hide his feelings about her. He shifted in his chair. His eyes misted. "That's when I spotted her. I saw Emily and she was alive."

Jon covered Dan's arm with his hand. "Are you okay?"

"It was one of the most overwhelming moments of my life. I could see why she easily stood out in a crowd of children." Dan was developing a personal relationship with Emily. She shared the most traumatic experience of her life with him. What made it worse was he saw her as an innocent child. Dan witnessed the fear in Emily's eyes, the last moments of her life.

"Wasn't there any way for you to warn her parents?" Elizabeth asked.

"Believe me, I tried," Dan took a deep breath. "Remember, no one was able to hear or see me. It was so frustrating. I was able to get on the merry-go-round, but I couldn't do a damn thing to help her."

Ted leaned forward. "How was someone able to kidnap her off a moving ride with her parents standing so close and watching her all the time? It doesn't make any sense. I'm assuming you saw who did it."

"I did. The person that abducted Emily was dressed in a monk robe. He snatched her off the carousel horse and swept her away. It only took a split second. He put his hand over her mouth and she disappeared under his robe," Dan said. "The last thing I saw was her eyes. She looked directly at me. Those big blue eyes looked at me with a fear that I've never seen before and hope never to see again. It's what she wanted me to see." Dan gritted his teeth as he recalled the moment.

"What did you learn from the trip except for the fact that she was abducted," Jon asked. "I have to agree with Angela, I thought you'd come back knowing something more about Brittney. That's all we care about."

Dan was worn out. He tipped his head back and sighed. "There was one thing at the very end. It was Emily's voice and she told me to find her."

"Find her?" Angela cried. "Find Emily? How do you expect to find a little girl that was kidnapped almost sixty years ago? Are you crazy? She's dead. Emily is a ghost." Angela was on her feet. She was holding on to her arm to keep her hand close to her chest. "What about my daughter? This is nuts." She looked at everyone like she was the only sane person in the room.

Dan shook his head. "I'm just telling you what she said. At least I think that's what she meant." He covered his face with his hands. "I'm positively drained."

"Come on Dan. I know you've been through a lot, but try to remember," Jon said.

All eyes were on Dan. He realized just how much they were depending on him. "The last thing Emily said to me was, now someone knows where we are. Find our remains and let us rest in peace."

Angela looked at Dan, her eyes begging for more than he could give. She began shaking so hard; she felt her knees knocking into each other.

Dan looked sympathetically at Angela. "Emily said that if I find her, I'll find Brittney. If I give her peace, I'll save Brittney."

"My God; she said that?" Angela cried.

Dan nodded.

Elizabeth noticed the crumpled bag Dan held tightly in his fist. "What's in the bag?"

"I took the doll with me, remember? I didn't want to walk around with it so I crammed it in this bag," Dan said.

Elizabeth took the bag from Dan's hand and opened it. "Where's the doll now?" she asked.

"I don't know." At that moment, Dan didn't care. He was tired and weak.

Jon rested his arms on the table. "Ghosts materialize through energy. Fear and anger is a form of energy. There's enough of that right here at this table for Emily to feed on."

He reached for Dan's hand and held it tightly. Dan in return reached for Leonard, Leonard took hold of Elizabeth, Elizabeth held on to Ted's hand and Ted took hold of Angela. Tears came to her eyes as Angela stretched her bandaged hand out to Jon.

"What do we do now?" Leonard asked.

Dan took in a slow even breath and tried to focus on the family sitting around him. The lights flickered on and off as he answered with the only response he could come up with. "We find Emily's remains."

Chapter Fifty-Two

Dan found it difficult to stay awake after breakfast and laid down for most of the morning. The rest of the day was spent talking about Dan's experience and sharing opinions on the situation, as well as developing a plan of action. After dinner, Dan called his mother and explained to her that he and Jon would be staying another night at the Michaels house. He didn't go into detail about what had occurred or why they were there. Instead Dan made it clear that the Michaels family was in deep spiritual trouble and he and Jon were doing all they could to help them.

Though disappointed, Grace was very proud of her sons. "I'll say a prayer for you and for that dear family. Do what you can for them. Dad and I will be here when you're ready to come home. By the way, I saw Father Luke last week. He was very indifferent to me. I think he has a lot on his mind. He was nominated for Bishop, you know."

"We'll talk when I get home. I have to go. I love you," Dan told her.

"I know, I love you too," Grace answered and hung up.

"I don't know about you, but I'm going to turn in early. First thing in the morning we have to go to the library," Dan announced after hanging up the phone.

"Why the library?" Ted asked.

"Hopefully we'll be able to find old newspaper articles about Emily's abduction. It's a start," he said.

Leonard and Elizabeth headed for the living room. "Good idea. I wish I'd thought of it," Leonard said.

Jon followed behind Ted and Angela as they turned out the lights and headed upstairs. "You should take a pain pill before lying down. It'll help you rest."

Angela didn't answer. She nodded her head and went to her room.

"Good night," Ted's smile was weak.

The house was still. Dan and Jon left the door to Brittney's closet open.

"I had no idea what I was going to do if you didn't come back," Jon admitted.

Dan smiled. "I would have found a way to come back, even if you were the only one who would be able to see me."

"Now, you're giving me the creeps. That would have been a heavy burden to carry," Jon said.

"I can't explain why I did it," Dan said. "I wasn't behaving logically. When I was in that closet with her, I felt every one of Emily's emotions. It was incredible; her sadness, her fear, her anger, even her denial in the end. It was so strong. Did you ever walk into a room full of people and feel completely alone?" Dan asked, and then he stopped abruptly. "I'm tired. I want to sleep now. We'll start looking for Emily's bones in the morning."

Jon nodded. "Hopefully, the morning will have cleared away some of the bleak, oppressive atmosphere she brought back with her."

"The only way that's going to happen is for us to find her remains and find out who and where her parents are," Dan replied.

Jon looked seriously at his brother. "Don't forget about Brittney. She is the real victim here."

For what it's worth...I hope I can help Emily escape from the hell she's been dwelling in for the past sixty years," Dan said.

Chapter Fifty-Three

The library was located in a musty old building that was shared with the town museum. The old grey stone building held a lot of vintage charm. When they entered the decorative wooden doors, Dan, Jon and the Michaels family were greeted with mixed smells of old books and pine.

The librarian seated behind the dark, cherry wood desk was a beautiful young woman. Her jet-black hair was pulled back in a snug ponytail and her complexion could be compared to a fine porcelain doll.

It was no wonder that Dan froze when she glanced up at him with a sinister warning in her gaze. He saw the depth of her soul in that moment, but kept it to himself and shook off the slithering chill. There was definitely something that attracted Dan to her, but he knew that it wasn't her striking looks.

"Hello, my name is Sherry. Is there something I can help you with?" The librarian smiled and pointedly directed her question to Dan, who appeared to be the spokesman for the group.

"We're here to do some research," he began. "We'd like to look at some newspaper articles from the summer of 1947."

"Everything we have dating that far back would be on microfilm." Sherry rose and continued to speak as she led them towards the back of the library. "Is there something specific you're looking for?" She opened the door leading to the basement. "Not too many people go down here anymore. Everything is open to the public, however. You're welcome to search through everything we have."

"We're looking for information about a little girl that was abducted from a carnival here in town. It happened back in 1947." Angela got right to the point as they carefully walked down the creaky old stairs.

"I hope the lighting is good enough down here," Sherry said. "This building is a historical landmark."

Elizabeth wrinkled her nose. "It smells musty."

Sherry smiled. "That's why we don't store books in this part of the library. It's an old cellar and there isn't too much we can do about it."

"If you'll just show us where to look, we'll take it from there," Dan said, anxious to get started.

Sherry glanced at the large bandage on Angela's hand. She pulled out a wooden chair and offered her a seat in front of one of the viewfinders.

"That looks like it really hurts," Sherry added with a sly smirk.

"Yes, it does." Angela guarded her hand.

"This is the section you need to look through. I hope it speeds up the search a little," Sherry offered.

Sherry took her time and explained where everything was and instructed them on how to use the viewfinders. "Help yourself; we're open until nine o'clock. I'll be up front if you need anything." She disappeared up the stairs and the door clicked shut behind her.

Dan sat down in front of one of the viewfinders. "Ted, start taking down the microfilm by dates, if you will. I'll load this thing up and we can start scanning the articles. The date on the flyer I found at the carnival was June twenty eighth, nineteen forty-seven."

A chill swept across the back of Angela's neck. "June twenty eighth is Brittney's birthday." No one commented.

Ted began searching through the rows of microfilm. "Dad, can you and Mom start pulling out the next group? There's an awful lot of material here."

Elizabeth jumped at the chance to help. "I'll go through the ones on the lower shelf and Dad can get the ones above me." The older woman pulled out her glasses and began her search. Everyone worked quickly and quietly.

"This is incredible," Jon said. "I didn't realize they kept all this stuff."

Dan scanned through several different articles from the year nineteen forty-seven. He read each one carefully and if there was one that was interesting or amusing, he would try to share it. It broke the monotony of the search.

"Has anyone found anything yet?" Angela asked as she continued to dig through the musty old cartons.

"So far, I've only seen articles about gangsters and alcohol," Dan said. "Hey, wait a minute. Listen to this. The annual carnival was held again at Wormwood Park. It was a lengthy run that began over the Memorial Day weekend and extended to June twenty eighth."

"It sounds like you found something," Angela said.

Dan believed that he had stumbled on the beginning of what they were looking for. "I thought it was going to explain what happened to Emily, but it only mentions the search, the closing of the carnival and the tearing down of the merry-go-round."

"Damn it, I know how her parents felt. I saw them. No article can describe the anguish Emily's parents went through." Dan pushed back his chair and stood up abruptly.

Elizabeth nudged Leonard and tipped her head toward Angela. Her face was drawn with torment. "We can't quit now. What about our torment? What about Brittney?"

A cassette jumped out from the bottom row, hitting Elizabeth in the knee. "Ouch! Where did that come from?" She bent to rub her knee and spotted the cassette on the floor between her feet.

"Well, I'll be darned." She picked it up, turned it over and read the faded sticker out loud. "June twenty eighth to July fifth, nineteen forty-seven. This might be what we're looking for."

Ted quickly snatched it out of her hand. "This has to be it." He fumbled with the case in an attempt to get at the microfilm inside. The raw anxiety in his eyes made Angela all the more excited.

"Here, let me do that," Dan offered and calmly took the cassette from Ted's clumsy fingers. He easily slipped the microfilm out of its case. "I hope this is it."

Dan set up his machine and everyone listened as he began to read aloud. "Charles and Sarah Thatcher refuse to believe that their young daughter Emily was not found during the intense search of the merry-go-round which led to the closing of the carnival. Emily Thatcher was reported missing on the twenty-eighth day of June from the revolving carousel that was located at Wormwood Park. At present, she's been missing a full week with no ransom note or leads. The Thatchers acquired a court order forcing the carnival to be shut down. The merry-go-round was disassembled; ordered by its owner. The ride is being held on a relative's property in a pole barn until the child is found. He is quoted as stating, 'The ride will not be reassembled until Emily is back with her parents.'

The search was extended to Lake Michigan, north east of town. Charles and Sarah Thatcher are offering a reward for information leading to the whereabouts of their five-year-old daughter, Emily. Anyone wanting to remain anonymous may contact the Thatchers through a post office box that will be posted daily in the newspaper for anyone wishing to volunteer information pertinent to this case."

Angela spoke first. "It certainly sounds like Emily was taken from the same park where the carnival is set up this year. There's only one park in town," she said. "It was Emily's fifth birthday too." She closed her eyes and let out a shuddering breath of air. "Is that all it says?" she begged. "Did they ever find her? Please tell me they found Emily."

"Here's something interesting. It's an article from a year after the incident," Dan said, interrupting Angela and realizing that he was venturing on thin ice.

"This might just give us some sort of lead. We can only hope that after a whole year of investigating, they at least have something to report," Jon said.

"For one thing, it says that they changed the name of the park from Wormwood to Willows," Dan read. "So, you're right about it being the same park, Angela."

"I was afraid of that," she shook her head.

Dan continued. "It also says that the Thatchers were so devastated over their loss that when their second child was born, they asked that the park be renamed."

"Thatcher is Mom's maiden name," Jon broke in.

"What does that have to do with anything? We would have heard something about Emily by now," Dan said quickly and leaned back in his chair.

"Yeah, you're right. Mom was an only child," Jon said.

Dan thought for a moment. "Actually, Mom did have an older sister that died before she was born."

"How do you know?" Jon asked.

"Right before I left for the seminary, we had a long talk. Mom didn't know much about her sister because Granny and Grandpa didn't talk about her. I thought it was weird, but I didn't see any reason to press the issue," Dan answered.

"Did your mother know how her sister died?" Angela asked.

"If she did, she didn't mention it," Dan said.

"Could it be possible that Emily Thatcher was Mom's sister?" Jon asked. Everyone's eyes turned to Dan. There was a deathly moment of silence.

"Think about it, Dan. No one ever said much about Mom's family. I didn't even know she had a sister. The dates sure do fit if Granny was pregnant with Mom when her first child was kidnapped. We might have stumbled on something," Jon searched his brother's face.

"Or maybe not," Leonard added. "Then again, taking care of Angela that day in the ER might have been a part of Emily's plan."

Dan thought about it. "It sounds crazy. It's too enormous a coincidence. But, I wouldn't put it past Emily to be capable of dragging us into all this."

"Emily's here," Angela gasped.

"I see her," Dan said.

"She scares me," Angela said.

"The more you search, the more you learn." Emily moved toward Dan. Her eyes squinted tightly as if she were looking directly into a bright light.

"Our time is getting short. If my soul isn't put to rest soon, I will need a body to harbor my wandering spirit." Emily's voice was deep and throaty, unlike that of a child.

Dan tried looking at Emily through the bright light she was standing in. He couldn't tell if she was actually outside or inside of his body.

Suddenly, her voice sounded as if it were in his head. It felt like a soft feather, being pulled out of his ear as her words brushed against his cheek. "Odd, isn't it? Let's not sit idle or all will be lost."

There was a deep sadness in her voice as Emily faded back into the darkness of his thoughts. The utter gentleness of her action pulled Dan closer to her and at that moment, he wanted to know her.

Chapter Fifty-Four

The musty, stale, odor of the antiquated library basement harbored an eerie coolness that reminded Dan of the cabin they used to go to at the lake when he was a boy. Though the memories were good, there was an odd premonition that would send him home with unexplainable nightmares, lasting for weeks. His own parish priest, Father Luke Phillips brushed it off as attention seeking when he tried to talk to him about it when he was about fourteen years old. Dan brushed the thought away.

He was no longer in control of the viewfinder where they searched for information about Emily Thatcher. The articles flew past him in a blurred mass. All were newsworthy, but to Emily, they were nothing more than boring stories.

Suddenly the screen froze. The article in front of Dan instantly increased in size and posed, ready to be shared. Emily's life and death was an open-end book with no closure.

Dan read aloud. "It's been over a year since the abduction of Emily Thatcher, daughter of Charles and Sarah Thatcher. A horrible string of events followed her abduction. Five more children, of the same age, vanished in the surrounding area and still, there are no suspects. They appear to have simply disappeared without a single clue. Hopes of ever finding any of them are slim to none."

"That doesn't prove that Brittney is with all of those missing children, does it?" Angela asked through tears and hysteria.

Dan didn't answer; he didn't know.

Ted wrapped his arms around Angela, his own fears weakening him. "Have we learned anything?" Ted asked.

Dan let out a sigh. "That guy dressed as a monk holds some important answers. He has secrets that need to be revealed."

"Shouldn't he be about Granny and Granddad's age?" Jon was trying to put the pieces together.

"I don't really know." Dan sounded irritated and turned to Jon. "What do you think about the possibility of our mother actually being Emily's sister?"

"What do you mean? Why would it matter?" Jon was surprised that Dan brought it up in front of the Michaels' family. "I thought we agreed that it would be too great a coincidence for something like that to be true."

Emily appeared directly behind Dan and stepped forward into his body. The small features of a beautiful child appeared like a projected image over Dan's face. No one moved. Jon noticed how the dimple in Dan's cheek and the one in Emily's cheek lined up perfectly. He couldn't tell if it belonged to Dan or Emily. Her ghost had taken over his body.

Everyone kept still, afraid for Dan. Jon maintained his distance but challenged the invading spirit. "Damn it! What do you want, Emily? We know who you are and what happened to you. So what is it you want us to do with this information?"

Emily had walked into Dan's body without his permission. She attempted to force Dan out of his mortal shell, but he put his soul to sleep and she couldn't reach him in his dream like state.

"Can't we talk without you being in there? You have no business invading his body. He didn't invite you," Jon demanded.

That was the way it was supposed to be. A spirit shouldn't be able to take over a living person's body without their permission. However, Emily was strong enough to defy the spiritual laws.

"Where's Brittney Michaels? You aren't planning on taking over her body, are you? Her parents are here to fight you. You saw how strong Angela's bond is with her daughter. You'll never be able to succeed with that plan," Jon continued to question Emily.

The librarian entered the room just as Emily began to speak. She watched silently from the door, fascinated by the events taking place and unwilling to interrupt.

Angela approached Dan's body as he sat upright in the chair. It was the eyes that terrified her. They were opened, but they were the eyes of someone who was in a deep sleep.

"Please tell me where Brittney is," she pleaded with the fragmented spirit.

Everyone felt a breeze that carried the scent of popcorn and cotton candy that over powered the dank smell of the basement.

Angela cried. "There's just no reasoning with her."

Emily's voice bellowed from Dan's open mouth, repeating her demands. "Give me peace, Dan Markos. It is up to you to find my mortal remains and lay me to rest."

Emily's spirit exited Dan's body as easily as it had entered. When she vanished,

Dan slumped down in his chair.

A loud thump caused everyone to turn. The young librarian had fainted and hit the floor. Jon moved quickly to her side and cradled her head in his lap. "I think she's just dazed." He heard her moan and watched her shallow breaths. Sherry moaned and opened her eyes slowly. Jon's face hovered over her. When their eyes met, he had the uncomfortable feeling that she was hiding something.

"I'm sorry, I didn't mean to walk in on whatever it was you were doing. By the way, what were you doing?" The young woman sat herself up and looked at everyone who was gathered around her.

"What is it you think you saw?" Dan asked.

"There was some sort of ghost. Am I right? It looked like a little girl," Sherry said.

Angela became very defensive. "It isn't any of your business. It's our problem and we're taking care of it." She turned to Ted. "Do something. We can't let her ruin this. We have to find Brittney."

Angela's words frightened Sherry. "What are you people talking about? What are you up to? Who's Brittney?" The librarian was able to get to her feet. She backed away from the group of strangers.

Dan quickly intervened. "Don't get the wrong impression. These are good people. They're just trying to find out about someone who was abducted many years ago. She's somehow related to us and we're simply interested in what happened to her."

"I saw something," Sherry said.

Jon stepped over to Angela. "None of us saw anything, did we?"

"That's right. It would be your word against all of ours. I'd advise you to mind your own business and forget what you think you saw here," Ted spoke firmly.

Sherry took a step backward toward the stairs. She started to climb and stopped. "I understand. You don't have to worry about me. I just work here." Before leaving, she looked at Dan and spoke to him with her mind. "I saw what I needed to see."

No one else heard her last thought. They all followed the young woman up to the main floor of the library and left quietly.

The air outside was refreshing. "You don't think she'll be a problem, do you?" Jon asked Dan as they headed for the car.

"There's nothing we can do about her if she does say something. Who's going to believe her anyway?" Dan said.

Everyone agreed that bigger problems lay ahead. "I have an idea," Dan said as he squeezed into the back seat next to Elizabeth. "Let's go to the carnival. I want to see the merry-go-round. I'll tell you if it's the same one I saw when Emily took me back in time. If it is, we might be able to find out more there."

"Good idea," Leonard said.

"Have these ghosts actually attached themselves to us?" Elizabeth asked.

"I think there's a reason that we've all been brought together, whether it be temporarily as a pawn or for her further use. It just surprises me, how much power these spirits hold," Dan answered.

Elizabeth continued. "I read once that ghosts can actually attach themselves to a living person for their convenience."

"I believe that's true," Dan said. "It's one of the arguments I maintained with the Catholic Church. But, I also believe that they are selective on their choice of individuals. They need someone with familiar qualities or who are personally appealing to them for their purpose."

"What does Emily want with Brittney?" Angela asked.

Leonard sounded tired when he spoke. "There's a single thread connecting all of us now. It's a stitch in our lives that Emily has woven and manipulated with great skill. Whatever strength I have left, I will spend on saving my granddaughter."

"That's very intuitive," Dan said. "What we have to remember is, at any time, Emily can pull on that silky string of life she was somehow able to dangle us from and create more chaos."

"Hopefully this whole ordeal isn't simply for her entertainment," Ted added.

Angela turned around from the passenger's seat up front and faced Dan. Reaching back, she covered his hand with her own. "No matter how this turns out, I want you to know how grateful we are to you for coming all this way to help us. I feel like I'm losing my mind." Her eyes softened.

"I appreciate you recognizing why we're here," Jon added.

"Let's stop at the house, I'll make something to eat while everyone gathers what they need," Elizabeth suggested.

"I need to get something for pain before we go to the park," Angela added.

The wheels were in motion. The Michaels family had been introduced to the netherworld, a dead zone, neither heaven nor hell, a place for bodiless souls.

Dan leaned his head back. He realized there would be no more restful moments for him until this was settled. The cold, icy breeze that covered his face assured him that Emily was still close by. Her subtle reminders would keep him on track until he was somehow able to calm Emily's spirit and help her soul to cross over.

Chapter Fifty-Five

When they entered the park, the now familiar, melodic tune coming from the merry-go-round echoed through the trees like hundreds of gentle, angelic voices.

Dan could feel Emily's excitement. It seemed to flow through him, stimulating all his senses.

"I believe Emily is happy that someone actually knows what happened to her," Dan said hopefully.

"She should be. I'm just wondering why she avoided going into the light in the first place," Jon added. "That part bothers me."

Dan kept his thoughts to himself so as not to confuse and distract everyone. Deep down, he knew he was the one Emily was searching for all along. She would stop at nothing to get what she wanted, but he still didn't know what that was.

They headed in the direction of the merry-go-round. Dan's legs felt heavy. Each step was becoming a chore. He didn't want to complain, because he wasn't sure what was happening.

"Angels or other beings of The Light assist souls to find their way, but for some reason, Emily resisted."

"What?" Jon asked.

"Oh nothing, I was just thinking," Dan said.

"You know, what happened to you in the library was really creepy, Dan,"

Jon whispered. "Shit, Emily was able to walk right into your body and use you. It was the most disturbing thing I ever saw."

"I know. I was in there watching her and unable to do anything about it," Dan replied. "What bothers me more is the fact that I didn't allow it. Two souls have to agree to something like that. It was too easy for her."

The merry-go-round loomed ahead. It was more magnificent than Dan had remembered. "I hate to think of what might happen if we don't fulfill Emily's demands."

Dan focused on the carousel as he headed towards it with a driven force. "I'm sure that this is exactly the same merry-go-round I saw Emily riding when her abduction took place," he exclaimed. "I know it's the same tune. It gives me strength to know that I'm the one capable of meeting this challenge."

The others followed. Ted and Angela were hoping they would find Brittney. Each wooden figure passed gracefully in time to the music. It was hypnotic, watching the horses take turns going up and down in perfect synchronized rhythm, methodically moving and alternating between rows. In the small spaces separating the horses, Dan spotted a little girl standing in the inner circle of the ride.

He spoke calmly. "Angela. Come here."

"What is it? What do you see?" she slipped up beside Dan and gazed from one horse to another, searching each character for Brittney.

"Don't move too quickly. I want you to look past the horses and tell me if that's Brittney standing in the center of the ride." Dan tried to remain calm so as not to panic Angela.

Angela looked past the horses to the center of the carousel. She nodded her head vigorously affirming Dan's discovery.

"What do we do?" The words stuck in her throat. Her chest heaved as she tried to stifle her cries.

"You do nothing. I'm going to try to get to her," Dan instructed. He never took his eyes off the child. "Don't tell the others yet. I'm sorry, but I don't want Ted rushing in and doing something foolish and you know he will. Stand here and watch me. Please, you have to trust me with this."

It was hard, but Angela nodded and continued to stare at Brittney as she desperately repressed the urge to run after her daughter. Her body shook from head to toe with adrenaline racing through her veins like a line of gasoline catching fire. "I'm here, Brittney. Mommy's here," she whispered frantically.

Dan stepped forward and Angela took hold of his arm. "Just so you know, I'm not leaving here without her." She released her hold and Dan leapt onto the moving carousel.

He grabbed hold of a pole to steady himself after boarding the platform. The ride began to pick up speed.

Dan tried to create a mental picture as he worked his way toward the inner circle of the merry-go-round. His thoughts played havoc with him. Father Luke Phillips came to mind. His judgmental and biased words came flooding back. Dan tried to shake the thought. "I have to concentrate on what I'm here for. I'll have to deal with him when this is over."

The merry-go-round was picking up speed uncomfortably. Dan tightened his grip on each pole. The muscles flexed in his arms as he continued to move between the horses. The closer he maneuvered himself to his objective, the faster the ride spun.

The mirrors on the inner structure reflected off the lights in a blinding array of colors. Dan had to avert his eyes from their intensity, but he didn't want to lose sight of Brittney. "Why are you doing this Emily? Why won't you let me get to her?" he called out. With each step forward, wind hit him in the face with a breath-snatching force. He bowed his head and plowed through.

"Brittney Michaels!" Dan tried calling to her.

The other children on the ride screamed in horror as the run-a-way carousel went faster and faster. The bigger children were hanging on tightly. Adults clung desperately to the smaller riders. The wooden horses became animated, barring their teeth and turning their heads from side to side. Their coats gleamed with what appeared to be sweat.

On the ground surrounding the ride, parents, spectators and workers were a blur. Dan could no longer see Brittney. Emily's image blocked his view.

"Stop it Emily," Dan yelled against the forces driving him back. "Why are you fighting me?" His goal at this point was to make it to the inner circle. With one courageous leap, Dan flung himself off the ride. He hit the ground hard and tumbled swiftly into one of the mirrored panels. Stunned for a moment, he assessed himself and decided nothing was broken. He sat up and waited a moment before trying to get up.

The operating attendant, who was in the center of the ride, rushed over to him. "Why'd you do such a stupid thing? Are you hurt?"

Dan accepted the young man's assistance in getting to his feet before he countered. "Why'd you let that ride get out of control like that? Don't you have a way to slow it down?"

The carnival worker backed away from Dan. "I did. I was taking care of the problem when I saw you fly off the ride like some sort of maniac!" He defended himself while sizing Dan up.

Remembering Brittney, Dan spun around and started searching for her. "Where's the little girl that was standing in here?" he asked.

"What little girl? No one is allowed in the center of this ride but me. You must have hit your head. I sit over there and control the merry-go-round so bozos like you don't mess around and get hurt."

The carousel attendant nervously looked around for help. Dan held up his hands to show that he meant him no harm. "Listen, I saw a little girl standing in here. If you don't believe me, ask her mother. I was trying to get to her."

The young man backed away from Dan. "I have to stop this ride."

Dan turned his attentions back to locating Brittney. He cupped his hands around his mouth. "Brittney! Answer me."

The ride had slowed to almost a complete stop. While the music continued to play, the young man operating the carousel jumped on to the slowing ride to assist children and parents off the horses and directed them to the exit. Dan went to the control box. It looked just like the one he saw on the merry-go-round from almost sixty years ago.

Ted and Angela joined Dan in the center of the carousel. They were out of breath and frazzled.

"Where's Jon?" Dan asked.

"He went to find out who the owner of this thing is," Ted answered. "What are you doing in here? I couldn't believe what just happened. I'm surprised no one was killed."

Dan turned to Ted. "I'm looking for Brittney. We thought she might be somewhere on the merry-go-round." He looked at Angela. Her eyes were wide and she was staring with her mouth opened. Dan followed her line of vision and saw what had caused her to freeze.

Ted, Angela and Dan stood in front of one of the plated mirrors. Instead of seeing their own reflections looking back at them, they saw Brittney standing with Emily and the group of strange little girls.

Disturbing emotions and dark images swirled in each of them and clouded their thoughts. Ted pounded on the glass in an attempt to get to his daughter.

"Stop it," Dan ordered. "It's just an illusion. Emily is using it to intimidate you. She's causing you to react irrationally. When you're out of control, she can step in and take charge. We have to use our heads and figure out a way to get Brittney back without disturbing the realm she was sent to as a living, breathing person. Your daughter is alive and walking among the dead."

Chapter Fifty-Six

Dan, Ted and Angela stood in the center of the merry-go-round gaping into the mirrors at their daughter with Emily and the other little girls when an officer approached them.

"What are you people doing in here?" he asked.

Dan instantly took over the conversation. He was sweating and out of breath from the whole ordeal, but he knew he had to think quickly and get them out of there.

"I was helping these people get their little girl off the merry-go-round. That could have been quite a catastrophe. They thought she fell off her horse and I offered to assist them," Dan said.

Emily and the other children were watching from inside the mirrors. No one but Dan, Jon, Ted and Angela were able to see them.

"I'm sorry. I thought my little girl was in danger. I panicked and these gentlemen helped me," Angela added.

"Where's the child now?" the officer asked.

Ted was surprised at how easy it was for Angela to fabricate a story. Being visibly shaken up from seeing Brittney in the mirror convinced the officer that her statement was viable. Angela behaved like a typical hysterical mom. "I sent my daughter to the car with my parents. We stuck around to see if there was anything we could do to help."

"We can handle it from here. Everyone has to clear the area so we can get someone in here to find out what happened. The ride is closed," the officer said and waited for them to leave.

Dan looked back at the mirrors. The children were gone. However, before they left, he noticed an indentation. It was definitely a handle of some sort. *There is a door! Why didn't I see it before? I can't chance sticking around. We'll have to come back later tonight after the carnival closes.* Dan held his thoughts close.

"Let's go," he said. Jon walked in front of him. Dan would have to keep the knowledge of the handle to himself until they were far away from everyone at the scene.

Angela thanked Dan openly for the sake of appearance in front of the officers. She took Ted by the arm and led him away from the ride.

A loud clap of thunder exploded, followed by a drop of rainwater. Everyone picked up their pace as they headed for the parking lot where Leonard and Elizabeth were already waiting.

Once in the car, Angela began to cry. "We aren't leaving, are we? You saw Brittney in that mirror, I know you did."

"Of course I saw her. I saw Emily and the other children too, but we can't do anything about it right now. Jon needs to tell us if he found out anything when he went snooping around about the merry-go-round and we need to stop by my parents' house to ask my mom a few questions," Dan spoke as if he had everything planned out.

"What about Brittney? We know where she is. We can't leave her here," Angela cried. Ted sat in the driver's seat waiting for Dan's response.

"We have to be very careful not to arouse any suspicion. No one will believe us if we try to tell them the truth about what's actually going on. I realize how you feel. But first, we need to gather some vital information and we have to wait for everyone to leave this place for the night. Then, we'll come back together, after dark," Dan said firmly.

Angela glanced back toward the merry-go-round. "I'll be back Brittney. Now that I know where you are, nothing will keep me away." She buried her face in her hands.

Dan saw the strange black woman dressed in a long-flowering, African-looking garment. She was wearing a vibrant, multicolored headscarf. The woman glanced back over her shoulder and nodded her head with a peaceful smile that barely creased her lips as she headed through the trees toward the merry-go-round and vanished right before his eyes.

Chapter Fifty-Seven

The rain poured out of the sky, coming down in sheets. Angela leaned her head on the window and let the beating raindrops lull her. "I'm going home without Brittney. I can't believe it. What kind of mother am I?"

"I know what you think you saw, Angela," Dan began. "It wasn't real. If there were something solid for us to grab on to, we would have had your daughter. You know that."

Angela didn't hear a word he said. All she could think about was her loss. "I feel like a part of me has been ripped away."

"Your wounds will heal with time. What about mine? Where do I find justice?" Emily's voice left a trail of unrest with Angela.

When they reached the Michaels home, Dan and Jon got out and went over to Jon's car. "We'll see you later. Jon and I are going home for a short visit and I'm going to talk to my mother about our grandparents."

"What about them?" Jon asked.

"I need to find out if Emily is related to Mom. If she is, then it will explain a lot about why we were dragged into this whole ordeal," Dan said to Jon. "I have to find out what it is Emily is really after."

Ted helped Angela and his mother out of the car. Elizabeth leaned over to Ted. "It looks like that cut is bothering Angela again. I hate to say anything to her because she's so defensive right now."

Ted nodded and gently took her arm and led Angela to the house.

"See you soon." Ted waved at Dan and Jon.

"I can make you some chamomile tea if you'd like, Angie," Elizabeth said as she followed them into the house.

"Thanks Mom. That would be nice," Angie said.

Dan and Jon waved at the sorrowful family. Dan rolled down the window. "Don't worry, we won't be long. Be ready to go to the park as soon as we get back."

Leonard stayed outside. "I'll be right in," he said. He watched Dan and Jon drive away. A head of blond curls turned slowly from the backseat of their car. Instead of seeing the face that should have been a beautiful child, Leonard witnessed the sunken, hollow dark pits that glared at him from a withered, skeletal head.

"What is your motive, little girl? All I see right now is rampant malevolence." It was difficult for Leonard to rid himself of the look on Emily's face when she peered at him from the Marcos's car. Leonard tapped his pipe on the side of the porch before returning it to his pocket and quickly went into the house. He locked the door as if by doing that, he could keep Emily out.

"Is everything okay?" Elizabeth asked. She was waiting for Leonard when he came into the house. "If you want to go home, we can. I don't want you getting sick. You look like you just saw a ghost."

Leonard smiled at his wife's keen observation. He didn't answer. There was nothing more to be said. It wasn't over, Emily would be back.

Chapter Fifty-Eight

As soon as they were down the street and away from the Michael's house, Jon jumped all over Dan.

"What the hell do Granny and Grandpa have to do with Emily? Mom doesn't know anything, Dan. You can't drag her into this. She's too weak. I don't want her involved with Emily."

The thought of Emily being related to his mother had been weighing heavily on Dan's mind. "Think about it. We didn't have any cousins or family of any kind on Mom's side, just Granny and Grandpa. I asked Mom about it before I moved to Italy."

"What'd you ask her?" Jon questioned.

"I asked her if she had any sisters or brothers," Dan said.

"And..." Jon pressed.

"She told me that she had a sister that died before she was born, but she didn't know anything about her," Dan said.

"Didn't she know what her sister died of? Wasn't she even interested? I mean, come on," Jon couldn't understand why his mother wouldn't have wanted to know more about her sister. "What was the big secret? Even if she had been kidnapped, Mom should have known about it."

"You know, it was a long time ago and I really don't remember the entire conversation. I actually didn't care why she died and forgot all about it," Dan admitted.

"So that was all she said?" Jon asked.

"That was all that was said; however she did go on about how she was raised very strictly. She wasn't able to leave the yard as a kid and couldn't even date in high school," Dan recalled.

Jon wasn't settling for any of it. "It was just that period of time. Girls were all sheltered back then."

"Now that I think about it, I feel very strongly that there was more to it. Here's what I seriously think," Dan began. "Mom's sister was Emily Thatcher. It isn't a coincidence that we were brought into this mess with the Michaels family. If what I assume is true, we are Emily's nephews and she feels that Mom owes her."

"And why is that?" Jon asked.

"Mom lived," Dan answered simply.

"That's scary," Jon said. "Who do you think that guy in the monk outfit is?" Jon realized that monks and priests were a touchy subject in the Markos household. He didn't want to offend his brother.

"Our hooded visitor is most likely the one who kidnapped and possibly murdered Emily. He's the epitome of evil. I really feel that the cloak was just a cover up to mask his real intentions. It was a disguise. Whoever is under that cloak is NOT a real priest. What a freak to use the order to hide his criminal behavior."

"What now? What do you think brought her back?" Jon asked.

"I don't know, but I don't think it was him," Dan answered. "Emily is the one who wants justice. Somehow, she was able to break free from his hold. I hate to say it, but I think Mom might have some answers. She just might be in the one who's in danger."

Dan's revelation frightened Jon. "That's a lot to think about. If that's the case, we have to do something."

"Did you learn anything about the merry-go-round when you checked on it at the information tent?" Dan asked.

"First, I asked the guy working there, who the owner of the merry-go-round was," Jon said.

"What'd he say?" Dan pressed.

"This girl that was standing behind him, acted like I was some sort of spy or something. She whipped around like she'd heard a gunshot and started questioning me like I wanted to buy the thing," he answered. "It was really weird. She wanted to know what I intended to do with the information and made me feel very uncomfortable. She sounded paranoid now that I think about it. Why would she care? She just worked there."

"I take it you didn't confront her about her response?" Dan asked.

Jon hesitated before he went on. "Funny thing about that girl, she looked like the same woman we met at the library. You, know, the librarian Sherry?"

"I don't see how that could be possible. We left her at the library. She was working," Dan said. "You have to be mistaken. Did the girl at the carnival ever tell you who owned the merry-go-round?"

"If it was the same person as the one we met at the library, she acted like she never saw me before. But I'm telling you, Dan, it was her," Jon insisted.

"How can you be so sure?" Dan asked.

"For one thing, she knew all about Emily being abducted and how the owner had the ride disassembled and put into storage. She said the pole barn is still standing. It's the one by Welby's meat market," Jon said. "She actually got into it after all that rudeness and talked about everything like it was an urban legend. There were other people staying to listen to her story. It was actually very bizarre."

"I know just where that meat market is. Didn't they have a big fire out there?" Dan asked. "I thought I saw something about it when we were scanning the articles in the library. It was right after the carousel was put in storage that someone tried to burn the place down. I guess they tried breaking into the pole barn first and when they couldn't get in, they decided to torch the place. Fortunately, the fire never reached the merry-go-round and all it suffered was some smoke damage," Dan recalled.

"According to the woman at the carnival today, the merry-go-round was new at the time it was taken apart," Jon continued. "She also said that it was a one of a kind. In fact, it was the only one in the country with the one piece, mirrored center."

"She said that?" Dan asked.

"I can't remember everything, but she did mention the fact that the owner of the carousel didn't own the pole barn. The building belonged to a relative."

"I wonder why that would make a difference. He didn't have anything to hide. Was there anything else?" Dan documented everything Jon told him on a small tablet he kept in his shirt pocket.

"I wonder if our hooded friend started that fire."

"He certainly had motive. Whatever he was trying to get rid of might still be in the center of that ride. There has to be a way to get behind those mirrors and I might just know how to do it," Dan said.

"I wonder who she is and why she would know so much about it." Dan said. "It doesn't make any sense that someone who wasn't close to the situation would be that informed. If it was the same woman that we saw at the library, it wouldn't be just a coincidence that she was at both places during our investigation," Dan analyzed.

Jon continued telling about his experience exactly how he remembered it. "She even knew that the guy who owns the merry-go-round now is from Chicago. He bought it at an auction recently and renovated it before setting it up at Willows Park. She said that she personally watched them reassemble the merry-go-round and mentioned how worried she was about them accidentally breaking one of the mirrors. They used a huge crane to place the center structure where it sets and she claimed that it's all one piece," Jon concluded.

Dan listened intently. "Right now, my main concern is with the door leading inside of the central mirrored section. I'm sure it isn't just a decoration. We have to get in there tonight," Dan said. He was thinking about the handle he saw.

"We also have to find out what, if anything, Mom knows about Emily." Dan arched his eyebrows. "I'm almost certain they're sisters. There's even a slim chance that Mom knows what happened to her. Hopefully, she'll be able to tell us something."

"Have you lost your mind? I don't think so," Jon said. "Mom has such a gentle spirit. She couldn't know anything about Emily. If she did, she would have talked about her."

"We'll see. Mom might not realize how much information she has. Even though she never talked about Emily, Mom might be able to recall something she overheard as a child. You know how kids are? If they were really sisters, then Granny should have had a picture or something belonging to Emily. I'm almost certain that Mom will know something," Dan concluded.

Dan didn't mention the ghostly vision of a little girl sitting in the seat behind Jon's with her long blond curls and lifeless eyes. He knew that Emily could read his mind. Her spirit was not at rest. She was there for some sort of closure.

It wasn't your fault, Emily... You were only a little girl.

Chapter Fifty-Nine

Jon used his key to open the front door of his parent's house. Robert Markos was sitting in front of the television watching a baseball game and eating popcorn.

"Your mom is in the den going through boxes of old photos. You two might want to leave your shoes by the front door," he reminded them.

"Sure dad. Who's winning?" Jon asked while kicking off his shoes.

"Well, you know it isn't the Cubs," he chuckled. Robert was a die-hard Cubs fan. He watched every game they played through thick and thin, always wearing his worn out Cubs hat. Grace didn't like him wearing it in the house, but that didn't matter if a game was in progress.

Jon laughed, walked into the den, grabbed a big throw pillow from the love seat and plopped down next to his mother. "What're you looking at Mom?" Grace was sitting with her legs curled to the side of her on the floor, going through a box of old snapshots.

"Your timing is perfect. I'm so glad you're both here. You're just in time to go through some old photographs with me," she exclaimed. "Come on Danny sit down. I'm putting them in different stacks according to who's in them and when they were taken."

Dan noticed that off to the side were some older pictures that he hadn't seen before. "Who are these people, Mom?" he asked and picked up the pile of black and white snapshots.

Grace glanced up. "Let me see," she said and began to examine the well-preserved photographs.

A smile creased the corners of her mouth. "Why this is your Granny and Grandpa when they were young." Her voice softened and she let out a sigh.

Dan and Jon moved in closer. They looked at each other with great anticipation.

Grace explained who the people were in the photographs as she flipped through them. Interrupting her, Dan reached for one that had slipped from the bottom of the pile. He couldn't take his eyes off the little girl in the photo.

"Look at this, Jon. Who's this Mom? Why haven't we seen these pictures before?" Dan asked.

"They were up in Granny's attic. I couldn't bring myself to go through her personal possessions after she died. It seemed so invasive. I've just recently started taking my time with her things and seeing what I want to keep. What you boys don't want, I'll give to the church," Grace said.

"Do you know who this little girl is?" Dan fished for a name.

Grace held up the print in her hand. "Well, like I said, these two young people are my mother and father. Not quite like you remember them. They were a handsome couple, weren't they?"

Dan leaned over and whispered in Jon's ear. "Those are the two people I saw at the carnival when Emily took me back to 1947. It's true. Emily is mom's sister."

He pursed his lips and patiently waited for his mother to tell him who the little girl with the long blond curls was. "Mom, we need to know who this little girl is. Do you know her name?"

Grace leaned back in the chair, puzzled by her son's abruptness. "My parents suffered a horrendous loss," she began. "I would have had an older sister if Emily didn't disappear."

"Emily Thatcher was your sister?" Dan felt that he was experiencing a complete psychotic breakdown. He laughed out loud. "Unbelievable!"

Grace was oblivious. She stared lovingly at the picture of her parents. "I really do miss them. Especially my father," she said softly. "You know my maiden name was Thatcher. I never knew

Emily. She was gone before I was born. It was such a shame," she said.

"What happened to her?" Dan inquired in a soft tone to encourage her to talk.

"I only heard bits and pieces about it. I remember my father saying that she was exceptionally beautiful. I always wondered how I looked to him, in comparison. That was silly of me." There was a hint of pain in her words. "But, they never discussed her in front of me. On occasion, I overheard them talking. My mother would be crying. That's what usually got my attention."

Grace spoke reverently about Emily. "Your granny wanted to believe that Emily was taken by someone who couldn't have a child of their own and had a lot of love to shower on a beautiful little girl like Emily. By them never finding the body or having a burial, they never actually thought of her as being dead. She was simply missing."

"Did you actually hear Granny say that or is it what you assumed?" Dan asked.

"I suppose it's how I interpreted what I overheard. What difference does it make?" she asked. A prominent v-shaped indentation creased her brow.

"None, I suppose," Jon answered. "What about you? Didn't you ever wonder about her?"

"I don't know, I suppose. But, I'm sure that whoever took Emily, killed her," Grace answered.

"Wow, that's a pretty strong feeling," Dan said.

"Of course, I was young when I first heard about Emily, but even then, I just knew," Grace was solemn.

There was enough adrenaline flowing between Dan and Jon for them both to run a marathon. "I feel like there's a deep dark secret that our family has kept very well hidden. This is incredible. Why haven't we ever heard about Emily before?" Jon asked.

"I guess I never mentioned her, because I didn't know her. I grew up an only child. If anything, I'm the one who felt betrayed when I found out that I had a sister. She was someone I could have grown up with. I'm not saying my parents were negligent. But, I think I had a right to know about her." These were suppressed feelings that Grace had harbored for many years. Jon and Dan were surprised at how easily she expressed them.

The hairs on the back of Dan's neck bristled. He shook from the icy cold feeling of tiny fingers on his back. "I do believe we have company."

Jon quickly looked up. "Mom, you're completely aware of how Dan and I can see dead people, right?"

"And you both know that I don't see anything, I don't want to see anything, and I don't like hearing about it," she replied with a slight tremor in her voice. Grace thought for a moment about the group of little girls that she had seen earlier, huddled on the front porch.

"We know how you feel Mom and we usually don't talk about it in front of you, because we respect your feelings. But, we do have something very important to discuss," Dan said.

"What do you mean? What could I possibly tell you?" The look on his mother's face was worrisome. It made Dan feel sick inside to have to bring up her relationship with Emily. He let out a sigh, realizing at this point, his mother was the only one who could shed some light on the situation.

Dan took hold of his mother's small, age-worn hand. His eyes met hers and at that very moment, he felt so much love for her. "I'm sorry about having to drag you into this and it's totally up to you whether you want to talk about it or not. Neither Jon nor I would ever do anything to intentionally make you uncomfortable. Please, believe me when I say that it's not our intention to cause you any pain or worry. You don't have to answer us if you don't want to, but you just might be able to help us out with the problem we're dealing with in regards to the Michaels family." Dan chose his words carefully.

"It's okay, Danny. I don't understand, but if I can help in any way...it sounds extremely serious," she said softly as she looked back and forth between her sons.

"The Michaels family came to Jon for help after a visit to the hospital when Angela, the mother, was hurt trying to help her daughter," Dan began.

Grace tried to keep an open mind. "What do they have to do with me or my sister?" she asked, totally at a loss.

It sounded odd for Grace to use the phrase, 'my sister', in any tense. Jon jumped in. "The reason Angela was at the hospital was because she had to have a pretty good size piece of glass taken out of her hand from a window that was broke by the ghost of your long lost sister, Emily." The room fell silent for a moment. It sounded completely ludicrous.

Jon continued, "The cut was very serious. If the doctor couldn't get the glass out in the ER, Angela would have had to have surgery. I was her nurse," Jon added.

"Do I know her? Again, what does all this have to do with me?" Grace asked sincerely.

"Emily's spirit was there. She followed Angela to the ER. I saw her," Jon explained.

Grace shuddered. "What makes you think that the ghost you saw was Emily? I'm assuming it was one of those roaming spirits you and your brother are always seeing."

"It was the same little girl as the one in your pictures." He pointed to the black and white photo of Emily with Grace's parents.

Dan held up his hand in the direction of the fireplace. Grace repositioned herself to see what he was looking at. She didn't see anything out of the ordinary.

"What are you doing, Danny?" Grace asked.

"Emily's here, Mom. She's the problem we've been talking about. Emily wants us to find her remains so you can bury them with Granny and Grandpa. I know it sounds unbelievable, but she somehow found her way back from the dead and is walking among the living." Dan was trying to break it to his mother in a gentle way, but there just didn't seem to be a sane or easy way to put it.

Grace leaned forward and whispered, "I never saw her, but I've always felt that Emily was around, especially when Granny was alive. I think my mother had the same gift you and your brother share. When I was a little girl, I would hear her talking to someone when she was alone in her room. It sounded as if she were speaking to a child."

"Why didn't you ever say anything?" Jon asked.

"I don't know. I didn't want to be caught listening. I didn't want to get in trouble," Grace answered. "I remember sometimes looking for my mother. Sometimes she'd be in her bedroom with the door closed. It was those times that I'd sit outside the door and listen to her or if I didn't hear anything, I'd peek in and find her sitting in the rocking chair next to her big oak dresser. Those were some of the rare occasions when she was in her best moods. Sometimes we'd just smile. I even heard her laughing in there."

"How old were you?" Dan asked.

"Oh, I was probably about four or five years old. I wasn't sure who Emily was at that time, but my mother always talked about her in the present tense. Not to me, of course," Grace said.

"Who was she talking to?" Jon asked.

"Herself," Grace answered. "Or so I thought at the time. Your Granny never let Emily's spirit die. She's the one who kept her alive and with her."

"That's why she couldn't cross over," Jon suggested.

Grace pursed her lips and took a deep breath. "It wasn't until I was older that my father told me who Emily was."

"Gosh Mom, that had to be quite a revelation. Didn't you ever want to try to find out what happened to her?" Jon asked.

"Oh no," Grace replied quickly. "Emily was a loving memory that kept my mother sane. I never saw her picture until I was grown and by then, it just didn't seem to matter. I found a large oil painting of her in the back of my mother's closet when I was looking for a pair of boots. I asked Granny who she was and I was told it was a picture of her daughter. Imagine that! Her daughter, not my sister. She took the painting away from me and put it back where I found it. I felt as though I'd discovered a dirty little secret," Grace said.

Grace looked at the photo of Emily and her parents. "Growing up, I had no idea that this little girl was my sister."

"That's pretty strange, Mom," Jon said.

Grace shrugged. "My mother asked me once if I ever saw Emily around. I wasn't sure why she asked me or what she meant. I didn't really know what to say, because I was still clueless about Emily. She told me that she used to see her and talk to her. It was as if she were telling me a wonderful secret. So, I never shared it with anyone. I guess as I got older, I just figured that my mom had lost a little piece of her mind when she lost Emily." Grace folded her hands neatly on her lap. "It scares me to think about it. But now you're telling me that you see Emily too. So, maybe she wasn't so crazy after all."

"So, Granny had the gift of discerning spirits," Dan laughed.

"At least one that I know of," Grace replied. "I suppose if you boys can see ghosts or whatever you want to call them, then no one can say that your Granny was out of her mind."

"Why didn't we ever spend much time with her?" Jon asked.

"We didn't know if we could trust her alone with you boys. Not that I ever felt she would hurt you. Grandpa would never have allowed anything to happen to either of you boys. But, she talked so strangely about Emily the older she got. Your dad figured that she was pleasantly confused and he wouldn't allow you boys to go over without us." Grace spoke matter-of-factly. "They didn't ask to take you places or have you over like most grandparents do and I didn't push it."

"You realize that Granny most likely really saw Emily?" Dan was very excited about what he had just learned. "It's just possible that Granny didn't treat Emily like she was dead, so Emily might not have realized that she was actually a ghost. Granny probably blocked the thought from her mind to save herself from really going insane. I think she was protecting herself in the only way she knew how. You said yourself that Emily's body was never found," Dan said.

"What a legacy to pass on to her grandsons. That makes us like kindred spirits," Jon laughed. "Granny had to know that Emily was a ghost. Heck, she never got any bigger or older. I don't think Granny was nuts. I think she just didn't want to let go and found a way where she didn't have to. Grandpa obviously didn't share the gift of seeing Emily; but he loved Grandma so much that he let her live out her fantasy contently instead of seeing her mourn the loss of her little girl."

"Sounds like a good book," Dan said with a smirk.

"What you say might very well be true. I do know that my mother would never have done anything to send Emily away," Grace pondered the subject.

"That's it!" Dan shouted. "Emily didn't know what to do or where to go when Granny and Grandpa died. She tried going to you, Mom but you couldn't see her. I'm right, aren't I?" Dan felt he had made a huge discovery. "Mom, Emily tried to confide in you, but you don't have second sight and you couldn't see her. You said that you sensed her around though. Her presence was strong enough to be felt, but she couldn't materialize for you. She's stronger now."

"What do you mean?" Grace asked.

"Emily was desperate to find a way to be reunited with your parents, her parents. You were the natural tie. But, when she couldn't get through to you, she did the next best thing," Jon added and looked at Dan with an over exaggerated grin.

"I think you're right. That's where Jon and I come in," Dan spoke sincerely to his mother.

Grace was clutching the small, gold cross that hung from a chain around her neck. "You boys are frightening me."

"Oh Mom, don't be afraid. Be happy for Emily. I'm going to try to help your sister cross over," Dan said. "I'll be able to help the Michaels family return to normal and reunite Emily with your parents and guess what? You're going to help," he smiled.

Grace hadn't seen Dan so excited in a long time. "Where is she? You said Emily was here," Grace asked.

Dan leaned closer to his mother. "Emily, you're stronger now. Can you let your sister hear you? Let her know that you're happy right now."

Dan, Jon and Grace sat quietly listening to the giggling voice of a child. "Can you hear her, Mom?"

"Is that really my sister? Is it Emily?" Tears welled in her eyes. "I feel bad that I can't tell her that I love or miss her. I can't say something that isn't really true. But, I didn't know her," Grace said. "What do I do?"

"Talk to her. You have a once in a lifetime opportunity that may never happen again," Dan encouraged.

"Emily, I don't know you, but you're my sister. I never had the chance to love you. I had to grow up an only child when I could have grown up with you. So, in a way, I was robbed too. I was robbed of knowing you and having a friend to share my life with." Grace couldn't see Emily, but she could hear her laughter. Emily's voice filled the room. It was the same laughter that haunted Grace's dreams while she was growing up. Now she felt comfort in her sister's voice.

"Where is she Danny? Can she hear me?" Grace asked.

"She's standing right in front of you, Mom," Dan said. He moved in close to his mother. For some reason, Dan didn't share the joy in their meeting. Something felt desperately wrong.

Chapter Sixty

Robert poked his head in the doorway to see what everyone was doing. "Why don't we all go to a baseball game one day. It's easier to see on television, but you can't beat the smell of a ball park."

"What do I tell your father?" Grace whispered in Dan's ear. "I don't know how to begin to explain what's going on."

"Then don't," Jon answered abruptly. "Just tell him we're looking at old pictures and visiting shadows of the past."

"What shadows?" Robert walked up behind Dan. He could tell that Grace was upset about something.

"After the boys leave, I'll tell you what's been going on. I think I'd like to try to explain it to you myself," she said.

"We have to go back to the Michaels house after dinner. We'll talk more about this tomorrow." Dan got up and stood next to his father.

"I have a stuffed, roasted chicken with dressing and mashed potatoes in the oven. It should be ready about now." Everyone headed for the kitchen. Grace glanced back to see if she could catch a glimpse of Emily.

Jon saw her and put an arm around his mother's shoulder. "All in good time Mom."

Dinner was delicious and everyone stuffed themselves. Dan asked to be excused, "Thanks Mom; that was incredible, as usual. We really have to be going though." He looked at Jon and glanced at the kitchen clock. It was the same clock that had hung on the wall in his parent's kitchen as long as he could remember. Things just didn't change in their house. The feeling of comfort clung to him as he left the room.

Jon rose and added, "We'll be back. See ya later Dad."

Dan turned and addressed his father. "We don't seem to be having much of a visit. I'm sorry. I promise I'll make it up to you both. Jon and I need to help this family and I feel good about it," he said.

"Then, that's what you should do," Robert smiled at his oldest son. Dan gave his father a big hug.

He left Robert standing quietly on the front porch looking after him. There was a light sheen in Robert's eyes as he watched his sons get into the car.

Dan rolled down the window. "When this is finished, we're gonna take you and Mom fishing up at the cabin. We haven't done that in a long time. While we're gone, see if you can find our old fishing poles and my tackle box. They should still be in the garage."

Robert smiled. "That's a great idea. I'll do just that." Robert turned his attention to Grace who had stepped out to the porch to wave goodbye to her sons. "Gracie, would you bake some of that homemade bread you used to make? It always made the best sandwiches when we took the boys to the lake."

When they closed the door, Dan thought, *that ought to keep them busy for a while. I think we'll all enjoy getting away after we get this thing settled with Emily.*

To his brother he said, "We have to hurry and pick up the Michaels' and get over to the park."

"I know."

"You heard me tell Dad that we're all going up to the lake for some fishing when this is over," Dan glanced at Jon.

Jon shrugged. "That might be fun. I haven't thought about the cabin or fishing in a long time. What made you think about it now?"

"I don't know. I'm glad that Dad didn't sell the place," Dan admitted. "We had some great times up there when we were kids."

"Yeah, but I think we went up there more often when Granny and Grandpa were alive," Jon stated. "It was their place. They left it to Mom. So, what made you think about it again?" Jon probed.

Dan didn't want to get all mushy about how comfortable he felt being back in his parent's house with everyone there. He decided to change the subject. "You know, on one hand, it was hard for me to leave the priesthood. There are days when I wonder if I made a mistake. A lot of my older parishioners still call me Father. I lived in the rectory and went through some very soul searching, routine rituals every day. It was a huge part of my life. It's who I was and it was a good place for me to be at the time. Maybe I should have stayed and fought it out."

"That's pretty deep. It sounds like you're still struggling with it," Jon said.

"Not really. I guess now I can think about a family of my own," Dan said.

"What's so bad about that?" Jon asked. "You were the one who always said you wanted four or five kids."

Dan's smiled. "I did, didn't I?"

"Do you think Ted and Angela are ready? I'm anxious to get to the park," Dan said. "By the way, did you happen to notice any additional security while you were nosing around today? You know, like guard dogs?" he raised his eyebrows at the thought.

"First of all, back to our conversation. You don't have to explain yourself to me. Personally, I'm not ready for a family yet. It sounds like you are. Other faiths do it. Did you ever think of changing religions? I mean if it's why you quit being a priest, try being a minister of another denomination," Jon suggested heartily. "And no, I never thought about dogs or security officers. We'll have to be careful and have a common response ready in case they're patrolling the park," Jon added.

Dan's response was quick. "It's worth the risk if Emily allows Brittney to return home to her parents."

"What about those other girls? Shit, we've done everything she asked." Jon pulled into the Michaels driveway. They sat quietly for a moment. "We sure have a long night ahead of us."

"You've got that right, little brother. Let's get started." Dan got out of the car first.

They walked up to the Michael's house, rang the doorbell several times and waited impatiently. "I wonder where they are. They knew we were coming back. I told them to be ready to leave when we got here." Dan peered into the front window.

"It's dark in there. I hope they didn't do something stupid like going over to Willows Park without us," Jon complained.

Just as they were about to leave, the porch light came on. Elizabeth opened the door. She was in her nightclothes.

"Where is everyone?" Dan asked firmly. He looked around the darkened house and walked past her.

"I don't know. I thought they were waiting for you," she said. "Leonard and I went to bed so we could be rested in case the kids need us for anything later on. We were finally able to get some sleep."

Dan and Jon were disturbed over the thought of Ted and Angela not waiting for them. "This is crap. I don't understand why they would go out there without us," Jon's words shot out of his mouth in a spontaneous display of anger.

"They did say they would wait," Dan reminded Elizabeth.

"Maybe they misunderstood you. They might have thought you were going to meet them out there," Elizabeth replied.

"Ignorance is different than innocence. They asked us to help and we really need to be with them at the park." Jon always said what was on his mind, unconcerned with the consequences. This was no exception. "We would have given them a time if that were the case."

On that note, headlights careened eerily across the front of the house. A car door slammed and while hastily coming up the walk, Angela said, "We're glad you're still here. I hope you weren't going to leave without us."

"Ignorance, huh?" Elizabeth said in a huff. She spun around and stepped heavily up the stairs.

"We were afraid that you might have taken off without waiting for us," Jon said, putting aside his previous assumptions.

"Did you find out anything from your mother?" Angela asked.

"We'll talk in the car," Jon said anxiously.

"It's been quiet since you two left. It scared us more to think that maybe Emily was gone for good without giving Brittney back to us." Angela searched Dan's face.

"Where'd you guys go?" Jon asked as they all piled into his car.

"We went out to pick up a few things for tonight," Ted said and swung his duffel bag on the seat between him and Angela.

"What's in the bag?" Dan turned around and asked.

"I bought flashlights, batteries, walkie-talkies, and rope. We even found these clips so you don't have to carry anything. Your hands are free." Ted demonstrated everything as he spoke with renewed confidence and determination in his voice. "Most of this stuff was Angie's idea, in case we get separated."

"Great, thanks a lot." Jon said.

Dan didn't care about gadgets and supplies. He was lost in thought and extremely concerned about what was going to transpire at the park.

"When we get there, we can't waste any time," he said. "This might actually go smoothly; however, we have to be prepared for that almighty monkey wrench."

"Jon, I want you and Ted to go around the merry-go-round in opposite directions. It's important that you keep watch, so Angela and I can get inside the center of the mirrored structure. I know there's a way in. That inner construction is sturdy. It holds up the carousel, but I have feeling that it was used for something other than just support."

Angela turned to Ted. "We can't let anything go wrong. Brittney's life depends on us. We have to find her and get her out of there. I won't go home without her. Not this time." The look on Angela's face was something Ted had never seen before.

"I know," Ted said. "Dan, what do we do if someone is there? I think we all need to have the same story ready."

"Good point," Dan answered. "You have to somehow detain them. Tell them that you were out walking your dog, it broke off the leash, and you were trying to find it."

Dan was anxious to get to that handle and find out what was behind those mirrors.

"You can even stall them by trying to get them involved in the search. That'll give us some valuable time, if we need it," Angela added..

The closer they got to Willows Park, the stronger Dan could sense Emily's presence.

"Umm, what kind of dog are we looking for?" Ted asked, matter-of-factly.

"I'll leave that one up to you," Jon said as he pulled into the outer parking lot. "Hopefully, there won't be anyone here to deal with."

They loaded the batteries into the flashlights and walkie-talkies. "I'm glad you thought about this stuff. Is everyone ready?" Dan asked without hesitation.

Ted kissed Angela. "We're as ready as we'll ever be."

Angela walked away with Dan into the blackened park. She tightened her hold on his hand and clutched her bandaged limb to her chest snuggly. Shadows of the stoic carousel horses seemed to emerge out of nowhere as they approached the phenomenal merry-go-round. It appeared larger and more intimidating in the dark. "The ride seems to have taken on a life of its own," Angela whispered.

Ted and Jon followed like sheep, close behind. "We're in this together now, like a tightly linked chain," Dan whispered. "No matter what we see or hear, there is no turning back."

Chapter Sixty-One

Taking their appointed positions, Ted and Jon ventured out into the shadowy darkness, back to back moving in opposite directions around the outer perimeter of the merry-go-round.

"Yell if you need me," Ted whispered to Jon on his first step.

"I have a flashlight, a walkie-talkie and I'm walking point, around a merry-go-round in the middle of the night. What's the worst that can happen?" Jon mumbled as the darkness swallowed him up.

The night air was refreshing. Ted's eyes strained through the blackness as he kept a look out for predators.

Dan and Angela climbed up on the merry-go-round platform and walked between the horses as they headed for the center of the ride. When they reached their objective, Dan jumped down first. He helped Angela off the platform, careful of her bandaged hand and then turned to face the mirrored panels.

Not thinking, Angela turned on her flashlight and was startled by the bright reflection that bounced off the mirrors. Dan spun around and grabbed her wrist roughly and forced it down.

"Turn that off," Dan whispered harshly. "The mirrors will reflect your light all the way back to the road. You might as well just shoot off a flare."

Angela immediately turned off the flashlight. Her voice quivered, embarrassed by her actions and shocked at Dan's abrupt response. "I'm sorry. I didn't think about that. It's just so dark." She choked back hot tears.

Dan ignored her explanations and turned back to the job at hand. "I know I saw a handle on one of these mirrors when we were here earlier. It has to be here someplace," he mumbled as he ran his hands up and down each panel aggressively.

"Do you really think Brittney is inside? Maybe she can hear me if I bang on the glass," Angela spoke in a low voice with renewed optimism. She cupped her hands around her eyes and pressed her face against the mirror in an attempt to see through the glass. "Why can't we just break one?" she snapped at Dan.

"I don't think so," Dan's response was quick. "I don't want to spend time in jail and owe these people a fortune for damages. What explanation would we give for our actions? Keep the flashlight pointed down and help me find the mirror with the handle."

Dan stopped what he was doing and stood perfectly still. "Listen, do you hear that?"

Angela froze in place.

"I think I hear music," Dan replied. "The carousel is starting to move."

"There isn't anyone by the controls," Angela whispered and aimed her flashlight at the empty chair next to the control box. She was careful not to shine the light on any of the mirrors.

All of a sudden, the shrill cry of a child rang through the park. Angela jumped and grabbed Dan's arm. "God help us!"

Dan frantically returned to his search for the door handle. Whether it was sheer luck or the hand of God, his right hand slid into a grove. "I think I found it," he cried out.

Angela shoved Dan out of her way, madly running her good hand over the mirror until her fingers met with a small glass ball that fit neatly into the palm of her hand. With her fingers wrapped firmly around it, she twisted it back and forth several times before the mirror began to move.

"Angela wait," Dan called, but he couldn't stop her. She was already pushing on the mirror, shoving it inward with her shoulder. It opened. With Dan close at her heels, Angela stumbled inside.

"My God, woman; I'm amazed that his whole thing didn't collapse around us," Dan scolded.

Angela ignored the reprimand. She was finally inside. She turned the flashlight toward the corners and began searching the odd shaped cubicle. "I think Emily started the music, because she didn't want anything to stop us. Brittney, are you in here? It's mommy. I'm here to take you home." Her voice went up an octave, no longer afraid of being heard. Nothing and no one was going to stop her from finding her daughter if she was in there.

A glow illuminating the room slowly grew brighter. The air became heavy and the small cubicle was hot and humid with a pungent stench that together, made breathing difficult.

A short cot was on one side of the room and neatly stacked boxes lined the walls.

"Look at these old cartons. They're set up like some sort of antiquated filing system," Angela said. "They're even labeled." She squatted to eye level and began to read each one out loud.

"Names!" she cried, moving quickly from one stack to the next. "They're girls' names."

Dan pulled out his flashlight and looked at one of the labels. "Did you notice the dates?"

Angela was unable to pull herself away. "The years are all different, but the month and day are the same. June twenty-eighth, Brittney's birthday," Angela announced.

A small round table stood next to the cot. Stacks of envelopes, tied neatly with ribbons were piled on top. Dan blew the dust away before opening the first one.

"Look at this," he said. Dan handed Angela an envelope, which contained photographs of a little girl on one of the carousel horses. She looked to be around five-years-old.

"She's riding alone," she noted. After staring at the first photograph, Angela began anxiously thumbing through the rest. Dan knew what she was looking for. "All these children," she cried.

"Let's not mix anything up. We need to examine the contents of each box and see if we can correlate them with these snapshots," Dan instructed.

She studied each picture more carefully now. "Look at the faces of the carousel horses. They have an arrogance about them I never noticed before."

Suddenly, the music outside became louder. Dan glanced out the open panel and noticed that the horses were beginning to take on realistic characteristics. "I wonder where Ted and Jon are. They need to see this."

The air was getting warmer and more stagnant. Dan wiped away the sweat that was dripping into his eyes when he noticed the door begin to close.

"Don't let that door shut! We won't be able to get out," Dan yelled. He pushed past Angela and wedged the little table into the opened panel. He looked out at the carousel horses. They had become silhouettes against the moon lit night.

"Shouldn't we call Ted and Jon?" Angela asked. "I don't know where they are. They should be seeing what's going on from out there," Dan said.

Each time the beautifully carved bench on the merry-go-round passed, Dan could see someone sitting in a brown hooded cloak. He redirected Angela away from the opened panel.

"We can't go out there right now. Do you have one of those walkie-talkies on you?" Dan asked. Angela handed the small wireless communicator to him.

Dan warned Ted and Jon about the visitor. "We see him," Jon answered. "The merry-go-round is moving but none of the lights are on. Hopefully no one will spot it. What did you find in there?"

"There's a cot in here, stacked boxes, photographs. See if you two can get in here," Dan said and turned to find Angela on her knees. She was listening intently to something.

"Can't you hear her?" Angela cried.

Dan listened as the sobbing that seemed to ooze from every corner of the small enclosure got louder.

"It's Brittney; I know her voice. She's in here some place. Help me find her," Angela insisted.

Dan couldn't believe his ears. Angela was right.

"How's your hand?" he asked.

"It hurts like hell," Angela cried.

"Come on, I'll take you out of here and come back and finish myself," Dan said.

"No way, I've come this far. You don't understand, I'm not leaving here without Brittney." Angela composed herself and haphazardly wiped her face with the back of her hand. She jerked away from Dan and began searching behind the stacks of boxes.

"Mommy, is that you?" It was Brittney.

"Yes Britt, I'm here. Where are you, baby?" Angela cried hysterically.

Brittney's voice sounded like it was only a few feet away. "We're all here Mommy; me, Emily and all the other little girls."

Chapter Sixty-Two

Ted and Jon waited for an opportunity to jump on the merry-go-round together. They weaved between the horses, leaped off into the center of the ride and headed for the mirrors.

"Dan! Angela! Where are you," Jon called. He shined his light into the opening. "Is everything okay in there? Did you find anything?"

Jon and Ted entered the mirrored structure and turned their flashlights on Angela and Dan. "Did you see that hooded creep? He was on the merry-go-round for a while. We were keeping an eye on him," Ted said.

"I saw him," Dan answered.

Jon noticed that Angela's hand was bleeding again. He tore a swatch of material from the bottom of his shirt and tied it around her injured hand. "I hope you didn't tear those stitches open. I'll change the dressing when we get home and take a look at it."

"I heard her, Ted. Brittney was calling me," Angela said.

"Where is she?" he demanded anxiously. "What are all these boxes?"

"We haven't examined the contents yet," Dan said.

"What are you waiting for? It's hot as hell in here," Jon's curiosity was getting the best of him.

Dan tried to explain. "Each wall has a stack of boxes that are labeled with a different child's name. First we found a stack of envelopes. They had pictures of little girls about Brittney's age. They were each riding the merry-go-round alone. I'll show you."

He walked over to the first stack of cartons and read the label out loud. "June twenty-eighth, nineteen forty-five. This must have been one of the first children abducted."

Everyone stood and listened reverently as Dan read each child's name. He reached for the top box. The first one contained more pictures. "Man, this guy must have stalked these kids. There are several snapshots of the same little girl. They're random shots too. She didn't pose for any of these pictures. This must be Nicole Darling. Her name is on the front of each box in this stack." He passed her pictures around.

Angela stared at them. "Poor little thing. Look at her. She doesn't have a clue what's going on."

"Open the next one," Ted coaxed. "This is taking too long."

Dan reached in and pulled out a long braid of hair tied in a faded pink ribbon.

Angela covered her mouth with her good hand in an attempt to muffle her scream. "What sort of animal are we dealing with?"

Dan didn't wait; he jerked on the next box. It was stuck to the one below it from age and dampness. The cardboard started to tear. He reached in and pulled out a piece of clothing. "This must be her dress. It's old, the material feels thin; I don't want to tear it. The police are going to want everything in order and this creep set it all up for them."

"Who said anything about the police?" Ted asked. "We have to find Brittney first."

Angela slid her hand over Ted's arm and quietly whispered, "We'll deal with them later. Let's find Britt." Her forcefulness and strength surprised Ted.

"Look at those little shoes," Dan commented. He put everything back in the box as he found it.

"Well, this is the last one. What else could this creep have saved?" Dan said as he pulled out the bottom carton. He tugged slightly to free it from where it sat. As soon as he had hold of the box, the heartbreaking wailing of all the lost children filled the room. Dan lifted the lid to the old carton and found it filled with the human bones of a small child.

Angela's knees buckled. She held on to Ted's arm for support.

Jon moved swiftly to the second row of boxes. Each time they started on another stack, they went right for the bottom box and found more bones.

The children's cries echoed louder as each one's remains were discovered. "Maybe now, they'll be able to cross over. We've found their remains and their spirits can be set free. They've been locked away in here for so long. Hopefully each one will be identified and given a proper burial. What a glorious find!" Dan cried.

Angela didn't care about any of the lost children. All she wanted was her daughter. She beat Dan to the last stack of boxes and tore open the bottom one. "Look," she screamed, "More bones."

Ted, Dan and Jon stared at the wide-eyed, crazed woman. The box tore and the contents spilled onto the floor. Pictures of a beautiful little girl with long blond curls scattered over the bones, exposing her identity.

Dan reached down and picked up one of the pictures. He raised his eyes and said, "My God. It's Emily. She did it. She led us to this morbid mausoleum. These are the abandoned remains of Emily Thatcher. She brought us here and revealed her tomb."

Chapter Sixty-Three

Angela was drawn to an unexplored corner of the tomb by the faint sound of moaning. She stumbled through the empty boxes and discovered yet another set of photographs.

"Oh my God, Ted," she screamed. "These are pictures of Brittney," Angela kicked the boxes aside and found Brittney curled up in a fetal position. She was shaking and barely covered with an old blanket.

Ted ran over and lifted his daughter off the floor. They turned to face none other than the hooded figure that now stood in the middle of the enclosure. Their expectations of a leachy creature with latch hooks for fingers evaporated. Under the loose fitted hood was the twisted, careworn face of an old woman.

The revelation astonished everyone. Angela yelled out, "My God, she looks like an old distorted version of the girl we saw in the library."

Brittney remained quiet in her father's arms. Emily appeared and glided gracefully toward them. Angela reached out with her good arm and wrapped it protectively around her daughter, causing Brittney to release a slight moan.

"God have mercy, what have you done to her?" Angela demanded.

Dan stepped between Emily and the Michaels family. "Brittney belongs here in the present with her mother and father. You don't belong here Emily. You're a memory to be visited and shared," he said cautiously, knowing full well of her ability to retaliate.

"I'm sorry for your suffering and loss, but we can't change what happened. There's no longer a place for you among the living, not now or in the future. You appear to linger only to cause fear and torment as your tormentor did. That makes you as evil as her."

Angela reared her head and faced Emily. "You won't have Brittney. I'll take you to hell personally." Her words were venomous.

"This is where it ends, Emily. We found your remains. Now, one way or another, we're going to get the hell out of here. Let these people go home in peace," Dan pleaded.

Angela quickly gathered the photographs of Brittney and noted a lock of hair tied together with a pretty pink ribbon. She picked it up and gritted her teeth at Emily. "This is more than simply a spiritual battle."

Angela continued to face Emily and the monstrous woman under the hooded cloak. She raised her one good hand up toward the heavens and began to pray out loud. "Merciful Father, who art in heaven; help me now in my hour of need," Dan joined her. He reached into his pocket and held the silver cross up to face the forces of evil that surrounded them.

Jon stood next to his brother and mumbled, "There's strength in numbers, but I suggest we get the hell out of here!"

Brittney's eyes flickered open. She was relieved to find herself cradled in her father's arms. "Mommy, where's my doll?"

Ted clung tightly to her as they rushed for the opening in the structure. It was their one and only escape. "We have to get Brittney out of here," Ted yelled as he pushed his way through the now inky darkness.

The light that a moment ago allowed the group to witness their surroundings was gone, creating a black barrier between them and the doorway. Ted pressed Brittney to his chest. "Come on Angie, run. Run, damn it!" he commanded.

Dan grabbed Angela by the arm and began dragging her with him. Jon wedged her between himself and his brother. They followed Ted out of the warm, humid enclosure into the center of the carousel where the sweet, life invigorating, night air filled their lungs and made it easier for them to breath.

They had barely made it through the narrow opening when Dan saw the unknown black woman who had become a noted part of the mystery surrounding Emily Thatcher. She held the single mirrored panel open until they were all out safely.

The music had reached ear-shattering intensity. Ted bounded up onto the moving platform with Brittney, making his way through the wooden horses that were now galloping in place. As he brushed up against them, he could feel their warm lifelike bodies and strong, rippling muscles. He found himself trying to stay out of the way of their bucking back legs.

"How can this be happening?" he cried fearfully, struggling to get to the edge of the carousel with his daughter.

Brittney's eyes were wide open now. Ted called back to Angela as he reached the platforms edge. "Hurry, Angie!" For a split second he felt as though he had abandoned his wife. Ted looked down at Brittney and said, "Wrap yourself around me baby and hold on as tight as you can. No matter what happens, don't let go!"

Brittney burrowed her face into her father's chest and clung on for dear life.

Her muffled screams served to push Ted harder and without hesitation, he jumped off the carousel with Brittney plastered to his sweaty body.

They hit the ground hard and he lost his hold on her. Ted and Brittney tumbled fast and hard into an agonizing roll. Then they stopped suddenly as if unseen hands held them back from flying into a huge oak tree. He looked up, stunned. No one was there.

Ted immediately looked for Brittney. Incredibly, she was standing in front of a tree looking none the worse for wear for what she had just gone through. It looked as though she was smiling at someone. Her small face was tipped up and her chin seemed to be resting on something. He couldn't see Leeza as she lovingly cradled Brittney's cheeks in her barren hands.

Ted's only thoughts were focused on getting Brittney out of the woods and to the car. He ran over to her and grabbed Brittney by the hand, not giving her a chance to say a word. Together, they took off running through the moon lit woods. The tightly knit trees made their journey that much harder.

It all happened so fast. Ted yelled back to his wife, "Come on Angie, move your ass, we have to get to the car."

His lungs burned and every muscle in his body screamed as he tore through the woods, stopping only to swoop up his stumbling daughter. He had to push fear and panic for Angela aside as he forced his stinging legs to keep going. His choice to drive forward was irreversible. Angela, Dan and Jon would have to make it out of the woods, on their own.

Dan and Jon faced the dilemma of getting back on the moving ride from the inner circle with Angela, who only had the use of one hand.

"I don't know if I can do this. It's moving so fast and if I fall, I can't catch myself," Angela uttered fearfully.

There was no time to waste. With one on each side, they spontaneously took a firm hold of Angela's arms and, by the grace of God, all three made it onto the speeding platform.

Dan realized that Angela wouldn't be able to jump off alone. The horses began to whinny and stomp their enormous hoofs in place. It looked as though, at any moment, they would break free and bolt wildly in a stampede. With no time to stop now, they fought their way between the carved horses transforming around them.

When they reached the outer edge of the platform, Dan called out, "When you jump, tuck and roll."

Jon had one arm locked around Angela and the other hand gripped tightly to a pole. "I'm going to let go of Angela. You'll have to hold her alone," he yelled.

"Just jump!" Dan hollered, his adrenaline surging.

When Jon hesitated, Dan impulsively shoved him as hard as he could, causing Jon to fall off the merry-go-round. Dan immediately turned to Angela. "When I count to three, let go of the pole."

"I'm terrified! I can't!" she cried.

Dan's only response was, "You will! We'll do it together." He was too strong for her to resist. Angela realized there was no other way. Dan locked eyes with her and began, "One, two, three." With his right arm wrapped tightly around her waist, they both leaped off the wild, spinning carousel.

As they hit the ground, Angela broke free from Dan's hold and rolled over and over through the dirt and gravel, into the weeds.

Jon limped over to where Angela laid face down in the leaves and dirt. The make shift bandage he had tied around her hand was torn and hanging freely.

"Are you okay?" Jon asked as he slowly turned her over. "Can you get up? We have to get out of here."

Every part of her body hurt. Her hand throbbed, but it didn't compare to the sharp pain she felt in her right hip and shoulder. Angela moaned as he helped her to her feet. She had to struggle to gain composure.

"Can you run?" Jon asked.

"I'll try," she said, spitting chunks of dirt.

"Do it for Brittney," Jon coaxed and they limped off through the woods toward the car.

The car was just beyond the tree line. When they finally approached it,

Angela bent over and lost the contents of her stomach. Ted spotted them and ran to her. "Thank God, you made it."

They looked back through the trees and could only see glimpses of the out-of-control ride. The lights and action of the merry-go-round could be seen from the road. It was only a matter of time before the police were alerted.

Suddenly, they heard sirens. "Shit, it's the police. They'll be here any minute. We have to get out of here." Ted pushed Angela toward the car.

"Where's Brittney?" she cried.

Before Ted could answer, the mirrored center of the merry-go-round exploded, sending multitudes of tiny, glistening pieces of broken glass into the sky. The full moon cast its glow on the area creating an eerie illusion of fireflies in frenzy.

The voices of children giggling could be heard echoing throughout the night's darkness. Their joyful laughter rang throughout the park as the spirits of all the children were set free.

To everyone's relief, Dan showed up during the shower of splintering glass. Angela looked at the area above the trees that encircled the once magnificent merry-go-round. What she saw left her speechless. She silently tugged on Dan's shirt and pointed to where Emily hovered over her once secluded tomb.

"Why isn't she leaving with the rest of the children? What does she want now?" Angela cried.

They all stared as Emily's long blond hair floated freely in the wind like spun gold. The other children glided through a beam of light that carried their spirits through the night sky.

Angela rushed to the car and opened the door to the back seat where Brittney waited. With tears streaming down her face, she got into the car and reached for her daughter. "I'm so thankful that you aren't with the rest of those children," she cried and cradled her daughter.

Jon followed Angela's droplets of blood into the car. He tore more fabric from his shirt and removed the soiled bandage from around her hand. After quickly rewrapping the wound and securing the cloth, he said, "I'll tend to that properly when we get home. We have to get out of here right now."

Jon got into the driver's seat and started the car. Ted slid into the back seat, on the other side of Brittney. Dan just started to get into the passenger seat alongside Jon when a voice came echoing through the branches of the dense forest surrounding them.

"Bury my bones, Dan Markos. The deed is not complete."

It was Emily's voice. Dan leaned his head wearily on the car door. He knew what he had to do. "I have to go back. Hurry and give me something to wrap her skeleton in."

"Like what?" Jon asked anxiously as the sound of the sirens grew closer. "You can't go back into that mess, Dan. The police are on their way."

"Shut up and give me your jacket. You're wasting time," Dan demanded harshly.

When Jon didn't move, Dan grabbed his brother's jacket and looked sternly at him. "Get them out of here. I have to go back or we'll never be rid of Emily. I promised!"

"Be careful," Jon called after his older brother. "We aren't going anywhere. We'll circle around and meet you on the other side of the woods. We'll watch for you along the tree line."

Dan nodded and bolted back into the dense forest. He headed for what was left of the carousel and prayed that he would be able to salvage Emily's remains before the police got there.

Chapter Sixty-Four

Dan reached the merry-go-round before the police. He took a moment to look around. The only thing destroyed was all of the mirrors. The main structure looked like a small wooden shed.

The ride had stopped revolving and the wooden horses were nothing more than beautiful painted replicas. Time was of the essence. He wasn't ready to explain any of this. All he wanted was to get Emily's remains out of there.

The black woman with the saintly smile stood holding the door to the center structure open for Dan. She motioned for him to come in.

As he approached her, Dan saw light reflecting from her lifeless eyes. He knew it was coming from her very soul. .

"You know why I'm here?" Dan asked the older woman. She smiled and nodded.

Dan entered the shed-like building and was thankful for the full moon. It shone through wide cracks in the walls. "Where are you Emily?" Dan moved quickly through the stuffy enclosure searching for the carton labeled Emily Thatcher. He didn't have far to go. Emily stood in the center of the room with her remains stacked neatly at her feet.

Dan spread Jon's jacket on the floor and blessed the bones while wrapping them securely. He zipped the jacket closed and tied the sleeves together, carefully tucking it under his arm.

As he rushed for the doorway, Dan bumped into the cot. A large pillow fell on the floor. He grabbed it and quickly shook the pillowcase off. Even after finding the material to be fragile, he decided to use it. Dan carefully stuffed the jacket and its contents into the delicate fabric before leaving.

When he reached the doorway, Dan turned and gave a final farewell to the other skeletal remains. "I'm sorry for your tragic endings. I'll say a special prayer for each of you." He crossed himself and turned to leave only to find himself faced with yet another obstacle. The hooded figure anchored herself firmly in the center of the doorway, blocking his only means of escape. The brown hood was tossed back, exposing the woman's twisted features with horrifying, dark, hollow sockets where the light of life once shone.

Leeza stood close behind the tormented soul. The old black woman presented no threat, but beckoned Dan to come to her. With no other options, he ran right through the disgusting creature that turned out to be just an illusion. He would let nothing stop him from taking Emily's remains out of the tomb that for years harbored her darkest secret.

He took a deep breath and sighed with relief as the night's fresh air hit his face. "You can't hurt anyone anymore," he called back to the old woman that disappeared into the shadows.

The sirens were blaring as he ran into the darkened woods. Police cars moved in fast and tore through the trees to the area where the merry-go-round stood shattered. Once out of their line of vision, Dan turned and watched the officers surround the once-beautiful carousel. *Holy Father, that was close!* Dan watched silently for a brief moment while he caught his breath. "Wait until they find the rest of your companions, Emily. Hopefully, they'll all eventually be identified and laid to rest," Dan spoke quietly to Emily's remains.

He followed the soft glow emitted from the lone black woman who led him silently out of the woods. "I don't know who you are, but I'm deeply grateful for your presence. You must love Emily very much," Dan spoke to the illuminated figure before him.

A voice that can only be described as the caressing softness of a breeze, responded, "That I do, sir; that I certainly do."

The night was warm and Dan was sweating. He suddenly felt the presence of an unseen force on either side of him. With no control over his own movements he found himself being carried swiftly and silently through the trees.

Dan looked down at his feet. They were barely touching the ground. His toes brushed the dirt and leaves as he continued to move gracefully out of the woods. He thought about what he was carrying and held on tighter to the bundle that was securely nestled under his arm.

Chapter Sixty-Five

Brittney squirmed off her mother's lap and sat safely between Ted and Angela in the back seat of Jon's car.

"I'm hungry Mommy," she said.

"That's a good sign," Jon said as he anxiously waited for his brother to come out of the woods.

Brittney leaned her head on Angela's shoulder. "Be careful honey. My hand is very sore," Angela whined.

Jon chewed nervously on his fingernails as he scanned the length of the tree line. "Try holding your hand above your heart for a while, Angela. Damn it. The cops have to be there by now. I hope Dan got out of there in time!"

"Why don't we circle around to the other side of the park and see if we can spot him?" Ted suggested. "I hope he was able to find Emily's bones in the merry-go-round. That was quite an explosion."

Jon nodded. "Not to mention the fact that he had to make it out of there and into the woods without being seen. Shit, he could be sitting in the backseat of a police car right now."

"Give him time," Angela said. "It's dark out tonight, plus it's even darker in the woods."

"Those sirens sounded close when we left," Ted said. Angela poked him in the ribs.

Jon ignored Ted's remark. "Dan will be lucky just to find his way out of there and into the field. I hope he doesn't get turned around and end up back by the merry-go-round."

Ted tried to relax. They had their daughter sitting safely between them. "Dan should be showing up any time now," Ted said.

"I don't know whether to sit here or drive around and look for him. Where the hell is he anyway?" Jon said. Ted and Angela glanced at each other but remained quiet.

"Dan seems very intelligent," Angela said.

"Oh, he is. He's the smartest and most honest person you'll ever meet, not to mention loyal. When we were kids, he couldn't tell a lie. It would weigh so heavy on his conscience that he'd end up telling on himself. I wasn't surprised at all when he announced that he was going to be a priest. We talked about girls and stuff, but at the time, he just wasn't interested. He had a burning desire to help others. When I say that he wanted to save the world, I mean it literally." Jon kept his lights off and started the car.

Angela spoke up out of curiosity. "If you don't mind me asking; why did he give up the priesthood?"

Jon paused. "I'm not sure. I know there was some problem between him and Father Luke Phillips. I don't know the details and I don't care. I only know what a terrific person Dan is." Dan's morals are high and his ethics are even higher. When he graduated from high school, he announced to my parents that he was going to become a priest."

"How did they feel about that?" Ted asked.

Angela spoke from a mother's point of view. "You want security and love for your children when they become too old for you to give them what they need. It must have been hard for your parents to stay impartial with his decision."

"Dan was so dedicated to the church that he moved to Italy and took a position in one of the cathedrals in Rome," Jon boasted. "He knows there's life after death, because of his ability to discern the spirits of the dead. His choice to become a priest was his way of choosing sides, so to speak."

"He's obviously gifted and has a gentle spirit. I certainly feel honored to know him," Angela interjected. She smoothed Brittney's hair back from her face and kissed her forehead. "All of this is so hard to believe."

"We need to find Dan. If he isn't here in the next few minutes, I'm going out to look for him. You can take the car and go home," Jon shifted nervously.

Ted sat up and added, "The police are bound to suspect something if they spot the car and find us loitering around here. "Why don't we drive around the entire park one more time before giving up? I'll keep looking for Dan while you drive and Angie can watch for the cops."

"Where's my doll Mommy?" Brittney asked.

"I don't know honey. We'll look for it later. We have to find Dan first," Angela said.

Jon crossed the intersection and cut through the gas station. He was driving down Dogwood Lane behind the park making one more pass when Angela spotted Dan at the edge of the wood line. "Slow down, I think I see him," she shouted.

"Pull into the parking lot over there by the One Stop. I'll jump out and go get him," Ted said.

Jon pulled into the One Stop and turned off the headlights. Ted quickly got out of the car and turned back to Brittney. "Stay close to Mommy. I'll be right back."

"I'm glad that Ted wore dark clothes. I can barely see him out there," Angela said as he disappeared into the darkness.

Jon strained fretfully to see if he could spot Dan. "I hope they hurry. We need to get out of here."

Ted ran through the parking lot and scurried through the open field to where Dan was crouched down just outside the tree line in front of the woods.

Ted saw him and called out, "Dan, over here."

Dan was relieved to see Ted. He stayed low and moved as quickly as he could over to him. "I'm sure glad to see you. Where's Jon?"

Ted pointed to where the car was parked. "Did you find Emily's bones? This place is swarming with cops. We have to get out of here, now!"

Dan chuckled at Ted's comment knowing all too well where the police were and how close he came to meeting them personally.

They hurried back to the car and Ted jumped in. He was sweaty and out of breath. "That was scary, but sort of exciting," Ted spoke through a surge of adrenaline.

"Where's Dan?" Jon asked just as Dan knocked on Jon's window.

"Hurry and open the trunk," Dan ordered.

Jon reached under the dashboard and pulled the lever to pop the trunk. Dan put the filled pillowcase into the back of the car. Before closing it, he noticed a small bony prominence poking out from a tear in the fragile material. He gasped as he recalled how he felt Emily's remains move and squirm beneath the tightly bound cloth as he ran through the woods.

Dan closed the trunk and slid into the passenger seat. He leaned his head back on the headrest and blew out a hard burst of air. "Thank God that's done."

"Are you okay?" Jon asked.

"Let's just get the hell out of here," Dan said.

Jon slowly backed the car out of the parking space. He turned on the headlights and headed in the direction of the Michael's home.

"The police must have found all those bones by now." A heavy sigh followed Dan's words.

"It's like we cracked this really important homicide and we'll never even get credit for it," Ted said.

"Actually, we just might get some recognition in this case," Dan added.

Ted sat forward in his seat. "What do you mean?"

"Somehow, Jon and I are going to have to present Emily's bones to our mother so they can be buried with our grandparents," Dan explained. "This is far from over. We can't just go to the cemetery and dig up our grandmother's grave. Those remains are going to have to be positively identified before they're buried, for one thing."

"You're right. I didn't think that far ahead," Jon replied. "So, how are we going to explain all this? By the way, we have our dead aunt's bones in the trunk of my car, who as a matter of fact, has been missing for over fifty years?"

Dan's snappy comeback sounded as if he'd already thought it through. "First, no one can possibly blame us for the kidnapping and murder. Once they identify who the remains belong to, it will put us all in the clear. We weren't even alive when it happened. Someone is going to have to listen and believe us."

The car choked and sputtered. "Hold on Emily. We'll think of something." Jon gripped the steering wheel. "If not, I'm sure you'll find a way."

No one laughed. It was late and they were all exhausted and traumatized over what they'd just been through.

"We'll take you home and then Jon and I are going back to our parent's house. We can all use a good night's sleep. We'll talk to our mom in the morning and give you a call to let you know what's going on," Dan announced.

Dan looked over his shoulder at the Michaels family. They sat huddled together in the back seat. It was good to see them safely together. Angela moaned some sort of response through her discomfort. A quick glance at Brittney sitting snuggly between her parents gave Dan a sense of victory.

During the ride home, Angela dozed off with her good arm wrapped around Brittney. The slamming of the car doors woke her up.

"I don't think you'll have to worry about Brittney disappearing again. I'd keep a close eye on her for a while though. We don't really know what's she's been through or seen; but kids are pretty resilient. It might all just seem like a dream to her." Dan's smile shone with empathy.

"Do you really believe that Emily is gone for good?" Angela raised the question.

"I really hope so," he started. "I don't see why not. We did what she wanted. If anything, it wouldn't surprise me if Jon and I became the targets of her misdirected anger until what's left of her in the trunk gets buried. Hopefully, once that's done, she'll be able to rest."

"It's food for thought." Emily's voice was meant for only Dan to hear. No one else reacted to the words that buzzed past his ear like the irritating wings of a small bug.

"The sooner this is over; the better. I don't feel comfortable with the remnants of Emily's earthly body in the trunk of my car," Jon said frankly.

"We need to make a definite decision about that, for sure," Dan agreed.

Ted took Brittney from Angela's arms and carried her to the house. "I can't thank you two enough for everything. Ang, don't be too long," he said and went inside.

"Things are going to be different now that we have to bring our mother into all this," Jon said. "I still find it incredible that Emily is her sister."

Dan sounded more concerned than surprised when he added, "The whole thing is so bizarre. I need to stay close to her for a while. She never dealt with ghosts and death very well."

Jon nodded. "We can help her go through the rest of Granny's things. She won't mind and maybe we'll learn something in the process."

"The main thing is, your daughter is safe at home. Now, maybe you'll be able to get your lives back to normal," Dan said sincerely.

Angela gave each of them a tight hug. Her eyes were filled with tears.

Jon asked, "How's your hand? I can take a look at it if you'd like before we leave."

"No thanks, you've done more than enough. I think the bleeding's stopped and I'm going to take one of those pain pills when I get in the house and lay down with Brittney." She smiled at Jon, but there was a look of doubt in her eyes. Angela let out a sigh. "I hope this won't be the last we see of you two. We'd like to think that we made a couple of good friends. It isn't every day that you get called upon to go on a ghost hunt. Maybe you can come over for dinner one night after this is over and done with."

Both men smiled. "You can count on it," Jon responded politely. Dan nodded.

Angela went into the house and closed the door. Dan felt good about leaving them alone. He knew Emily wouldn't be a problem to the Michaels family anymore because, while walking back to Jon's car, he could see her head of blond curls waiting patiently for him in the back seat.

Chapter Sixty-Six

The night was unusually silent. There wasn't even the slightest breeze to cause the trees to rustle their branches . Dan and Jon left the Michaels family alone to heal. A lot had transpired since Jon's first meeting with Ted and Angela. However, what was yet to come weighed heavily on his mind.

"What the hell did I get us into? There are human bones in the trunk of my car. I can go to jail. Imagine if we get stopped by the police on the way home. What then?" Jon asked in a worried shaky voice.

"Calm down. I have a feeling our problems have only just begun." Dan was mentally preparing his next plan of action when out of the corner of his eye, over his left shoulder he saw something move. "Either my peripheral vision is playing tricks on me or we have a passenger."

Immediately Jon looked in the rear view mirror. "I don't see anything." However, when he turned around, he saw Emily sitting in the center of the back seat. Her strikingly blue eyes shone through their darkened sockets of death. "What's she doing here? I don't like not being able to see her in the mirror."

"At least the Michaels family will get a good night's sleep. I think they're safe from Emily now," Dan let out a long sigh.

"She isn't gonna leave us alone, is she?" Jon asked.

"I'm positive that she's just protecting the precious cargo in your trunk. We can't blame her for that. It took her a long time to make someone find those remains. No, Emily isn't going to leave us alone until we finish what we were compelled to do. I'll keep an eye on her; you just drive." Dan spoke calmly in response to his brother's query.

They headed for home. "I suppose you're right, but I'm confused about something. Didn't that dramatic exit Emily made back at the park mean that she was free? I thought she would have taken that opportunity to cross over with the others. Why is she still here?"

"I don't have answers for all the mysteries of life, let alone death. For some reason, Emily feels that our family failed her and she isn't settling for anything less than what she came for. I just hope she doesn't think that we owe her something more," Dan said thoughtfully.

"Like what?" Jon asked.

"I'm not sure, but Emily is driven by a goal that has to be fulfilled. It could be dangerous for us not to cooperate."

As Jon drove home, Dan leaned his head back. He didn't look back at Emily again. Instead he pushed away the image of her controlling eyes. and visualized Emily's spirit. The blue was starting to show through the sockets. She was too close to the light of life.

"God only knows how long her search has been going on or how much she knows about Mom. She has no more conception of time now than she had in life. It doesn't give us hope of any rest until everything is settled and Emily gets what she came for," Dan mumbled.

"Jon, I need to ask you something."

"What now?" Jon asked wearily.

"Did you see the black woman that was holding the mirrored panel open for us at the merry-go-round? Who do you suppose she is?" Dan asked.

"I caught a glimpse of her once, but for some reason, I haven't had a lot of connection with her. Is she with Emily or some sort of guardian angel that's following you around?" Jon replied, feeling oddly disgruntled that he didn't connect with this unknown spirit like Dan did.

"I believe she's with Emily. She appears to love her unconditionally and seems to reprimand, guide, and protect Emily. I'm going to try to find out who she is. Mom might know," Dan remarked.

"What would she be protecting Emily from? Emily's a ghost. What could possibly happen to her?" Jon gave a mock laugh.

Dan turned to look at the impish spirit who appeared to be listening to everything they said. He answered Jon as simply as he could. "Herself."

Chapter Sixty-Seven

It was late by the time Dan and Jon returned home. Grace greeted her sons with an anxious smile and hugs. She didn't ask them what they'd been up to; she was just glad to have both of her sons home.

"Now that you're both here, I thought I'd show you some of Granny's things before you go to bed."

"What's that? I don't remember seeing it before?" Dan asked when he spotted a small antique trunk under the picture window.

Grace turned toward the chest. "Dad helped me get some of Granny's things down from her attic. I still haven't decided what to do with their house and everything in it. Maybe there are some things you boys would like before I make any decisions," she said.

Dan and Jon inspected the curiously alluring trunk. "You have the most comforting dark brown eyes, Mom. I don't think I ever told you that," Dan said seriously.

"Thank you Danny. You have my mother's blue eyes. I always wished I had them. But we seem to want what we don't have." A light shade of pink added a glow to Grace's pale, smooth skin.

Dan knelt on one knee and tugged firmly on the old lock that securely sheltered his grandmother's secrets. His instincts told him there was more than just old letters and trinkets inside. "Mom, where's the key to this lock? How could you stand not knowing what's in here?"

"I thought I'd wait for you and your brother to come home so we could look inside together. Dad wasn't the least bit curious and I wanted someone to share it with. Your Granny wasn't very materialistic, so I'm not expecting anything spectacular," Grace said.

"Come on, where's the key?" Jon asked.

"Years ago, Granny gave me an unusually shaped key. It was very unique and I didn't want to lose it, so I tucked it away in my jewelry box. For reasons I never really understood, there was always a heavy sadness in her eyes that kept a wedge between us. She took good care of me, in fact, she was overly protective at times and an absolute nervous wreck whenever I was out of her sight. But, I grew up feeling more like a possession than a daughter," Grace recalled sadly.

"I'm sorry. I never realized that," Dan said sincerely.

"Anyway, when she gave me the key and I was told not to use it until after she died. So, that's what I did," Grace spoke matter-of-factly. "She wore the key on a pink ribbon around her neck for as long as I can remember. Oddly enough, taking care of her took a toll on my dad and he died before she did. That's when she gave the key to me and made me promise that I would put it in a safe place," Grace finished with a sigh.

"Did you know about the trunk?" Jon asked.

"Yes, it always sat at the foot of her bed. I wasn't allowed in the room whenever the trunk was opened," Grace replied.

"Now, how strange is that? Didn't it make you want to see what was in it all the more?" Dan asked.

"No, I was just happy that she entrusted the key to me. It made me feel special and I put it away like I was told. My father moved the trunk into the attic when she was too sick to go through it anymore."

"Holy cow Mom," Jon said. "Dan and I would have opened that lock as soon as the key was in our hands," he laughed.

"Speak for yourself little brother," Dan smiled.

"Sometimes her words could slice like a sharp knife. When she gave me her precious key, though it might sound lame to you, I treasured the privilege of keeping it safe. It was the key to her private thoughts," Grace sighed.

"You really have some issues, Mom," Jon said casually.

"Why didn't you ever tell us about any of this?" Dan asked.

"Oh, I don't know. I didn't want to share such a depressing old story." With that, Grace opened her hand and let the decorative old key drop and swing from the worn ribbon.

Jon approached the trunk. "We never spent a lot of time with her and Grandpa. Maybe we'll learn something about them."

"I hope so, but my main interest is in learning more about Emily," Dan said with renewed attention.

All at once, Jon stopped cold. "I should have known."

Emily hovered over the mysterious old chest with her feet barely brushing the top.

Dan's instincts told him to wait before acknowledging her openly in front of his mother. He directed his thoughts to her.

I know you can read my thoughts. You also know what's in the contents of this trunk. I'm doing the best I can, but I'm starting to worry about your intentions.

Grace placed the key in Dan's hand and with a slight tremor in her voice she said, "Go ahead, open it. Please be careful. I don't want anything damaged."

"Okay, you look at everything first. Then, we'll go through it." The key slid easily into the lock. "It fits perfectly. Let's see if it works."

Emily moved behind Grace. She appeared so lifelike. Fear gripped Dan and his stomach clenched. He had the fleeting thought that Emily's intentions toward Grace were threatening and he called out, "No, don't do it."

"Don't do what?" Grace asked. "Open the trunk and quit acting so dramatic. I told you, my mother didn't have anything worth much."

Dan glanced at Jon. What Grace didn't realize was the one thing her mother, Sarah, had that meant more to her than anything in the world, was Grace herself. Perhaps Grace never knew how much her mother really loved her. Maybe Sarah knew. She could have been protecting Grace.

Dan turned the key and the lock fell open. As Dan started to lift the lid, Emily immediately slammed it shut.

"What the hell?" Dan addressed Emily. Grace saw what happened, but didn't see Emily.

"Danny, I asked you to be careful," she said.

"Sorry Mom," Dan said. Emily moved back to Grace's side. Dan and Jon felt very nervous having her lingering so close to their mother.

Jon blew out an exasperated breath of air. "Let's just do this."

Dan slowly lifted the lid and cautiously reached into the trunk. He pulled out a stack of faded photographs and handed them to Grace. Dan and Jon kept silent and waited patiently as Grace looked at each picture. Tears welled up in her eyes.

Robert entered the room. "Pull up a chair Dad. We're just going through Granny's trunk," Jon said.

All three gathered around Grace. "Do you know who these people are?" Dan asked.

"This is my mother and father when they were young. It must have been taken before I was born." Grace began to recall out loud the familiar faces.

"It looks like they're at a carnival," Robert added as he peered over Grace's shoulder. "Who's the little girl?"

Grace turned the picture over and read the inscription. "It's my mother's handwriting. I recognize it. It says, Charles, Sarah, and Emily Thatcher. June twenty eighth, nineteen forty-seven," she read. "It must be my sister Emily. I wonder why they kept these pictures locked up in this trunk." She turned the picture over and studied it. "It's peculiar, yet sad to see someone who was loved by my parents before I was born. Look at my mother's face. It looks like she adored Emily," Grace marveled. "I never actually saw her this relaxed and happy."

It bothered Dan to see his mother hurt over the pictures. "May I see that, please?" He reached for the photo, recognized Emily and handed it to Jon.

"Yep, that's her," Jon agreed, glancing over at Emily who stood in front of them now.

"What are you talking about? How would you know?" Robert asked.

Dan took Grace's hands in his and spoke soothingly. "Mom, your sister is here right now. It's the reason Jon called me home to help him. Emily has been raising havoc with the Michaels family," Dan explained. "We've discovered that it wasn't a coincidence that Jon and I were dragged into Emily's plan. She's been trying to get back here for a very long time."

Jon interrupted quickly, "There's no question that Emily is Mom's sister now."

Dan looked past his mother at the frail little spirit that once lived and loved. "She was the little girl that Granny and Grandpa lost."

"Why is she here now?" Grace asked. "I don't see her, do you Robert?"

Dan continued thumbing through the pictures of Emily at the carnival. "This was her last day with them. See the merry-go-round?" Dan showed the picture to Jon.

"I've never seen another one like it, except for the one at Willows Park," Jon agreed.

Dan suddenly came across a photo of a woman who appeared to be the same as the one who wore the hooded cape. "Mom, by any chance, do you know who this is?" He handed the picture to Grace.

Grace studied the photograph of a woman that Dan recognized to be the hooded fiend, possibly the one who posed as the librarian and the woman at the information booth, all one and the same.

Grace turned the photo over, "Susan Young, summer of forty-seven." She paused and thought for a moment.

"I remember hearing my parents talk about her in the privacy of their room.

She was their neighbor. If I'm not mistaken, she even lived with my mom and dad for a short time after her husband died."

Dan was extremely careful not to scare his mother, but his excitement was hard to hide. "Please, tell me whatever you can remember hearing about her. Take your time and think about it, because it's really, really important."

Grace looked at the picture of Susan Young and responded thoughtfully. "From what I gathered, she had a daughter that died when the little girl was five years old and believed that her child was poisoned by one of the neighbors. I overheard my mother say that Mrs. Young became obsessed with the idea to the point that eventually, she was sent away to a mental institution."

"That's interesting. Could that Mrs. Young person have suspected Granny of poisoning her little girl?" Jon questioned.

"I don't know why she would. My mother was a very quiet, church-going woman, and Mrs. Young remained friends with her long after Emily disappeared." Grace spoke protectively about her mother. "Now remember, I was young when I overheard most of this."

"What else can you recall?" Jon pressed.

"Her husband died of some sort of stomach ailment. I'm sure that he was stressed out over losing their child," Grace added. "Mrs. Young stayed with my parents until my mother became pregnant with me. I do know that she was asked to leave their home. I guess it was too much for my mother because she had also lost a child."

Robert reached for the picture. "She wasn't a very big woman," he commented.

"No, she wasn't," Jon glanced at Dan.

"Do you know why Mrs. Young stayed with Granny and Grandpa?" Dan asked. "Were there any relatives she could have lived with?"

Grace could only speculate. "Apparently not. I think they all went to the same church. After she lost her child and then her husband, my parents felt sorry for her and they did have a big house. It was the Christian thing to do."

Dan continued going through the trunk. He reached deep into the family heirlooms and wrapped his fingers around something cool and hard. When he pulled it out, he stared in disbelief at the familiar icon.

"Jon, look at this." He held up his cross. "I thought I lost it at the merry-go-round," he smiled and picked a few slivers of broken mirror bits out of the inscription on the back. "Incredible," he remarked.

Emily's ghostly spirit continued to linger around Grace. Jon reached into the trunk and pulled out the rag doll. "This looks like Brittney Michael's doll," he said, totally amazed. He turned the doll over and read the inscription, "To Brittney from Nana. I can't believe it."

"What are you two talking about?" Grace asked. "No one's been inside that trunk since Granny closed and locked it years ago."

Dan pulled a thick book out of the bottom of the chest. He ran his eyes over the fragile pages and said, "It looks like some sort of diary."

"May I see that?" Grace reached for the book. "Maybe this will tell us something," her eyes flashed as she thumbed through the pages.

Dan watched his mother. " People usually write their deepest and sometimes darkest thoughts in their diaries. You might not want to share everything in there with us."

Jon wasn't as reluctant as his brother to delve into his grandmother's personal thoughts. "Read it Mom."

Grace sighed. "It's after midnight. I'm sure you're both exhausted, I know I am. I'd rather wait until morning."

"If we're taking a vote, I'd like to hear what's in it now," Jon was all wound up.

Robert intervened. "There is no vote and I think it's enough that your mother has the book. It'll keep till morning. Come on Grace; let's go to bed. You can read it tomorrow. That book laid there all this time; one more day won't change anything."

An icy breeze hit Dan in the face causing him to shudder. It scared him to think that what happened in his apartment in Italy could start again now. *I haven't forgotten about you Emily. Please be patient.*

Grace was already on her feet. With Robert's arm securely around her waist, the decision was made. "We'll see you boys in the morning. Sleep well."

Jon whined at Dan. "How can we sleep now? It isn't fair. Up until now, all we've had was hunches. That book might give us some hard evidence."

"It's Mom's decision. I'm tired too. Morning will come soon enough." Dan turned from Jon and saw that Emily was still behind his mother.

The look she cast back at him was nothing more than sheer evil. He could actually feel the bitter hatred Emily emitted and it was all directed at Grace.

But far worse was the shadow that rose from behind her small spiritual frame. It hovered over Emily, dark and grinning. Rotted flesh appeared to hang from its pointed teeth and a leathery, forked tongue darted from its evil grin which was focused on Grace. Dan was afraid of the demon for his mother's sake. He knew then and there that he was in a spiritual battle for his mother's very soul.

Chapter Sixty-Eight

"I want to know what's in that blasted book," Jon whined childishly.

"You will. Mom was extremely overwhelmed, in case you didn't notice. She needs time to digest some of what we threw at her. We'll talk about it in the morning. By then some of the shock should be worn off," Dan replied.

He was surprised that Jon hadn't mentioned the demonic figure that arose from Emily in the hall. "Did you happen to notice anything when we followed Mom and Dad?"

"Only that she had that damn book with her," Jon volleyed with another immature remark.

"Stop it!" Dan ordered harshly. "You didn't see the horrible demon that Emily brought with her?" Dan continued.

"No, did you? Why wasn't I able to see it? I see everything you see, don't I?" Jon lowered his voice.

"Usually, but I think this one was meant for me," Dan said cautiously.

"What do you mean?" Jon asked. "I think Emily is messing with you. Don't let her do it. You know better than to allow that to happen."

They stopped at their bedroom doors. Jon whispered from across the hall, "Doesn't it feel weird, all of us here like this again?"

Dan nodded. "I'm really tired. I'm still on Italy time. I need to get some sleep. We have a huge day ahead of us tomorrow."

"Don't worry about that thing you saw. Emily is just trying to scare you. We can't let her single us out. Our strength is in numbers, remember?" Jon reinforced Dan's own statement.

"You're probably right," Dan said, but deep down, he knew better. He closed his bedroom door, dropped his clothes on the floor and turned down the covers on the freshly made bed.

Dan lay down between the cool, fresh smelling sheets and thought about how different his mother's soft brown eyes were from Emily's icy blue ones that glowed through the blackened sockets of death.

The only light in Dan's room came from the soft afterglow of the moon that shone through his window. Emily's silhouette could be traced in a vivid shadow, standing at the foot of his bed. Determined to get some rest, Dan closed his eyes and boldly said, "Good night Emily."

It didn't take long for Dan to fall into a dream like state. Instead of peaceful rest, Dan found himself in the middle of a psychic battlefield. He was in a frigid room that resembled a walk-in freezer. It contained one small trunk and several carefully stacked boxes.

In his dream, Dan reached for his neck and snatched off his stiff white collar and laid it on an antique trunk that sat in the middle of the room.

Immediately, the boxes began spilling their contents. Images of the children belonging to the freed remains flashed before him as their bones piled up quickly, making it difficult for him to move. The calcified body parts began to wrap tightly around Dan's limbs, restraining him.

All attempts to climb out of the pile were futile and before he knew it, they were around his chest, then neck until finally the unclaimed mound of bones buried him alive.

Out of the depths of his skeletal tomb, Dan called out to his Lord for help. Fighting with every bit of spiritual strength he had, Dan was finally able to claw his way to the top and free himself.

Skulls were lined up on the floor looking up at him. They all turned in unison and stared at Dan through their empty sockets with jaws drawn back in a sinister, evil grin.

The room in his nightmare became claustrophobic and suffocating. Dan's mind raced with reenactments of the children's failed escapes. This is only a dream. I have to wake up. I have to bury Emily's bones.

He woke with a start. His breathing was fast and heavy as a voice trailed through his waking thoughts. "It isn't enough. I want more."

Dan threw back the covers and sat up in bed. After rubbing his face hard with both hands, he ran his fingers through his thick, wet, matted hair and let out a deep, hard sigh. After a few moments, Dan straightened himself and sat cross-legged. He pondered Emily's words, spoken as he was coming out of his deepest sleep. 'I want more.'

The house was quiet. Dan's room was stuffy. Even the clock on his nightstand seemed to have stopped ticking. He got up and walked over to the window. Cool beads of sweat slid down his back. Dan snatched a tee shirt off the chair by his desk and slipped it over his head. As he opened the window and inhaled the cool, sweet night air, Dan felt revived. He knelt alongside the window seat.

"Protect me from my predator, Father God. Keep me whole and healthy of mind, body and soul."

Dan went back to bed and pulled the sheet up snuggly around his neck. Before closing his eyes, he gazed at the full moon that hung suspended outside his window, turned his back to the glow and fell back to sleep.

Chapter Sixty-Nine

Dan was awakened by a light tapping on his bedroom door.

"Danny are you up?" It was his mother's loving voice. He smiled.

"Yes Mom. I'll be right out," he answered.

He rolled over and tried to focus on the clock through the sleep sand in his eyes. The familiar image of Darth Vader's black helmet faced him. The clock was a gift for one of his younger birthdays. It told him that he had slept long into the morning.

"It's after ten o'clock. I can't believe I slept in this late."

He thought about everything that had transpired and Emily's bones that were still wrapped carefully in Jon's jacket, bound and stashed in the trunk of the car. "How can I explain this to Mom?" He sat up, hung his legs over the side of the bed and contemplated getting up.

Before he was able to get to his feet, Jon burst into the room. "Come on you lazy bum. When are you going to get up? Mom wouldn't let me bother you this morning," he said sarcastically in a sing song manner. Jon wiped some syrup off the corner of his mouth. Dan could smell the sweet scent of maple when Jon plopped next to him on the bed.

"You ate already?" Dan turned to face his younger brother.

"You bet I did. Did you think I was going to wait for you? Get up. Mom won't read from Granny's diary until we're all together. I think she was looking at it when I got up. It doesn't look like she slept very well. Come on, hurry up," Jon annoyingly urged his older brother.

"There are pancakes on the table and a fresh pot of coffee if you'd like some." Grace stepped into the room and glanced around. "Not much to do in here but make the bed. Jon's been up and showered for hours. I know you have some business to take care of today, but I think after you shower, we can start reading from my mother's diary."

Dan responded anxiously, "I'll take a cup of coffee and we can go ahead and get started. My shower can wait. But first .

Do you mind if I go to the bathroom and at least wash my face?" Jon was about to say something, but Grace gently touched his arm.

"Of course you can. We'll meet you in the living room," she said and lead Jon down the hall. Robert was waiting for them in the living room. It appeared that everyone was more than ready to hear what secrets Sarah Thatcher hid in her private journal

Grace made up a tray with coffee cups, her old, familiar ceramic cow creamer, a sugar bowl, and a pot of freshly brewed coffee. She brought it into the living room and set it on the coffee table. Dan entered the room just as everyone was taking a seat.

Grace sat down in her chair, next to the fireplace and asked, "Do you believe in the power of dreams?"

Dan and Jon answered in unison, "Yes."

"Do you also think that if you discuss your dreams, they'll come to pass?" She asked shyly.

"I certainly hope not," Dan added. "If that were true, I'd be in big trouble after the whopper I had last night. I'd just as soon forget about it. Sometimes, you can't be sure what's real and what isn't in a dream. I do know that when we're awake, things are tangible. We perceive through our senses. When we're asleep, we see what's really there, but beyond our reach."

Grace held her mother's diary tightly in her hands. "I never knew this diary existed. My mother had a lot of secrets. It bothers me that even as I got older; she never felt it necessary to share anything personal with me." Grace spoke softly as she opened the well-preserved leather book. "She must have started this shortly after they lost Emily. I can understand why she would do that, but what I don't understand is all the secrecy. My parents swept all evidence of Emily under the carpet, so to speak, as if she never existed."

"Everyone deals with loss differently," Dan offered his professional opinion.

"I suppose," Grace sighed. "Well, here goes," she said before beginning to read her mother's private thoughts out loud.

Chapter Seventy

April 18, 1948

It's been ten months and the pain hasn't gotten any better. I sit in this rocking chair and try to remember how it felt to hold my precious little girl in my arms. I go through all that's left of Emily; some scattered photographs, her hairbrush and the nightgown she wore the night before her disappearance. It still holds her smell.

Susan continues to say foolish things about Emily. Her incessant whispering drives me crazy. I fear there is something wrong with that woman. She insists that she sees Emily around the house. I'm afraid of her. I'm certain that she is out of her mind or that she's trying to make me go mad. I don't know why I ever agreed to let her stay with us.

April 21, 1948
Susan doesn't seem to be able to differentiate between the loss of her own daughter and our Emily. Her behavior is becoming stranger every day. I think I'm pregnant. I haven't told Charles yet. It's becoming harder to hide my growing middle. Susan had the nerve to ask me at the dinner

table, right in front of Charles if I was putting on weight. Charles didn't comment. He wouldn't. He's too much of a gentleman to do anything so crude. But, it makes me wonder if Susan knows. I don't want her to know. I don't want her around my baby or me.

April 24, 1948

I have to tell Charles that I want Susan out of this house. This morning I watched her walk over to her yard. Her house is empty and it's beginning to show signs of vacancy. The yard is a bit unsightly. I thought she might be feeling better and was going in, but she didn't. I watched her by that awful hemlock bush. She was taking clippings from it.

I told her years ago that it was a poisonous weed that grows wild and it was dangerous to have around the children. She pretended not to know a thing about the hemlock plant when her husband asked her what it was. I should have spoken up then. That was before he became ill. She had such a beautiful little girl.

She's insane. I can't have her around my family, especially my baby.

April 26, 1948

Today, Susan called me a worrywart when I warned her about the plant. I hope she wasn't stupid enough to cook with the leaves or flowers on that poisonous bush. Her daughter and husband both died of unknown causes. Stupid or clever? I know I'm not being paranoid.

April 28, 1948

Susan finds it necessary to go over to the house and tend to that hemlock bush every day now. She acts like she loves that plant, but I know better. Everyone thinks she just needs something to care for right now. No one will listen to me. I have to watch her all the time. The more I think about it, the more I feel that her infatuation with that vile plant is the reason her husband had constant stomach ailments before he died. I don't think she wanted me to know about that. He complained about it to me once when I was outside with Emily. I saw Susan watching us from behind the kitchen curtain. I won't have her in my house another minute. My God, she knows I'm watching her. She just glanced at the house. God forgive me if I'm falsely accusing her, but the facts are adding up.

April 30, 1948

Susan must have had something to do with Emily's disappearance. I wish Charles wouldn't treat me like I'm the one who's out of my mind. He is patronizing me and I know he wouldn't believe me right now. If only I could tell him what I know.

That boy across the street, I think his name is Luke Phillips. He was snooping around the neighbor's house and looking at her hemlock bush. I hope he didn't touch it. It's poisonous. I shooed him away and he looked terrified when we made eye contact. Stupid boy... I'll have to remember to keep an eye on him. I wonder what he was up to.

May 1, 1948

She has to leave today. Susan is coming. I can't let her catch me writing in my diary. If she knew about it, she would try to find it and read it. Then she would know that I found out about her. I'm convinced she'll try to hurt my baby. I have to hide this book. I'll lock it in my trunk. I can't even tell Charles about the baby until she's gone.

May 2, 1948

Susan caught me writing in my diary today. I have no other choice but to expose her for what she is.

May 3, 1948

My heart is so heavy today. I went up to the attic. Everything is still where I left it, except for the doll. I searched everywhere. It's gone. I'm sure that Susan took it. I never gave Emily the rag doll I made for her birthday. Her presents are still unopened in the attic. She never came home from the carnival for her party. I know asking Charles about it will only make him angry. He still won't share his feelings with me. He'll be furious if he knows I was in the attic going through her things. I put all of Emily's pictures in my trunk now. What if by God's grace, Emily comes home? What if by some slim chance, they find her? I have to wait. I have to be careful and protect this baby I'm carrying.

I just looked up and Charles is standing in the doorway watching me write. There are tears on his face. We have to talk. I hope he believes me.

Chapter Seventy-One

Tears weighed heavily in Grace's eyes as she finished reading from her mother's diary. "These pictures aren't in color, but I imagine Emily had my mother's eyes. I remember them being the color of blue sea glass." A black and white photograph of Emily was stuck between the last two pages of Sarah's diary.

"She did," Dan said with a warm smile. "I wonder if the boy, Luke Phillips that she mentioned is the same one that is the priest at our home parish. That would really be something."

Jon shook his head. "No wonder your parents kept that whole mess from you while you were growing up. Who'd want to expose their child to all that grief and drama?"

"I feel badly, because after all they went through, it only made it harder on them to raise me," Grace said. "My poor mother. It had to be horrendous for her trying to hide her fears from everyone, not to mention the pregnancy."

"You realize that this diary not only holds information about Emily, but it has some incriminating facts pertaining to their neighbor, Susan Young," Dan said. "We should probably take it with us today. I wonder if it really was Father Luke who grew up across the street from your parents. He might even know things about Mrs. Young that no one is aware of."

"You don't suppose she really poisoned her husband and child with that hemlock plant, do you?" Jon asked.

"I don't know. This is the first I'm learning about it," Grace said.

"Granny was most likely right about her neighbor," Jon stated. "It makes sense. What a sneaky little creep Father Luke was." Jon laughed out loud.

"It stands to reason that if she was able to kill her husband and child, Mrs. Young killed Emily too. She was obviously mentally ill. If Granny hadn't been so suspicious, none of us would be here today," Dan concluded.

"That's certainly a scary thought," Robert interjected.

"What about all those other little girls?" Jon asked.

"We aren't sure of anything. We're only speculating at this point. That's why we need to get as much information about Granny, Grandpa and Emily as we can," Dan added.

"And don't forget Susan Young," Jon mentioned.

"Not to mention our dear Father Luke," Grace added.

"Is there anymore in the diary?" Robert asked as he reached for Grace's hand.

"No, that's it," Grace closed the book. "My mother appeared to have very good instincts," Grace stated.

Robert leaned in closer to the conversation. "You never really know a person."

Jon spoke up in reference to the poisonous plant. "We get a lot of calls in the ER pertaining to children or pets eating plants in their yards, but not too many cut it up and serve it for dinner," Jon said sarcastically.

"I would hope not," Grace added.

"One raw leaf of the hemlock has enough poison to kill a child," Jon explained. "So, it could easily be hidden in a salad or sandwich."

"My mother never shared any of this with me. Mrs. Young was already gone by the time I was born." Grace sounded relieved.

"What do we do now?" Jon asked while rummaging through the rest of the things in the trunk. "Look at this picture." He held up an old photograph of a very young and attractive Susan Young with Emily. "It's obvious that Emily knew her. This must have been taken shortly before she went missing."

"Both my parents have passed. We'll never really know the truth," Grace sighed as she placed the diary back in the trunk.

Dan cleared his throat. "Mom, I think now is as good a time as any to tell you and dad the real reason I came home from Italy."

Jon couldn't imagine how Dan was going to tell them about Emily. Dan felt that Emily was harboring dark feelings toward his mother. Grace was in grave danger if he was right. "Maybe it would be easier if Emily helped us," he suggested.

Grace crossed herself. "Is she still here?"

"Oh, she's still here. I'll bet a year's salary on it," Jon answered smugly. "It's totally up to her whether or not she allows you to see her. Angels or spirits come and go all the time. Whether or not we see them is left to their discretion."

"I'll testify to that," Dan added.

"Do you think Dad and I can see Emily?" Grace asked.

Emily faced Grace as she hovered next to the old trunk that her mother had kept locked all these years, hiding her very existence. They were sisters, yet they looked nothing alike. If anything, Grace could be Emily's grandmother.   Emily watched Grace intently as she thumbed through their mother's private photographs and diary. It was Sarah and Emily's secret. Now, Grace had invaded the privacy that was shared only by the dead.

Grace lived the life that Emily should have lived. Emily reached for the diary and held it up. The worn book hung suspended in the air like a magic trick.

It opened slowly and the pages began to fan swiftly.

Grace looked on in amazement. "Is that you, Emily?"

Emily was totally infuriated with Grace. She tossed her head flippantly toward Dan. Her ghostly features were twisted with rage. She began spinning around in a furious frenzy. Everything in the room turned and moved from its original position. Robert reached for Grace and clung to her protectively. It was hard to be heard over Emily's loud wailing.

Grace covered her ears and leaned on Robert. "Make her stop," she cried. Jon went to the other side of his mother and blocked the flying objects that Emily was hurling.

"Knock it off Emily," Jon yelled.

Suddenly everything stopped cold. Emily's eyes, hard as flint, stared at Jon and his father as they embraced Grace. She looked at Dan for the first time and cried out in torment.

"Help me, Dan Markos. Help me or suffer the consequences." Her raspy voice floated out of her twisted mouth as each word carried her pleas.

Dan looked at his mother. "Can you hear her Mom?"

Grace lifted her chin cautiously. "Yes, I can. Is it really Emily?"

Dan couldn't hide the sympathy he was feeling for Emily. "She's crying out for help. She needs us."

Grace glanced at her disarrayed living room. "Where is she? Why is she reacting to me in such a horrible way?"

Dan lowered his voice as the noise in the room began to dissipate. "She's standing in front of you holding her arms out. I think she wants you to hold her. Emily is jealous of the life you had with Granny and Grandpa. The life she was robbed of."

Robert tried to protest. "What if she hurts your mother? Look what she did to this room."

Jon placed his hand gently on his father's shoulder. "Dad, please stay out of this. Mom will be fine. If she wanted to hurt her, she would have already done it."

Grace was trembling as tears soaked her face. She stood cautiously and held out her arms. "Is this what I'm supposed to do?"

Grace smiled and let out a nervous giggle. "I feel foolish. Oh my, I think it's her. I feel something cool. It's like I'm holding one of Granny's feather pillows."

Dan smiled. "That's Emily. You're holding your sister. This is the first time the two of you ever connected."

Grace closed her eyes and was allowed to feel the tiny frame of what was once Emily's mortal body. She held on to the invisible form. The only warmth came from within herself. "I don't know how to explain what I'm feeling. There's nothing solid to hang on to. It's like trying to hug a cloud," she smiled through her tears.

"I wish I could see you," Grace said to Emily.

For a brief moment, Emily allowed herself to be visible to Grace as the beautiful child she once was. Then, she faded slowly from sight.

"How do you feel?" Robert asked.

Grace was still smiling. "It was like standing in front of an opened window on a cool fall day with the breeze blowing gently on my face."

"Before Emily can cross over, she has to let go," Dan said. "I'm not quite sure she's ready to do that."

Grace wept. For the first time, she was able to grieve for her lost sister.

Jon felt a wave of dread as he thought of Emily's remains wrapped securely in his jacket. He imagined her terror, before life slipped from the very body that lay broken and lifeless in the trunk of his car.

What is it you really want, Emily? What could you possibly want with Mom?

Going through Sarah Thatcher's diary and finding the evidence needed in her private trunk made it all the more important for Dan to get Emily's remains properly identified and buried.

"Mom, we're going to the cemetery to find out how to go about having Emily's bones buried with Granny and Grandpa. It's what Emily wants and I'm sure Granny would be happy about it too," Dan announced. "Hopefully, she can cross over and finally rest in peace."

Jon stood alongside Dan and added, "Emily wants to be reunited with her mother, your mother. We need you to come along, because I'm sure we'll need your consent."

Dan and Jon explained everything to their parents from the first encounter with the Michaels family, to their predicament with Emily, Brittney and the merry-go-round.

"So what you're telling us is that you have possession of Emily's remains?" Grace asked. She was very calm and showed more interest than emotion in her question.

"Is that what you're hiding in the trunk of your car?" Robert asked as his mouth dropped open and he shook his head in disbelief.

"I don't know how anyone is going to believe us, but we have to go through with this. Emily won't allow us to stop now," Dan explained.

Robert and Grace listened to everything their sons had to say. It took a while to absorb it all before Grace said, "If you repeat that story to anyone, you're both going to end up in jail. You're in a lot of trouble, in case you don't realize it. Your story is absurd, irrational and totally unbelievable," she went on. "I listened to everything you said with an open mind. I even witnessed the paranormal activity, but I don't know how you're going to convince anyone that what you said is true."

Dan tried to reassure his mother. "Emily didn't bring us this far to have anything go wrong. I'm depending on her to step in for the final round. She's very close now; I don't think Emily is going to let anyone stop her from getting what she set out for."

Grace picked up her purse. "Whatever happens, I'll be right there with you." Her mother's diary sat on top of the now closed trunk. There was a picture of her parents with Emily sticking out from between the last two pages. Grace picked it up and glanced around the living room.

Everything was back in place. "I don't know if I'll ever be able to stay in this house alone again."

Robert walked out to the car with his sons. Jon opened the trunk and showed him the tightly wrapped jacket. From one corner, a small bony prominence protruded as proof of what they had just revealed.

"Oh boy," Robert said as Grace approached the car. He gave Grace a kiss on the cheek and turned to go back in the house.

"You're not coming with us?" she asked.

"I don't like any of this," Robert answered. "I'll wait here and hope I don't get a phone call from the police department."

Robert stood on the porch and watched them drive away. Grace sat in the passenger seat up front. She faced Robert and blew him a kiss.

Robert could see the back of Dan's head as they drove away. Next to him, turning slowly to expose her identity was the face of the little girl from the black and white photographs. He was able to see her, plain as day. It's what Emily wanted. A quick bolt of fear shot through him and Robert turned away.

He went back into the house and opened the drawer of the end table next to his recliner. His hands were shaking as Robert pulled out a rosary and quietly began to pray.

Chapter Seventy-Two

The cemetery was only fifteen minutes from the Marcos house. It was laid out above the city on top of a beautiful hill. An iron fence surrounded it, isolating the hallowed ground.

When they arrived, Jon paused a moment before passing through the gates. He looked at Dan. "This is the most active place I've ever visited. Emily should be able to gain a lot of strength here with all the energy in the air. These spirits almost feel solid."

"Let's go. I'm sure there won't be any problem burying Emily with my parents," Grace said.

"The problem is going to be proving that the bones we have in the trunk belong to your sister without making this appear to be some sort of sideshow," Dan said. Emily sat quietly in the back seat. Dan ignored her. "I've been thinking about how to approach these people and there simply isn't an easy way to do it."

"First things first, we have to get the okay to reopen Granny's gravesite before we can do anything else. Then, we have to go to the police with Emily's remains and tell them our story. Do you know what you're going to do if they don't believe us?" Jon glanced at Dan in his mirror as he parked the car in front of the cemetery office.

"I don't think we'll be alone during any of our discussions, do you?" Dan responded, deep in thought.

"Emily can really screw us if she wants to," Jon said quietly.

"I don't think that's part of her plan." Dan glanced at the ghost sitting beside him who appeared more clear and lifelike than he had ever seen her. "We have to get this done soon though."

"I wish I could see her like you boys do. I would feel better just knowing that she was actually around to help prove your story," Grace said. "Yet, I never saw anything before and I don't think I would tolerate seeing the spirits of dead people around me all the time."

"We understand, Mom. It can be overwhelming for us at times," Dan responded.

"Like now," Jon added. "I don't like being here and being able to see hundreds of roaming spirits. Their energy is remarkably high in the cemetery. I'm sure Emily feels it too."

"Hopefully, we can bring her some closure," Dan said thoughtfully. But deep down, he was beginning to doubt that this was going to be the end of it. "Let's drive past Granny and Grandpa's graves before we get started."

Jon drove to the area where his grandparents were buried. The long headstone sat on a small knoll halfway into the cemetery. As they approached the gravesites, Dan and Jon noticed Emily standing between the two plots.

"Just out of curiosity, do you see my parents?" Grace asked. She reached in her purse for a tissue.

"No as a matter of fact, I don't," Dan said. "If they crossed over into the light, their spirits won't be lingering here on earth."

"I don't see them either," Jon said. "It might be one of Emily's reasons for having a bad attitude. They didn't wait for her," Jon added.

"Think about it. If Granny didn't accept the fact that she was dead, why wait?" Dan rationalized.

"We better get started. We have a lot to deal with." Jon turned the car around and headed back to the office.

Dan was the spokesperson. Once inside, he extended his hand in a non-threatening fashion and glanced at the name on the manager's desk. He started out with a positive attitude.

"How do you do Mr. Dalcour. I'm Dan Markos. This is my mother Grace and my brother Jon." He approached the man wearing a broad smile.

Randall Dalcour stood to greet the Markos family. "How can I help you?"

Jon closed the office door. It was a long conversation with the manager of the graveyard. There was a lot of speculation about how they came into having the bones of a small child in their possession. More important was how they knew it was Emily Thatcher.

Dan explained the situation with Emily the best he could, downplaying the paranormal events, fictionalizing some of what happened and assuring the man that they were taking the bones to the police for identification before they were buried.

"That's quite a story." Mr. Dalcour's response was better than Dan expected.

"We realize it's hard to believe and we still have the police to deal with, but the sooner we get these bones buried, the better it will be for all concerned," Dan continued, not backing down from the man's suspicious tone.

"May I see the remains? I'm assuming you have them with you," Mr. Dalcour faced Dan with a note of challenge to his voice.

"Of course we do, they're in the car." Jon opened the door for his mother and followed her out to the parking lot with Dan and Mr. Dalcour behind them.

Jon opened the trunk and Dan carefully unwrapped one corner of Jon's jacket, exposing the skeletal remains.

"They belong to a child alright," Mr. Dalcour said.

"I imagine there's a lot of red tape to go through to reopen my mother's grave," Grace said.

Mr. Dalcour turned to her and said, "The police will have to positively identify these bones and release them to me before we can even think about opening your mother's grave. I hope you all realize that this isn't a simple matter."

Dan watched Emily as she hovered over Jon's car. Suddenly, heat lightning appeared to connect the trees throughout the graveyard in an amazing dot to dot extravaganza. Emily's arms were pressed tightly to her sides as the smell of burning wood coursed through the cemetery.

"It looks like we have some sort of freak storm," Mr. Dalcour said. "I hope we don't have a fire in here with all these old oak trees."

The sky flashed with an array of colors, followed by loud claps of thunder. An ancient oak stood next to the office. Before they could think to move, a huge branch from the old tree snapped and hung suspended directly over them. Everyone crouched down and covered their heads, but nothing happened. Emily remained over Jon's car parallel to the large tree branch.

"I don't like thunderstorms," Grace said without looking up. "They frighten me."

Mr. Dalcour stood as still as a stone, staring at the branch. "Did you see that?" he asked, shocked and amazed by the incident.

"I tried to tell you," Dan began. "It's Emily. It's her way of warning you of what she's capable of if things don't go her way."

Mr. Dalcour nodded his head. "As long as everyone's alright, I'm going back into the office. I'll wait to hear from the police before starting any arrangements." He hurried inside, keeping his back to what was happening in the graveyard.

They all got back into the car. Jon started the engine and drove away from the threatening branch. He watched in his rear view mirror as it dropped, crashing to the ground with a force that splintered the sturdy limb.

Dan sat back and thought about how close they came to actually being injured. He thought about what had happened to Angela's hand and his fears for his mother's well-being escalated. Emily's threats were becoming more menacing.

Now, the worst lay ahead. What version of the truth could he possibly invent to tell the police? Running the story through his mind, it came to Dan that he sounded like he was expelling a collective fantasy. How many versions of what he was about to reveal would be shared amongst those he had to tell? Each person would add more and more colorful strands to the fabrications and in the end, who would really believe them?

Chapter Seventy-Three

The Markos family drove away from the cemetery shaken over her last warning. She could have easily killed them.

"Now, all we have to do is convince the police about everything that has happened. I can't imagine how we're going to pull that off," Jon said.

"For once, I'm hoping that Emily shows up," Dan spoke as he pondered on Emily's building capabilities.

"It felt so awful seeing those little bones in your trunk," Grace maintained, though no one seemed to share her pity.

"Are you okay with this Mom?" Dan stuck his head between the two front seats and reached for his mother's hand. "I realize that you haven't got a clue about what's actually going on here. In retrospect, we aren't completely out of the dark when it comes to Emily."

"I don't have much of a choice, do I? It was a blessing for me to be able to grow up with my parents, marry your father and have you boys. Emily was victimized in more ways than one and I think she blames me for having what she missed out on," Grace said softly.

Dan felt the same way. He was surprised that Grace realized how Emily felt. "She wasn't the only victim. Your parents suffered a tremendous loss and so did you, Mom. You were raised as an only child, without the companionship of a sibling, the love of a sister and the safe, loving emotions your mother had to keep in check for fear of getting to close to you. She couldn't handle another tragedy after losing Emily. That was her first born child."

Grace thought for a moment before asking, "Do you think that Emily suffered at the hands of that sadistic murderer?"

"We don't know. At this point, after reading the diary, we suspect that she was poisoned, but no one really knows," Jon said.

"That's right, the hemlock plant," Grace said.

"This is all Emily's doing. She's had almost sixty years to plot and plan this out," Jon added.

"The police are going to want solid facts. That's all they go by. It's one thing to believe what isn't true and another thing to refuse to believe the truth. We're going to have to be on our toes when we talk to them. We can't sound like ghost chasers," Dan emphasized.

It was almost eleven o'clock when they pulled up to the police station. Jon clenched the steering wheel of his car and sat motionless.

"What's wrong," Dan asked.

"What if we go in there, tell them we have the bones of a little girl in the trunk and they slap us in handcuffs and throw us in jail? What if they don't give us a chance to explain?" Jon was starting to panic.

Dan took a deep breath before starting. "First, we aren't going to just march in there and tell them we have the bones of a little girl in the trunk. Don't talk unless someone asks you a specific question. Let me handle it."

"Oh my..." Grace followed Jon's lead and started to breath heavily.

Suddenly, without his assistance, Jon's car door opened. He looked into the mirror and Dan was smiling. Jon felt a hard shove and found himself outside of his vehicle. He walked to the front of the car and stood there. Dan followed suit and held the door open for his mother.

"You can come with us and deal with them or stay here and deal with Emily," Dan said.

Grace tucked her arm around Dan's and glanced back at Jon. He was following slowly wearing a look of dread. "Come on Son. If anything happens, I'll take the blame."

"What in the world...you'd let Mom go to jail for you?" Dan tried making Jon feel guilty.

Jon ignored Dan's remark and asked, "Do you even know what you're going to say?" His legs felt heavy. "I think I'm going to be sick."

Dan entered the police station with a false sense of confidence and stepped up to the desk. There was an officer standing behind a glass window that Dan decided was bullet proof because the glass was so thick. The uniformed man spoke through a voice piece.

"What can I do for you?" the officer addressed Dan.

"We'd like to speak to a detective," Dan replied.

The officer asked, "What's this pertaining to?"

Grace stepped up to the glass. "We need speak to a detective, please. Tell him we won't talk to anyone else."

Dan was surprised at his mother's boldness, but it seemed to do the trick. The desk sergeant slid some papers under the glass.

"Fill these out and I'll get someone for you to talk to," he instructed.

The area where they waited was small. There were three closed doors to the right. Two police officers observed the Markos family suspiciously. It didn't help lower Jon's stress level at all.

It seemed like forever before a couple of plain clothed men entered the waiting area through one of the closed steel doors. Dan, Jon and Grace all turned abruptly to face them.

"These are the people I was telling you about." The desk sergeant left the two detectives with the Markos family and went back to his position.

The first detective extended his hand to Grace. "How do you do; I'm Lieutenant James Sullivan. Please, come back to my office where we can talk."

James was a short, middle aged man that presented himself very professionally. Lieutenant Sullivan led them back through the heavy steel doors into a hallway where the single office doors had glass windows identifying what department they belonged to.

Jon's first instinct was to turn and run. Dan placed his hand firmly on Jon's elbow and directed him slowly through the doorway into the hall.

They stopped in front of the door with Detective Bureau written in bold black letters on the clear glass panel. Under that were four names with Lieutenant James Sullivan listed first. He held the door open as they entered one at a time.

Chapter Seventy-Four

There were three chairs positioned in front of Detective Sullivan's desk. "Take a seat," he said. His chair looked old and comfortable. He sat down, took a pen from his jacket pocket and opened a well-used tablet that sat on top his desk. There was a desk phone to his right and several stacks of manila folders scattered in front of him.

The Lieutenant set up a small tape recorder and glanced up at the three people sitting in front of him. Detective Sullivan reached out and turned on the tape recorder. "This will run until our interview is over."

Dan didn't wait to be asked. He uncharacteristically blurted out, "My name is Dan Markos. We're here to have a child's remains identified for burial. We believe they belong to my mother's sister, Emily Thatcher. She disappeared almost sixty years ago. They're in the trunk of my brother's car."

Dan realized how awkward he sounded but continued, "This has been very difficult for us. After we finish explaining everything, we hope you'll help us."

The detective leaned forward, laced his fingers together and rested his hands on the desk. "Is your brother's car out front?" he asked calmly.

Detective Sullivan glanced over at his partner, who had stopped what he was doing to listen.

"This is harder than I thought it would be. You must get crackpots in here all the time, but I assure you, we are very serious and on the level," Dan pleaded.

They couldn't tell whether Detective Sullivan believed Dan or not because, he showed no emotion. He opened his tablet and began taking notes. "Let me get this straight. You say that your sister is dead," he addressed Grace.

"Yes, for over fifty-eight years now. I wasn't born when the kidnapping took place," she answered.

Detective Sullivan looked at his partner. "Take the keys to Mr. Markos' car and check it out."

Matt came over to the desk and held out his hand. Jon surrendered his keys without prompting.

"If we find the remains that you spoke of, do you have an explanation as to how you came in possession of them?" The detective was as cool as a cucumber when he addressed the Markos family. He showed no emotion.

"We'd like to explain. Please, allow us to tell you everything from the very beginning," Dan said humbly.

Detective Sullivan remained composed. He nodded his head to Dan.

"The explosion of the merry-go-round mirrors at Willows Park all ties into this. If they haven't already located them, there are several other skeletons in the center structure of that ride." Dan kept talking. Detective Sullivan looked around to make sure there were police officers standing by to witness the statement Dan was making.

Dan explained everything that he thought was pertinent.

"That's quite a story," the detective said when Dan appeared to be finished.

Dan leaned back in his chair. Jon and Grace sat quietly. There was nothing more to say. The detective went over his notes, trying to make sense of them.

"The thing is, we have to be able to identify the bones that we brought to you as positively belonging to Emily Thatcher before the cemetery will open our grandmother's grave. We have to bury her remains in the same gravesite, because that's what Emily has demanded." The more Dan talked about Emily, the less credible his story sounded.

The detective chose his words carefully. "You claim to be here to surrender the remains of a child that you believe to be your long lost sister. Is that correct?" He addressed Grace.

"Yes sir," she answered. There was a slight quiver to her voice.

"This presumed relative should be about sixty years old now, if she would have lived," the officer continued.

"Correct," Dan answered.

Jon was the only one who couldn't bring himself to speak.

"Do you all live together?" Detective Sullivan questioned.

"No sir. I live in Italy, my brother Jon has his own apartment and my mother lives with my father here in town," Dan had a quick answer for every question asked.

"I feel that you seriously doubt our story," Dan said.

The detective was stalling while Jon's car was being searched for evidence of foul play.

Sensing his weakness, Detective Sullivan zeroed in on Jon. "Can you tell me how this child died?"

With more composure than he thought he was capable of, Jon responded appropriately. "No, we were hoping that you could tell us."

Grace leaned forward. "Emily was my older sister. I didn't know very much about her. We never met. I only just recently learned about her kidnapping. I have some old photographs and we did find my mother's diary. She mentioned a woman named Susan Young. She was their neighbor at the time of my sister's disappearance. Also, my mother wrote some interesting statements about a hemlock bush and poisonings," Grace added.

"We're going to have to confiscate that as evidence and hold on to it until we're certain there isn't any involvement on your part. None of you are to leave town unless you check with me," Detective Sullivan ordered.

"Are we in trouble? Are you going to arrest us?" Jon sat up straight in his chair. He looked pale.

"I don't have anything to hold you on, yet. By the way, you said there were more bodies inside the center of the merry-go-round at the park. How do you know this and how do you know that the bones in your trunk belong to Emily Thatcher?" He looked from one set of eyes to the next.

Jon spoke up spontaneously, "We were led to the location by Emily's ghost. Her remains were in a box in the center structure of the merry-go-round at Willows Park. There were carefully arranged stacks of old cartons. Each stack was labeled with a name. There are pictures of the individual children with personal belongings such as clothing and there's even a piece of their hair. There's enough evidence for your whole forensic team."

Detective Sullivan listened with interest and wrote down everything Jon said. His doubt of their innocence was becoming obvious by the way the lieutenant paused and looked at the Markos as a group.

"If you don't believe us, I'm sure that Emily will be more than happy to convince you," Jon said.

Sounding like a threat, Lieutenant Sullivan responded. "What's that supposed to mean?" He reached for his phone, but it slid just out of his reach. He looked at the Markos family members as if they had something to do with it. His hand was still stretched out toward the telephone.

"Is this some sort of trick?" He stood and stepped toward the door. Just as he reached it, the door slammed hard in his face, shattering the glass pane.

Grace rushed to the officer's side. "Are you alright?" she asked. The incident shook her up. "Emily," she cried. "Stop it right now. How are we going to get this man to help us with you acting this way?" She turned back to the officer.

"Now, if you'll please listen and try to understand what we've been going through. You have to remember that Emily is still actually only five years old and doesn't know any other way to get what she wants. It appears that she was a very spoiled little girl and used to getting her way," Grace added.

Detective Sullivan looked cautiously around and asked, "What does she want?"

"Justice," Dan stated simply. "She's a five year old child that was kidnapped from a carnival ride and never found until now. She made that possible. She also made certain that each one of us played a part in her discovery. I'm sure that if you look into this case, you'll find there's a reason for your involvement. We'll give you the dates and events. Just give us a chance. By the way, we aren't sure that Emily realizes that she's dead."

Grace smiled sincerely at the puzzled officer. "One thing is certain. Emily wants her remains buried with my mother. That's what this is all about. It took her over fifty years to come back and be reunited with our parents. I don't think you or anyone else is going to be able to stop that from happening."

Detective Sullivan went back to his desk. He put his hand on his chair to pull it back and met with a strong resistance. "Emily?" he asked.

"Yes, she's standing with both hands on your chair," Dan answered. "We also should have told you that my brother and I have a gift. We can see dead people."

Detective Sullivan didn't know what to believe. "I guess we'll have to take this a little more seriously."

Dan nodded. "How long do you think it will take to identify the remains as belonging to Emily Thatcher?"

"It's all very complicated," he began. "There are a lot of departments I need to get in touch with. Is she still here?" Detective Sullivan looked around his desk.

"I've been a detective for many years. I've never dealt with anything like this before and I have to tell you, I don't believe in ghosts. Yet, I can't explain what's happening," he said.

Grace laid her mother's diary on the detective's desk and pushed it slowly towards him. "I hope you're able to find something useful in here. Please let me know when I can have it back."

"I'll get in touch with you when the forensic team is finished identifying the remains. If they turn out to be your sister's, we'll release them to you for proper burial," he responded with a lack of expression. "There is still the problem of explaining to the chief how you came about having these bones in your possession. It isn't going to be easy convincing him that you were led to them by a ghost," the detective exhaled slowly. "This could still be just a trick. I'm not saying that I believe everything you've told me."

Jon spoke seriously. "We know there's some sort of time limit for Emily. She can become quite convincing when things don't go her way."

"If you were a believer, I could go deeper into what has occurred over the past few days," Dan said.

Detective Sullivan listened and watched as the other police officers were being held in the hall by an unknown force. They weren't able to get into the detective's office.

"It's as if they've run into a brick wall," Detective Sullivan observed. "If this is a trick, you're very good."

Dan shook his head. "For now, I can only tell you that Emily will stop at nothing to get her bones laid to rest in her mother's gravesite. I intend to see that it happens. I also think that somehow, you're involved with Emily. It's why she brought us to you. If not you, then someone close to you. We'll see. It will all be made clear, soon."

Chapter Seventy-Five

Detective Sullivan led the Markos family out through a back door. The door they entered was currently being cleared of broken glass from Emily's recent outburst.

"I have a police car waiting out front to take you home. Your car will be returned to you when the forensic team is finished with it," Detective Sullivan explained. He paused a moment, "I'm not sure exactly what happened here today, but I will be watching you closely. If, by some slim chance, this story of yours about Emily Thatcher is true and she is haunting you...from what I can figure out; at the worst moment of her life, she must have been overwhelmed with terror."

"Why do you say that?" Dan asked.

"She shared it with us today," he said.

Dan nodded in agreement. "Somehow, Emily found a way to return after all these years. I find her endurance and courage unimaginable. Our mission was set from the moment we were secured and we've been on her schedule ever since. She's not to be underestimated."

"From what we experienced here, I'd have to agree with you," the detective added. "However, there seems to be something more. I think she's capable of greater things. That's only IF she is in fact, real. Something or someone has a strong influence over her."

Dan thought about the black woman who always seemed to be around when they needed help. "It's odd how much you've learned about Emily in such a short time."

The detective left them at the back door. "You'll be hearing from me. I'm going to go back through the old and closed files to see if I can find something pertaining to those missing children."

"I'm sure that the articles we gave you from the library will help," Dan said.

"I'll definitely check them out for authenticity and any leads," the detective responded firmly.

Sounds of chaos erupted from behind the detective and they all looked back. Jon quickly stepped out the door gently guiding his mother by her arm.

Dan shook his head sympathetically and said, "I'm sure within a few hours, you'll decide to put a rush on this investigation."

The look Detective Sullivan gave Dan was hard to explain. "Like I said before, if this is some sort of trick, you people are really good. However, if Emily is for real and has been waiting since 1947 to be put to rest, then who am I to stand in her way. I don't see her, but I won't deny hearing the voice of a child close to my ear."

Dan knew exactly what he was talking about. "Just heed her warnings." The door closed with a heavy thud. It could only be opened from the inside.

Dan caught up with Jon and his mother as they headed around the side of the station to the car that was waiting for them out front. There was a police officer standing next to it.

"I'll be driving you home," he said as he opened the back door.

Jon bent and whispered in his mother's ear. "Have you ever had to sit in the back seat of a police car before?" There was a bit of mischief in his question.

"Just get in before someone we know sees us," Grace ducked into the back seat and slid over to make room for her sons.

The police officer wasn't very talkative on the ride home. He'd been given a quick briefing about their situation and was either instructed not to say anything or simply didn't want to get involved.

"There's a dark shadow on this case," Dan spoke quietly to his family. "Nothing is worse than a monster that abducts children and then kills them."

"I hope they keep it out of the newspaper," Jon added.

"I didn't even think about that," Grace mumbled.

The officer spoke up. "My name is Scott. I apologize for listening to your conversation, but I couldn't help overhearing. With all the commotion going on earlier at the station, the reporters have already started sniffing around. They can smell something like this from miles away," he half chuckled. "You don't have to tell me how you did all that if you don't want to, but I'm no fool. I know there's no such thing as ghosts."

Dan, Jon and Grace braced themselves for something horrendous, but nothing happened. Obviously, Emily had more important things to work on. It almost scared them that she appeared to be gone; at least for now.

"We don't want people to think we're crazy," Grace said. "I'm worried about spectators and gawkers who are under the impression that they're going to experience something supernatural."

Scott attempted to reassure the family. "If anything like that happens, call us right away. If we have to, we can send a car out or assign someone to watch your house until this is settled."

When they reached the Markos residence, the police officer got out of the squad car first and opened the back door for them.

Robert stood up from the porch swing where he was waiting for his family to get home when he eyed the police car.

Jon spotted a man with a camera standing on the sidewalk. The officer reprimanded the pedestrian and sent him on his way. "I'll be sure to tell Detective Sullivan about this. He might be able to detour these people somehow."

Scott nodded and adjusted his black baseball style cap that had 'Police' written in white block letters across the front. "In the meantime, you might want to stay indoors, keep your doors locked and your drapes drawn. There's a lot of thrill seekers around."

Officer Scott got into his squad car and looked back at the Markos house. They had gone inside as instructed and closed the curtains. A chill ran across his shoulders when Scott witnessed a dark shadow hover over the length of the Markos home. It wasn't over any other house. "These people give me the creeps. There's something spooky as hell going on and I'm not sticking around to see what happens." Without hesitating, he drove away and didn't look back.

Chapter Seventy-Six

Detective Sullivan immediately ordered every member of the Markos and Michaels family to submit DNA samples. The closest forensic lab was three hours away, which meant that it might take some time to get the results. Once Emily's remains were identified, the only thing needed to move the earth above Sarah Thatcher's grave was a signature from the next of kin, which would be Grace.

The funeral arrangements kept everyone in the Markos family busy for the next couple of weeks. Father Luke Phillips, their parish priest, agreed to say the Requiem Mass for the services requested for Emily's remains.

"I spoke with Father Luke," Grace announced at the dinner table one evening. "I hope that's alright with you, Dan. I know there was a problem between the two of you at one time. He was hesitant, but he finally agreed to do the service for Emily."

"That's okay." It was all Dan said.

Newspaper reporters initially rushed in with their over exaggerated articles and photographs that captured stolen glimpses of the Markos family. It was difficult keeping the ghost hunters at bay.

Grace sat at the kitchen table after returning home from the funeral parlor. The whole ordeal was more overwhelming than she had anticipated. Dan sat down across from her.

"It was difficult picking out Emily's casket. It resembles a beautiful doll bed," Grace began. "I don't think my mother would have handled this very well."

"It drives home our own mortality," Dan said.

Grace let out a heavy sigh. "Emily should be very pleased with everything we're doing for her." There was a note of distaste in Grace's voice.

Dan watched his mother closely. For a moment, he could almost recognize Emily's features as her expressions casually altered. Her usually small, brown eyes suddenly appeared large, round and distinctly sunken in with dark circles that favored a charcoal color. It was Emily's intent to scare Dan.

He couldn't believe what he was witnessing as Grace's straight, slender nose widened, shortened and turned up slightly. Her skin turned a sallow shade of gray, giving her a ghostly appearance. Grace's soft, round face became elongated and slender with high, flattened cheekbones. She was beginning to look like a cartoon caricature of Emily.

Dan pushed away the shock and fear and instead remained calm. He scanned the area around his mother. I don't see her but that doesn't mean Emily isn't here. What is she up to now?

"Let's all go out to dinner tonight, my treat," Dan suggested.

Jon poked his head into the kitchen. "How about Italian?" Jon had taken some time off work while his brother was visiting. He missed his apartment, but had agreed with Dan that they should stay close to his mom right now.

Grace pushed her chair back from the table. Her response was sharp. "Now my cooking isn't good enough?" She stomped toward the door and mumbled, her voice barely audible, "Just get it done. Bury my bones with MY MOTHER!"

"What did she say?" Jon asked, shocked by his mother's remark.

"Have you seen Emily lately?" Dan asked.

"No, why have you?" Jon answered.

"I'm not sure, but keep a close watch on Mom," Dan warned.

"Crap," Jon said. "No wonder dad's been spending so much time out in the garage."

"I think he's cleaning up our old fishing poles," Dan remarked and headed for the garage.

Dan came up behind his father, "What're you doing Dad?"

Robert had four or five fishing poles taken apart on his workbench. Without looking up, he responded harshly, "I have to get these poles ready if we're going up to the lake when this is all finished. Your mother..." he hissed through clenched teeth.

"You aren't blaming Mom for this mess?" Dan pulled up a stool and sat next to his father.

"Of course not, but she's been acting different lately. Your mother is the sweetest person I know and she's been so angry and irritable lately. I just want everything to get back to normal. Enough is enough," he frowned. A crease ran along the length of Robert's forehead.

"Be patient with her Dad. I'm sure, it won't be long now," Dan smiled. "Can I help you with anything? My old tackle box should be out here somewhere."

"It's over there on the bench. I'm finished out here for tonight," Robert said. He wiped his hands on an old rag and went into the house.

Dan was left standing alone in the garage. Without warning, the lights went out, the garage door came down slowly, and the temperature plummeted to a chilling cold. Dan was getting tired of the frigid attacks.

"What the hell?" His teeth chattered as he spoke. "We've performed like marionettes for you Emily. This has to stop."

Dan tried to orient himself in the dark with one hand out in front of him as he stared hard into the blackness that was closing in on him. He felt a cool eerie mist next to his cheek. It felt alive. There was a warmness that could only come from mortal lungs. "I don't know what you're up to, but you need to know that once your bones are buried with your mother, you have to go into the light. It's over Emily. This is the end."

Dan went into the house hoping to see his mother in the kitchen, but apparently everyone had lost their appetite. He walked through the house to see if anyone was still up and found Jon out on the front porch.

The evening sky was filled with twinkling stars and a moon so full and bright that it cast eerie shadows across the yard.

"Did Mom and Dad go to bed?" Dan asked.

"I guess so," Jon bit into an overstuffed sandwich. "What's going on with Mom?"

Dan let out a sigh. "I'm not sure. We have to stay close to her though."

"It's almost over," Jon said. "This whole ordeal has been way too creepy. I'm sorry for bringing you into it."

"I don't think you had a choice. This has been planned out for years. Emily has manipulated every detail," Dan said.

"How's your faith holding up?" Jon asked.

"Why would you even ask me that? I'm still very strong in my faith. I wouldn't have been able to make it through everything Emily has confronted me with if I wasn't," Dan answered without hesitation. "I think Emily is getting stronger and she realizes it. The sooner we seal that casket and bury her, the better."

"Is that how you both feel?" Grace stood behind the darkness of the screen door silently listening to her son's conversation. Her eavesdropping startled them.

"Come on out and sit with us Mom. It's a beautiful night," Dan scooted over on the porch swing and patted the seat.

"What did you mean by that question?" Jon's manner wasn't as subtle as his brother's. "Of course it's how we both feel. Won't you be glad when this is over?"

Grace stepped cautiously out on to the porch. The moon glow fell directly on her face and she shot a defiant look at Dan. Her image was imbedded so deeply in his mind that when he closed his eyes, he could still see her piercing blue eyes on the inside of his eyelids and it sickened him.

In an attempt to divert Emily's conspicuous intimidation, Dan chose not to respond to her cruel attack. Instead, he redirected his thoughts from the tormenting transformation to the simplicity of sitting outside on a warm summer night and enjoying the sweet smelling air.

Emily wasn't going to allow herself to be undermined. She had a determined and willful spirit. It was apparent that Emily was not only making a severe impact on Grace's personality, she was able to take control of her body. Then, Grace stepped directly in the path of the moon's glow and Dan watched as her eyes slowly converted to their natural, soft, brown color.

Chapter Seventy-Seven

The sharp ringing of the telephone pierced the deadly silence of the late hour. Dan rushed to answer it. "Hello."

It was Detective Sullivan. "Sorry for calling so late." Dan heard a flicker of hope, along with a trace of excitement in his voice.

"No, no, please; don't worry about it. This is good news, I presume?" Dan took a deep breath and waited impatiently to hear what Detective Sullivan had to say.

"Forensics was able to identify some of the missing children. It's been very intense and unusually emotional around here," he began. "They tracked down family members that made it possible to retrieve medical and dental records. It's been quite an ordeal locating the families of these unfortunate children."

"That's great, but what about the ones from the trunk of Jon's car? Were they able to identify them as belonging to Emily Thatcher, my mother's sister?" Dan asked point blank. Though grateful for the others, he mainly wanted to know if they had found Emily's remains or not. He felt that there would be hell to pay if they weren't.

Jon and Grace entered the house. Robert stood just outside his bedroom door. They all waited patiently for the detective's report.

"The forensic team still has a lot of work to do, matching all the uncovered bones with the right children. However, I'm pleased to say we'll be taking Emily's remains to the cemetery and turning them over to Mr. Dalcour for burial, first thing in the morning. She has been given top priority." The detective sounded genuinely relieved.

"That's great news," Dan gave a thumbs-up sign to his family.

"I'm delivering her personally. It's the first thing on my agenda," the detective added. "These past few weeks have been rough, if you know what I mean."

"I'm afraid I do," Dan said. "I really appreciate you calling. I'll pass the information along to my family."

Instead of hanging up or saying goodbye, there was a moment of silence at the other end of the line. Then, after an audible sigh, Detective Sullivan said, "I spent many long nights going through old files. The information you gave me from the library helped."

Grace rudely interrupted Dan. She spoke directly into his face to be sure that the party on the other end of the line could hear her. "What about Mother's diary? Tell him not to forget that in the morning. I want it back."

Dan shot his mother a shocked and disturbed look.

Detective Sullivan acknowledged Grace. "Tell your mother that I'll drop the diary off on the way to the cemetery. I also think I should warn you that the media is going to take every opportunity to blow this entire case out of proportion. You need to be prepared for more reporters."

"Thanks again for all your help." Dan hung up with a feeling of victory and relief.

"Maybe we can all finally get a good night's sleep," Robert said as he turned to go back to his bedroom.

"After Detective Sullivan drops Emily off at the cemetery, I'll call the Michaels family. We can stop by there after we finalize the burial arrangements and share the good news, if it's okay with you," Dan suggested to his mother, who didn't appear to care one way or the other.

"Good idea," Jon said and headed for his room. Grace lingered a moment.

"What's wrong Mom?" Dan asked. "I thought you'd be happy."

"I have mixed emotions," she responded softly.

"What do you mean?" Dan sat down on the rocking chair. He was watching his mother closely as she spoke. Grace appeared to be back to normal; however Dan wasn't sure he trusted what was right in front of his face. Either way, Dan was afraid for his mother. He wouldn't be able to rest until Emily actually went into the light.

"It's going to be difficult to see my mother's grave reopened," she began. "But worse than that is the thought of watching them put that little coffin, filled with the bones of my sister, down into the ground. I guess in my own way, I'm grieving the loss of Emily. Can that be possible? I didn't even know her," Grace looked sincerely at Dan. Her eyes shone a soft, warm brown.

"I'm tired and we have a big day tomorrow. Why don't you get some sleep?" Dan said.

"Sure," Grace turned to go down the hall. "What's that?"

Dan went over to the object lying in the middle of the hallway floor. He bent down and picked up Brittney Michael's rag doll.

"I don't want to get into anything tonight. I'll take this with us and we can return it to Brittney tomorrow after we leave Mr. Dalcour. This all needs to stop. Once Emily is buried, we're going to take that trip to the lake and relax. I'm looking forward to it, aren't you?" Dan asked.

"Yes, as a matter of fact, I am," Grace smiled. An uncharacteristic giggle followed her remark. Dan watched as his mother skipped playfully to her room. She didn't bother to look back at him. After Grace closed her bedroom door, Dan stood in the hall looking after her.

"You're a wicked spirit Emily. You think you've gotten strong enough to conceal yourself from me, but you aren't that smart. You're still playing games but you don't belong here and you are not welcome. I admire your strength and stamina for making this all come together. You've done something tremendous. You were able to come back from the worst moment of your life and find within your spirit the capacity to bring your family together to help you solve this mystery. You've accomplished a miracle. But it's finished. Your battle is over."

Chapter Seventy-Eight

Early the next morning, Detective James Sullivan pulled up in front of the Markos house. He glanced at the front porch and immediately recognized the group of small children huddled closely together in the corner. After all, he'd witnessed their presence several times over the past few weeks. He recognized their sunken faces and their large, dark, lifeless eyes. They haunted his nights and invaded is dreams.

The detective took his time getting out of the car. The air was hot and dry and the sun beat down relentlessly through the cloudless sky. He took a white handkerchief from his breast pocket and wiped beads of sweat from his forehead. His left shoe made a dull flapping sound as he walked up the short sidewalk leading to the Markos house. "A loose sole," he mumbled aloud and smiled at the unintentional pun.

Another police vehicle pulled up behind Detective Sullivan's car. The officer remained in his squad, waiting for orders.

Detective James Sullivan averted his gaze from the children with the hollow stare as he stepped onto the porch and rang the doorbell. The Markos family appeared immediately and welcomed him in with warm greetings.

"Good morning detective, please come in," Grace said.

"I'd feel more comfortable if we could all sit down," he said and quickly moved past Grace into the house.

"Of course." Robert motioned for the man to take a seat. "I'm Robert Markos, Grace's husband." He extended his hand to the detective.

"Would you like a cup of coffee?" Grace offered.

Detective Sullivan accepted a cup of hot, dark coffee. "This has been quite an experience," he began. "There are some things, I'll never admit to having seen during the past few weeks. I haven't slept much and I really hope that once this child's remains are buried, this shit will end."

"I'm curious," Dan said. "I'm sure that she's harassed you. It's what Emily does. But, were you able to actually see her?"

"What he means is, she doesn't allow everyone to see her," Jon added. "Emily's actions are still those of a typical five-year-old."

Dan continued. "Emily is growing stronger the longer she's around us. It doesn't matter who it is; she will literally suck the life out of anyone who tries to obstruct her plan. The weak can't survive around her. We have to take whatever measures necessary to get her remains buried and make sure that she crosses over into the light."

"Like all those other little girls?" the detective asked.

"You've seen them too?" Dan asked.

Grace sat up in a straighter, more aggressive position. She listened intently to the men as they talked.

James Sullivan leaned forward and lowered his voice. "Cops see things differently than other people. We're always looking for a sneaky move or guilty gesture. The law teaches us that a person is innocent until proven guilty. Through a cop's eyes, you're guilty unless you can prove otherwise. It's dangerous for us to let our guard down, even for a moment."

"How do you sleep at night?" Dan asked.

"With one eye open," he answered with a straight face. "And once I got involved with Emily, not at all." It was apparent by the dark circles under his eyes. "Emily gets into your head when you try to sleep and doesn't let you forget her. She's ruthless. I don't agree with you about her acting like a five-year-old. No five-year-old can accomplish what Emily does."

"What do you mean by that?" Robert's asked. "She's actually just a little girl, isn't she?"

"I never thought I'd say this, but Emily wants your soul. It seems to give her strength. So, you don't sleep, you don't rest, you don't dare let your guard down. I had to steal moments of rest just to survive by avoiding her eyes. I did learn that much." Detective Sullivan stood and handed Sarah Thatcher's diary to Grace. "Good luck." It was obvious that he was deeply disturbed by his experience. "I don't think it was a coincidence that we were all drawn together in this case."

"Why do you say that?" Grace asked.

"As with a lot of police officers, I come from a long line of cops," he began. "I followed in my father's footsteps just as he did. They loved what they did. My dad would never sit behind a desk like I do. He needed to be out there on the streets," he spoke with pride.

"Go ahead, tell them why you're here," Grace's abruptness took her family by surprise.

Dan watched his mother closely. He knew that Emily was now able to use Grace's body.

"I noted the dates on the newspaper articles you gave me." He pulled one of the articles out of his pocket. "My father was the police officer on duty the day that Emily was kidnapped. His name was mentioned several times."

Grace paced back and forth in front of the detective, making him very uncomfortable.

"The kidnappings left everyone scared. Anyone's child could be next. My dad called several times a day from work to check on us. We weren't allowed to leave the yard. If my sister or I couldn't go, my parents stayed home," Officer Sullivan explained. "Do you understand? It was my father's case. It haunted him until his dying day. Emily never let him rest. Everyone thought it was his mind. Mom died thinking Dad was hallucinating. I wish he could have lived to see me help end this."

Dan and Jon watched Emily enter and leave Grace's body. She lingered around the detective's chair.

"Have you always been able to see dead people?" Jon asked.

"No never." His response was fast. "I have only seen Emily and those other children."

"Have you seen her here today?" Dan questioned.

Detective Sullivan answered wearily. "Yes, she's become quite the center of attention around me lately. I see her at home, at work, in the car; she makes sure that my thoughts are completely on her at all times." He looked back and forth between Dan and Jon. "You are the only ones I would ever admit this to. Emily blames my father, along with anyone else who was there at the time of her abduction, including her parents."

"What makes you say that?" Jon asked.

"She visited me in my rare moments of sleep. I saw the merry-go-round, her parent's frantic search for her, and my father's failure to find her before it was too late." James Sullivan Jr. hung his head. "It was his only huge failure as a police officer."

"Before you came to visit me at the station, I was about to take a leave of absence from work," the detective was unbarring his soul. "She had already started introducing herself to me in subtle ways."

"Like what?" Robert asked.

"I'd enter the kitchen and all the cabinet doors would be opened, the tea pot would start whistling and I never filled it or turned on the stove, things like that." He shook his head. "I thought I was losing my mind. I needed to find out if I was having a nervous breakdown. Then, you and your family showed up and the pieces started coming together."

Dan and Jon sympathized with the officer. Grace leaned on the back of Robert's chair. "Are you chewing gum?" Robert asked.

Grace snapped the gum boldly in his ear and stood up. "Did you ever find Susan Young?"

"Yes, I did. She died in a nursing home a few miles from here," he replied. "They said that when they found her, she looked like she'd been scared to death," He said. "Her husband and only child preceded her in death. She did have a half-brother. He was younger than her and is still alive. I visited him a couple of days ago. He gave me some photographs of Mrs. Young when she was a young girl. He also said that when she died, she was stark raving mad." James Sullivan reached in his pocket and pulled out a short stack of pictures.

Grace quickly came around the chair and snatched the photos out of his hand. She stared at the pictures. "I never suspected her of anything so evil. She looked like such a nice lady. I played with her little girl."

Detective Sullivan was trained to pick up on subtle remarks. His eyes met with Dan's. Dan pursed his lips and shook his head back and forth in a warning gesture.

"I can vouch for the fact that a criminal isn't always a goon in a trench coat. They don't throw off warning signs or have their intentions tattooed on their foreheads. However, they dwell on their prey and their movements are precisely planned. When you grow up in the home of a police officer, you learn early to be suspicious of everyone. Predators can be a close friend, a family member, the person behind you at the grocery store, or your neighbor."

Dan nodded. "I heard a lot of confessions when I served the church as a priest. I council people that are sex offenders, murderers, pedophiles; the list of criminal behavior is endless. However, I still think that the worst offender is the one who violates a child."

"What about Emily? How were you able to identify her?" Grace asked.

"There was still some hair on the skull and she had fingernails. They found a familial match to the DNA samples you provided. One of the forensic artists made a sketch of what Emily might have looked like if she would have lived. She was beautiful."

"Oh, she was perfect alright," Grace added.

Everyone ignored her behavior. Robert just figured it was stress, but Dan knew better.

"If it wasn't for that ghost making my life so damn miserable, I can honestly say that I wouldn't have believed a word you said," Detective Sullivan spoke cautiously. "I do have to say that she kept me on my toes throughout this entire investigation."

With that said, the detective was ready to leave. He turned slowly and asked, "By the way, do you have any idea who the black woman with the head scarf is?"

No one could give him an honest answer and he was anxious to leave. He needed to get outside into the warm sun. It felt like the temperature had dropped twenty degrees.

"I'll send an officer in with the papers you need to sign. Then, I'm going straight to the cemetery to turn over Emily's remains to Mr. Dalcour for burial. By signing the papers, you will be accepting full responsibility for your sister's remains. Are you willing to assume that responsibility?" he asked through chattering teeth.

"Yes, I understand perfectly," Grace answered.

Detective Sullivan continued inching his way out the front door as he spoke. Just standing near Grace caused him to shake harder from the continuous drop in his body temperature. "Why is it so damned cold in here?"

Jon leaned over and whispered to Dan, "Is it my imagination or is this guy starting to turn blue?"

No longer able to tolerate the frigid cold, the detective stepped out of the house and directly into the sun. The officer waiting outside brought the paperwork up to the porch for Grace to sign. He stared at the frost hanging from the scant mustache over Detective Sullivan's upper lip.

Before leaving, Detective Sullivan addressed Dan. "If you would come down to the police station later on this week, I'd really appreciate it." He rubbed his hands vigorously together. "I don't know what's happening, but I'm about to freeze my ass off." He could barely get the words out.

Emily appeared out of nowhere. She remained suspended over Detective Sullivan, stealing his heat. Grace and Robert were oblivious to what was going on, while Detective Sullivan was now able to see Emily clearly.

Dan knew that Emily had stepped out of Grace's body. She was able to enter and leave his mother's mortal shell whenever she wished. The changes weren't only in Grace's character. Dan could identify physical manifestations as well.

The detective stood nearly frozen in place in front of the Markos front porch. "Over the past few weeks, I've been pushed, shoved, bitten and tripped, humiliating me on the job as well as in my home."

Dan nodded at the man with empathy. "Jon and I can see her. Emily is here. Our parents aren't able to visualize her, however. She's tormenting you because she wants justice. I'm afraid that the sooner we get her buried the better for everyone. I don't think Emily is satisfied with what we've done. She wants more. We can't delay the burial any longer."

Emily spoke so only Dan, Jon and Detective Sullivan could hear her. "You can bury my bones Dan Markos, but you can't bind my spirit."

"Please hurry," Dan pleaded.

"I'm on my way," the detective could only move his eyes. His joints began to ache and burn.

Dan tried the only way he knew how to deal with unruly spirits. "Leave our home Emily. You are NOT welcome here. We've done what you asked, now go to the cemetery and wait by your mother's grave."

Though her retaliation could have been worse, Emily spun to face the black woman who stood with opened arms in front of Emily's spirit. She cast a look back at Dan that was filled with hate and forewarning before disappearing.

Detective Sullivan felt relieved as his body began to defrost. His clothes were drenched. It was just a reminder of what had occurred. He took off his wet jacket and draped it over his arm.

"Are you okay?" Dan asked.

"Hell no. I'm going straight to the cemetery to get rid of these damn bones. Then, I'm going home to soak in a hot tub of water. If you don't do anything else," he addressed Dan. "Put a rush on that burial."

Dan watched as the detective got into his car and drove away. He thought about the wicked way Emily behaved around his mother. "I'll do everything I can to put an end to Emily's unholy visitation."

Chapter Seventy-Nine

Dan, Grace and Jon visited the cemetery later that morning. What was left of Emily Thatcher arrived earlier, as Detective Sullivan had promised. Emily's little bones were already placed in the casket that Grace had selected. The funeral director and Mr. Dalcour were scheduling the date and time for her services.

Dan insisted on no delay. The burial was to be the following morning. Sarah Thatcher's gravesite would be opened and she would accept the bones of her first born to be laid to rest above her own casket. It was almost over.

After completing the arrangements, they made a visit to the Michaels family. Angela greeted them looking rested and refreshed. "Come on in. It's good to see you," she said. "Ted and Brittney are in the kitchen."

Ted stood and extended his hand when he saw Dan and Jon. "Hi, how's it going?"

They introduced Grace to the Michaels family and finished greeting and welcoming each other.

"How's Brittney?" Dan asked.

Angela glanced at her daughter, who was in the process of shoveling a piece of waffle, dripping with syrup into her mouth.

"Except for not being able to find her doll, everything seems to be back to normal. No more unwelcome visitors, if that's what you mean."

Dan brought up his arm and held out the rag doll. When Brittney saw it, she came running to him.

"Mommy, it's Abby," she squealed.

Ted looked puzzled. "Where'd you find that?" A familiar bolt of terror caused him to clench his stomach.

Grace smiled sheepishly. Angela was extremely uncomfortable around her. They all sat down at the kitchen table. Angela offered coffee but didn't extend her welcome any further. There was a cold wall slowly building up between her and Grace.

Dan kept a close eye on his mother. She left her seat and walked over to Brittney's play area. She trailed her hand over the books, crayons, and puzzles letting her fingers linger possessively.

"The funeral is tomorrow," Dan announced, attempting to get his mother's attention. "We're having a small service at the cemetery, if you'd like to attend."

"I'm sure it was a relief to be rid of Emily's ghost," Jon added. "I know it will be for us."

"Our lives will never be completely the same again," Angela said sadly. "We're still on guard and I can't let Brittney out of my sight. If she's up in her room, I can't work down here. I always have that suspicious red flag that pops up, causing me to drop what I'm doing and run to find my daughter."

Grace approached Angela. "It must have been horrible for you to think that you'd never see your little girl again." Her voice sent cold chills up and down Angela's spine.

Angela rubbed the hairs down on her arms. "I can't imagine what your mother went through," she retaliated. "What time is the service tomorrow? I don't want to miss it." Angela never took her eyes off Grace as she spoke.

"We're supposed to meet in front of the cemetery office at ten o'clock tomorrow morning. That Luke Phillips boy is doing the ceremony. Isn't that right Danny?" Grace rolled her eyes in a very immature fashion.

"You never knew Emily, did you?" Angela asked.

"No, she was gone before I was born. I just recently saw pictures of her," Grace answered casually. "She was really beautiful."

Angela redirected the conversation to Dan and Jon. "Detective Sullivan talked to us for quite a while when we went in to give our DNA samples."

"It was as if he couldn't get enough information about Emily and everything leading up to us finding her," Ted sat at the table with his hands folded in front of him.

Jon nodded. "I'm sure. Emily made that man earn his pay these past few weeks."

Angela smiled at Brittney. "She's our only child. Detective Sullivan did more than listen to us. He seemed to absorb every word we said."

"To me, Emily is simply a name. We never bonded like normal siblings. I didn't even have a visual of her accept for a few black and white photos," Grace remarked casually. "My father locked away my existence after I disappeared to protect my mother, as well as his own sanity."

"I beg your pardon?" Angela asked. She didn't know if she heard Grace right.

Dan immediately stepped in and changed the subject. "The detective said they think it was a neighbor. I saw a picture of her. She looked pretty normal to me. I can see how no one would suspect her of anything."

"Oh, I don't know about that. From, what I've been reading in my mother's diary, she was afraid of Susan Young. She felt very strongly that there was something wrong with her."

After a pause, Grace continued subtly shifting her eyes. "Mom should have been more careful. She should have told Daddy about her. You have to be careful when it comes to your little girl." Grace looked deep into Angela's eyes, as the temperature in the room dropped.

"It's funny how blond Emily's hair was in contrast to yours, not to mention your brown eyes," Angela commented. "You and your sister were like night and day."

"Look at Dan and me," Jon jumped in. "I have a more olive complexion with dark hair and my eyes are just like my mother's. Dan got the surfer boy look," he joked in an attempt to lighten the mood.

Dan stepped up behind his mother and whispered, "What's going on with you?"

Grace smiled up at her oldest son. "I think Danny looks a lot like Emily. Especially after seeing pictures of her. Yes, right down to that deep dimple in his right cheek." She giggled out loud like a little girl. It freaked everyone out.

Jon looked at Angela's hand. "By the way, how's your hand? I see you still tend to favor it."

"Actually, I go to physical therapy once a week. I can't completely close or make a fist yet, but it's coming along," she replied.

Jon reached out and held Angela's hand in his. "It sure left a thick scar."

Angela looked at Jon and answered strongly, "Actually, that's okay. It's a constant reminder of what happened. It helps me keep my guard up."

Angela placed a protective arm around Brittney's waist. Dan felt a definite tension between Angela and his mother. He had to admit that Grace wasn't acting like herself and he didn't know whether to blame Emily or not.

"We better be going," Grace glanced around the room. Brittney skipped over to her play table and started working on a coloring book.

Grace slid over to Brittney and peered over her shoulder. "Is that hard?"

Angela heard Grace's question and moved in closer to the older woman. An overpowering feeling of apprehension suddenly encompassed her. Their eyes met and Angela expressed her fear without uttering a word.

Standing alongside Grace was like standing in front of an opened freezer door. Angela opened her mouth to speak and stopped when she saw her own breath puff out in front of her. She took hold of Grace's hand. "My God, you're as cold as ice."

Grace pulled away from Angela's grasp and looked at her through a set of entrancingly blue eyes. It caused the tiny hairs on Angela's neck to bristle, but she stood firm.

"See you tomorrow at the cemetery," Grace smiled.

"I wouldn't miss it for the world," Angela held her ground and maintained eye contact with the older woman until Grace stepped aside and followed Dan and Jon out of the house.

Chapter Eighty

The day of Emily's burial had finally arrived. Dan's eyes snapped open long before the alarm had a chance to go off. Everyone in the Markos household quietly prepared for the funeral, each holding their own thoughts and feelings regarding what was about to take place.

There was no nervous chatter or recollections of memories to share about Emily. Not even a muffled sniffle or a stray tear was shed as they left for the cemetery.

Conversation was minimal. Silence permeated the inside of the car. Everyone was mentally exhausted from the entire situation. No one was sure what lay ahead.

The cemetery loomed above the city on the North side of town. It could be seen a mile away. On the front gates, angels were ornately carved into the thick wrought iron. The walls surrounding the cemetery were half stone, topped with iron bars, spaced evenly between limestone pillars as if they could contain the spirits of the dead. When they drove through the entranceway gravel crunched noisily under the weight of the car, slightly startling everyone into awareness. An overwhelming aura, emitting sheer energy, caused each individual to question whether they should turn and run or simply succumb to the unwelcomed force.

On the other side of the gates, a huge, marble cross stood in the center of a circular drive and seemed to welcome all who entered.

Grace had purchased a small stone Cherub that held a heart in its plump little hands where Emily's name was now engraved. This would mark her final resting-place.

"Mr. Dalcour told me the marker will be placed on the gravesite once it's covered and the ground settles," Grace said meekly. She was lost in thought as they came closer to the place where she had already laid her mother and father to rest. Now, the ground would be disturbed once more. "One grave, two bodies."

"Are you okay?" Robert laid his hand over Grace's and gently squeezed.

"I was just thinking about the cherub I bought for Emily. I think Mother would have liked it," she sniffled and dabbed her eyes with one of her mother's embroidered handkerchiefs.

"Mr. Dalcour asked for a picture of Emily. I tried to choose one that would look right on the grave marker," Grace let out a gasp when she reached in her purse and pulled out the black and white photograph.

"What's wrong Mom?" Dan asked quickly.

"Nothing, I thought I forgot something, but it's okay. Everything has to be perfect today," Grace tried to remain calm as she slid the photograph back into her purse. I know that isn't the photo I picked out. I took my time selecting just the right picture of Emily.

The child in the photograph wasn't Emily. It was Grace when she was five years old. *Oh my God, Emily wants me to be buried in the ground above our mother. She wants my life.*

"I thought that placing the figurine right in front of Granny and Grandpa's tombstone would be more appropriate than simply attaching a plaque to their marker. That way, Emily will be recognized individually for who she was," Grace chattered nervously. The closer they got to the gravesite, the higher her anxiety level spiked.

"Mom, what's the matter? You're acting strange. If this is too much for you, we'll take care of it. Dad can take you home. Leave it to Jon and me," Dan offered.

Grace slowly opened her purse and took out the black and white snapshot of herself when she was a little girl. She handed it to Dan and he examined it closely.

"Is this the picture of Emily you want to give to Mr. Dalcour?" he asked.

"Look at it," Grace cried desperately.

Robert reached for the picture that was causing so much commotion. "This is ridiculous. You're taking it way too seriously. This is a perfectly good picture of Emily. You've done quite enough. She should be glad we're going out of our way to make certain she gets buried with your mother. We should have just had her cremated and been done with it. You didn't even know her, for crying out loud."

"Come on Dad," Jon said as they pulled up to the opened grave. "This has been hard on everyone. Let's just get it over with."

Robert handed the photograph to Dan. "Take care of this, will ya?"

Dan looked at the picture of the little girl with the long blond curls. It was definitely Emily. "It's a good enough photo, Mom. Don't worry about it. This will be over soon and then we can go home and get ready for the fishing trip. I'm looking forward to going back up to the lake," he said and silently prayed.

Grace thought for a moment. *Emily is playing tricks on me. I'll have to be more careful. Of course she doesn't mean any harm by it. She's just a child.*

Once out of the car, they were greeted immediately by Mr. Dalcour. He lead them to the chairs that were lined up in front of the opened gravesite that was shadowed by a huge old oak tree.

"Your family can sit here. Take as much time as you need. I'll get the priest, so he can begin the service."

Jon saw the Michaels family pull into the cemetery and went to meet them. Robert stood behind Grace's chair with his hands on her shoulders. "I hate cemeteries. It just doesn't seem fair that we all have to end up here. It's so damn depressing."

Dan sat next to his mother. "How are you doing?" he asked.

"Is she here?" Grace looked sorrowfully into her son's eyes.

"Yes, as a matter of fact, Emily is standing next to Granny and Grandpa's headstone. I'm sure everything will be fine once the priest begins saying the words needed to help ease her transition to the other side," Dan said.

"I'm worried Danny," Grace spoke quietly, under her breath as her son leaned in closer to hear her.

Dan realized that there were changes taking place with his mother and he needed to stay close to her. "What's on your mind, Mom?"

"I think Emily realizes that what she's finally found isn't half as important as the act of trying to find it. Do you know what I mean?" Grace sighed.

Dan shook his head. "Not really, but I think you're wise to be cautious of her right now."

A lone tear slid down Grace's cheek. "Emily's life wasn't characterized by the moment of her death, but by all the moments of my life."

Dan felt a flush of heat rise in his face as the realization of his mother's words began to sink in. "That's plain foolish. I won't let it happen."

Detective Sullivan stepped up from behind the tombstone. Dan rose. "My life has changed since I met you and your family," he said. "I discovered a part of me that I never knew existed. I'm here in hopes that once Emily Thatcher is put to rest, things will go back to normal."

"Thanks for coming," Dan said. "Are you able to see her?"

"Yes, unfortunately I am." He turned his head to witness what he hoped was the final time he would ever see Emily Thatcher.

Dan stepped over to his grandparent's headstone and approached the ghost of the black woman who always appeared to be watching Emily with the loyalty and instincts of a mother. As usual, her attention was on Emily.

"I can see you," Dan began in a gentle whisper. "Who are you and why are you here?"

The black woman scurried behind a taller neighboring tombstone as if she were caught in a place she shouldn't be. Dan followed her.

"Please, if you're here to help Emily cross over, you're more than welcome," Dan extended the invitation to the black woman who wore the same colorful scarf on her head, tied neatly at the nape of her neck.

"I am Leeza, Emily's governess. Be aware, she doesn't want to go. Emily has been a free spirit for too long. She has kept me from entering the light and as long as she refuses to go, I am doomed to follow her for the rest of eternity. She needs a place to set her spirit. All is free for the taking. But be aware; Emily preys on the weak," the woman warned. She turned and stepped back behind the headstones as if it were her proper place.

Dan went back to sit beside his mother. Emily's sights were set on Grace. Grace was the weak one.

Chapter Eighty-One

"I didn't think it would be this difficult seeing my mother's grave reopened like this," Grace whispered to her son. "I wish I felt more of a loss, but the fact is I'm just doing this for my mother and father."

"I'm sorry, Mom. It'll be over soon," Dan said.

Robert remained behind Grace; his hands nervously squeezing her shoulders. Her sons flanked each side.

Detective Sullivan remained by the Thatcher's headstone. Ted and Angela Michaels stood respectfully on the opposite side of the burial plot, facing the Markos family.

Emily levitated over the opened earth where her casket would soon be lowered and covered with cool, dark dirt.

Everyone took in a quick breath as the priest approached the gravesite. The highly anticipated moment had finally arrived. The tiny white casket was slowly lowered to just above Sarah Thatcher's newly exposed coffin.

The funeral director and Father Luke Phillips stood at the foot of the grave. "I'll try to be brief. Many things are forgotten when a life ends. It's a miracle that Emily's remains were located after all these years. I'm aware that none of you actually knew this unfortunate child. Unless you're forced to listen to those who have passed before us, you don't know if you're being drawn to the entity by even the slightest bit of familiarity or if your souls have bonded. However, there is one among us who knows Emily Thatcher intimately. He's the one who will welcome her home with open arms. Let us pray."

The ceremony was short and informal, as the priest had promised. His words were comforting and reverent as Emily was given her final rights.

Grace cried for the injustice that Emily suffered at the hands of a supposed family friend. She wondered what her life would have been like if Emily had been around to grow up with,

405

and the years of anguish her mother would have been spared. Finally, Grace cried for all the other little girls that suffered because of the same evil woman.

All at once, the ropes gave way and the small casket fell the short distance meeting the lid of Sarah's coffin with a loud thud. Now, Emily's casket sat directly on top of her mother's. The clanking sound of the boxes touching caused Grace to cringe. She released a low moan.

Emily's crying could be heard by all. It was the pitiful sobbing of a lost child.

Father Luke crossed himself and addressed the Markos family. "I hesitated before accepting the responsibility of performing this ceremony," he raised his voice. "There are circumstances here that are questionable to the church."

Dan cocked his head. "What do you mean, Father?"

He spun around and faced Dan. "This is against all that is holy. You profess to see ghosts and the spirits of dead people. It's no wonder the church asked you to step down as a priest. I'm sorrowful for having to say these things to you and I had no intention to confront you. However, I've experienced some inexplicable incidents over the past few weeks, since I accepted this formality that has caused me great concern."

"Do you mean to say that you've been visited by Emily's ghost?" Dan questioned the man who had stood in judgment of him and his gift of discerning spirits.

"I'm not sure," the priest answered in a whisper.

"Do you see her now?" Dan pursued his questioning.

"I've averted my eyes from the devilish sight, because she terrifies me and challenges my faith," the older priest bowed his head and walked away without giving Dan a straight answer.

"Oh Danny," Grace cried. "Help me! I'm fighting for my life. Emily wants me to trade places with her. I can't do it! She thinks I should feel guilty for having lived."

Dan and Jon stood shoulder to shoulder in front of their mother. Robert moved the chair out of his way and continued to stand behind Grace, who was now up on her feet. They watched Emily float over the gravesite that now held the only proof of her mortality.

"We're trying to give you a decent burial Emily. I'm sorry that you were robbed of your life, but now you must leave this earth. You hid from the light all these years, now you must go to it!" Dan cried out to Emily's spirit as he watched the older priest continue to walk swiftly to his car.

Leeza stepped out from behind the tombstone. "Go to the light child. Your mamma and daddy are waiting for you. It's time to go home."

Grace felt herself being pulled forward toward the opened grave. "No! Stop it Emily. I don't want to die. It isn't fair, I want to live."

Her words only seemed to infuriate Emily more. She continued drawing Grace toward the unearthed hole.

Robert clung tightly to Grace. He called out to Father Luke for help. "For all that's holy, help us. What kind of man of God are you?"

Father Luke had reached his car, but was unable to get in. "What holds me here?" he called back to Dan.

"The strength of the other side," Dan answered.

"She's evil. I can taste her venom," Father Luke was terrified. Sweat ran down the sides of his face.

Dan confronted the older priest, ". How can you judge us and deny that her spirit exists? Can you actually accept the position of Bishop when you can't even face the other side? If you believe that there is a heaven; you must realize that there truly is a hell!"

"Can she hear me? If I face her, will she smite me?" The priest's voice cracked when he spoke.

"Do you believe us when we tell you that we have been given the gift of discerning spirits? Do you still judge me for that, because up until now, you've been incapable of visualizing them yourself?" Dan flung the questions at the priest angrily.

"Do you admit that I was wronged by the church for being honest and confessing my gifts of the spirit or did I simply tell it to the wrong person? I trusted you Father and you betrayed me." Dan poured his heart out to the man he had known all his life, and who had crushed his dreams of the priesthood by exposing his God given gift to the Bishop as something wicked, dirty and evil.

Father Luke Phillips had been their priest for years before Dan decided to join the Catholic seminary. Emily was using his physical senses to berate and humiliate him. Father Luke cried out, "The cold is nearly unbearable."

"He feels," Emily's voice flowed from her mouth. "He can speak when taunted."

"Can't they stop that incessant music? It sounds like we're at a carnival instead of a funeral." Father Luke covered his ears as the melody from the carousel blared throughout the graveyard.

"He hears," Emily echoed with sarcasm.

"The stench of perfume is so pungent. It can't be the flowers. It's taking my breath away," the priest gagged on his words.

"He can smell," she giggled as her words grew with intensity. Father Luke was forced down to one knee.

"Stop this insanity. This isn't fair. I loved you as a child. I thought my heart would break when you disappeared. There was nothing more for me to live for. I never loved another woman after you. Now please, go back to the grave. You don't belong here. Your very existence is an abomination," he glanced up from his kneeling position and found himself looking into the side mirror of his car.

What Father Luke saw in the mirror scared him more than the ghost of Emily Thatcher. His eyes were filled with fear and his face was distorted from shame, exploitation of his lack of faith and remorse.

"He finally sees," Emily's words were loud and clear.

"Dan, it was my accusations that caused you to be ridiculed and judged unfairly. It was my disbelief that caused your faith to be questioned. However, you remained civil to me and never revealed my lack of discretion to your family or to the church," Father Luke confessed through painful tears. "I apologize for judging you. I'm sorry for my weakness and arrogance."

"Do you believe me now Father?" Dan called out, desperately waiting to hear the words that would clear his name in the church.

Everyone stood silently staring at the man who had humbled himself out of fear and Emily's reprimand.

"I don't claim to understand. I won't lie and say that I'm completely in control of my faculties at this very moment however, I admit to witnessing the spirit of this deceased little girl, who holds me fast." Father Luke didn't dare raise his head. He was all too aware of his cowardliness and lack of faith.

Grace cried out in one last attempt to save herself. "Help me, Mother. I need you. Please take Emily home."

Sarah Thatcher's tormented soul rose from her now disturbed grave. Grace was able to witness the magnificence of the moment, along with everyone present. Emily's spirit cried out for the mother she longed for. Her tortured, distorted features, that moments ago horrified her group of witnesses, relaxed as she melted into her mother's vision. Their transparent spirits entwined as they floated freely through an opalescent mist.

"Emily, go with Mother." The toes of Grace's shoes pushed some loose dirt into the opened grave as she was drawn closer to the edge. If Emily didn't stop, falling in would be inevitable. Her voice escalated in sheer panic as she envisioned the earth closing rapidly over her face. "Please Emily stop, before it's too late." Tears streamed down Grace's cheeks.

Sarah remained suspended over her own grave, her spirit spiraling haphazardly with Emily's. Charles grief stricken manifestation rose and joined them as they reveled in the glory of the reunion.

For a brief moment, Sarah made contact solely with Grace. Their eyes locked and Grace gasped uncontrollably as she was able to feel all the tension, fear and dread that her mother had carried throughout her life finally being released.

With awe inspiring her words, Grace wreathed, "I see them. I see my parents with Emily. They're really together. Oh, I love you so much, Mom. I miss you Dad," Grace could barely spit out the words, but her heart was bursting with emotion.

Robert placed his arm around Grace's shaking shoulder and gently guided her away from the opened grave. He couldn't speak. The spiritual presentation had struck him mute.

Everyone present witnessed Emily's reunion with her parents. They all appeared just as they were that horrible day when Emily was plucked out of their lives. Their youthful spirits entwined and wound together as their voices cried out with jubilation.

It was unbelievably exhilarating to see the enormous, white downy wings of the angels as they encircled Charles, Sarah and Emily. Sarah's human features blurred in and out as did Charles. Their souls were no longer trapped here on earth. They were finally being led by a legion of Heaven's angels toward the light that would finally release their lost and wandering souls.

But Emily, who although she apparently relished the long sought after reunion with her parents, appeared to steer clear of the light.

Dan turned to his mother while the vision of the trio began to dissipate in the mist. "It's finally over. We did it, Mom. We actually reunited Granny, Grandpa and Emily."

Grace had relaxed into Robert's hold. A tiny wrinkle appeared between her eyebrows and the corners of her mouth lifted in the suggestion of a smile. Dropping a single red rose into the grave, she whispered softly into Dan's ear. "Is she really gone?"

Dan smiled. "Emily is safe in the arms of her mother. That's all she wanted, isn't it?"

But then terror gripped Dan's very soul as his sweet, loving mother raised her face to meet his, her strikingly blue eyes driving deep into his heart like a sharp spike. The familiar musical tune from the merry-go-round began playing methodically throughout the cemetery. It was carried on a breeze that circled the Markos family, bringing a chill that caused them all to shudder.

Dan put his face next to his mother's ear. "I'll fight for you, Mom. I promise, I'll spend the rest of my life keeping you safe from Emily."

"Never say you weren't warned," Emily's voice brushed past Dan's cheek, bounced off his face and landed in Grace's ear. Only the two of them heard Emily as she promised, "You're not going to like what happens next."

EPILOGUE

Dan Markos sat under an Olive tree gazing at Felicia as she chased their five-year-old daughter, Sophia around the park. *She looks so much like her mother.* But more than that, it was Sophia's soft, warm, brown eyes that tugged at his heartstrings. She reminded him of Grace. Dan missed his mother.

"She would have loved you," he mumbled under his breath.

His thoughts overwhelmed him with sadness as they drifted back to the day at the lake, following Emily's burial. She had been laid to rest, but her soul consumed his mother's body, forcing Grace's spirit to take shelter somewhere unbeknownst to him.

Dan recalled that first morning at the lake. Rising early, he made breakfast for everyone. His mother picked at her food and suddenly jumped up, leaving her half-eaten meal to run outside, letting the screen door slam behind her.

He could still visualize her skipping down the dirt path that lead to the lake. Dan bit the inside of his lip.

He left his father and brother deep in conversation over a map of the lake and walked down to the water with a heavy heart.

"Show me how to skip a rock, Dan," he remembered her voice as if it were yesterday. "I can't do it."

Though it looked like Grace, she spoke and acted like a five-year-old child. Dan knew that his mother was no longer with them. Emily had stolen Grace's body.

Robert and Jon stepped out on the porch and his father yelled down to them, "We're going to town to get some bait. We won't be long."

Grace began jumping up and down, screaming, "Wait for me; I want to go to!" She took off running after Robert's car. He was already driving away and hadn't seen her trip and fall on the dirt path leading back to the cabin.

Dan immediately called out to her, "Mom, are you okay?"

When she didn't answer, he used a sharper, more aggressive tone, "Emily!"

"What?" she snapped back and glared at him through her piercingly blue eyes. She pushed herself up to a standing position and brushed the dirt off her clothes.

They were alone, he recalled. The water on the lake was calm and quiet that day. Dan could still feel how the words stuck in his throat as he choked them out. "Let's go for a swim, Mom. You always loved swimming in the lake."

Then, for the last time, he looked at the shell of what was once his loving mother.

Dan sighed deeply as he recollected that day with her. He had taken off his shoes and socks and stripped down to his swim trunks. The water was cool against his bare skin when he jumped in first.

"Come on, Mom. Let's swim out to the island and back. It'll be like old times. I'll race you," he coaxed.

He felt as if he'd been punched in the stomach as he remembered how the tears burned his eyes when he dove under the water and started swimming toward the island.

"You can't beat me," the voice that called to him from the shore was that of a child. He heard the splash when she hit the water, but he never looked back. Dan just kept swimming, taking his time and stroking the water methodically.

When he reached the island, Dan pulled himself up on the bank, laid his face down in the grass and sobbed. She never made it.

Dan vividly recalled lifting his tear-streaked face from the wet grass. Then trembling, afraid to look back, he turned his head ever so slowly and saw, nothing. The water was smooth as glass.

"Daddy, look at me," Sophia's voice snapped him back to the present. She was sitting on top of the sliding board.

"I see you honey," Dan's words came out choppy from the lump that had formed in his throat. Sophia pushed off and slid down swiftly. She ran giggling to his opened arms.

When Sophia reached Dan, he scooped her up and she wrapped her little arms around his neck. In a voice that was all too familiar, but not that of his daughter, he heard her say, "Can I ride the merry-go-round?"

Made in the USA
Monee, IL
30 November 2022

18872965R00233